THE STORM OF SEA AND SKY

Book Four - The Sunstone Saga

Nicolin Odel

CONTENTS

To all those who have shown me their unwavering support and are taking the time to read these pages.

My heartfelt gratitude goes out to each and every one of you.

Chapter One

CORSAIR

Simon flew unhurriedly through the sky over the enchanting waves of the Isles of Tal'tulu. The vibrant jade islands, adorned with impossibly white beaches, cast a spell on the azure-blue water. The fresh ocean breeze was invigorating as he scanned the sea below for signs of a sail. Finally, he spotted three crimson sheets gracefully gliding across the waves, the white V-shapes of their wakes trailing after the vessels. Simon leaned toward the ships, and as he descended, he noticed a fourth vessel ahead of them.

No, not a ship. The oblong olive head of a massive swimming sea beast burst from the water and crashed back down as it surged through the waves. Mist and foam spewed from its head each time it surfaced. Two sleek crimson sailing ships were gaining on the creature's flanks while the third stayed close behind.

From above, Simon could see the ships herding the beast directly toward a crescent-shaped cove on one of the islands. They were trying to surround it and cut it off. By the time Simon was close enough, the ships had done just that. Smaller boats had been launched, and men and women were closing in, hurling harpoons and firing arrows into the thick skin of the creature.

Simon heard it cry out in pain. It was a dreadful noise of fear and hurt and a frantic need for life. He stopped mid-air, his heart wrenching for the poor thing. It struggled, dived, and thrashed, but the dozens of piercing rope-tied projectiles were pulling back, and he could see the creature's exhaustion beginning to win out along with its lifeblood.

Suddenly, a shrill horn blasted and echoed through the cove as four black sails rounded the bend of the far side of the crescent-shaped island. The sudden appearance of the new ships was a surprise, their black sails a stark contrast to the azure sea. An ebony and golden-yellow flag flew from the main mast of the new vessels. Swords crossed before a black bird with its wings spread wide, but the bird's face was a skull wearing the oddest triangular hat with crossbones upon it. All this on a turmeric-yellow field.

The crimson-sailed ships went into a panic. The boat let go of its lines on the beast and immediately fled back to the larger vessels, some even choosing to head for shore instead of being caught. The closest of the red ships was not so lucky. Seeing it had no time to flee, it turned to face the oncoming vessels. Unfortunately, it turned into the wind, and it was sluggish in the water.

The black ships closed. Two were nearly upon the hunter's boat, aiming to come up along each side of the stranded vessel. One of the black ships had a cobra figurehead, its fangs exposed viciously.

Dunnian. Simon vanished into thin air as he came very close, close enough to see the people franticly scurrying along the decks and up the mast of the vessels.

Massive harpoons thrummed and shot out from the bow of the crimson ship at each of the pirate vessels. One struck the railing of the closest black vessel, and a man was staked in a burst of gore and carried along with the projectile. The other bolt glanced harmlessly off the curved bow of the cobra-headed ship.

Hundreds of meagrely clad pirates with rattling jewelry of beads, feathers, bones, and gold, men and women alike, jeered and hurled grapples across to fasten the vessels together. The men's shirtless, suntanned muscles and chests glistened with sea spray and sweat. Most were clad only in short linen trousers but had beads and bone wrapping around their wrists, ankles, and necks. Simon could tell the woman wore more beads and adornments than actual clothing. Only their breasts and waists were covered in colorful, extravagant, but minuscule garments. All carried a multitude of weapons on their hips.

More of the pirates began to swing across on ropes, their swords and axes flashing as they landed on the deck of the crimson ship, and blood began to spill. Most of the pirates were of Tal'tulu descent, but there was also the odd Xamidian. All of the crimson shipped crew were of the latter.

Are these hunting ships all from Xamid? Simon pondered as he watched the crimson ship quickly overwhelmed by ferocious shouting corsairs. They cut down their foes in a deadly, brutal manner.

A small group of the hunters had gathered near the stern deck and were bravely fighting to their deaths. Somehow, they held the pirates at bay as they tried to climb up the steps to the higher level.

Then, there was a cheer from the corsairs as a man with the same oddly shaped hat displayed upon the flag swung across from the cobra-headed ship. The Tal'tulu man had so much gold, silver, beads, gems, and other trinkets decorating his hat and body that Simon wondered how he could move about. He also noted, with great attention, that the man's dark chest and chiseled abdomen were molded nicely into a 'V' at his waist, and he glistened with sea spray. There was a wicked-looking cutlass in one hand and another clutched between his teeth as he soared over the heads of the sailors below. The man landed on the stern deck among the Xamidian hunters, and his swords *ripped* into them as he lay about himself. Blood splashed as he spun and hacked and kicked in a whirlwind of death—beheading one man and gutting another.

The screams echoed into the sea air, and the pirates surged up to the aid of their captain. "Captain Kai!" they bellowed in unison.

The next thing Simon knew, all but one of the hunters lay dead on the deck. He stayed silent and watched, hovering nearby.

The last hunter was a dark-bearded Xamidian. Stern and grizzled. He held a finely ornamented saber at the ready.

"You're the last defiler. Surrender or die," Captain Kai said with a cold tenacity. His vigorous chest and toned arms heaved after the exertion.

Simon couldn't help but gaze at Kai's raw physicality. He had an air about him—an attraction.

"Cursed fucking corsairs," the Xamidian man spat back at Kai. "We're trying to run a Skrull-damned business! Why do you have a death wish upon us?"

"Our brethren, the *Erin Okun*." Captain Kai waved a cutlass toward the beast lying still in the waters. Blood drifted through the waves around it, washing the dead creature slowly toward the shore. "Their numbers dwindle, and *you* are the source of this."

"Fucks to that thing and fucks to you! Fucking pirate bastar—"

The man's words were cut off by a sucking gurgle as one of Captain Kai's cutlasses flashed with impossible speed as it carved red through the man's throat. He gaped for a moment, dropping his sword and clutching at his neck as blood gushed from him and between his fingers before he finally fell to the deck of his ship.

"Throw the bodies overboard. Loot what you will!" Kai shouted at his pirates. "Rudie, have a skeleton crew bring this ship back to Keeya's Refuge and get her outfitted to return to active duty with a full crew."

"Aye, Captain," a woman said with a nod and hurried off, shouting his orders.

Captain Kai strode to the railing at the stern and looked out at the dead beast floating in its blood.

Simon hovered closer.

He heard Kai speaking in a near whisper, "I'm sorry, *arakunrin*. I didn't make it in time."

"The poor beast, no living creature need be put to such a gruesome death," Simon agreed aloud.

Captain Kai's cutlasses appeared in his hands as he spun about. His eyes scanned about for the source of the voice. "Who's there? Show yourself!"

"Uhm," Simon said hesitantly. "Only if you promise not to cut me down."

Kai squinted suspiciously, slowly circling toward where Simon's voice came from.

Simon moved as Kai did, hovering slightly above deck, sure to keep his distance from the lethal pirate. "I come in peace. I'm not one of these hunters. I've come from much further away. From Aurulan. Please, Sir Kai—"

"*Captain* Kai," he corrected. "Very well," he sighed resignedly and sheathed one of his blades on his hip. "I won't be killing you today. Now show yourself, sorcerer."

Simon let the invisibility spell fade; he held up his hands in a motion of *I mean you no harm*.

"By Chike's shaft! You *are* a bloody sorcerer." Kai exclaimed, then was upon Simon as swiftly as the words came from his mouth.

Simon reacted too slowly, trying to fly up as fast as possible. He felt Kai's firm grip on his ankle as he ascended. Then, he sank back down to the deck under the captain's weight. Something thudded into Simon's stomach, and the air rushed from his lungs. Then, the weight was atop him, and his face was forced down into a puddle of blood on the hardwood of the deck.

"Ha! A simple prey is a sorcerer, it seems," Kai laughed from where he kneeled on Simon's back, his hand pushing his head down.

Skrull's balls, he's quick. Well, isn't this a predicament? Strangung. Simon pushed away from the deck with all the might he could muster with the strength-enhancing spell. He surged up, flinging the surprised pirate off him. Simon turned to see Kai nearly tumble over the rail. He grabbed the captain's flailing arm before he could fall, and Simon pulled him against his chest.

There was a silent moment when neither Simon nor the entrancing pirate captain moved a muscle. He smelled of the sea, the tang of salt spray, and a cool mist on his sun-kissed cheeks as they brushed against Simon's own. Then, the moment was gone. Simon felt Kai's muscles tense as he jerked away, pushing Simon back.

"What's the meaning of this?" Kai rebuked; his face flushed. "You trying to seduce me, you damned devil man?"

"What? No." Simon shook his head, still baffled by their brief but intriguing embrace. "No. Of course not! I'm a married man. I didn't want you to fall."

"I'm the King of a fucking pirate fleet. You think I can't swim?"

"I never said that."

"You thought it."

"Sir—"

"Captain! Have you gone, daft man? You will address me as captain when you're on my ship."

"Of course, *Captain*," Simon corrected himself. "Please, let me tell my tale."

Captain Kai tilted his head curiously, then shook it. "Not now, can't you see I'm a little Skrull-damned busy?"

Simon opened his mouth to retort.

Kai's finger covered his lips. It was calloused and rough and tasted of brine. "Shush now, devil man. Move to my ship, *The Mamba's Mouth,* and see me in my quarters at nightfall. Until then, either pitch in or make yourself scarce." With that, Kai moved off in a stimulating display of agile, taunt-muscled movement, grabbing a line and swinging back to the black-sailed ship from where he had come.

Simon still stood with his mouth open. Unable to speak, he looked on after the captain, entirely *enchanted*.

Simon did his best to stay out of the way of the bustling pirates. He watched as they put out boats into the waters and surrounded the corpse of the *Erin Okun* in the Tal'tulu dialect, or *Sea Elephant* in Auru. He watched as they surrounded it, holding torches, they chanted and sang. An elevating prayer rose as dusk began to fall. Simon saw Captain Kai leading the procession. Piquing his curiosity, he again became invisible and flew close to observe them.

"We return you to Chike, the warrior of the sea."

The corsairs sang, waving their torches as they did so:

Chike, Chike, the warrior of the sea
He fights for freedom, he fights for peace
He wields his trident; he raises his shield
He strikes the tyrants; he makes them yield

Chike, Chike, the warrior of the sea
He stands for justice, he stands for truth
He leads the rebels, he inspires the youth
He challenges the oppressors; he breaks their chains
He liberates the captives; he ends their pains

Chike, Chike, the warrior of the sea
We honor his memory; we honor his name
We sing his praises; we sing his fame
We follow his example; we follow his way
We carry his spirit; we carry his flame

After the song ended, there was a moment of silence before Captain Kai spoke again. "We will not let your body go to waste, *arakunrin.*" He nodded, and the pirates began harvesting the creature for meat, bones, fat, and oil. Long into the night, they toiled.

Simon was dozing off on a bench before the captain's quarters on *The Mamba's Mouth* when a kick to his foot jolted him awake.

"Devil man? I'm surprised you didn't fly back to wherever you came from," Kai said, a half smile on his lips.

"Ahem, of course not." Simon stood, brushing himself off. "I desperately need to speak with you."

Kai opened the door and gestured to him. "After you."

Simon smiled and hurried into the room.

The door slammed shut behind him, and he turned just in time for Kai to push a knife against Simon's throat as his lips locked against Simon's. There was a sweetness to Kai's mouth, like honey. Simon tried to pull back in his surprise, but his legs butted into a low bed, and he rocked back.

Kai's other hand grasped between Simon's legs as he toppled him over onto the soft bedding. Then Kai was atop him. The knife sliced the threads of the fastened buttons of Simon's shirt with swift precision. Kai straddled Simon and removed his vest-like top in one fluid motion. The captain's sculpted body glistened in the dim light of a lantern, the shadows playing on his muscular lines. "Chike's shaft," Kai groaned. "I've been thinking about you ever since you embraced me so. I *desperately* need you too...devil man."

"I—wait—" Simon protested.

Kai tossed the knife aside as their lips met once more. *Vigorously.*

What about Saudett? I vowed never to do this again. But gods, this man...and it's been months. Simon tried to summon resistance to his limbs with little effort before he found himself relishing in the passion. *We had an agreement. I'm allowed to do this.*

Kai swiftly pulled off both of their trousers.

Simon returned the fervent caress as Kai took him in. *What's one last time?*

Then, Kai was groaning and oscillating his hips deeply upon him.

By Hettra's holy tits, it's been a long time. He's Skrull-damned attractive...and zealous...and...and...fuck.

Kai trembled atop him, arching toward him.

"Gods...oh no," Simon stammered. "Skrull's saggy balls, I'm sorry. That was too quick."

Kai lifted a leg, hopped off Simon, and stood beside the bed. He then gently took Simon's head and guided it to his substantially exposed member.

They both moaned and groaned as Simon brought Kai to completion.

Kai gasped with pleasure, then released Simon's head and flopped beside him on a pillow, pulling the covers up to his chin. "Thank you, devil man. It's been a long day, and that was an enjoyable quick finish to it in full. Sleep well, sorcerer." The captain closed his eyes and did not say another word.

Simon lay still, shame rising as a single thought bubbled up within his mind. *Saudett.*

Chapter Two

ENGULF

Hata Vasara took hold of the massive chunk of stone that had fallen from the walls of Keep Crystalia during the battle. It had crushed a homestead in the city below the keep, Aerion. The home of the Himin-dvergar. She gripped the rock and lifted it with all her mental might. Lifting her hands, the stone began to rise from the wreckage. The amber gem in the breastplate of her armor flared warmly as she walked, still holding the boulder skyward. She walked through the city, past other burnt-out homes from the less recent blue firebombing, toward the edge of the floating island city. Once there, she hurled the massive stone over the side and watched as it turned into nothing more than a speck, falling through the clouds and into the oceanic world below.

Teras's thunder, we have much work to do. Aerion needed to rebuild. Keep Crystalia required repairs to many of its defensive capabilities. Especially the many magically infused arbalests that had been lost to the forces of Hear-fan Skaad. The people needed to heal and regroup. *The Children of Skaad are still out there preparing for their next attack.* Hata wanted to scratch at the itching burns still wrapped and healing with the malachite flakes beneath her armor. The burns had been all across her arms, torso, and legs from her battle with the humanoid man who used a terrible corrosive dark magic. *He nearly killed me. Lucky for me, Raine was there to save me.*

My Raine. The Queen of the Himin-dvergar. A strong and straightforward ruler. An isolated ruler. Once Hata had spent time with her, she found Raine to be a solitary but striking and caring woman. *What is she doing right now?* As the image of Raine's soft, dark, freckled, *naked* body came to Hata, a voice called out.

"Sky-lass!"

Hata looked to see Rorik Windbeard waving at her as he approached from the direction of Keep Crystalia. The feisty rotor-wing pilot hurried over to her; bandana pulled down from his stubbly chin as he panted with exertion. "We need you on the walls. The queen wants to send out a detachment of rotor-wings to see what the Skaad bastards are up to. She wants you to come with, just in case something like *that* man appears again."

"All right, let's go!" Hata exclaimed eagerly. She was itching to get back into the fight. To rid the world of the Ryk Lân of the evil forces of Skaad. "We don't want to keep her waiting."

"Luminar's light, sky-lass, give me a minute to catch my breath."

"Here." Hata scanned the surroundings for another piece of rubble and found a broken collapsed wall. She found a sizeable flat piece and stood atop it. She beckoned to Rorik to join her on the surface of the fallen wall.

He took her hand and did not let go as they levitated into the air and flew up toward the massive walls of Keep Crystalia. The magnificent crystal veined walls were scarred from the battle. Mainly where Hata had fought with the hooded man and his violet fire; as they soared upward, Hata looked toward where the enemy commenced their attack—the direction of the Wayfarers Gate. The islands in that direction were shrouded in dark navy clouds. The thick smoke nearly covered the horizon. *They're still out there planning their next move.* Hata brought the slab of stone to rest on the bulwark of the keep.

"Thank the bright beard that's over," Rorik sighed as he knelt and patted the ground. "I missed you, dear friend."

"You're a rotor-wing pilot," Hata snorted in amusement. "How can you be afraid of a little hovering through the air?"

"That's completely different, Sky-lassie," Rorik retorted. "When I'm in the cockpit, I have absolute control."

Hata stifled a chuckle. "I still don't get it, Rorik Windbeard."

Rorik shrugged and motioned for her to follow. "Come on, they're waiting on us."

Hata followed the Himin-dvergar man across the battlements. She soon spied ahead a few dozen rotor-wing aircraft, ready to depart. As they approached, blue and red steam hissed from vents, and the magically powered engines rumbled to life as propellers began to spin into motion atop the two-person vessels.

Raine Stormfall stood with arms crossed, tapping a foot impatiently before her rotor-wing. Her brilliant gemstone armor glimmered in the sunlight. As she saw Hata approaching, a smile flashed across her features before she pointed to Rorik and then at another rotor-wing.

Rorik hurried off to join his partner, Bryn Sparkheart, in their aircraft as the contraptions began to take flight.

Raine embraced Hata as they met, looking up into her eyes.

Hata couldn't help herself, and she leaned down for a kiss.

Raine returned it, and they lost themselves momentarily before Raine righted herself. "Come, let's see what these our enemies are scheming," Raine called over the loud thumping. She turned and hopped into the cockpit of the flying machine directly behind her.

Hata climbed up and took the seat behind Raine. Her long legs were cramped and uncomfortable, and her armor didn't help. Raine had said they were rebuilding the fleet and would commission a larger cockpit for Hata's size, as she was much taller than the average Himin-dvergar, between four and five feet tall.

The rotor-wing thrummed to life and lifted into the air. The other crafts were hovering, awaiting their queen to lead the way. They ascended at an angle, and the small fleet fell behind Raine's rotor-wing. They soared over a dozen islands; some interconnected with the massive chain bridges that the forces of Skaad had used to move their ground troops across the sky-island world. Then, a solid wall of dark navy clouds loomed before them. Violet lightning flashed through the shadows of the smoke. It was unnaturally spherical, encompassing an enormous mass of the horizon.

A rotor-wing came up alongside them, and two Himin-dvergar turned their heads to await the queen's orders.

Raine motioned for them to scout ahead.

The craft moved forward alone. As the rotor-wing came within reach of the spherical navy cloud, the lightning flashed violently, and the smoke suddenly stretched out like fingers and engulfed the scouting craft. Violet energy arced through the smoke, and there was an explosion with a muted sound. The tendrils receded.

The rotor-wing and its crew were gone.

No. Hata felt sorrow for those two lost souls. *Teras, return them to the mountain. What evil has Hear-fan Skaad conjured here?*

Hata watched from behind as Raine's head shook back and forth in disbelief and guilt. Then the queen motioned again, and the small fleet of rotor-wings turned about and retreated to Keep Crystalia.

"What can we do against such a thing?" Someone called from the back of the throne room.

"It's concealing the Wayfarers Gate."

"Nay, it's protecting it. It has engulfed the damned thing."

"Can the Sunstone do nothing?"

Hata straightened from where she stood at the bottom of the steps leading up to the throne where Raine Stormfall sat, chin propped on a gauntleted fist as she leaned on the arm of the throne. Raine was staring straight ahead, lost in thought. The crowd of Himin-dvergar nobles muttered among one another or shouted out their concerns brashly.

Someone repeated the question, "Sunstone? Can you do something about this?"

Hata took a deep breath and prepared herself to answer.

"We cannot send the Sunstone to her death!" Raine barked, slamming her fist into the arm of the stone throne. "She would befall the same fate as any of us who would enter the dark magic that Hear-fan Skaad has created."

"Then what would you have us do?" a voice came from within the crowd.

"Two things," Raine said flatly. "First, we must rebuild our defenses and prepare for another attack tenfold that of the last. We will rally the other cities of the Himin-dvergar and gather our forces here. The great cities of Skyforge and Zephyrion. We need the full might of our peoples at our back."

Murmurs rippled through the crowd, some of agreement, others of unease.

Raine's voice became solemn. "Secondly, we must seek the aid of magic that can contend with the darkness of Skaad."

"The Crystal Elves," someone whispered close to Hata.

"The Crystal Elves. The *Kidekorvat*," Raine repeated more loudly. "We will send a delegation to seek their aid. They have cultivated the magic of the isles without harvesting it from the earth as we do. They have their beasts to contest with the shadow."

More whispers of disquiet. "The Kidekorvat have banished us from traveling in their lands. They say we harm the world itself by mining the gemstones."

"They're damned arrogant bastards!"

"Feckin' elves."

"They hate us. It's the bright beards blessing that we're not at war with them, too."

"Enough!" Raine's voice boomed over the concourse. "I have spoken. See it done."

With that, the nobles of the Himin-dvergar began to disperse. Soon, only a handful of guards stood at attention as Hata looked up to where her partner sat.

Raine's eyes met hers, and she smiled tiredly and beckoned to Hata.

Hata quickly strode up the steps and took Raine's hand, pulling her to her feet. Looking deeply into Raine's beautiful chestnut eyes. Hata leaned close and whispered, "I want to kiss you."

Raine's gaze moved to the guardsmen, then back to Hata. "You know how I feel about openly displaying our affection, Hata."

"The nobles are gone. It's just the guards."

"It doesn't matter *who* it is, Hata," Raine's voice was grave.

"All right," Hata sighed in defeat. "Come, it's getting late. Let's get you out of that armor." Hata led Raine toward the back stairs that led up to the queen's quarters. Raine let herself be pulled. Her heavy armor clanged as she plodded after Hata tiredly.

Hata waved a few hand servants away as they entered the queen's living quarters. *Our living quarters.* Using magic, Hata quickly removed her armor, let it float through the air, and fastened it to an armor stand in the corner of the dressing room.

Then, she unfastened the thick leather and steel clasps holding Raine's gem-infused armor together. She liked to do this manually, *without* using her powers, when it was Raine's body in question. The gauntlets revealed Raine's steady tan hands, and the vambraces fell to the floor. The pauldrons clattered to the stone floor, and Hata let her lips touch Raine's neck. There was still a heavy gambeson covering the woman's arms and chest beneath.

Raine sucked in a sigh of relief and pleasure.

Hata's hands worked at the back clasps of the breastplate. Once undone, Hata moved in front of her queen, grasped the bottom edge of the heavy plate, and carried it a few paces away. She turned back, and the quilted gambeson covering Raine still looked nearly as heavy as the armor. A hole was sewn out in the center of the quilted pad between Raine's breasts. The magic gemstone that aided the armor's wearer needed to be in contact with skin. Hata eyed Raine's cleavage a moment too long before she pulled the gambeson up over Raine's head.

As the padded tunic came off, Raine's arms fell to Hata's shoulders.

Hata let the tunic fall behind her as their lips met, wrapping her arms around Raine's waist and pulling them together fervently. Hata began undoing the tasset around Raine's waist, their lips still locked together.

Raine pulled her lips away and put a finger to Hata's mouth. "My love, by the bright beard, we both need a bath first."

Hata paused momentarily before saying, "I don't care. You're stunning; you're mine, and I want you as you come."

Raine's cheeks flushed as she blinked, then nodded slowly.

Hata finished undressing her lover and pushed her back onto the massive bed in their sleeping chamber. Then, starting from Raine's lips, Hata made her way down, inching, kissing, and caressing just as someone had shown her so long ago until tantalizing pleasure engulfed them both.

CHAPTER THREE

CONSTRICTED

SAUDETT TIGHTENED HER WINGS around her, trying to keep warm in the cold darkness of her prison cell. *How long has it been since he threw me in here? Days? Weeks? Years?* She hadn't seen Hear-fan Skaad since he killed Nyxal and imprisoned Saudett as a traitor to his cause. Deep underground in the Skaad Lân, in a prison cell cut into the earth with not so much as a bucket to defecate into. Occasionally, one of those deformed, stunted creatures would come about and slop a pile of muck into her cell for her to eat. It was a soupy, chunky mixture of blackened ground meat and who knew what else. She had no choice but to eat it if she wanted to live.

The dark was filled with ceaseless wails and cries that reverberated endlessly, a haunting symphony that persisted day after day. As Saudett had been forcefully carried to her cell, she had glimpsed many other creatures; some she had never seen the like of before. Some humanoid. Some not. Many had been wrapped in bandages with extra appendages surgically grafted to their bodies. Saudett shuddered at the thought, even though she had willingly let the Lord of Shadow do the same to her. *To give me these wings.*

She constricted the dark leathery wings closer as she sat back against the wall. *What will I do when Hear-fan Skaad finally comes for me?* The last thing he had said…

"You killed my son. You will bear me another."

Saudett couldn't stop trembling as she clenched her hands together in fists beneath her cloak of wings. *I saved Hata's life. It was worth it.* She consoled herself, but still, her hands shook uncontrollably. *Any minute now, that vile bastard will appear and have his way with me. Raped until I come with babe once again. I can't do it...* She had already lost one child, Simon's child. The man who loved her the most. What would he think of her now? *I killed our child. I fell in with the enemy.* Her breath shortened as hysteria began to spiral her thoughts out of control.

Footfalls padded slowly in the cavernous room that made up the prison, nearly stifled by the constant wails of other prisoners. Saudett flinched, withdrawing further into the corner and covering herself. She peaked through a crack in her wings, watching as a shadow came into view outside the bars of her cage. It was tall, well-muscled...with tufts of fur.

Darkclaw Marah pressed their face against the bars and sniffed. "We have your scent, Lady Saudett."

"Marah!" Saudett gasped in surprise and ran to the thick steel bars, reaching for the Volkinn.

Darkclaw Marah's long, taunt, fur-covered arms stretched through and embraced Saudett.

Saudett pressed into Marah's warm chest. They smelt of the woods, fresh air, and the leaves rustling in the wind. *They also smelt of blood.* The fur around their mouth was stained crimson and black. But they looked incredibly healthier than the last time Saudett had seen them. When living in the underground complex Hear-fan Skaad called home, Marah had not been thriving, taking little food and spending their days cooped up in Saudett's chamber. Hear-fan had brought Saudett and Darkclaw Marah to the Wald Lân, a world of vast woodland, rivers, and lakes—an untouched sanctuary. Marah's fur shined with vibrance, and their body was stern against Saudett.

"We're sorry, Lady Saudett," Marah rumbled. "We were hunting in the Wald Lân and lost our sense of self. We do not know how long it has been. Finally, one day, as we were on the hunt, we came upon the Gate and remembered all."

"Hettra's mercy!" Saudett exhaled. "It doesn't matter. You're here now. Can you get me out of here?"

"We will try."

"Thank you...thank you. Please help me. That *man* could come for me soon."

Darkclaw Marah's head turned quickly as they let out a low growl, then dashed into the darkness.

The scraping stride of one of the stunted creatures soon approached, accompanied by the squeak of rusted metal as it pulled an iron wagon filled with the blackened muck that passed for food. As it gripped a shovel and began to heave a muck pile into the cage, Darkclaw Marah's clawed fingers grasped the creature's head from behind and, in one quick, brutal motion, snapped its neck with an audible sucking *pop*.

The creature fell limp to the floor, the shovel clanging against the bars as it fell.

Darkclaw Marah's ears pricked and turned, listening for a moment. "Hells," Marah hissed. "Something is coming to investigate. Wait for us, Lady Saudett." With that, Darkclaw Marah picked up the dead creature's body and vanished again into the shadows.

After a moment, two more stunted creatures came shuffling into view, followed by one of the molten rock-like skinned ones. These were rare; Saudett had only once seen one and killed it in the Valley of Hasiera as it sought out Hata. It was humanoid, yet its face was featureless other than the glowing amber-red eye sockets. *Which Lân do these things come from?* Saudett pondered.

The fire-like eyes stared at her through the bars, then gazed around the hallway.

One of the hunched creatures rapped the bars with a stick of rusted black metal and croaked, "Where is the *Child* assigned to feedings?"

Saudett did not answer.

"Filthy human," the other hunched one hissed. "Tell us what you did to our brethren!"

"Silence, fools," the rock-molten humanoid rumbled, its voice grating to the ears. "Listen."

A barely audible *bang* echoed down the hall, followed by a faint scream from far away.

The molten creature's eyes flared with crimson light. It touched the two small, hunched *Children*, and all three began to sink into the ground. Then they were gone, and the prison was silent for a moment.

Something donned on Saudett about how the creatures had sunk into the earthen floor. *That's how they hid in the Burning Sea and moved through the ground during the sunlit hours. That's how they ambushed us in the Moreas Lân. These strange rock-like creatures have that ability and can use it on others.*

Her stomach groaned as she sat waiting. She waited for the sounds of fighting. The wails of her prison mates soon returned, drowning out all else. What felt like an eternity passed as she waited for Darkclaw Marah to return. *Maybe they had been killed or thrown into another cell.* Saudett waited and waited. She waited to be violated. Fear gripped her once more, and her hands continued to shake. Trying to keep her mind off the dark thoughts, she crept forward and crouched over the small pile of gruel that had managed to make it into her cage before Darkclaw Marah had slain the creature. Saudett kneeled over the pile, wings wrapped around her. Using her fingers, she spooned the vile nourishment into her mouth.

A howl reverberated down the corridor.

Darkclaw Marah killed another hunched creature as they came upon it in the dark, slamming the feeble thing against steel cell bars with a loud report.

The sound quivered down the corridor, and the thing shrieked in fear.

Marah cursed inwardly as they tore out the flailing creature's throat with a savage bite. The black blood tasted of rust and rot. Marah let the thing fall, crouched low, and listened. *More will come. We must move.* Marah continued to stalk through the dark corridors. The scents of death and decay hung in the musty air. *We will circle back toward Lady Saudett.*

Suddenly, there was a faint earthy scent growing in the air.

Rock-like hands shot out of the ground and grasped Marah by the ankles.

Marah began to sink. They clawed at the earth, trying to pull themselves free. They managed to push up against the pressure, but suddenly, two hunched abominations were there, striking Marah with black iron bars. Marah let go of their struggle against the force pulling them downward to shield themselves from the blunt weapons. Their legs submerged. Their chest submerged. Darkclaw Marah let out a howl of frustration just before their head sunk into the earth, and greyish darkness surrounded them.

Somehow, they could breathe. Marah twisted and turned but could only see a grey-black mist.

A flash of red light appeared momentarily, and then something slammed into Marah's head, and true darkness took them...

...Darkclaw Marah awoke sometime later, strapped to a table with iron manacles. They could not move their head or limbs.

The stunted creatures moved about the chamber, fiddling with various cutting tools.

Frustrations burned through the fur on Marah's neck as they let out a howl of utter failure.

The creatures began to cut and saw into Marah's flesh.

Chapter Four

SON

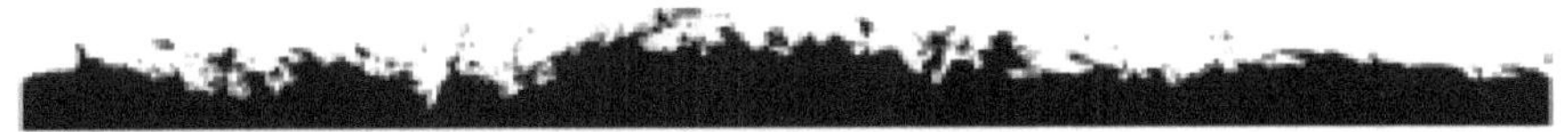

Ien-fan Skaad stepped through the Wayfarers Gate and into the Ryk Lân. After decades he had been recalled from his post in the Fjoer Lân. He clenched all four fists as he strolled across the iron-planked bridge to the next island; a massive wall of thick navy smoke surrounded the islands around the gateway. Bolts of lightning arced and flashed through the roiling shield. *Is Father keeping this magic active? That must be taking a toll on him.*

A disgusting *Child* groaned as Ien-fan walked by it to the next, larger island. *Why had Father insisted on naming all his followers his Children?* Of Hear-fan Skaad's blood children, Ien-fan was the first. Twade was long dead. Now, Trije-fan had been killed as well. Ien-fan hadn't heard the details of his death and imagined it was one of the reasons his father had finally summoned him here. *I am the last of true-blooded children. I've lost both my younger brothers now...when will this senselessness end?* They had been conquering Lân's for nearly a century, starting with Father's home, the Hiel Lân. The Hiel Lân would have been the most problematic in a full-out war. The Iban'mael were far too scientifically advanced and powerful in aspects of magic incantations. Father had wanted to take them by surprise and snuff out their existence in one fell blow, and he had done exactly that.

Father had planned and gathered their forces for years to crush the Iban-mael. Ien-fan Skaad remembered that day.

Ien-fan Skaad charged through the Wayfarers Gate into the Hiel Lân.

A man dressed in armor standing beside the portal turned in surprise.

Ien-fan's axe came down on the man's shoulder and sunk deep. Blood sprayed as his other axe came in low and hacked in at an angle. Then, he pointed with his lower two hands and released duo *Scua Bael Cnytells* at point-blank range into the man's body. The violet-black fire drilled through the soldier as his eyes clouded and death took him.

The horde of *Children* poured out of the Wayfarers Gate and into the city streets. Townsfolk who looked just like Ien-fan fled, their four arms flailing as they screamed in terror and fell to the claws and teeth of the *Children of Skaad*.

Are these not my people? The same people who exiled Father to that wasteland. Ien-fan stood and studied the sprawling city around him as the Children did their work. Massive structures of glass and metal towered around him. *Scua Afléotan,* Ien-fan incanted internally and began to rise into the air. The city stretched as far as the eye could see. An enormous central citadel engulfed his vision at the innermost point of the city. His father had said that the Hiel Lân was relatively small, a habitable moon, as he put it. Yet the entirety of this world was populated. *We must leave none alive.*

An explosion of violet light ignited nearby, and smoke billowed in the air at multiple points throughout the city. Father had initiated the invasion from many Wayfarer Gates that dotted the metropolitan.

Ien-fan leaned toward the citadel as he soared through the air. *That is where the Wayfarers congregate. But first…a little arbitrary destruction. Scua Ad Cliewen.* The black-violet flaming spheres plummeted down upon the city, colliding with one of the tall glass structures and melting metal and glass alike before exploding outward. It groaned and collapsed in on itself with a spew of dust and debris. *Again.* Another blast of heat buffeted him as the fireball struck. *Again!* Hundreds of people died beneath him. Slowly but surely, he floated toward the central citadel, leaving a path of death and devastation in his wake.

Suddenly, a flash of white caught his eye as strings of bright fire leaped up at him from below. He rolled in the air, the flames nearly grazing him as he dove toward the perpetrator. Ien-fan thundered down, thudded, and skidded across the fine stone-paved street where he had seen the spell come from. He leveled his axes at the ready, scanning the area. Nothing moved. *No people. No Children.* There were many pools of black ooze where the *Children* had recently perished.

He heard something shift behind him and turned too late as a force slammed into his side, hurling him through the air. Ien-fan crashed through the glass window of a building, shredding him as he landed violently.

"Fuck me," Ien-fan mumbled painfully as he rolled over and pushed himself to his feet. *Strangung.* He felt his body strengthen, though it wouldn't heal his wounds. His lower left arm hung limp, broken. He was about to enchant the healing spell when he heard glass crunch beneath feet nearby. He looked up and still saw nothing. *Gesihp.* He enchanted the true-sight spell as the Iban'mael Wayfarer came upon him.

Her drop kick flew toward him.

Ien-fan was ready this time and raised his axes in a crossguard before him. His magically strengthened muscles stopped the attack, but it still sent him sliding back through rattling glass with such a powerful impact. As he caught his balance, the woman was upon him once more.

Her four fists struck him with deadly, trained precision, accompanied by quick, powerful kicks.

He danced back and swung both his axes down at her.

She twisted, and two jabs rocketed into his abdomen, though his black metal armor took most of the force.

Ien-fan grimaced and hissed through his teeth, rushing forward, swinging his axes in a rage-induced fury.

She smiled, and her movements blurred.

He found himself face first on the floor, then her weight was atop him, an arm wrapped around his neck in a deadly hold. *I can't breathe.* He pushed and clawed at her arm. As his vision darkened, he closed his eyes and desperately incanted a spell. *Scua Gicela.*

The arm grip on his neck went limp, and the weight rolled off him as he gasped for breath.

The razor-sharp shards of black ice pierced her body as if they had grown out of Ien's back and she had fallen upon them. One jutted through her mouth and out the back of her head. Blood trickled down the tinted ice.

"Fu—fuck me," he panted, trying to catch his breath. He picked himself up and found his axes. Then he healed his broken arm. Finally, he stepped back into the street. Before flying off, he turned to the building with the dead Wayfarer—*Scua Ad Cliewen.* The sphere of flame engulfed the structure, which burst into flames as he again soared up into the skies of the Hiel Lân. *By all the hells, it's going to be a long day.*

Not a second later, he saw blasts of elemental magic down below. Ien-fan descended toward the turmoil. A large force of *Children* was giving ground under the assault in a narrow street. A single figure at the head of the *Children* was taking the brunt of the magical attacks from a small group of Iban'mael at the end of the road. Ien-fan saw his younger half-brother Trije-fan Skaad deflecting white flaming streaks of fire with his violet fuming hands as he slowly tried to advance. Trije's hood had been thrown back, and blood dripped from his lips as Ien-fan shot past him overhead and crashed into the line of Iban'mael, axes flaming to life.

The enemy looked like peasants. Physically, they looked like Ien-fan and his father but dressed in dirty, plain tunics, trousers, and aprons. A large building on one side of the street had a large opening, and Ien-fan caught a glance of strange metal contraptions and scaffolding reaching up around the oddly shaped things.

The Iban'mael panicked and screamed in fright as he landed among them, cutting a young woman down instantly.

"Fight!" Someone bellowed from among the Iban'mael, and to Ien-fan's surprise, the scattering people turned and renewed their defense. White flames licked from their fingers as they pointed at him. Ien-fan surged forward as a stringing volley of white-fire shot past him or deflected against his blackened *Scua Lind* shield of magic. He tore into them with his dual flaming axes. Blood splashed, and people screamed for the last time. They did not put up much fight. As he coldly cut them down, he realized these people were non-combatants. Labourers trying to defend their homes. *They're just people trying to survive.* He had a sudden sense of admiration for these people. *Even the average townsfolk of the Iban'mael can use magic.*

"Fiends!" came a cry from the open building.

Ien-fan turned to see a man dressed in a strange metal suit. The suit was massive, with piston-like bars of yellow-painted steel connecting the limbs to the torso. The man was entirely engulfed in the contraption, his face covered by a bulky helmet with a black plate of glass where his eyes should be. His footfalls thundered and cracked the pavement as he picked up speed, swinging a massive steel girder with all four arms.

Hells, I don't think the Scua Lind barrier could take a hit from that. Ien-fan rolled aside as the metal-clad man let loose a rushing swipe at him. The man crashed through the wall on the opposite side of the narrow street. Dush spewed forth from the new opening around him.

Scua Bael Cnytells. Ien-fan fired his violet streaks of flame into the dust where the man had vanished. Once. Twice. Thrice. He squinted as the dust floated about, unable to see if he had scored a hit on his adversary.

Then, the massive steel beam shot out of the obscurity and collided with Ien-fan directly in the chest. *Strangung.* His barrier shattered at the impact of the girder, and he grabbed the massive projectile with enhanced strength. Still, he felt his ribs crack, and pain burst inside as he was thrown back into the open factory building. His vision blurred as he lay there, barely able to breathe.

The ground rattled as the metal-suited man stomped toward him.

Ien-fan Skaad could do nothing. He looked up at the strange hanging rectangles on the ceiling of the large building, which gave off unnatural light.

Then, there was a hissing sound and a gurgling scream. Violet steam drifted at the edges of Ien-fan's vision. Then, there was a massive *thud,* and a limp metal-clad hand flopped on the ground next to him. Slowly, he turned his head to see the metal-clad man lying in a violet fuming heap. The helmet covering his head had corroded inward, fusing the man's skull with the metal itself.

Trije-fan stood over the body, hooded, smirking down at Ien-fan. "I should have left you to die, Ien. I had this under control; we were all assigned different gates and areas of the city to exterminate. Why are you in mine?"

Ien-fan closed his eyes and painfully put a hand on his chest. *Scua Gehae.* The violet-gold healing *burned* away the pain. He felt his ribs knit themselves back together. Trije had always been jealous of Ien as he was envious of his relationship with Twade, their father's second son. Twade and Ien had grown up together. Trije had come along nearly two decades after his older brother.

As the healing took hold and his lungs began to fill fully again, he sighed and said, "I saw you were struggling, little brother."

"I had everything under control!" Trije hissed and turned and stalked away. "I will prove to Father that I am his strongest son."

Ien-fan pushed himself to a seated position and breathed slowly. "You do that, Trije." Though his little half-sibling had already gone out of earshot. Trije's jealousy and ambition toward their father had pushed them apart. Trije rarely spoke to either Ien or Twade. *Twade, on the other hand…is the only friend I have. My only true brother.* He was honestly the only one Ien could speak to about anything and everything. Something was knotting within, and something was wrong with what they were doing here in the Hiel Lân. Ien-fan had always followed his father mindlessly, but this campaign of vengeance was different. *I need to speak to Twade.*

Ien-fan walked back into the street as *Children* flowed by in droves, following Trije. Ien took to the skies again and set his sights once again on the towering citadel in the city's center.

Ien-fan Skaad stepped into the command tent surrounded by countless numbers of his father's *Children*: the grotesque lumbering beasts and hounds of the Skaad Lân. The grey-skinned, ape-like creatures who were taken from the Wald Lân, and most of their bones were surgically replaced with metals. Thousands of the Grot Lân peoples, the Nyra, were perched in the crystalline trees across the floating islands. He saw none of the earthwalkers, the molten-stone humanoids from Fjoer with their magical affinity to the earth.

Last of all, his long-dead kin, the once Iban'mael. Iban'mael, who had been captured during the invasion of Hiel. They had been tortured, their wills removed as their bodies had been grafted to the massive insect-like blue-burning creatures. Another native of the Fjoer Lân. These massive insectoids had been too savage to domesticate and train for war. So, his father had to merge the Iban'mael prisoners, removing the insectoid's head and brain to be replaced by the half-torso of his kin. Giving them deadly scythe-like blades on their upper arms to defend themselves.

Abominations, Ien-fan thought as his father looked up at him in the dim light of the tent.

"My child," Hear-fan Skaad said from his seat in a comfortable-looking cushioned chair.

It was taken from the Hiel Lân, no doubt. All of Father's niceties were taken from our homeland. Aloud, Ien-fan said, "You called for me, Father?"

"I did." His father said as his eyes fell on the obsidian gem hanging around his neck, emanating a dark aura. The Lord of Shadow's upper hands were open and focused on the gemstone. Pure violet-black intensity reverberated from the thing.

"What are you doing, and what do you need of me?" Ien-fan asked bluntly, eager to be out of his father's presence.

"I am maintaining this barrier around our forces as we construct new siege equipment to confront the Rykling defenses. The Himin-dvergar are a more formidable race than I first perceived."

"Those barbaric little peoples put up a fight?" Ien-fan asked in surprise. He had heard that the people of the Ryk Lân were merely miners and did not know the true treasures their magical island world wrought.

"They have advanced far in the last hundred years. That and they had aid from a human. A human I also underestimated. This Hata. This *Sunstone*, as she calls herself." Father clenched his lower hands repetitively as the rage built in his voice. "But no longer, we will come at these squealing rats with the full might of my Children."

"Will you not deal with them in person? Why send for me?"

"Indeed, I will be *dealing* with this matter in person. But I have another task for you. That task is the Earste Lân."

"The humans?"

"Gaelin Yesnala is the primary adversary. The humans are his pawns. I would have you remove him permanently and destroy the Wayfarers Gates residing in the Earste Lân. I will waste no more time with that Lân of recklessly breeding insects."

"Your will be done, Father. Do you have a gate pointed to that Lân?"

"One, but I'm afraid you must do a little digging."

"Digging?"

"The Sunstone collapsed a mountain atop it."

"Father, can we not simply use the Fjoer Lân's earthwalkers?"

His father blinked, and his face reddened before he visibly calmed himself with a sigh. "Ien-fan, you are my most prominent and promising offspring, the only true blood Iban'mael of my lineage. It was wrong of me to keep you in Fjoer for so long. Alas, my vision was clouded, and I did not see all the tools I had available at my disposal. If possible, bring Gaelin Yesnala to me alive. I have words for him before he dies a slow and painful death at my hand."

"Your will be done, Father." Ien-fan nodded his head and turned to leave.

"One more thing," Hear-fan said, a hint of amusement in his tone. "A human woman is being held in our dungeons. I've meant to pass on my seed to her, but I cannot leave here at this time or for the foreseeable future. Please see to it in my place."

Ien-fan did not answer and nodded again before pushing through the tent flaps. Within, his hatred for his father seethed. *Am I to rape this woman as you did my mother?*

Chapter Five

SATIATED

Simon's eyes fluttered to wakefulness with the shouts of sailors and the thuds of running feet on the deck outside the captain's quarters. He swung his legs over the side of the bed and found his discarded shirt and trousers on the floor. He dressed quickly while moving to the door, squinting as the bright sunlight seeped through the crack, and stepped outside.

Pirates moved about the deck as the ship coasted toward an island. It was not just any island but a city of gangplanks and boardwalks. Simon saw coral stone houses with intricately carved wooden balconies lining the waterfront. Colorful fabrics fluttered from windows, and the scent of spices—cinnamon, cloves, and cardamom—permeated the air. The roofs were thatched, providing shelter from both sun and rain. Stone towers reached up at intervals with large trebuchets and ballistae built atop them. A white sand beach curved in on one side of the pier where smaller fishing boats and people hurried about. Children splashed in the surf and dug holes in the sand.

As *The Mamba's Mouth* glided into the bustling harbor, he saw a mosaic of vessels. Small dhows with triangular sails, their hulls painted in vibrant patterns; sleek pirate frigates with black and yellow flags snapping defiantly; and merchant ships laden with exotic goods.

"Bring her in steady!" Captain Kai's voice came to him from above and behind.

Simon turned and ascended the stairs up to the stern deck.

Captain Kai stood with hands behind his back, rocking on his heels beside the helmsman whose firm hands guided the ship into port.

"Ah ha! The devil man awakens at long last," Kai said with a grin.

"Captain," Simon greeted cheerfully. "I haven't slept that well in ages, to be quite honest. Especially after such a *vigorous* welcome and all." His eyes danced down Kai's enticing body before he could catch himself.

Kai's grin widened. "You will have all the comfort and pleasures you desire at my home once we've fastened ship. For now, stay out of the way."

"I've been meaning to ask—"

"Man, the rigging! Ready to secure lines!" Kai bellowed over him.

"Aye, Captain!" the answering call came from all hands on deck. The crew moved in such synchronized movements that Simon thought sea ghosts may possess them.

Colorful flags signaled from a tower in the center of the docks.

"Five points to starboard, Silas," Kai mumbled.

"Aye, Captain," the helmsman answered with a nod.

Lines were cast to the waiting dock workers, who wrapped them on the pier and hulled on them to bring the ship to the side of the dock. Finally, *The Mamba's Mouth* came to a gentle rest.

"You have shore leave for the day," Kai ordered as his crew gathered before him. "Report to my manor by noon for wage pay, then be at ship come morning light."

There was a raucous cheer from the sailors as they began to pour onto the docks.

"Welcome to *Keeya's Refuge*, home of the *Gilded Crow Corsairs* and many more of that ilk," Kai said, gesturing to the city. "This is the home of we who aim to release the Sea of Xamid and Isles of Tal'tulu from Xamidian oppression."

"Is it truly that bad?" Simon asked curiously. "I thought Xamid strived for knowledge and peace above all."

"As long as it lines their precious Sultan's coffers, the bastards will resort to murder and pillaging. The Xamidians have a stranglehold on trade, fishing, hunting, and military sea dominance. We fight back for the people of Tal'tulu, who will do nothing for themselves."

"Hmm, I never knew," Simon pondered aloud. "Perhaps this is why many Tal'tulu immigrate to Aurulan. Forced to leave their homes in search of a better life."

"Quite perceptive." Captain Kai's brow arced at him. "At any rate, I will hear you out now, devil man. Let's get a drink, shall we?"

"By Skrull's saggy scrotum, I sure could use one."

The captain led Simon down the dock and into the city proper. People bustled about, and fish sellers were set up with market stalls. Their wares were hanging on poles of wood behind them. Others were selling jewelry, some fine gold and gems, others of bright sea shells and bones. The town elevated as one traveled further into it.

Kai stopped near the end of the docks at the tower that took up the central pier.

An older woman called to him in greeting. "How fares you, Kai Bahari?"

"Harbour Master," Kai said with a nod. "We've reclaimed the oil and meat of an *Erin Okun* killed by hunters not far from here and looted their holds as well. You will see it unloaded and sold. Half the coin is to go back into the city reserves, and the other half is to me and my crew."

"I know the drill, my king," the old harbor master said. "Now, who's this scrawny, pale man with you?"

"Simon Meridio, Meridio Enterprises, First Otsoa of Hasiera, at your service," Simon announced with a sweeping bow.

"Enterprises? Otsoa? Hasiera? What're you on about, boy?" the woman snorted, then waved him away. "Be off with you; we have work to do."

"Come, devil man, of many enterprises and whatnots." Kai's hand rested on his shoulder as he led Simon away. "Let's rest at my home and discuss your plea." His hand crawled down Simon's back and found its way under the belt of his trousers to find a firm grip on his cheek.

Simon cleared his throat. "Ahem, Captain, there will be no more of that if you please. I'm married and do not desire to be with anyone else."

"Ha, that did not prevent you last night."

"You had a knife at my throat!" Simon exclaimed.

"But for a moment. Then you partook of our passion on your own accord."

Skrull's hell, he's right. I'm despicable. Simon stiffened and said no more and stood silently brooding. *Where are you, Saudett?*

Kai removed his hand as if sensing Simon's temperament and strode a few steps ahead. His tight trousers clung tightly to his dimpled ass, leaving Simon ogling after him. "Come this way."

They ascended the angled, crushed stone streets that crisscrossed the hillside, leading them to a vibrant market. With a casual air, Kai examined the colorful array of fruit and produce at the vendor stalls while Simon found himself laden with fresh vegetables and a few fish slung over his shoulder.

Children ran playing through the alleys and gardens, laughing as they went. An image of Saudett holding a babe formed in Simon's mind. *A little girl.* Suddenly, the baby was older; her black hair had grown out, and her beige skin was flushed with color. A toddler, walking, babbling. She played with a toy on the ground as Saudett hung the washing up. The little girl turned toward him. *'Papa!'* The image changed again. The young girl sat at the table in their quaint home. She was studying. Simon leaned over to see a sketch of a structure with measurements. She turned her head toward him. *'Father, I forget, what is the formula for roof pitch?'* The next thing he knew, the child had grown into a beautiful young woman, waving from horseback as she joined a caravan setting off for Al'Jalif. She was leaving to join the university and further her learning—

"Devil man?" Kai's words echoed through the image.

Simon's vision returned to the present. "Ahem, you were saying Captain?"

"We're here, welcome to my second home, as my ship, *The Mamba's Mouth*, is the first."

Simon's gaze lifted to a breathtaking sight. A magnificent garden unfolded before him, a narrow pathway cutting through the lush greenery. The quaint homestead, smaller than expected for a pirate king, was a charming surprise. The path was lined with clusters of swaying palms and banana trees, their leaves rustling in the gentle breeze. The stone structure ahead was adorned with brilliant flowers of various shades, blooming in a harmonious chorus and adding a vibrant, picturesque touch to the scene.

They entered the relatively small building, still more extensive than his small two-room home back in Dagad, but assuredly, this was no *manor*. A cozy sitting room met them with comfortable chairs and a small table made from the bones of some sea creature.

Kai immediately plopped down in one of the chairs, lounging casually, one leg dangling up and over the arm, the other spread wide before him.

It left nearly nothing to Simon's imagination with the significant bulge between those legs. *Gods.* His face flushed as he found a seat across from the provocative pirate.

"Tell me your tale, devil man. How did you come to the Isles of Tal'tulu, and what brings you here?"

"Skrull's balls, where should I start?" Simon sighed.

"At the beginning."

"The beginning? Ha. It feels like ages ago." Simon nearly got lost in memories of old, of before all this. Finally, he began his tale. "Well, it all started with a terrible dream..."

Simon went into far too much detail as he told of all that had happened to him since that dream of drowning. He now realized that Gaelin Yesnala had planted that dream in his mind to bring him to the Wayfarers Gate in Hasiera. Still, Simon told the tale as it was. There were multiple interruptions as he went on—disruptions in the form of knocks at the door. The first was a chest of coins a dock worker dropped off. The second was a group of Kai's sailors from *The Mamba's Mouth*, seeking their wages.

Captain Kai was in high demand, and many others came knocking at his door for advice on anything from this matter to that. The hours went by as Simon spoke, and Kai still listened intently.

Simon had got to the part where they had returned from the Moreas Lân and restored water to Hasiera when Kai stood and beckoned him to keep speaking as he entered a second chamber. Kai began chopping vegetables and cleaning the fresh fish he had purchased. He unstopped a dark bottle of rum and poured a draft for each of them, adding a thin slice of ginger to the wooden cup.

Simon sipped at it. "Hells, that's good." It was sweet, and the ginger gave it a little extra kick.

"One of Tal'Tulu's primary commodities is Gold Cobra Rum, as sugarcane is abundant on our islands and the distilleries used to run day and night. Recently, Xamid has been withholding trade with our peaceful countrymen, claiming piracy is the cause."

"Ah, I see. Therefore, Xamid blames you and yours and further constricts their hold on the island nation."

"It has turned many people to the other side of our rebellion against Xamid. Tal'tulu merchant vessels are barred from dealing with Xamid until *we* are dealt with. The Tal'tulu are forced to journey north to the ice flats to trade with the Nunara or circle further through northern sleet storms and perils to the western coast of Aurulan and into the *Mer d'ombre*. It takes months, a treacherous journey that rarely makes much profit. Our very own people want us to turn ourselves in." Kai suddenly slammed his fist onto the table where he was preparing food. "Fucking bastard Xamidians."

"Thus, you resort to more raids, more piracy. It is an unending loop, the snake biting its tail, as they say."

"We do what we must to survive." Kai splashed some oil into a pan that was heating on the hearth. "The Xamidians are slaughtering our waters, in turn destroying our livelihood."

"What of further east?"

"Ships that try to find the coast of Aurulan by that route never return. It is said to connect to the *Mer d'ombre,* the Sea of Shadows. But I doubt it. More likely, those ships fall off the edge of the world. We stopped sending them on that voyage centuries ago."

"Skrull's balls, then an agreement must be negotiated with Xamid. Surely there is some formal written accord after all these years?" Simon said, pacing as he took another sip of the rum.

"There is no ruling class in Tal'tulu." The finely chopped vegetables sizzled as Kai scooped them into the pan. He then sprinkled a mixture of seasoning upon them.

Simon's mouth watered as the scent hit his palate.

"Every island is of itself," Kai continued, "and every town makes its own decisions. We are separated, yet we are kinfolks to one another."

"How do these towns govern themselves?"

"They have gatherings of elders and townsfolk to discuss matters which need attention. But honestly, they do not even do much of that. Most people live their lives going through the motions. They'd rather ignore the issues at hand, the politics of it, and sit on their arses in the sand drinking fucking rum all day."

"It sounds like you've put much thought into all this."

"I run this town and a few island settlements around it. If I'm not killing Xamidians on the decks of their hunters and warships, I focus on making my islands a better place for those who live there."

"That is an admiral goal, dear captain."

"Chike's shaft, devil man, we aren't on deck." Kai's eyes twinkled, and he looked Simon over with a ravenous necessity.

"Hells, I don't know the rules." Simon cleared his throat—*this man.* "Dear *Kai,* then," Simon felt his neck and face brim with heat. "Let me finish my story. We can devise a solution to your struggles to benefit all parties involved, Tal'tulu and Xamid alike."

"You speak of beasts of the night and other Lân's." Kai patted a different mixture of seasonings on the neat fillets of the ocean fish. Then, he pushed the sizzling vegetables aside and delicately laid the fish in the center of the searing pan. "What in Skrull's hell does that have to do with me and my people?"

"Oh, far more than you think, for if we don't succeed against this enemy to mankind, this Lord of Shadow, Hear-fan Skaad, then he will destroy our world and all those who live here."

Kai paused in his tending of the hot iron pan with toasting seasoned vegetables and fish, which, by the gods, smelled Skrull-damned delicious, and looked up at Simon. "Is it that dire? As you put it, you casually appear on my deck and seek aid from a band of pirates in a war in some far off Lân. You need to talk to your king or the fucking Sultan of Xamid. Perhaps if he is distracted with this, that will give me and mine some room to fucking breathe. Why ask me?"

Simon paused. *Why indeed? Why ask a handful of pirates to fight for him?* From what he'd gleamed of Tal'tulu, there was no fighting force, standing army, or navy. A thought came to him. He tilted his head questionably. "How many ships do you command, Kai?"

Kai's eye twitched slightly as he plated the fruits of his labor. His answer was almost a whisper, "A few dozen."

"A few dozen?" Simon exclaimed. "Thirty-six ships?"

"Fifty-five as of yesterday. That is only those who fly my flag and do my bidding. That does not include my alliances with other pirate bands."

"There are others?"

"Old Keen Eyes has the most prominent fleet after my own, the bastard half-breed. But he is a ruthless eel who will attack any vessel on sight. I can't control him, let alone seek his aid."

"Well, I'll be damned," Simon muttered in awe. *The pirates are the Tal'tulu standing navy. That's why Xamid is so intent on disassembling them.* "Therefore, you have fifty-five vessels under your direct command, and you said you oversee a *few* islands around here. Just how many of those are inhabited?"

"My territory covers some twenty or so minor villages, though most of the hundred or so islands have some residents, be they farmers or fishers."

"Skull's balls, man, you're *already* a king. You already rule a nation."

"Bah, devil man—"

"My *name* is Simon." He interrupted sternly. "You must speak to Xamid in peace and spearhead a trade deal with them."

"Devil—" Kai stopped and sighed. "Simon...I do not speak for all of Tal'tulu. The most inhabited isles are under Keen Eyes' control. It's not even so much of an island as it is the most significant land in our seas. Thousands of people live on Tal'tulu's Spine. It is an interconnected snake of landmass that cuts through the Isles at an angle from northwest to southeast. My territory is located southwest of the spine, closest to Xamid."

"At the forefront of the struggle."

"Yes," Kai's voice was sullen.

Simon noticed Kai suddenly looked exhausted. Simon's eyes fell on the two plates of fish and vegetables cooling as they spoke. He smiled reassuringly. "Come, let's not let this fine feast wrought by your delicate hands go to waste."

Kai caressed the callouses of one of his open hands with the other. He tilted his head and gave Simon a mischievous look. "Delicate?"

"I mean, sturdy...uhm, deadly—"

"Chike's trident, you're easy to unsettle, *Simon*." His name came from Kai's lips like sweet syrup. Kai handed him the wooden plate and strode back into the sitting room, where he placed his platter on the low table. He leaned over it and began eating.

As Simon sat and took a bite, he realized how hungry he had been. Despite the slightly cool temperature, the flavor of the dish was exceptional. The vegetables were perfectly seasoned, each bursting with a unique blend of spices. And the fish, with its crispy edges, was the perfect complement to the vegetables. Simon savored every bite, feeling satisfied and content. Before he knew it, he leaned back, hands across his stomach in pure bliss.

Kai left and returned with the bottle of rum, pouring them another round. Then, to his surprise, he sat down beside Simon. He rested his head on Simon's shoulder, and his solid chest pushed against Simon's arm. One of Kai's hands wandered between Simon's legs.

Simon felt a shiver of desire tingling through him.

Kai's lips touched his ear. "*Simon.*"

Gods. His trousers were immediately pitching a pavilion...*as they say.*

He closed his eyes and pictured Saudett. Saudett and the babe. Saudett and *his* daughter. He opened his eyes and shifted away from Kai. "I'm sorry," he said, taking Kai's hand as he did so. "You are a handsome, glorious man, Kai, and I want you, but I can't do this again."

Kai stood and calmly pulled a string from his waist, letting his trousers fall free at his feet. A tangle of jewels and beads adorned Kai. He sat back down beside Simon and crawled toward him temptingly. "You've already broken your vow to your spouse." His voice was a low groan. "Would one last time change anything now?"

By my goddess Hettra, I beg forgiveness. Their lips met as Kai pushed him onto his back. *What's one last time?*

Chapter Six

SAPPHIRE

The wind buffeted Hata's face as she sat behind Raine in the newly outfitted rotor-wing. The engineers designed the new machine with more space for Hata's long legs to stretch underneath Raine's seat. Another new feature was the explosive canisters in a compartment below their seats. Bryn Sparkheart's experiments had been successful. He had rigged the canisters to ignite on impact with the ground. The mixture of reactive magical gemstone dust caused considerable destruction to whatever was nearby when it exploded.

We need everything and anything we can use against Hear-fan Skaad, Hata thought as they broke through the cloud cover. They had been traveling for three days. A dozen rotor-wings and their crews accompanied the queen to meet with the crystal elves, the *Kidekorvat.* They had yet to see any sign of them.

As the sun set again, they approached a craggy island of large, jagged stone formations surrounded by ominous clouds. They descended upon it and landed on rugged terrain of sharp, broken crystals jutting from the earth in a chaotic pattern. Himin-dvergar hopped out of their rotor-wings as the propellers puttered out and inspected their machines for any damage or wear and tear.

A larger craft bringing up the rear, sporting eight propellers shuddering overhead, came to a rest with a heavy *thud,* small crystal formations shattering under its flat footlike landing gear. People poured out, rolling casks of ale and carrying crates of food.

They think with their bellies before all else, Hata thought amusedly as the Himin-dvergar began striking fires and setting out small folding stools.

Raine strode past Hata with determination, *or frustration,* in her step and up the ramp into the large flying vessel. Hata hurried after her, grabbing two freshly poured mugs of ale from a crate near a newly broken barrel. She took a satisfying sip from the sloshing beverage before carefully walking up the ramp, balancing the two mugs.

Hata found Raine leaning over a table of maps nailed down to its surface. Her brow creased in concentrated dissatisfaction. *She looks so pretty when she's angry.* As Hata approached, Raine grunted in frustration; her fists clenched on the tabletop. "We should have found *Valon Vuori* by now."

Hata stopped, her mug of ale held at mid-sip to her lips. "*Valon Vuori?* That's awfully close to the name of my people, the Vouri."

"Well, the damned crystal elves do speak your language. *Valon Vuori* is the name of their city. It resides within a mountain. I have only been there once, when I was very young."

"A mountain city?" Hata sputtered, coughing on her ale. *Exactly like Oitilla,* she thought as she wiped ale from her mouth and chin onto her sleeve. "And they speak Vouri?"

"Thank Luminar that we've been brushing up on the old tongue with you since your arrival," Raine muttered as she moved an odd trinket with a spinning needle across the map table. "Though it would be nice if you learned our language too."

"I—I've been practicing!" Hata said in broken Himin, then switched back to Vouri. She held out the other mug of the rich ale to Raine, who smiled and took it from her waiting hand. "At any rate," Hata continued. "These crystal elves, I mean the *Kidekorvat,* seem to have much in common with my people. I can't wait to meet them."

"Pray to Luminar that we are well received, let alone find the whereabouts of their home." Raine paused for a moment and looked up at Hata. "Hata, my love, there is something I need to tell you before—" The room shook and lurched to one side. The entire ship lifted at an angle and fell back into place, throwing Raine off her feet, her mug of ale splashing to the floor.

Hata instinctively steadied herself, molding the heavy tungsten greaves protecting her lower leg to grow stilts outward at her feet. When the tremors to the vessel passed, Hata quickly aided Raine back to her feet.

Outside, desperate shouting could be heard, followed by the sputtering ignition of engines and propellers whirling to life. A rib-rattling roar overcame the sounds of people panicking.

Hata and Raine ran down the ramp as Himin-dvergar retreated up toward them.

"Get the ship in the air, or we'll all be stranded here with that thing!" One of the engineers urged her comrades on. "Start the engines!"

Raine grasped the engineer's shoulder, shaking her. "What thing? What's happening?"

The woman pointed up and past the large airship. A giant shadow loomed beyond it, rock and crystal reflecting the flickering firelight in the dimming night.

"Glimmergast," Raine whispered in severe awe, staring at the shimmering scales of the serpentine creature. When the beast shifted, parts of it seemed to vanish from sight. Its pitch-black eyes glistened on a massive head that slowly opened, revealing curved dripping fangs. Its head shook, and a mane of crystal spines expanded behind those pit-like eyes.

"To the air!" Raine shouted, pushing Hata toward their rotor-wing.

Hata stopped and faced the gaping maw of the snake. She focused on the earth around the creature, lifting her hands. She willed massive rock slates to rip out of the ground directly before the Glimmergast. Dust spewed out as the earthen force erupted before them. Hata strained to see through the darkness and dirt spray. She squinted, peering at where the serpent had been.

It was gone.

A rumbling hiss came from overhead and behind her. A sparkling mist spewed out over the Himin-dvergar camp. It rained down on them gently.

Hata lifted a hand as the glittering mist sleeted around her. Her hand then froze in place. *I can't move.* She willed her legs and arms to move. They did not. Desperately, she reached for the earth. *Nothing.* A warm wind caused her spine to shiver, and a foul stench came on the wind. Drops of shimmering saliva fell into her vision. Two long fangs overhead.

Then, a sharp, piercing scream suddenly cut through the air, filling the surroundings with an eerie sense of a rising storm. The fangs retreated, and the looming shape of the Glimmergast came before her, but its head was held high, and its mouth was open skyward.

Hata felt the hair on her arms prickle.

The air seemed to compress in a long line directly above the Glimmergast's head at an angle. There was a thundering burst in the air, and a shockwave cut a hole in the dark cloud cover. A javelin of lightning surrounded by crackling air hurled from the expanding circle of cloud—the searing lance shot through the sky, impacting the head of the Glimmergast with such force that the bolt erupted out the other side in a spray of blood and chunks of flesh. The serpent's long body twitched and spasmed, then lurched and fell, crushing a rotor-wing beneath its massive bulk.

Hata gazed upon the magnificent dragon. Arcs of electricity crackled and dwindled at its gaping jaw as its focused energy dissipated from the compressed, concentrated blast. Its translucent wing span covered the starry sky as it soared above them. The magnificent creature had crystal-like scales shifting between deep cobalt and cerulean blue shades, and vibrant gemstones grew in shining patches across it. When the moonlight glimmered on the being's hide, it refracted into a mesmerizing dance of azure and indigo. The scales resembled storm clouds in clear skies, like a churning cyclone. It dove toward them with a roar, and its wings beat the air, clearing the shimmering mist away from the paralyzed onlookers.

Hata feared it would attack again as she felt her fingers twitch with renewed movement. The dragon landed heavily near the corpse of the Glimmergast. That's when Hata noticed the flapping cloak of azure on a figure perched behind the head of the dragon, reins in hand. The figure slid down the back of the dragon and gave it a reassuring pat before striding directly toward Raine and Hata.

The blue dragon began to bite and tear into the flesh of the Glimmergast with predatory desire.

As Hata gained movement to her arms and legs, she caught the dragon's eye, one of the twin pools of glowing liquid cobalt. It watched her even as it devoured the flesh of the dead beast. Its gaze felt like the sky was peering into her soul. Hata shivered in awe and felt herself being sucked into the gaze.

"Do not stare too long into a Sapphire Stormwings regard." A man's sultry, soft, yet somehow sophisticated voice broke Hata's concentration. "You may succumb to the gale of her wrath."

Hata turned her head to the man speaking perfect Vouri. He removed the fine azure cloak covering his head to reveal brilliant red hair, combed and braided with a warrior caste knot—*a Vouri braid*. Dark lightning bolt tattoos decorated his face. *Like fathers and mothers.* He was tall and had slender limbs, but his muscles were tense, visible through his tight leathers and what looked like shining blue dragon scales on his shoulder pauldrons and bracers. He looked as if ready to spring forth to combat in a heartbeat.

"We thank you for your aid, Brother of Dragons," Raine answered bluntly. "We would all be swimming in Glimmergast guts without your timely intervention."

"Timely indeed," the man said.

His skin was as fair white as Hata's but unfreckled, and his face was *too* smooth and elegant. The pointed ears were odd yet fit the man's look quite naturally. *He is intensely beautiful for a man. Teras's thunder, I have so many questions.* She would have to wait. It was not proper to interrupt her queen while she negotiated.

"I've been wondering," he continued, "what a wandering patrol of these loud, obnoxious contraptions have been doing in our skies since yesterday." He gestured off-handedly to the larger of the flying ships. "I do say, I've never seen one of this size."

"You've been watching us for an entire day? By the bright beard, why did you not reveal yourself?" Raine demanded impatiently. "I am Queen Raine Stormfall of Crystalia Keep and the Himin-dvergar. We come seeking your people."

"Dear me," the man bowed, his red braid dangling nearly to the ground as he crossed a hand over his chest. He carried a delicate bow and a quiver of arrows on his back, and Hata caught a glimpse of a fine gemstone sword hilt and a dagger beneath his cloak as he righted himself. "I apologize, Queen of the Himin-dvergar. I am Taivaseläin, kin to Safiiri." He turned his head to indicate the dragon. "I suppose it can only be that ominous sphere of darkness and ruin that would make one such as you swallow your pride and turn to the *Kidekorvat* for aid."

"You know of that too?" Raine's voice elevated with each word from her lips.

The dragon lifted its head, dripping raw meat dangling from its jaws as it turned to regard Raine.

Hata put a hand on Raine's shoulder reassuringly. *Be patient, my love.*

Raine sighed audibly and took a deep breath before continuing, "We're gathering *all* of the Himin-dvergar to our stronghold, and still, I fear it will not be enough against the threat we face."

"*Please*," the man sounded disinterested. "Queen Stormfall, save your breath for the elders. I am but a soldier coming back after a long-running patrol. We shall take flight at first light. It will be my *unending* pleasure to take you to *Valon Vuori*. For now, get some rest." With that, the man turned and strode back to the feeding dragon.

"Damned arrogant elvish bastards," Raine muttered as the man moved out of earshot. Though Hata thought she saw his head twitch slightly, he continued away from them.

The dragon's massive head curved down to greet him, and he spoke a few words.

"Well, thank Teras, he saved us," Hata said. "At least he's got that going for him."

"I suppose," Raine said, leaning against Hata wearily. "Come, I'm tired and hungry. Let's get a bite and retire for the night."

Hata's heart was racing excitedly at discovering these new people and their ties to the Vouri. Even though she knew she couldn't sleep much, she smiled and took Raine's arm, leading her toward the rekindled fire. The aroma of hot Himin-dvergar stew bubbling on the fire permeated the air, making her mouth water. Hata sat with her bowl beside Raine and ate as her mind wandered back to the *Kidekorvat*—the dragon-riding elves.

Half a day came and went as they followed Taivaseläin and his Sapphire Stormwing, Safiiri. They passed countless cloudy islands of crystal forests and gemstone rock formations. After long last, Taivaseläin signaled to them with one hand as he guided the massive beast through the air, reins in his other hand.

Raine returned the signal.

The azure dragon began to climb, and Raine aimed the rotor-wing into its wake as it ascended. The beast and elven rider disappeared into a thick cloud cover. As their aircraft was immersed in the mist, they held their breath for what seemed like an eternity, praying they followed in the right direction. They finally broke into the open air again to the spectacular sight of a massive floating island in which the ring of clouds had obscured around its base. It was an immense mountain.

Dragons flew to and from the landmass, and the mountain *drifted* through the sky.

That's why we couldn't find it, Hata thought. *It's a moving island.*

As Raine steered the rotor-wing to approach, the blue dragon leading them let out a cry, which was returned with an answering cacophony of draconic music.

Once closer, Hata saw dragons of emerald-green scales reflecting the sunlight. Others had iridescent opal scales that shifted colors as they soared through the winds. There were golden dragons, their citrine crystals glowing like miniature suns. Yet more with an even deeper gilt, a mix of earthen tone, rock-like growths on their backs and limbs.

"They're beautiful," Hata said aloud, but the thudding of the propellers drowned her out.

Raine trailed closely behind the mighty Sapphire Stormwing as they soared through the vast sky. Their aircraft was flanked by the other rotor-wings, which fell seamlessly into formation behind her. The large multi-propellered craft brought up the rear. Ahead of them loomed the towering mountain island shrouded in a thick veil of mist. As they approached, Safiiri veered to the left, leading them straight into a hollow opening in the mountain's side. The tunnel seemed to swallow them whole, enveloping them in darkness as they delved deeper into the earth.

Then, a light twinkled ahead. Hata shielded her eyes with her arm as the light grew brighter and brighter. Finally, they emerged into a massive cavern that took her breath away—the sight before her was awe-inspiring—a stunning city that seemed alive and beating with energy. A light tunnel seeped in from above, lit up the crystal growth within the cavern. Everywhere she looked, there were gemstone trees that glowed with an array of spectral colors, casting a beautiful glow across the entire cavern. And majestic dragons were perched in nests upon the walls all around the city, their scales glistening in the warm light. The city of elves, *Valon Vuori*.

They descended to the ground next to where the blue dragon had landed on a flat surface near one of the large gem-like trees. Hata noticed elegant window openings on the trees and large, intricately carved double doors leading out. People emerged and began hurrying toward their group as the propellers stopped their unceasing thumping.

Raine climbed out of the rotor-wing and waited as the other Himin-dvergar gathered behind her. Hata stood at her side, still wondering at the sight.

Taivaseläin's dark cloak fluttered behind him as he nimbly disembarked from the neck of his colossal dragon.

Safiiri tilted her head towards him, and he patted the beast's snout affectionately.

Watching from a distance, Hata could see the faint movement of Taivaseläin's pallid lips as if he were conveying some message to the dragon. Suddenly, the dragon lifted its head and spread its wings, generating a powerful gust of wind that crackled with energy before soaring up into the air.

A posse of elegantly dressed crystal elves lined up ahead of Hata and company, and Taivaseläin fell to a knee before them, a hand to his chest.

"Elders," Taivaseläin said. "I present the Queen of the Himin-dvergar. Raine Storm-fall."

Raine stepped past the prostrated Taivaseläin. "May your beard never tangle in the winds of the high skies."

"And may your crystals always catch the light of the eternal sun," one of the elders replied, his long silver hair falling past his shoulders. His golden eyes flickered toward Hata, and then they returned to Raine in a split second. "We've heard the reports of malicious intent at your threshold. For we knew it was only a matter of time before you would come seeking the assistance of the *Kidekorvat*, Queen Stormfall."

Hata saw Raine's shoulders stiffen, her hands clenched tightly at her sides. Abruptly, the queen of the Himin-dvergar fell to her knees. "I beg of you, help us."

Chapter Seven

UNSOUGHT

A shadowed figure stood within her prison cell, the silhouette of four arms looming over her.

He's finally come for me. Saudett's heart hammered in her chest at the realization. Terror gripped her, and tears streamed down her face as she began to sob uncontrollably. "No. No. No. Please, no."

The four hands reached out for her.

Her piercing scream tore through the silence, echoing in the darkness.

"I'm not here to hurt you," a gruff voice said, his hands waved in a calming motion. "One moment." One of his hands flicked its fingers, and a soft globe of warm golden light grew from nothing. A bearded man looked at her, his inverted eyes watching her, his lips in a solemn line. The lips moved. "What has he done to you?"

"Please don't hurt me," Saudett begged. "He will have his way with me until I am with child. I can't have a child, not with him. Please don't bring me to *him*."

"To Hear-fan Skaad?" His white pupils glimmered against the golden light. He stayed where he was; hands still held up to indicate he would not touch her.

"Please..." she murmured.

"Did you know he raped my mother too," the man said softly. "I'm the fruit of his violation."

Saudett looked up at the stranger. Blinking through the tears, she finally *looked* at the man. She saw a young man's complexion resembling his father's, with a pale grey hue that almost appeared blue. However, his skin had a rough texture, as if it had been exposed to the sun's harsh rays for too long. To add to his rugged appearance, he sported a thick, tangled black beard and hair that seemed completely unkempt, giving him an air of wildness. He wore weathered and beaten black leather armor.

"My father was banished here for that crime, banished to the Skaad Lân. The crime was so rare in the Hiel Lân that my people, the Iban'mael, did not know what to do with him. They were enlightened and egotistical, thinking such a thing would never happen in their superior post-scarcity society. A world where everyone had everything they could ever want or need. Alas, it was still not enough for my father."

He never told me why he was banished. Saudett recalled her long dinner conversations with Hear-fan Skaad and how he had manipulated her into empathizing with him and his exile. Abandoned and starving, he feasted on the residents of the Skaad Lân, and out of petty vengeance, he destroyed the Heil Lân—his people.

The man continued to speak. "A decade or so after my birth, though in human time I would still be a toddler, my mother had me sent away to join him in his exile. She could not bear to look at me without being overwhelmed with unbridled hatred."

"You were a constant reminder of what he did to her," Saudett finally said.

He jolted in surprise at her response and then nodded solemnly. "Indeed, I was. I was too young to know anything. He raised me in his image. I grew up knowing nothing of my past, a proud son of an ambitious father. A conqueror of *worlds*. I discovered my past as we extinguished the lives of our people." He paused, stretching out one hand with the palm upward. "Can I show you?"

Saudett hesitated. *This could be a trap. He's luring me in. He's HIS son for Skrull's sake!*

"I would have done it by now if I meant to fulfill my father's bidding and maintain our family's bloodline."

"He sent you in his stead? To *rape* me in his stead?"

"He did."

"You will ignore his bidding?"

"He needn't know I refrained. As long as you play the part. Just as *he* does not know that *I* know of my mother." He chuckled abruptly. "Fuck me, that's a mouthful."

"Why do this for me?"

"I have murdered in his name. I have committed genocide in his name. I have pillaged and enslaved dozens of Lân's in his name. I will not repeat the very cause of all this pain and torment."

"Why stay? Why continue to serve him at all?"

"Because I am selfish and a coward. It's rather simple. I want to live."

Saudett paused, pondering this man's words. *He seems genuine, but so did Hear-fan Skaad. Is he toying with me?* "Why should I trust you?"

He paused momentarily, his face betraying his thoughts with a sorrowful expression. "I—I don't know. I've been alone for so long. When I saw you huddled in the corner, I couldn't do what my father bid. When I saw you there, I thought of my mother, and the words spilled out. I've never told anyone of my mother. There was no one *to* tell. Perhaps it is that you, humans, are the closest beings to the Iban'mael that we have met biologically. Molten rocks don't make decent confidants, and the other *Children...*" he gave a distasteful snort.

"What's your name?" Saudett asked, her curiosity getting the better of her.

"Ien-fan Skaad. The first son. But by all the hells, the name my mother gave me is Malix."

"Malix?" Saudett asked as she reached out a hand. "What did you want to show me?" Her fingers came to rest on his open palm, and light flashed before her eyes.

Ien-fan Skaad burst through the wall near the base of the towering citadel with fuming violet *power*, showering rubble everywhere as he took in his surroundings. He didn't have long to look as a barrage of concentrated razor-sharp air came at him. *Scua Lind.* A dark shield of magic crackled into existence around him as he flung himself to the side. A few blasts struck him, and his shield shook and pulsed. It could only take so much.

Soldiers were covered from head to toe in white and red armor like nothing he had seen before. The oddly smooth helms covered the entire head, a strip of black glass where their eyes would be. Plates of the same hard-shiny material covered their chests, shoulders, and thighs. But it was not metal. It glistened in the white light that unnaturally filled the chamber. The soldiers pointed white rectangular objects at him, and another barrage of *Windan* ripped toward Ien.

He twirled mid-air and let loose two blasts of *Scua Windan* in return.

The soldiers dived behind a low wall as stone and debris exploded around them. One of the soldiers took the blast in the shoulder. It knocked him back but did not cut into his flesh as it should have. A broad-shouldered man with decorations on his armor gave encouraging orders to the dozen men and women. He carried a massive sword on his back.

Ien-fan ground his teeth. "Fucking hells, I'll need to get in close."

The soldiers were guarding a large door to another chamber. They peaked over a low wall in front of and on both sides of the door, letting shots of the compressed air loose in intervals. The attacks were too quick and numerous for Ien-fan to dodge them all, and his barrier of dark light reverberated and cracked.

He tried to move forward but found himself unable. *So be it. I'll try something different. Wincian.* As Ien stepped forward, he disappeared and reappeared ten feet ahead of where he had just been. The *Windan* blasts zipped past him. He took another step and blinked ahead another ten feet.

The soldiers shouted in distress. Their attacks tore up the chamber, shooting debris everywhere except on Ien himself.

Then he was in their midst. *Strangung. Scua Byrnsweord.* His axes ignited in violet fire, and his muscles bulged as he hacked and slashed through the soldiers. Blood painted the chamber.

His enemies drew metal sticks with sparking energy crackling from their ends. The batons were held in their lower hands as their uppers continued to aim the *Windan* weapons at him. One fired a shot from near point-blank range.

Ien-fan's shield crackled in duress but held. He twisted and kicked the weapon out of the soldier's hands before coming full circle with his two flaming axes, searing through two arms and cleaving into the man's chest.

The man gave a muffled grunt as blood gushed, and he fell dead to the floor.

A blast of *Windan* impacted Ien-fan's back, sending him stumbling forward into two more soldiers who lashed out with four batons. When the sparking tips hit his barrier, somehow, they *passed* through it.

Pain lanced through Ien-fan as one of the batons hit him in the arm. He roared in fury and retaliated with a double overhead swing, chopping through the enemy soldier's upper arms at the shoulders.

The woman screamed and stumbled back as one arm thumped to the ground and the other dangled precariously, still attached as blood spurted from the wound.

Ien-fan ducked in the nick of time as a massive sweep of a two-handed sword cut through the air above him. The blade sizzled with that sparking energy that seemed to ignore the magical shield.

The burly man wielding the weapon grunted with exertion, bringing the great sword back to chop down on him.

Ien-fan sidestepped and surged forward, slamming his shoulder into the man's chest, hacking down on the man's leg with one axe as he did so. The strange plate of armor slowed the blow, and as it reached flesh, the man roared in pain, wrapped his two right arms around Ien-fan, and peeled him off.

Ien-fan rolled, trying to get to his feet, only to be leaped on by more waiting soldiers. Their batons sparked painfully into his back. His magical shield shattered into nothingness. One knelt on him as the rain of blows kept falling. Whoever was on his back grasped Ien painfully by his short topknot, pulling his head back.

The large man lumbered over, raising his two-handed sword to thrust it into Ien's face.

Fuck me, looks like this is it, then, Ien-fan thought without resistance.

A violet-black string of fire pierced the neck of the large man, and a sizzling gurgle emerged from his throat as the sword clanged to the floor. A second hiss ignited, and the soldier atop him rolled off. Dead. Another *hiss* and *snap* followed by more. Soon, the chamber was silent except for Ien-fan's heavy breathing.

"I do not understand your fascination with killing in such a barbaric, close-range fashion, big brother."

Ien-fan pushed himself to his knees as he looked at his younger sibling through strained vision. He managed to pull a wry grin. "Well, fucks to you, Twade."

His brother, Twade-fan Skaad, floated casually a few feet off the ground. Refined, unblemished robes of violet and shadow hanging past his feet. He grinned back at Ien.

"Perhaps you should learn to walk, little brother. Else you become feeble," Ien-fan mocked. "Get your hands dirty once in a while."

"Ha," Twade sniffed loudly. "And spoil my outfit? Utterly ridiculous."

Ien-fan came to his feet and stretched, picking up one of his fallen axes. He sighed impatiently, "Well, I thank you for the save, but we need to get back to work."

"Do you not ponder why our father has us eradicate these people who are the same as you and he?" Twade-fan asked nonchalantly, floating toward the doors to the next chamber. He began inspecting the heavy metal construction that appeared fastened tight. "The Iban'mael. Are you not one yourself?"

"They unjustly banished him." Ien-fan joined Twade at the door, but there was no handle and nothing to pull on. Pushing on it did nothing. "We seek retribution." Twade's question had been running through Ien's mind since he had slain the first Iban'mael Wayfarer he had come upon.

Twade played with his braided white hair that dangled down the front of his robe. "Of course, of course. But surely the destruction of our people, though I am only a half-blood, is a bit extreme, is it not?"

He's right, Ien-fan thought, but instead, he felt he needed to defend his father. He spun toward his brother, leveling an axe at him. "What're you implying?"

"Ha-ha," Twade laughed nervously, then smiled warmly. "Blind faith is simply so unbefitting of anyone, dear Ien. Master the art of thinking independently." He gestured, and corrosive, violet fumes spewed from his open hand onto the door. The metal began to *hiss* and *pop* as it melted away.

Ien-fan stepped back to avoid the corrosive magic. *Father has never given me a tangible reason for his exile.* He always managed to avoid the subject, preaching his rage at the unjust treatment of himself. *Twade and Trije at least knew their mother.* A human woman whom they had long outlived. They had watched her grow old and feeble, wandering the underground halls of their father's stronghold. Until she had passed peacefully in bed. *Who was my mother?* All he knew was that she was Iban'mael. *I'm one of these people who I so ruthlessly murder.*

Ien-fan walked after Twade, floating ahead of him through a curving, gradually inclined hallway, absent-mindedly lost in his thoughts. They were on a lower floor of the central tower, this hallway seeming to wrap around the tower's circumference, leading upward while chambers made up the center column of the tower.

They came to another door on the side of the hall, which Twade made short work of. They entered a room full of sizeable globes of different colors and odd flat plates of glass with moving words and images upon them. The globes floated above desks or workstations and rotated slowly. One was of greens, browns, and blues, like land and sea. Another was of dark grey swampland and snaking rivers. One was of crimson lava and volcanic rock.

"What's all this?" Twade wondered aloud.

Ien-fan approached a piece of glass with the image of a woman, her nearly blue-skinned face creasing with age. *Asecgan,* Ien enchanted internally and the words began to make sense in his mind.

Elynor Thalriss – Ryk Lân – *Tasked with documentation, research, and negotiation with the Himin-dvergar and Kidekorvat. Protect from otherworldly threats, if necessary, but do not engage in inter-species conflicts and politics.*

The image flickered and changed to that of a man with a grey hood shadowing his features.

Gaelin Yesnala – Earste Lân - *Tasked with documentation, research, and negotiation with humans of different racial backgrounds and cultures. Protect from otherworldly threats, if necessary, but do not engage in inter-species conflicts and politics.*

It flickered once again to the image of someone he could not determine their gender.

Sylthar Vaelora – Moreas Lân - *Tasked with documentation, research, and negotiation with the Kadal and the fauna and flora of this Lân. Protect from otherworldly threats, if necessary, but do not engage in inter-species conflicts and politics.*

Twade came to Ien-fan's side, his eyes taking in the information quickly. "Well, this makes our task more complicated indeed. It appears there are Iban'mael Wayfarers spread across the heavens."

The glass changed repeatedly, showing them over two dozen people before finally coming to Elynor Thalriss again.

The floor suddenly shook. The shockwave felt like it originated from higher up the tower.

"Father was heading for the peak of this citadel. Shall we join him?"

"Yes, yes," Ien-fan muttered. "Go on ahead. I will clear these floors as I go. Join him swiftly." There was a red blinking box on the glass that Ien couldn't stop staring at.

"I mean, we could just level this entire citadel. It would be much faster than manually dealing with every Iban'mael we stumble upon."

"Father ordered us not to destroy it; there is much information here that he wishes to study."

"Ever the lapdog, eh, Ien?" Twade chuckled as he stepped back out into the hall. He then proceeded to detonate the tower's outer wall with casual grace. He waved to Ien, smiling as he floated out and ascended out of view.

Ien-fan touched the blinking red box.

Vagabond Wayfarers

The image of his father appeared.

Threnn Duskweaver – *Exiled to the Skaad Lân for the rape and violation of Nymira Kaelum, compounded by the odious and prominent ambitions of naming the Iban'mael as* *a master race over all others—seeking the subjugation or genocide of the denizens of countless other Lân's.*

The image flickered. A baby appeared on screen.

Malix the Unsought – *The product of Threnn Duskweaver's infringement.*

Ien-fan Skaad stared in shock at the flickering glass, looking at his younger self. *My name is Malix...*

Another explosion rocked the tower, sending tremors through its structure.

Saudett gasped as she pulled her hand away from Malix's. "Skrull's hell! He never intended for you to find out."

"No," Malix said coldly. "He will never know. Not until I find some way or someone who can stand up to him. He could brush me aside as if I am but an insect."

"I don't believe it. You're strong. I've *seen* it."

"Tell that to my little brother, Twade. Father killed him without so much as a dissatisfied blink."

Chapter Eight

KEEN

I'm a fucking bastard. Simon was utterly disgusted with himself. *I can't keep my Skrull-damned cock in my trousers. My sweet Saudett will never take me back. I'll never hold my child.* Simon paced back and forth on the deck of *The Mamba's Mouth*. The ship, followed by two others, was heading back to the island where the Wayfarers Gate was. Somehow, Simon had convinced Kai to pick up a few of his companions. *Skrull only knows what happens after that.*

The ship coasted leisurely through the blue-green waves. Sea birds cackled and followed above. They passed by the island where the hunters had killed the *Erin Okun*. There was no sign that a struggle had even occurred there. Simon recalled the direction he had flown in from and pointed as Kai prompted him.

Another hour came and went as they rounded another island. "Skrull's balls," Simon cursed. "I can't tell where I am down here." *Afléotan.* He took to the air, rising hundreds of feet above the ship. He immediately spotted the island where his people were gathered. The campfires gave off smoke, and he saw movement on the beach. That...and a *fleet* of ships anchored offshore. Black and light blue sails. Or was it violet? Small boats filled with sailors were moving to shore, and to his horror, he realized a battle was taking place there.

Simon pitched and dived back toward *The Mamba's Mouth* as the three ships rounded a point on the island, coming into sight of the dozen or so vessels. He was too late. Immediately, a handful of the other ships began to move to cut off the three Gilded Crow vessels.

Simon landed lightly on deck next to Kai. "Who are they? Enemies?"

"Keen Eyes," Kai muttered. "He is far too deep into my territory. Be on guard; you never know what this one will do. Though I doubt he has come in person."

"They're attacking my people on the beach."

"Well, what did you expect, *Simon*? We're pirates."

Kiana Ahmadi *danced* into the midst of the bloodthirsty pirates who had stormed the beach without a second thought to whom they sought to pillage. The white sands were stained crimson in Kiana's wake. A man's head rolled to the ground as another leaped at her, swinging a heavy spiked maul. She flowed like water under the strike, her sword moving with her body. The sand felt *right* between her toes. The man's guts spewed out as she sliced him open.

He screamed, dropping the maul as he grasped at his innards, trying to stuff them back in before stumbling and falling limp to the sand.

Three more enemies came rushing to meet her, swinging their long, kinked swords and jagged rusty axes. They flung themselves at her, sea-worn muscles clenching, veins bulging with exertion as they surrounded Kiana and attacked.

She *breathed*.

A blade grazed her cheek as she glided, simultaneously removing the hand of the offending weapon.

The man wailed in agony.

Kiana fell to a spinning squat, showering sand before her with her extended leg that left a divot in the silver silt.

A woman pirate coughed and spluttered as the grit hit her face, filling her eyes, nose, and mouth.

The tip of Kiana's blade moved in a silent flick.

The women froze. A second later, blood sprayed from the opening across her neck.

More pirates surged toward her, unphased by their comrades' deaths. Two charged down on her. Kiana tried to sidestep and back off, but the two came on furiously—caring little for their bodies, they collided with her, grappling her at the same time as stabbing at her with short, curved daggers.

Kiana's blade pierced one through the gut as both plowed into her, sending all three tumbling to the ground. The weight of the men crushed against her. Her breath was pushed from her body with the impact, and she tried to gasp, but nothing came.

A blade bit and sunk into the flesh below her right shoulder. Kiana could not scream as her vision blurred.

Another blade flashed and swished through the air, a sickening sound of flesh being carved and the cries of pain from her attackers.

The weight lifted, and Kiana blinked through tears to see Rakshak Zahir Al-Rashid as he kicked the limp dead body off of Kiana. Her mother, Anora Kafilah, was removing her blade from the other pirate.

"Close call, Sixteenth Otsoa," Zahir said, holding a hand out to her. "On your feet, we can't let the Vouri take all the glory."

Kiana took the hand offered and painfully found her footing. "My thanks, Rakshak." The dagger was still protruding from her shoulder excruciatingly. She ground her teeth as she thought of leaving it there and trying to stop the blood flow after the battle.

Suddenly, an old, grey-bearded, bent-backed man in white robes stood beside her. *Where had he come from?*

"Here now, young lass, I'll handle that." He unceremoniously yanked the blade free and pushed two fingers into the wound.

Kiana grimaced through the pain as *heat* bloomed within her. The blood seemed to rush from her entire body, causing a chill to grip every part of her except at the burning location of the wound, and she suddenly felt nauseous. She glanced down to see the older man's feeble fingers forcefully pushed out of the bleeding wound by new flesh that knit itself back together.

His two fingers slowly traced down the laceration like rubbing a smudge from her skin. Left behind was nothing but a dark scar on her brown skin.

"Excellent, young people do heal so quickly," the old man said with a wink as he turned away. He scanned the scene for a moment, then, surprisingly swift on his feet, hurried to a felled Vouri man and knelt beside him.

"The Theta," Zahir whispered as he, too, watched after the old man.

Kiana rolled her newly healed shoulder and looked to the battlefield.

A thunderous *crack* echoed through the air, and a lightning bolt exploded nearby, sending pirates hurling to land dead in the surf or upon the sand.

"*Hata!*" Baal Vasara's voice was a long, unnerving echo over the turmoil. The voice was broken as if it could not form the word correctly. It was the ghastly cry of a father seeking his lost daughter.

Flesh sizzled with electric current, and bones shattered before him. Tears streamed down his eyes. Baal's massive blue-tinge runic war hammer crackled with energy as it crushed through pirates in droves, accompanied by blasts of lightning with each strike. The long wail rose above the battle din, "HAAA-TAAA!"

Allies stayed well away from the massive man's wrath and sorrow as he waded through the enemy as if striding through a wheat field, scything grain shoots for harvest.

"Voitoon!" Brena hollered, leading a group of Vouri to tear into the enemies, trying to flank her mate. Their signature round shields, axes, spears, hammers, and swords spilled the pirate's blood in droves.

Kiana saw the grizzled veteran, the man Edvard, at Brena's side. He waved his broad sword and shouted to his people. "Shields!"

The line of Vouri warriors advancing doubled in size as others moved in behind, raising their shields over the heads of the first row. The line advanced. Arrows bounced off or thudded into the protective barrier's wood. Pirate blades tried as they might to penetrate the defense, only for the attacks to be knocked aside by a shield and followed by a retaliating strike of a Vouri weapon.

Blood soaked the sands.

The enemy was not prepared for the fury of the mountain people. They decimated the ranks of pirates, laughing with the thrill of battle as they did so.

I would not like to make an enemy of the Vouri, Kiana thought as she turned back to the raiders and continued her dance, breathing slowly and moving with grace.

Her mother joined her, and their movements nearly synchronized, carving two lines through the pirates as they flowed into the dance once more.

Zahir Al-Rashid followed, along with many warriors of Hasiera. He not so much as *danced* but expertly and, with precision, slashed down anyone who faced him.

The stone-weighted rope bolas of the nomadic Hasieran entangled pirates, toppling them to the ground before spears and silver curved swords fell upon them.

Besides the Theta, the magi of Aurulan and their soldiers held back near the beach tree line.

What are they waiting for? Kiana thought as she saw Captain Cad Dermont leaning against a palm tree, calmly watching her. *Nothing but her.* She nearly halted her dance as a shiver ran up her spine under his disgusting leer. Then she saw the Gamma.

Lila Parakeet, Gamma of the Council of the Aerie, dressed in a multi-colored, impossibly low-cut blouse and frilly skirt. A scantily clad, well-endowed, serving man held a colorful, lacey umbrella over her. Lila stepped forward and pointed at the beach.

Thousands of Vouri and Hasieran warriors charged down the sands out of the tree line to join the fray.

Kiana stared in wonder. *Where have they come from?*

The pirates hollered in terror and began to retreat, climbing into their boats and pushing off the beach, paddling with all their might.

"Voitoon!" the Vouri roared after them.

"Hasiera!" Kiana's people cheered in unison.

The reinforcements mimicked cheering and threats, but they were unnaturally silent. Even their movements made no sound. One of them walked right through Kiana as she stood in its way. *They're illusions.* The images turned and stalked back up the beach and into the trees, away from the sights of any pirates watching from the decks of their ships. They then vanished.

"Parley!"

Simon watched in awe as his people pushed back the assault of the Keen Eyes Corsairs off the beach. A shout nearby brought him back to his predicament. He returned his attention to the two ships flying violet-blue colors now flanking *The Mamba's Mouth.* Their flag was two half-closed eyes, one of the blue-violet shade and the other a golden brown.

"Parley!" Captain Kai shouted again across the decreasing distance to one of the Keen Eyes ships. "Hold the attack. This is Gilded Crow territory!"

Grapples flew across the expanse and hooked into the ship rail, pulling taunt. Arrows loosed, whistled, and buried into the deck at Kai's feet.

"Repel borders," Kai ordered as he unsheathed both cutlasses from his sides.

"Repel borders!" Silas, the helmsman, bellowed beside them.

The crew shouted their battle cries, weapons drawing as the two ships came together with a creaking *thud*, causing Simon to stumble. Corsairs leaped onto the deck, striking out at Kai's crew. They looked nearly identical, attackers and defenders. *Gods, how do they know who to kill?*

Two burly men landed before Captain Kai. He did not give them time to think, dashing forward, lashing out with his deadly blades. A lethal slice up one man's leg caused him to stagger and fall to his knees, only to receive a forceful front kick to his chest that sprawled him on his back.

The other man jabbed a sharp harpoon toward Kai, aiming to catch his innards on its barbed end.

Metal clanged as Kai swept away the attack with one blade and simultaneously sliced into the man's face, across his eyes, with his second cutlass.

The man screamed, dropped his harpoon, and grasped at his face as he stumbled away. Unable to see, he toppled over the railing and splashed into the waters below.

More enemy pirates leaped before Kai to challenge him.

Simon heard the clang and thuds of more grapples behind him on the opposite rail.

Skrull-damned pirates. Simon watched Kai battle the intruders as Silas and a few more crewmates joined him. *He seems to have this side under control. Afléotan. Lind.* Simon ascended into the air as the barrier of magic light surrounded him.

Enemy pirates froze, looking up and pointing him out as he hovered directly above the enemy ship.

That's right, you little bastards. Try this on for size. I think I saw that traitor Gaelin used this once in the Moreas Lân. Simon raised his hands over his head, and suddenly, fury overcame him at the thought of Gaelin and these pirates. *These sons of whores attacked my people.* The need to shout the spell with all his might grew within him. "*Firenleahtor...*"

A tiny sphere of near-white flame popped into existence above his hands.

"*...Ad...*"

It grew and grew until it was a hundred times his size. He heard distressed cries of fear below.

"*...Cliewen!*"

Simon *slammed* his hands down, and the flaming sphere's roaring heat was nearly unbearable as it plunged past him. The air shimmered and shifted, and his magical protective barrier rattled.

The spell first met the mast of the ship, which turned to ash as it did so. Pirates leaped into the sea as the sphere left nothing in its path. One man got tangled in the rigging and vanished as the fire took him in. It engulfed everything and sunk into the ship's deck, the wood burning away into nothing. Then, a geyser of steam erupted out of the center between two halves of a sinking ship.

"Skrull's balls," Simon muttered in disbelief at the destruction of the magic. There was a hint of utter satisfaction that washed through him. Screams came to his ears as he descended toward *The Mamba's Mouth.*

Pirates who had fallen into the sea shrieked and died as the water boiled them alive.

Hettra's mercy. I didn't mean to—

"Devil man!" Kai's voice came to him. "Chike's storm is with you! Yah!" Kai raised a cutlass. "Chike! Chike! The warrior of the sea!" His war cry was undulated with a vigorous spirit, and his crew took up the cry, cutting down and casting enemy corsairs overboard. Kai's crew pushed back and began to take the deck of the enemy vessel.

Led by Captain Kai, they chanted in rhythm as they *killed.*

"Chike! Chike! Warrior of the sea!"

CHAPTER NINE

BLOOD

"Teras's thunder, I never thought I'd see the day the proud Himin-dvergar would bow to us, the Kidekorvat," the regal male elven man said haughtily. His intricately decorated golden robe hung loose around his arms and legs as he gestured contemptuously. "And a *queen* nonetheless."

Did he say Teras? Hata wondered but held the eagerness within.

"Hear-fan Skaad has invaded the Ryk Lân once again," Raine answered stiffly, still on her knees. "Many years ago, we drove him out of our Lân, long before my time, but he has come again with a renewed vigor to enslave or eradicate us."

"I remember," the elder answered thoughtfully. "The time of the Wayfarer, Elynor Thalriss. It was assumed she died trying to retrieve the obsidian gemstone that exuded darkness."

"She led a squadron of Himin-dvergar through the Gate. We never saw them again." Raine bowed her head further. "But Hear-fan Skaad stopped his incursions into Ryk after that. He has returned and erected a magical destructive force around his war camp. We do not have time to reminisce. He is preparing for another assault. One that will make the last attack look like children at play."

Hata stood behind her lover, *wishing* she could say encouraging words, but Raine had explicitly told her to stay silent. Diplomacy was the queen's responsibility; she had studied and trained for it all her life.

"*Elder* Aerendyl, Brother to Ziraelthir," Taivaseläin said sarcastically. "The queen speaks the truth. I've seen the defensive cloud of shadow that *kills* anything that comes too close."

Elder Aerendyl's eyes narrowed at Taivaseläin.

The other elders turned and murmured together at Taivaseläin's affirmation of Raine's news.

Aerendyl turned to join them, and after a moment, his eyes glanced at Hata again. This time, he did not turn his head away. His silver hair framed his face, and his golden gaze studied her as he asked, "Who, by Teras, is this one?"

Hata saw Raine's shoulders stiffen, even through her heavy armor, but she turned her head and nodded to Hata.

Hata stepped forward. "I am Hata Vasara, the Sunstone of the Earste Lân. My world has many races of people, but mine are called the Vouri."

There was a gasp and more silent murmurs in the crowd of elves.

Aerendyl did not so much as flinch. "*Vouri*, you say? A simple misspelling of the word 'mountain' in our language. Are all your people as tall and lean as you?"

Hata thought back and realized most of her kinsfolk were quite tall, but most were burly and broad-shouldered, men and women alike. Miners and warriors who sculpted their bodies for decades, while Hata had shied away from such manual labors. *My mother must have been three stones heavier than me, even though we were the same height.* "Yes," Hata rejoined.

"And your people are exceedingly hirsute?" Aerendyl paused and slightly scoffed as he waved toward the bearded Himin-dvergar around them.

Most Vouri men had big, bushy beards and curly hair from head to toe. The women were similar. Aurulan 'manners' had been for women to shave completely. Vouri women did not care or bother about such a needy and inefficient task.

Hata nodded.

"There is a tale we wish to tell. But first," Aerendyl returned his attention to Raine. "Long ago, the Kidekorvat and the Himin-dvergar lived in harmony—trading and visiting one another with kinship in mind. We will aid you against this threat to our Lân in an extension to restore that kinship. It is long overdue." He paused again, then turned his golden gaze back to Hata. "In exchange for her."

Raine was on her feet in a heartbeat, hand going to the hilt of her sword at her waist. The other Himin-dvergar clambered at the ready behind them.

Taivaseläin spun, a long blade in one hand and a dagger held with a razor-sharp tip down in his other. Safiiri roared overhead, and Hata realized the dragon had been circling and *watching*.

"My, my," Aerendyl said, "you Himin-dvergar are so easily roused. We wish for the *Vouri* female to stay with us and learn our ways. That is, of course, after we have helped you resolve this conflict." He closed his eyes, and Hata felt...*something*. "I can sense her connection with the very earth she stands upon. She could perhaps become kin to a young Amberheart Drake. However, the kinship will take years to cultivate. Yes, that would be fitting for one such as her. One of both bloods."

"Both bloods?" Hata blurted out confusedly, unable to contain herself. "What do you mean?"

Aerendyl pointedly ignored her. "We will eat and rest and ride back with you to that monstrosity of a keep." His gaze was back on Raine now. "We will aid you, Queen Raine Stormfall, and repair our people's long-lost friendship. Though I fear it will take some time for us to get used to your unsavory manners." He gave a slight bow and turned, his elders turning in unison with him. They strode away so elegantly that Hata thought they were floating beneath their long robes.

"Arrogant fucking elves," Raine muttered under her breath. She waved a hand, and her people sheathed their ready weapons. Then Raine turned to Hata and looked up into her eyes. Distress swam in Raine's hazel regard as they glistened slightly, and her bottom lip trembled as she stammered, "I d-don't want to lose what I have just come to love."

Hata immediately embraced her. "You aren't going to *lose* me, Raine." Hata kissed her on the forehead. "I'll never leave you. Not for long anyway. But what you have said of the Kidekorvat and what Aerendyl has said himself has me intrigued. They are connected to my people somehow. I know it, and I need to know the truth."

Something flashed in Raine's eyes. *Apprehension?* "Do you promise not to leave me?" Raine pleaded, as her tears hid anything else from Hata's perceptions.

Hata stared into those imploring eyes and was lost in their beauty. She leaned in close and whispered, "I promise."

"Uhm," Taivaseläin cleared his throat awkwardly. "Will you dine with us?"

"Let's." Hata urged Raine on.

Reluctantly, Raine stepped forward, grasping Hata by the arm as they followed the company of elven elders to the base of a large tree. Crystals and gemstones intertwined with the very wood of the tree itself and its roots that curved in arches out of the ground around the base. Like a tree of living crystal. Branches shimmered with iridescent hues—opalescent blues, amethyst purples, and diamond-clear whites. As they approached the entrance, their eyes were immediately drawn to the exquisite white wooden doors. The intricate carvings on the doors were a sight to behold - they featured an array of patterns, such as stars, the crescent moon, and the depiction of a mountain soaring through the sky. The skilled craftsmanship and attention to detail were evident in every inch of the carvings. It was truthfully a work of art that left Hata in awe. It reminded Hata of the depictions of Teras back home.

With a gentle hand wave, Taivaseläin signaled the group to follow the elders and enter through the doorway.

Hata and Raine stepped into a massive feast hall. A *Vouri* feast hall, though much more elegant, was the furniture and décor. Columns of crystal-veined wood twisted to the high ceiling, and a curving staircase spiraled upward along the circumference of the inner tree. Instead of two long tables with a roaring fire between them, like back home in Oitilla, this hall sported a broad, long table connected with another at the far end. Like a giant 'T.' The table was made of crystal-flecked quartz or some such mineral. More long tables were set up on the righthand and lefthand sides of the chamber, accommodating hundreds of people. All were laden with delicious-smelling meat, vegetables, and fruits. Hata saw superbly dressed waitpersons in olive-toned uniforms endlessly moving about the room, pouring wine or replacing dishes. Elves sat on both sides, eating and drinking, but as Hata and company entered, all heads turned, and the feast hall fell deafly silent.

The elders silently moved to their seats at the top of the T-shaped table. Aerendyl stood and held out his hands in a welcoming gesture. "Welcome Queen Raine Stormfall of the Himin-dvergar into our humble home. Feast and be merry as we honor friends again to the halls of *Valon Vuori*."

Murmurs of surprise and curiosity rippled through the finely dressed elven feast-goers.

Taivaseläin led their group to the head of the main table, closest to the elders. Other elves cleared themselves out, making space for the newcomers and moving to the many available seats throughout the hall. Raine sat closest to the elders, and Hata sat beside her. Then, to Hata's surprise, Taivaseläin sat down next to her.

The elven scout immediately grabbed a goblet, and a servant appeared to fill his cup. He took a sip, and his whole demeanor seemed to relax. He smiled genuinely at Hata, his green eyes twinkling. "Drake-scales, I needed that. Sunstone, is it? Come now, have a drink."

The servant hovered over their backs, waiting. Hata hesitated only momentarily before holding her goblet and receiving a pour of the rich crimson wine. The servant moved on to pour Raine a glass as well. Hata looked down at the translucent ruby color of the wine, flecks of what she could only describe as stardust suspended within. She sipped. It had a harmonious blend of sweet and spicy, reminiscent of starlit nights, which left a lingering warmth. *Teras's thunder, I'm becoming quite a connoisseur of the fine wines of Ryk,* Hata chuckled within. Raine preferred wine over the traditional Himin-dvergar ales. Hata looked over to see her lover conversing quietly with the closest elder next to her.

Taivaseläin leaned back in his seat with a sigh, twirling the wine in his cup. "Ah yes, *Vanha Verta*, like the touch of a dragon's breath." He proceeded to down the goblet in one go. Then, he held his cup up once more.

"It has a pleasant taste," Hata agreed, taking it more slowly.

"A far better drink than what is served in the Himin ale houses, for that, I am sure."

"Honestly." Hata gave him a playful smirk. "I'd rather drink ale."

"Blasphemy!" Taivaseläin hollered teasingly. "But I suppose *their* palate has rubbed off on you, living with them as such..." he trailed off, and his tone became nearly inaudible, "or it's innately part of you."

"What did you say?" Hata asked, thinking she misheard him.

"More wine!" Taivaseläin called, and a server promptly appeared and poured.

These people are acting strange toward me. Hata wouldn't let the odd comments about her go. She put down her goblet and turned to the elven scout. Softly, she asked, "Taivaseläin, what did the elder mean when he said I was *'of both bloods'*?"

Taivaseläin chugged his cup again, and his cheeks and pointed ears became a rosy pink. He played distractedly with his ginger warrior's braid.

Hata's eyes lingered on the plait. "Why do you wear the same braid that many of my people, the Vouri, use?"

Taivaseläin turned to her, his face solemn through the flush of the wine. "There is a tale of old—a tale of our two peoples becoming one. The Himin-dvergar and the Kidekorvat. Unfortunately, this is why our relations were ruined many centuries ago."

"Come on, Taivaseläin, just spit it out," Hata prodded eagerly.

"Your people, the Vouri, as you call them, are the descendants of a group of Himin-dvergar and Kidekorvat who found love and joined together. They sired children who aged far quicker than their parents and looked oh so...well, like you. Human."

Hata's body stiffened, and her jaw dropped in disbelief. "I'm part Himin-dvergar and Kidekorvat? All my people, the Vouri."

Taivaseläin downed another goblet of wine, and the words emptied out of him. "The elders of the time were chauvinists. They tolerated the Himin-dvergar regarding trade, employment, and even collaboration. But to have our people sully their bloodlines fornicating with them. It was appalling." He slammed a fist to the table, his face enflamed with wine and *rage*. "Aerendyl was an up-and-coming, soon-to-be elder back then. He should have spoken out."

A hand touched Hata on the opposite shoulder to Taivaseläin. "Are you all right, my love?"

Hata abruptly turned to Raine, a flash of anger bubbling up. "Did you know?"

"Did I know what?" Raine asked, startled by the force of the question.

"That my people—that I am of your kind and theirs. That's why you all can speak Vouri. *Did you know,* Raine?"

The hall was eerily silent as Raine's eyes flicked about the room before returning to meet Hata's gaze. After a long moment, she spoke. "I suspected."

Hata stood, chair screeching in the silent hall.

"Hata, wait—" Raine started.

"I need to be alone," Hata exclaimed as she turned away from Raine in disbelief. How could she have kept that from me? Fueled by anger, Hata pushed open the heavy doors of the feast hall and stepped outside. Her neck and face were flushed red with frustration and betrayal.

Three earth-tone dragons awaited her, massive amber gemstones beating like hearts in their chests.

CHAPTER TEN

REASON

"FUCKING HELLS," JUDE NELON hissed through clenched teeth, his breath visible in the chill air. Snow was falling in a gentle rhythm on the mountain pass. The pain in his leg throbbed from the aching stump where his foot had once been. His makeshift crutch pushed excruciatingly into his armpit, most of his weight pressed upon it as he tried to keep his footing on the mountainside. "Skrull's sodden balls, when will this end?"

"Nearly there," the ranger, Kaplan Mir, answered Jude's rhetorical question. "I've caught a whiff of sea air; should be just over the next peak."

This man's optimism is increasingly starting to grate on me. It's always one more peak, yet we've been stuck in these Skrull-damned mountains for weeks.

"We can rest soon," Joanna Ohleoc said, trying to reassure Jude, even as she struggled to clamber up the rocks herself.

Gods, not you too. Jude rolled his eyes, took a deep breath, calmed himself, and pushed through the pain. His only solace was that the woman genuinely cared for him, even if he didn't want her pity. *She truly loves me. Fucks, she must be insane.*

"We need to make it to the other side before nightfall," Kaplan called back to them from the head of their little company. The man would constantly get further ahead, making the passage seem effortless. Then he would turn about and see his fellow party members struggling together, prompting him to jog back and put an arm under Jude's shoulder to help him along.

I'm starting to hate that non-disabled bastard.

"I fear we will not survive another night being hunted," Kaplan said as he hefted Jude's weight.

Fucking demons, fucking Children of Fucks. Night after night, the beasts came. Night after night, Joanna, Kaplan, and Jude either hid themselves or were forced to fight and flee. *And I'm more a hindrance than help. I'm Skrull-fucking done.*

Progress was agonizingly slow. Finally, after a few hours, they crested a ridge and saw the vast icy sea below them. Chunks of white ice drifted against the shoreline. Smoke wisped skyward near the rocky seashore, revealing a small town settled in a minor cove. The sight of the village was a welcome relief after the harsh journey. The smoke from the chimneys seemed to beckon them forward, promising warmth and shelter from the frigid mountain cold. A high wooden palisade wall surrounded the landside of the village defensively.

"It will be near nightfall when we make the village," Kaplan said flatly. "Let's pray to Qav's luck we reach it before the beasts find us."

"I fear it will be too late," Joanna said. "I will carry Jude down a different way." The woman's hands suddenly ignited in flames. "Go ahead of us, Kaplan. You'll make good time on your own."

"Skrull's balls, woman, you aren't just a pleasant face," Jude said enthusiastically. *Anything to bring this fucking journey to an end.* "We'll be down there in a heartbeat if you fling us off the mountainside."

"Well, it's the landing I'm worried about," Joanna muttered.

Jude hesitated, mouth hanging open.

"Are you certain?" Kaplan asked doubtfully.

"We need warmth, food and shelter. And we need it *now*," Joanna declared surely. "Come, Jude, hold onto my shoulders, and whatever you do, don't let go."

"I hope you know what you're doing," Jude said, dropping his crutch as he wrapped his arms around the woman's neck. With the lack of provisions, he had lost some weight since coming to the North Iron Belt, but he doubted Joanna could lift him alone. It would be up to him to not let go.

She turned her head and gave him a soft kiss on his cheek. "Trust in me."

The butterflies in his stomach churned with that strange new feeling of affection for her. He gave her a sly smile. "Well, if we fuck up the landing, at least we die together."

Joanna grinned back at him, and then heat bloomed below her feet and out of her hands. Then, it exploded in a display of power, hurling them skyward. Like a flaming shot from a trebuchet, they arced through the air, aimed directly at the village. The freezing air bit at Jude's face and through his clothing, even as the heat of Joanna's flames scorched at him. As they descended from their incline, Jude felt his grip slipping, his strength beginning to wane.

"Hold on!" Joanna cried through the buffeting wind.

Jude adjusted his hold, causing Joanna's course to pivot. He writhed, an arm wrapping around her neck on accident.

Her hands shot to his arm, the flames propelling them going out.

Jude let go.

They began to plunge, limbs flailing about through the air.

He tried to reach out for her, shifting his body, his phantom leg burning.

Joanna twisted and reignited her fire. She thudded into him and grasped him in such an embrace that one would think they were in bed together.

The rugged, serrated terrain of the mountain rose rapidly as it approached them.

With a scream, flames licking around them, Joanna let loose a second sudden detonation, sending them in another arching trajectory toward the sea.

Jude's eyes widened in terror as the icy waters loomed nearer and nearer. Joanna swiftly pivoted, her hand ablaze with flames, and turned him around just in time, so his back was facing the sea. An outpouring of scorching heat surged behind him, and then, with a stinging chill, the cold water enveloped him.

Kaplan Mir sprinted down the mountainside after the smoking projectile that was Joanna and Jude, holding Jude's crutch as he ran. *These two always act with such rash foolishness. They don't ever stop to think. They could have made smaller leaps to decrease the distance to the town more readily. Why risk their lives by hurling thousands of feet through the air? They are as stubborn as Kiana Ahmadi. Oh, Kiana. My Otsoa.* She was a fierce young woman, *too* young for Kaplan, to be honest. Her spirit flamed with determination, curiosity, and desire. She was genuinely astonishing. *And I dishonored her. I destroyed everything there was between us.* She had told him to leave. She never wanted to see him again. *Perhaps for the better.* A plume of steam had erupted in the distance at the village's shoreline. He shook his head from the thoughts of the beautiful image of Kiana in his mind and focused on Jude and Joanna ahead. *Qav's luck, they yet live.*

At a cautious run, it took Kaplan nearly an hour to descend the mountain and reach the closed and barred village gates.

"Hold there, stranger!" A gruff female voice called from atop the wall.

"My companions landed in the cove!" Kaplan shouted back. "Are they alive?"

"Teras's thunder. You mean the witch and the one-legged man that fell from the sky?"

The witch and the one-legged man. Kaplan withheld a smile as he pondered. *There's a story in that name.* He looked up but could only see a helmeted head bobbing over the wall. "Indeed, they are intact?"

"Hold there," the voice answered.

Moments later, one of the high log gates creaked open enough to let a few people hustle out. A broad-shouldered, heavy-set woman covered in sleek fur pelts appeared, wielding a long, vicious-looking glaive, followed by two others in similar garb. Her auburn-plaited hair and dark wave-like tattoos indicated she was Vouri.

She stalked up to Kaplan and pointed her massive weapon at him. "Far from home, Xamidian. What business have you in *Kiviranta?*"

"We flee the North Iron Belt and seek refuge for the night," Kaplan answered impatiently. "Are my companions all right?"

"Flee from what?" The woman shook the heavy glaive at him. "Are you convicts? The one-legged man has the look of a murderer about him, he does."

The other two warriors began to flank Kaplan. He sized them up, dropping Jude's crutch to the ground. The first was a burly man of golden tan skin and a scraggly black mustache, with the white fur of some beast on his shoulders. *His attire is of the Vouri, but his face is not.* The other was but a boy, pale, lengthy, and Vouri. He watched as they circled. *Ah, yes, hammer and anvil, though on a smaller scale.* Kaplan pondered idly before answering, "I never lie. There is something far more dangerous following through the pass. I suggest you prepare your defenses and make ready for battle."

"Teras's stones, we don't have time for this. Our people, the Vouri, live in those mountains. What could conceivably be chasing you?" She paused, eyeing her flanking companions. "Unless it's them you flee from? *Criminal.*" She gave a nearly imperceptible nod to her companions.

The burly man on Kaplan's left charged toward him, shield held up before him.

Ah ha, so you're the hammer. Kaplan's scimitar flashed into his hands as the man tried to drive him with his metal banded round shield toward the glaive-wielding woman. Kaplan took a feinting back step toward her, then spun toward the last of the three, the skinny boy with a flimsy fishing spear.

The boy's eyes widened in shock at Kaplan's sudden movement. He stabbed out with the spear, but Kaplan was already within reach. He thwacked the broad side of his scimitar against the boy's hand, and the spear dropped to the ground. Kaplan reached and grabbed the boy's collar to apprehend him as a hostage, only to see the sharp end of the glaive out of his peripheral. He let go and ducked under the strike. Then, the hardened wood of the other man's shield collided with him, sending Kaplan tumbling through the snow-dusted muck.

He turned the tumble into a roll and was quickly on his feet—scimitar ready.

The boy fled back toward the gates.

The two Vouri warriors circled him cautiously, like weary beasts.

Just then, an echoing cry broke the tension—an eerie wail from the mountain pass.

The two warriors stared through him, *passed him*, their weapons lowering.

Kaplan dared a glance back.

Navy smoke billowed skyward, and dark shadows moved down the rocky slope.

Kaplan pointed his scimitar at the approaching *Children of Skaad*. "I told you; I never lie."

Chapter Eleven

FLESH

"These are your people, Father," Twade-fan Skaad pleaded as Ien-fan, *no, Malix the Unsought,* entered the large chamber at the top of the citadel tower of the Hiel Lân. The dead were strewn about the chamber. Bodies of Iban'mael, some charred to a crisp, others sheared violently in two. One wall had exploded inward, a body crushed beneath the rubble, leaving a hazy violet city skyline in view with smoke billowing upward in snakelike tendrils.

A man was on his knees before Malix's father. One of his arms was missing, and he spat blood on the floor and then looked up at Hear-fan Skaad with a face full of utter revulsion. "Truly, you should listen to this vile half-blood. You commit genocide against your people. You're an abomination! *You...are...nothing,* Threnn Duskwea—"

His father's true name was cut off as Hear-fan Skaad's hands wrapped around the man's throat. "You did this to yourselves!" Father shrieked, spittle spraying the struggling man's face. "You exiled me to that wasteland, now I will do the same with Hiel."

Malix had never seen such unbridled rage in his father before.

"Please, Father, surely we should not kill all of them." Twade grasped his father's arms, trying to yank them from the man's neck.

"You dare defy your flesh and blood. I made you!" Father's black teeth glistened in a terrible grimace. "I knew it was unwise to breed with a human. Like this arrogant fool said...you're nothing but a *vile* half-blood." There was a sudden hissing sound, and then a line of violet fire pierced through Twade's back, directly from his heart.

"No!" Malix screamed, running to his brother as he fell limp to the floor, his violet robes pooling around him. Malix cradled Twade's head in his arms. Lifeless eyes stared back at him. "Brother! No... my brother." Malix shook him, tears falling on the pale skin of his younger sibling. He looked up in horror at his father. "How could you?"

Hear-fan Skaad snorted contemptuously as the other man fell dead at his feet, strangled to death. He stared down at his sons with indifferent regard. "Question me again, and you will meet the same fate, full-blooded or not."

A chill gripped Malix by the heart. Fear rippled through him. *I don't want to die. Not yet.* But at the same time, a candle began to burn within. *One day, I will avenge you, little brother.*

"Now come, let us burn this Lân to the ground."

"Your will be done...Father," Malix murmured in answer.

With that, his father, once Threnn Duskweaver, now Hear-fan Skaad, floated out of the open wall into the sky. Over the Lân he was born in. The Lân he was banished from. *For raping my mother.* Malix's father ascended out of sight. Moments later, thousands of massive violet spheres of magical flame rained down on the city below.

"We destroyed the Hiel Lân," Malix continued quietly, letting go of Saudett's hand. "Then he sent me to subjugate and hold the Fjoer Lân. This is the first he has sent for me in over a hundred years."

Saudett breathed slowly, regaining her composure from the vision. She had *been* Malix. She had felt his every thought and emotion during that time. His seething hatred of his father. His sorrow at losing his brother, his only friend. Those emotions still clung to her as she tried to keep the tears out of her eyes. Now, they sat in the dark prison of his father's making. Cautiously, she asked, "What're you going to do?"

"I will take you with me and proceed with the tasks he gave me."

"Tasks?" A ripple of apprehension trickled down Saudett's spine. *He will take me.*

"I will leave one of his children to relay the message that to ensure better you are impregnated; I brought you with me. I think that will calm any distrust he may have in me." Malix stood and stretched his four muscular arms. "His *other* task has directed me to your Lân. The Earste Lân. He has tasked me with killing the Wayfarer assigned there. Gaelin Yesnala. Likewise, I'm taxed with destroying any Wayfarers Gates I find. He grows tired of humans meddling in his plans."

"You're taking me home?" Saudett was flooded with relief and hope—the hope of escape. Simon's handsome face came to her, and she hesitated. His mischievous grin, his flowery flattery. *Gods, I do miss him. Could he ever forgive me?*

"Come, we'd best hurry. We will need the aid of one of Fjoer's molten earthwalkers to travel through the portal."

Molten earthwalkers? The thought of Darkclaw Marah fighting for their life trying to rescue Saudett came back to her. *Are they still alive?* She touched Malix's arm gently, and he flinched and pulled away. She tilted her head curiously but continued her thoughts aloud, "I have a friend from my Lân that came here with me. They are Volkinn, part wolf, part human. Have you seen someone like that?"

He looked down at his arm as if shocked by the touch before answering her. "No, I have not."

"They tried to rescue me, but one of those rock-like things went after them; I haven't seen them since. I suspect they were captured."

Malix grunted and gave a black-toothed grimace. Rolling his broad shoulders. "Come, let's check the other prison cells."

If not for his inverted eyes and the extra set of arms, he reminded Saudett much of Baal Vasara as she looked up at the tall, broad-shouldered man with his bushy black beard. "Let's."

They exited the cage, and a few hunched creatures immediately awaited them. One of them cricked its head at Malix. "Blood of Skaad, where are you taking the prisoner? The Lord has ordered us to keep her here until he has time to deal with her."

Malix shot the stunted being a glare that could kill. "That is why I am here. To *deal* with her in his stead. Do not question the Blood of Skaad."

It bowed repetitively as it cowered away from Malix's strong words. "Of course, I meant no insubordination."

"Where is the other from the Earste Lân, the wolf-like one?"

"That one is undergoing surgery. The Lord wished to dissect it themselves, but as you're aware, he is too busy."

Surgery? Dissect? A chilling panic churned in Saudett's gut.

"*Where?*" Malix's voice boomed with icy authority.

"Tenth level," the creature squealed. "Passed the breeding chambers."

"Send for an earthwalker to meet me on the surface."

"Of course, Blood of Skaad." The group hurried off to do his bidding.

"They're dissecting Marah." Saudett urged frantically. "We must hurry!"

"Quickly, this way." Malix broke into a run.

Saudett flexed her wings and propelled herself after him with a running leap and a mighty flap.

As they approached the platform that moved between the underground levels, the halls zipped by. Said platform was nowhere to be seen.

Malix did not pause. He jumped off the edge of the abyss and soared upward.

Saudett beat her wings and followed swiftly after him.

Malix landed on a ledge a few floors above the prison level and continued to run.

Saudett struggled to keep up, her breath straining and her muscles burning after weeks of idleness. They emerged into a 'birthing' chamber, pools of bubbling muck where the *Children of Skaad* grew to adulthood.

Stunted creatures scampered out of Malix's way with shrill cries.

A bestial howl of pain rang through Saudett, the sound coming from the chamber's darkness ahead.

Finally, they came to the room where Saudett had got her wings. There was blood everywhere.

Creatures huddled over Darkclaw Marah as they spasmed, twitched, howled, and *bled*.

Horror gripped Saudett. *No, no, no.* She rushed to Marah's side, grabbing one of the stunted creatures and hurling it aside. The other scurried away with a shriek at the sudden disturbance.

The Volkinn's skin had been cut and peeled back up one of their arms and shoulder. Marah's red flesh, where their fur and skin had been, was cut and bleeding in many places. *The bastards were skinning Marah alive.*

"Marah!" Saudett cried.

The Volkinn shook and thrashed as much as they could in their bindings. Suddenly, their eyes focused on Saudett. "We...we failed you."

"No," Saudett said regretfully. Shaking her head as she took Marah's good hand in hers. "You've saved me countless times. It's my turn to save you. You'll be all right."

Malix grasped the manacles and tore them away as if they were made of nothing more then thin threads. He stared down at the exposed flesh. Then, sullenly, he spoke. "I cannot save this arm, but I can save your life."

Marah's pained gaze found him and suddenly hissed in savage resistance. "He is of Skaad!"

"He is a friend. He is going to help us," Saudett pleaded. "Please, Marah."

Darkclaw Marah looked down at the flayed limb and sucked in a breath resignedly. "Do it."

An axe appeared and ignited in a magical violet flame. It split easily through Marah's arm at the shoulder.

The Volkinn screamed and spasmed, their back arching before they were overcome with pain and went limp. Unconscious.

Malix slowly placed two hands over the burnt flesh. His open, calloused, steadfast palms hovered inches above the blistered, bleeding flesh.

Saudett held her breath.

A surge of energy, a warm yellow-green glow, emanated from Malix's core and into his hands. The light enclosed Marah's wounds, weaving through the damaged tissue. It danced along the edges of their burns, stitching them with delicate precision. The scars began to form, tracing intricate patterns across the Volkinn's skin.

Malix's breath hitched, and sweat dripped down his temples. After what seemed like an eternity, the flesh healed. Malix let out a gasp of exertion.

Saudett finally released her breath in relief.

Then Malix flung Marah over his shoulder. The Volkinn's head lolled against his back, their tongue hanging out.

Saudett touched Marah's head and listened to the shallow but steady breathing.

Malix nodded and trotted from the vile room.

Saudett looked back at the disgusting tables, stained with blood. *What other unspeakable horrors has Hear-fan Skaad committed in this room?* She turned, praying to the Primus that she would never see this chamber again.

CHAPTER TWELVE

HEARTBROKEN

THE KEEN EYES CORSAIRS fled back to sea, tail between their legs. Fought off the beachhead, a handful of their ships scuttled into the sands of the bay. Half a dozen had escaped into the open ocean. Captain Kai had given up the chase, as many of his crew had been lost or wounded in the battle.

Simon sat beside Kai in a small boat as it rowed toward the beach.

"It would seem old Keen Eyes has thrown our alliance to the sharks, as they say." Kai deliberated as the boat came into shore. "Why would he have such a change of heart?"

Simon stayed silent, letting the pirate king focus on his thoughts. He was much too preoccupied with the welcoming party ashore. A group stood waiting for them on a patch of unstained sand where no blood had been spilled. Simon smiled fondly at the sight of his in-laws. Anora and Kiana Ahmadi stood, Kiana, waving enthusiastically to him as they approached. Baal, Brena Vasara, and Simon's loyal guard, Rakshak Zahir, were also there.

Shepherd's Eye, Cad Dermont, and the two council magi stood further back. The older man, the Theta, Cygne Caladrius, was in his white robes, though the ends of his sleeves had taken a crimson tint of blood and soil. The Gamma, Lila Parakeet…was nearly naked. She wore a long transparent shawl, almost dragging in the sands, showing off her impressively abundant, voluptuous body beneath. Only tiny strips of bright green cloth covered her womanly aspects beneath the shawl. With only simple flat sandals on her feet, she smiled and moved with a relaxed gait as Simon approached. A man, also bare for all but another strip of green cloth over his *significant* fortitude, held a large palm branch over Lila, keeping the sun from her.

Simon hopped from the boat and splashed into the shallow, warm water and onto the sands.

Captain Kai did likewise, striding beside him with a confident certainty that radiated about him. A hand rested atop one cutlass's hilt as they approached the group.

"Simon, you disappeared!" Kiana scolded, and at the same time, she excitedly embraced him. "You are the First Otsoa. It would be best to tell us what you're doing before abandoning us. *Please.*"

Simon returned the embrace warmly. Kai and Lila were staring icily into Kiana's back. "Ahem, little sister," Simon revealed. *That should settle Kai's temperament.* "I apologize. I sighted ships as I flew, and then next thing I knew, I was along for the ride."

"Well, at least you came back," Kiana said as she stepped back and looked at Kai. "Who's this that came to our rescue against those pirates? He has the look of one himself."

"And I am," Kai agreed, tilting his head questioningly and holding Kiana's violet gaze. He continued, "I am Captain Kai of *The Mamba's Mouth* and King of the Gilded Crow Corsairs. My territory consists of the southwestern half of the Tal'tulu Isles. However, it seems Old Keen Eyes has other plans for my territory."

"A king?" Cad Dermont asked as he stepped to the forefront, scratching at his salt and pepper stubble. "There was no king in Tal'tulu as far as I knew."

"And what is it that you would know of Tal'tulu?" Kai answered flatly. "Auru's don't concern themselves with our islands. Or are you Xamidian? You have the look of a half-breed about you."

Cad grunted something unintelligible.

"This is true," Cygne Caladrius interrupted Cad, nodding agreeingly in an elderly fashion. "Aurulan diplomacy reaches only so far as Xamid."

Lila strode forward, seeming to straighten her back and puff out her chest as she did so. "What use does a pirate king have to our cause, dear Simon?" To Simon's surprise, she came to him and gently touched his cheek.

The alluring aroma of her saccharine scent filled the air and wafted toward Simon, teasing his senses and stirring up a whirlwind of desire within him. Her boundless breasts brushed against him, and he felt his face and neck begin to heat up.

Kai wrapped his arm in Simon's, unapologetically trying to pull him away from Lila.

Lila hooked one arm on Simon's other side and put the other hand to her mouth in feigned shock.

"Both of you leave off! This man is married to *my* daughter," Anora Ahmadi shouted, a venom on her lips.

Dread suddenly bubbled within Simon. *Not only have I broken my vow of loyalty to Saudett, but I will also hurt Anora and Kiana in the process. Skrull's balls, I'm such a fool.* He had never spoken to Anora of Saudett and their extracurricular play, but he had shown his faithfulness to Anora's daughter since he had met the woman in Hasiera. *Now, I have betrayed their trust.*

"Oh?" Kai eyed Simon, a curious curve on his lips.

This is it. I'm done for.

"Did I not hear that our handsome leader was open to exterior stimulations?" Lila asked suggestively. "That he and his spouse both enjoyed the company of others."

"I—I," Simon stuttered.

"You are correct, Gamma," Cad Dermont said. "Even I have had the pleasure of Simon a time or two."

Bastard. Simon glared murderously at Cad.

"Really?" Lila turned her attention to the Shepherd's Eye captain, releasing Simon and taking a suggestive swaying step toward Cad.

"Enough! They have put all that behind them," Anora's voice elevated disparagingly. "They have a child on the way. No time for such filthy—"

"Shall we get back to the matter at hand?" It was Brena Vasara's voice that interrupted Anora. "It matters not who walks the mountain with whom. What matters is the threat we must face and the daughter we must find. What's your plan with these pirates, Simon Meridio?"

Baal grunted something incoherent behind his mate, leaning on the handle of his massive hammer with its runic warhead in the sand.

Anora's eyes, furious, did not turn away from Simon.

She knows. Simon looked away from his mother-in-law and returned to the task at hand. "Captain Kai has agreed to aid us in exchange for brokering a peace with Xamid."

"No, I've changed my mind," Kai said brusquely.

Simon turned to him, startled. "You won't help us?"

"Let me speak." Kai motioned his silence. "In light of Keen Eyes betrayal and now that I have witnessed you and your forces in action, we will instead aim to bring all of Tal'tulu under my control. Help me rid these islands of the Keen Eye Corsairs once and for all. Then I will help you."

There was a long silence that held the gathering.

Finally, Cygne Caladrius spoke, "A daunting task, to be sure. However, pirate politics may be far more straightforward than entering negotiations that could take months or even years with Xamid. Need we only deal with Keen Eyes himself?"

"Precisely, my friend," Kai said eagerly. He snapped his fingers.

One of his crew appeared from behind, holding a map before him so all could see.

Kai unsheathed a cutlass and pointed to a round dot on the largest islands. It was on the furthest northwestern point of Tal'tulu's Spine. Closest to Xamid. "All we need to do is take the port city of Jewelstrand. Well, take the town and *kill* Keen Eyes."

"And all his ships, peoples, and town steads will follow you?" Simon asked warily.

"They will follow," Kai returned. "*Pirates* always seek the strongest among us."

"Well?" Simon looked to his advisors. "What do you think?"

"What other choice do we have?" Brena said. "We can't sit here idly and do nothing; else you will begin murdering one another over who Simon will bed next. Why you are all so fascinated by such a flimsy man-child, I do not know." Brena turned, placing a hand on Baal's broad shoulder, and led him away.

There was an awkward silence after Brena's words hung in the air.

"Ahem," Simon cleared his throat unsurely. "It's decided then. We will join Captain Kai and take the town of Jewelstrand from his rival."

"My lord, who will stay to protect the Wayfarers Gate?" Rakshak Zahir asked.

Simon was startled, forgetting the stoic man had been there. He met Zahir's dark eyes. "Would you volunteer? Along with our brethren from Hasiera?"

"I would prefer to be by your side, my lord First." Zahir bowed, fist to chest. "But if you command me to stay, I shall obey."

"Thank you, Zahir."

"You will need someone with a bit more magical persuasion should the enemy strike through this Gate," Cygne said. "I will be needed for healing during the fighting for the port city. Lila?"

Lila Parakeet let out a regretful sigh. "Oh, I *dearly* wanted to accompany Simon. But yes, I suppose I can stay and continue to relax." She looked around at the blood-stained sands. "Though I must find a new beach to lounge upon."

"Very well," Simon said, command returning with his confidence. "Those of Hasiera will stay, and Cad will keep the Shepherd's Eye soldiers here as well. The rest of us will board Kai's ships."

"All those of Hasiera?" Cad asked with a questioning glance at Kiana.

"My in-laws will join me."

Cad's face contorted, and he turned and tramped up the beach like a child in a tantrum.

Lila swayed after him, her pallbearer struggling to hold the wide leaves above her. "Don't worry yourself, I'll be with you."

Kiana grinned at Simon, then made a rude gesture at Cad's back.

The gathering began to disperse after Cad and Lila. Kai returned to the boat, giving orders. A single figure stood still as stone as the others trickled up the beach and into the tree line toward camp. Her intense glare burned toward Simon.

"Anora," Simon held out his hands in a calming manner.

"How could you?" Anora's voice was heartbroken.

A flash of anger overtook Simon. *What my wife and I do in and out of our bed chambers is none of her Skrull-damned business.* He wanted to shout the words, but instead, he feigned ignorance. "I don't know what you are talking about, Anora."

"Did you fucking do it?"

"Do what?" Simon rebuked. "What are you accusing me of?"

"Did you *fuck* him?"

Simon threw his hands up with exaggerated emotion. "Of course not! What do you take me for? I am loyal to my wife, Saudett. I've put my past behind me." The guilt sickened him, but he would rather lie to Anora than lose her motherly affection. They had truly connected all those months ago when Saudett had reunited with her mother, and Simon had welcomed her and Kiana as a family into their lives.

"If you are lying to me, Simon, I swear, you are no better than Gaddard Kafilah was." Without another word, Anora turned and walked away from him.

Simon stood alone on the beach, taken aback. *Am I truly no better than that man? Saudett's father.* A man who tried to have his wife murdered. A man who fornicated in brothels as Anora worked for a living. A man who must have assaulted Anora on countless occasions. A man who did not respect her.

Simon fell to his knees, one hand gripping his chest. It was almost like actual physical pain was thrashing in his heart. His scarred left arm throbbed, and the back of his neck tightened.

I'm disrespecting Saudett by not honoring her wishes. I am no better than that disgusting bastard Gaddard was...oh gods, why can't I breathe?

The pain shattered into a million pieces in his chest, and Simon's face thudded into the sand.

Chapter Thirteen

Amberheart

The enormous amber gemstone nestled in the cavernous dragon's chest pulsated with a gentle, radiant glow, infusing the surrounding air with a comforting warmth. Hata found herself transfixed by the dragon's profound, luminous gaze – its eyes resembling twin orbs of smoldering topaz, capturing the essence of the soaring Ryk Lân. Each scale on the dragon's majestic form shimmered with a rich palette of golden earth tones, reminiscent of the breathtaking hues found in sunsets and mountain peaks. Of the trio, the first dragon was colossal, distinguished by its towering amber spines and horns, which were easily ten times the size of those adorning the two dragons flanking it. As it moved purposefully toward Hata, the ground trembled beneath its formidable weight, and she experienced an undeniable sense of their deep connection to the very earth beneath her feet.

Hata stood motionless as the colossal head drew near. It seemed as though, at any moment, it could strike and consume her entirely. She shut her eyes and released a wave of her earth sense, allowing it to radiate outward from her. The creature came to a sudden stop, withdrew, and then, with a magnificent display of power, all three dragons lifted their heads and let out a unified thunderous roar. The sound reverberated through the walls of the mountain, prompting other dragons to emerge from their perches, joining in with their triumphant calls. The chamber was filled with the resounding song of these majestic creatures. Hata gazed in utter amazement at the breathtaking sight.

A distant commotion arose behind her from the entrance of the feast hall.

The dragon before Hata, towering over the others, turned its gaze towards the tiniest of the trio. The youthful drake confidently approached, its inquisitive eyes studying Hata from just a breath's distance as it curiously sniffed the air.

Cautiously, Hata raised a hand.

The dragon did not pull away.

As her fingers brushed the scales between its nostrils, a warmth crawled up her arm and flowed into her. It felt the same as her connection with the earth. She basked in the power beating from the dragon's amber gemstone heart.

Suddenly, the beast emitted a strangely soothing, serpentine sound and nudged its head beneath Hata's legs, causing her to lose her balance and tumble precariously onto its snout. Before she could react, it deftly lifted its head, propelling her over its formidable spines and landing her safely on its broad back. Without warning, it surged forward, its massive wings beating with strength, carrying them into the air with breathtaking speed.

Hata found herself suddenly soaring through the air. Glancing downwards, she watched as the two earth-like dragons exerted tremendous effort to launch themselves into flight. A small figure staggered towards the clearing, and then the graceful azure scales of Safiiri glinted as she elegantly touched down beside her elven rider, Taivaseläin.

Hata clung tightly to shimmering amber spikes at the base of the dragon's neck as the fierce wind battered her face. The mighty creature soared higher and higher, its powerful wings beating rhythmically against the gusts. As they ascended, Hata caught glimpses of other magnificent beasts of varying colors and shades darting past her. The hole in the centermost peak of the mountain seeped sunlight through, and the dragon beneath her soared upward into the tunnel's shaft.

The bright light of day blinded her as they emerged into the sky.

The earth-shaking roar of the beast beneath her signified its triumph, as a continuous stream of dragons surged out of the mountain peak, resembling the eruption of a dormant volcano. The young dragon unfurled its majestic wings, holding them aloft to gracefully glide through the sky. It briefly turned its head to fix its gaze upon Hata, a glint of something enigmatic reflected in its eyes. Unlike the older, larger drake, this one's look seemed to convey a sense of mischievousness that intrigued Hata.

As though responding to her thoughts, the creature suddenly closed its wings and dove, beginning to spiral. Hata desperately tried to hold on as her body lifted from the creature's back during the fall. Despite her desperate attempts, her grip began to wane, and her clammy palms slid from the creature's sturdy spines. In an instant, Hata found herself plummeting through the boundless sky, utterly alone.

The dragon plummeted away from her.

An island was approaching too quickly for comfort. Hata calmed herself, reached for the metals in her armor, and took hold. *By Teras's might, I'm in control.* She urged the armor on, giving chase to the drake. Placing her hands tight to her sides, she dove after the beast. Surprisingly, she caught up, the space between them closing rapidly.

The landmass grew larger and larger below them.

Now, only feet away from where she had been perched on the dragon's back, she reached for it again. The amber gemstone in her breastplate reverberated as her hands were nearly inches from grabbing a spine.

Then she *felt* the dragon.

Its amber spines grew, extending and twisting out, allowing her to grasp them and pull herself into the safety of his scaled-back. Suddenly, the scales around her groaned and moved like tumbling stones about her hands and legs, trying to merge with the armor of her vambraces and greaves. She was stuck fast to the dragon's back. She felt her consciousness connect with his.

I am Kulta. He gave a magnificent roar of approval. *Who are you, little stone?*

Kulta, I like your name. I am Hata Vasara. Some call me The Sunstone. It's funny, I've always wanted a brother.

Kulta turned his head to regard her, then opened his wings again just before the ground reached them, and the halting force made Hata nearly lose her vision. Kulta, none too gracefully, landed with a skidding, scratching purchase. The scales released their grip on Hata's armor, and Kulta lowered his head to allow her to dismount.

As soon as her feet touched the ground, Kulta's tail *thwacked* hard into her back, sending Hata tumbling. Pain shot through her, but she grabbed hold of her armor and twisted mid-air to come to a halt.

Kulta's amber eyes no longer held their playful glint as they burned ferociously, watching her as he paced back and forth.

Hata slowly lowered herself to the ground. They were on a smaller plateau-like island, primarily flat with craggy crystal-veined stones jutting out around the entire edge of the landmass. The ground was torn apart, and there were scorch marks and other signs of magic-infused battles. Dragons, some with elven riders, landed on the arena's edges to watch. Others circled high above.

Hata focused on Kulta and sensed his emotions.

Prove your worth. As the thought hit Hata, Kulta roared and charged forward.

Hata slammed her hands to the ground. The earth rippled before her, and the ground beneath Kulta's feet turned to quicksand.

He gave a bellowing cry as he struggled through the muck. First, his legs, then his body sank.

I have him trapped. Hata was about to solidify the hold when Kulta's head lunged below the sinking sands.

His presence, his *earth sense*, disappeared from Hata's visualization as if he had melded with the earth. *How is that possible?*

The ground trembled beneath her feet, sending shockwaves through the earth. Suddenly, it exploded from under her, hurling earth and stones against her armor and pelting her exposed skin. Hata barely managed to propel herself upward as Kulta's menacing jaws snapped at her. Determined, Hata swiftly took to the sky, out of reach of the rows of deadly teeth.

Kulta followed, shooting from the earth in a geyser of dust and debris.

Hata soared overhead, turning to look at the enraged dragon. The amber gemstone in his chest began to flash rapidly as he chased. Hata changed course, diving back to the earth. *I have nothing to fight him with when we're in the air.*

As Kulta rocketed past, his wings beat furiously while Hata dove. With a thud, Hata touched down and quickly turned her gaze up at the sky.

Kulta came to hover directly above her, his mighty wings creating a wind beneath him, buffeting her. The light in his amber heart chest became a solid shine of golden red. Kulta opened his jaws wide. *Molten* rock spewed out in a torrent.

Hata's eyes widened in terror, nearly hesitating at the destructive force of such an attack. She slammed her hands to the ground and then raised them skyward in the nick of time. A thick slab of earth burst before her at an angle.

The molten superheated earth struck the wall and splashed and rolled around the sides next to her. Intense heat suddenly enclosed Hata. Her wall began glowing a white-orange, and the lava began seeping through. Hata stepped back, sweating profusely from the temperature and her own magical exertion. She screamed with effort as she erected a second, *thicker* wall behind the first. Then, two more to the sides, one with each hand.

For a few seconds at least, the heat subsided. On hands and knees, Hata bowed her head in defeat. *What can I do? I can't defeat him.* She stared at the earth below her and a thought came to her. *How had he disappeared into the ground?*

Become.

Hata's amber gemstone thrummed suddenly with red-yellow light as if speaking.

Become one with the mountain.

She reached *into* the ground…and began to sink—her arms, legs, and body. She closed her eyes as her head went under. When she opened them, it was pitch black, and then her vision slowly turned grey. It was like looking up at the surface of a lake from below the waves. *Somehow*, she took in a breath. She could feel the earth's minerals, gems, and stones around her.

Something rumbled overhead.

Hata looked up to see ripples of vibration stomping on the surface above her. She could see a hazy shadow of Kulta but more so sensed his heavy steps on the ground above. She felt his triumph, believing she had melted to ash.

Not worthy. Kulta's voice growled, somewhat disappointedly within her mind.

The amber in her breastplate pulsed again. The voice was that of both a caring mother and a stern father. *Gather the most vital pieces of me to you.*

Quartz. Topaz. Corundum. *Diamond.* Hata took hold of the trace minerals and pulled them to her. To a single spot. Around her fist. She clenched her jaw as the power surged through her. She propelled herself through the earth, gathering speed. She circled once. Twice. Faster and faster with each rotation. Abruptly, she pivoted. Up. Toward the ripples of Kulta above. Hata *exploded* fist first from the earth and, with untethered power, struck into Kulta's gut with a gemstone-encrusted fist. The force sent a shockwave through his scaled hide.

The dragon let out a piercing shriek and then doubled over, writhing in agony. After a moment, the great creature lay still, though Hata could still discern the steady rise and fall of its breath.

The dragons surrounding them roared in unison.

Safiiri landed nearby with a gust of wind, and Taivaseläin slid awkwardly down and stumbled toward Hata. He was obviously still drunk as he hollered, "Teras's thunder! What in all the hells? It should have taken years of training and time spent together before a kinship could be forged through battle."

Teras. He helped me. Hata fiddled with the amber gemstone in her breastplate as she ignored Taivaseläin and walked to Kulta. She knelt beside him and touched his neck near his head. One topaz eye opened to regard her. The warmth reached into her, and she felt his satisfaction at being bested. A renewed playfulness seeped through her.

You are worthy, my sister.

Hata sat down, leaned against Kulta's warm-scaled hide, and closed her eyes. Exhausted.

Chapter Fourteen

TAXED

"Archers!" Kaplan Mir shouted from the scaffolding behind the tall wooden palisade. Rain began to fall. He raised his bow, along with only a few dozen others, and loosed a volley. A *pitiful* volley into the roiling mass of bloodthirsty beasts. Still, they managed to down a handful of hounds and one of the hulking abominations. They let another volley loose and began firing freely into the enemy as they approached the wall.

The monsters screamed and thrashed at the thick timber logs. The grey, ape-like creatures leaped up but could not grasp the tall, rain and oil-slicked wood.

Qav's luck with this rain. Kaplan let another shot loose and watched as it sank into a lumbering hulk's head. The beast toppled to the mud, and its brethren took no heed, stepping over the corpse as it began to bubble and join with the muck. He glanced back to the town behind him. It was small, a few hundred people at most. They would not be able to hold out. There were too many of the *Children of Skaad* to fight off.

Kaplan's mind returned to his argument with the glaive-wielding warrior woman.

"Close the gates and begin evacuation," Kaplan had urged. "Do you have ships?"

"We must fight," the woman countered. "This is our home!"

"We will fight for as long as we can," Kaplan reassured. "But we must get those who cannot away before they're slaughtered."

Kaplan released another arrow. *Thank the Primus they listened.* Three longships with carved figureheads of long-dead warriors were being loaded with people and supplies at the town's rickety docks.

The beasts screamed, throwing themselves against the gate. It shook and swayed.

A dozen men and women pressed against it, trying as they might to hold it shut.

"I've sent the boy to warn our miners to return from the mountain. We must hold out until they return." The warrior woman with the glaive shouted up at him.

Kaplan did not answer. Instead, he stared as the massive insectoid, its back bright with blue flames, crushed through its allies straight for the gate. He turned, waving frantically at those below him. "Fall back! Get away from the gate!"

A few people there heard him and leaped out of the way just in time, but others were crushed under splintering logs and thick insectoid legs as the gate buckled inward.

"To the ships, hold the docks!" Kaplan shouldered his bow, unsheathed his scimitar, and sprinted along the wall. *From this angle, yes, I can make it.* He leaped out overhead of the massive burning beast, through thick oily smoke, directly into the blue flames.

Jude awoke to the sounds of screaming and the smell of burning. He threw off the bearskin blanket to find himself naked beneath. *Fucks!* He looked about frantically only to find his clothing drying near a hearth. The bandage on his leg had also been freshly tended to. "Fucking hells, I don't have a crutch."

Something moaned on the bed behind him. He turned and pulled the covers back to reveal Joanna. Stunningly naked as well. He blinked in surprise at her peaceful sleeping face and alluring curvaceous figure. She was a more prominent woman. Her chubbiness looked inviting...*and fucks, she is Skrull-damned beautiful.*

Joanna curled her knees up and groaned as the cool air touched her bare skin and gooseflesh rippled over her.

Gods.

A terrifying screech echoed outside the log building they found themselves in, pulling Jude back from his wandering thoughts.

Joanna's eyes shot open to see Jude staring at her. She sat up and instinctively pulled the fur blanket back up. "What are you doing?"

Jude shook himself out of his ogling and focused on the dire situation. "Fucking hells, I don't know. But there's fighting outside, I need your help." He pointed to their clothing. "I can't even dress myself."

Something banged against the door, and Joanna's embarrassment seemingly vanished as she leaped out of bed, grabbed the clothes, and tossed Jude's to him.

Jude pulled on his shirt, still slightly damp.

Joanna was half-dressed when the door burst open, and one deformed, hulking creature's horrid visage pushed its way in, deadly fangs dripping with hunger.

Jude watched in horror as Joanna got tangled in her dress. She stepped back and fell to the floor.

The beast lurched toward her.

Fucking fucks. With every ounce of strength he possessed, Jude hurled himself at the beast's side with an ungainly, one-legged leap. Their collision sent the creature stumbling and crashing down on top of him, knocking the breath from his lungs and sending waves of searing pain through his body.

The creature turned its ghastly maw on him, teeth sunk into his shoulder. He could do nothing. Not even scream.

Then, a spear of flame tore through the beast, through bone and flesh alike. Jude felt the heat of the magic. The creature lay dead atop him. Black ooze began to drip down on him.

Joanna hurried over and helped extract Jude from beneath the body.

"Skrull's balls," Jude finally said, panting for breath. "What in all the fucks is happening? The last thing I remember is hitting the water."

"The villagers must have saved us. In return, we brought hell down upon them." Joanna clutched at her head. "So many innocent people are dying." Joanna's back straightened, and her blue eyes glistened with resolve. "This needs to end. These abominations must be cleansed in fire."

Jude crawled back to the bed and leaned his back against it, one hand on his bleeding shoulder as Joanna strode resolutely from the tiny log home, leaving Jude entirely alone.

Kaplan's scimitar sank into the smoking, blue-burning flesh.

The creature let out a horrifying screech, its humanoid torso unable to reach behind it.

Fumes stung Kaplan's eyes and filled his nostrils. Flames licked up at him and began to burn. He pulled the blade free and rolled through the fire and off the side of the convulsing creature. It thrashed around, shrieking in pain. Its lifeless eyes found Kaplan, and the two scythe blades attached to the upper arms of the humanoid part of the creature struck at him in quick succession.

He swiftly dodged the first strike and blocked the second with his reliable scimitar. The impact surged through the blade and into his arms, but before he could retaliate, the monstrous beast lunged forward with startling speed. One of its colossal legs connected with Kaplan, sending him hurtling through the air.

He painfully thudded into the mud. *Damn.* He pushed himself up with his sword and got his bearings. A tide of *Children* poured through the smashed gates of the small town. The Vouri warriors had gathered and were falling back towards the docks. Then he saw a group cut off from the rest, being overwhelmed. It was the other archers on the wall he had abandoned when he had leaped from it. *Skrull's hell, I should have stayed and fought with them. Fool.* There were too many beasts in between him and the archers. He looked to the docks. A substantial force of Vouri with shields up had blocked the path leading onto the pier. One of the longboats had cast off while the others were still being boarded.

I'll join with those at the docks, and the archers, regrettably, must die while distracting the enemy. Hettra's mercy to you all. Kaplan broke into a run as the burning beast lurched toward him slowly, then fell, finally succumbing to its mortal wound. He saw hulks and hounds breaking through doorways into the log homes around him.

Three horrid hounds gave chase, quickly gaining on him. The first leaped for his exposed back, jaws snapping.

Kaplan rolled, simultaneously slashing his scimitar across the hound's belly as it barreled over him; its innards spewed out as it crumpled into a heap.

The second hound was upon him. Kaplan scrambled backward away on his arse.

The massive heavy head of a razor-sharpened glaive sheared the beast in half just before its jaws snapped at Kaplan's legs.

There was a bellow, and the burly shield and sword wielder from earlier crashed into the third Skaad-hound, sending it head over heels before sinking his blade into it.

The woman helped Kaplan to his feet. "Such a reckless Xamidian. Brave. You fight like the mountain caste."

"My thanks..." Kaplan breathed, catching his breath.

"Astrid. Astrid Kaarina." Her blazing blue eyes regarded him with amusement.

The shield man rejoined them. He sounded the broadside of his sword to the iron edging of his shield. "More are coming, little brother." He grinned a Baal-like grin through his long black mustache.

"And you've already met Nanuq Tornarsuk of the Nunara," Astrid said. "Though his heart is of a Vouri Thegn."

Suddenly, there was a howling, shrieking cacophony as the *Children of Skaad* charged toward the last line of warriors holding the docks.

"It was an honor to fight with you and your people, Astrid of House Kaarina," Nanuq said with a grin.

Astrid grunted in response.

At that moment, a pillar of fire erupted in the enemy's ranks. A towering inferno—churning in a vortex of flame. It consumed everything in its path, hounds and hulks alike—along with the Vouri log homes. Kaplan felt the air around him sizzle from the heat of it.

Joanna confidently emerged from a rustic log cabin near the docks. With a commanding motion of her hands, she directed the swirling inferno, her flowing black hair dancing in the fiery winds, and her eyes ablaze with determination. She took another step, decimating the *Children* who got in her way.

A grey ape-like beast leaped off the roof of the homestead she had just exited, crashing down with both fists. The force behind the blow upon Joanna was horrible as her head shot back, and her body pounded limp into the ground. The beast stood over her, shrieking and whooping, pounding its hands on its chest.

The pillar of flame vanished with a fizzling hiss.

Kaplan dashed forward. "We must help her!" He cried as the beast, hovering over Joanna's body, raised its fists again.

A dagger flashed through the air and sunk into the creature's back, and another bounced off its head harmlessly.

The beast roared and turned.

Jude Nelon leaned against the doorframe, grasping a bleeding shoulder.

Kaplan flung himself at the creature, his scimitar slashing into the grey-apes sinewy shoulder. The blade *clanged* against metal bones.

It reeled on him, slamming its powerful arm against him. Kaplan soared ten feet through the air and splashed into the muck. He groaned in agony, his body pounding as he watched Astrid and Nanuq thunder past him.

A mighty blow from the glaive cleaved into the beast's leg but again halted abruptly.

Nanuq charged head-on into the creature, the impact sending both man and beast crashing into the homestead's wall. With incredible strength, he pinned the beast to the thick logs, discarding his blade and using both arms to push against his shield. As he strained against the thrashing, roaring beast, he bellowed out, "Astrid!"

The glaive came down with such ferocity that the beast's head rattled even as the weapon glanced off the creature's steel skull. Metal glinted through black blood as the beast stopped thrashing for a moment. Another blow landed, then another.

Kaplan, breathing heavily as he found his feet, and went to Joanna, who lay unconscious.

Jude crawled toward her through the mud, tears glistening in his eyes. "No! Please don't die on me, Jo."

The repetitive clash of metal on metal rang out as Astrid and Nanuq beat the grey ape into lifeless submission.

Kaplan surveyed the area. Most of the creatures were dead from the flaming inferno of mage, Joanna Ohleoc. *Thank the Primus.* Still, more *Children of Skaad* streamed down the mountainside toward the village. "We must flee. Help me get these two to the ships."

A shout came from the opposite side of the village, and the gangly boy from earlier came running around the corner of a home. Two dozen sturdy-looking miners followed him, their large Vouri pickaxes ready.

"To the longboats!" Astrid ordered as she helped Jude to his feet.

Kaplan and Nanuq hefted Joanna and slowly approached the waiting ship. Ropes were thrown, oars hoisted, as a second massive wave of shrieking creatures breached the village. They looked back at the uncountable horde of death and destruction as the ship slowly crawled out to sea.

How can there be so many? Exhaustion and pain washed through Kaplan as he leaned against the curved hull. The Vouri people sat eerily silent. There were only the soft sounds of the oars pulling through the gentle waves. The smoking and infested village grew smaller as Kaplan dosed in and out of wakefulness.

OPAL

Saudett stared at the roiling red mist of the Wayfarers Gate. *I'm finally going home. I'll see my mother and sister. And Simon. He does love me, and he won't be angry with me over our child.*

"Blood of Skaad, these prisoners are not permitted to depart from the Skaad Lân," the gravel-like voice of the earthwalker standing before Malix was unwavering as its reddish glowing pit-like sockets regarded Saudett and Darkclaw Marah. "I captured the hound sulking around the prisoners' cell. Why would our Lord release them now?"

The platform groaned to a halt behind them, and a roiling mass of *Children* funneled through the knee-deep waters toward the gate to the Ryk Lân. It was constant. As soon as the platform emptied, it descended again to bring more creatures to the surface.

Oh, Hata, I pray to the Primus that you are all right. Saudett paused as guilt suddenly gripped her heart and tightened its hold. *I'm abandoning her again. Hear-fan Skaad is amassing his army to attack the Ryklings again, and I am running away after I swore to protect her.*

"My father wished me to extend our family line with this human," Malix said coldly.

That chilling fear overtook the guilt in Saudett. *That vile man is just through that gate to Ryk.* If she were to return to try feebly to rescue Hata...*he* would take her. Her hands began to tremble.

Malix continued reasoning with the earthwalker. "The only way to ensure that the *human* is to come with a child is to take it with me."

The molten humanoid turned its head slowly to Marah. "And the hound?"

Darkclaw Marah's fur bristled, and they hissed in a fury, clutching where their arm used to be. "We are no hound. We are Volkinn, and you have defiled us!" Marah looked ready to spring at the earthwalker and tear it asunder.

"Enough!" Malix bellowed, his eyes alighting with violet light before dimming as he calmed himself. He sighed deeply, "What is your name, earthwalker?"

"Bjarkeld."

"You will not question me again, Bjarkeld. I have lived among your people for decades. You should know I am the Guardian of Fjoer."

"I am aware." Bjarkeld's voice grated like stones tumbling down a mountainside.

"Then you will take us through this gate and leave us on the surface of the Earste Lân," Malix commanded. "*All* of us."

"So be it, *Guardian*." Bjarkeld turned and moved like slow-flowing lava through the red mist.

"Come now. We must be near him to earth-walk, or he will leave us behind." Malix held out his hand to Saudett.

She took it, and the trio hurried after Bjarkeld. Saudett held her breath as the mist engulfed her, and she entered a grey void. The distorted image of Bjarkeld and Malix ahead of her. She turned to see the skewed silhouette of Marah behind her. Malix squeezed her hand, and they moved vertically as if flying through a gloomy sky. They ascended through the grey world for far longer than comfortable. *This mountain had been massive.* How they could breathe was beyond her. They finally breached the surface into twilight, and a blast of cold air struck Saudett. Snow fell lightly around the massive crater in which they stood. Grey-white peaks rose around them—the North Iron Belt.

Without a word, Bjarkeld sank back into the earth, leaving the two poorly dressed battered prisoners, one with black leathery wings, the other a half-wolf one-armed Volkinn. And lastly, a magical, four-armed Iban'mael. The very son of the enemy of all peoples. Saudett felt a slight amusement as she took in their rag-tag group. *By the Primus, we're an outlandish and wretched little party.*

"Is all of your land so cold and barren?" Malix asked, visibly shivering. "I'm more accustomed to heat, if I'm being honest."

"Not all, no, the Earste Lân has many different environments. I much prefer the heat of the desert over this cold." Saudett wore the now-tattered clothing she had been wearing the day she was imprisoned. The day Nyxal, her loyal right-hand warrior of the Nyra, had died. The day Saudett had killed Trije-fan Skaad to save Hata. *It was worth it,* she told herself as the brisk mountain air bit at her skin through the shabby clothes.

"Fuck me, shall we leave this chill behind?" Malix asked, a grim expression on his face as he began to float upward. "We may have to carry you, Darkclaw."

"We will walk. You two may go on ahead. We will hunt for game as we go. Where is our destination?"

"Where indeed?" Malix mused, scratching at his curly beard.

"Will you still seek out the Wayfarer Gaelin?" Saudett asked curiously. "Would it not help us if he were on our side?"

"If I rid Gaelin Yesnala from this Lân, my father will leave it alone. Is that not the better outcome?"

Saudett stopped. *It is. Skaad wants to close the Gates and leave us be. But what about Hata and all those creatures of other Lân's that he has enslaved or has yet to slaughter?* Another thought struck her. "You would return to your father with Gaelin and leave me here? Will he not be furious?"

Malix slowly returned to the ground from where he had been hovering. His brow creased with pensiveness. After some time, he said, "Well, he may simply kill me."

"Then you should help us fight against him," Saudett pleaded. "With you, my husband, and Hata, we can fight against him."

Malix studied her, then sighed, "I will think about it. Either way, I wish to meet this Gaelin Yesnala. What is our course?"

"If this is where Oitilla once stood, the closest villages are southward in Aurulan," Saudett contemplated aloud. "We could head to the capital, Nidhaut. There is a council of mysterious magi there that could perhaps help us. Or at least give us some information."

Malix nodded. "Better than freezing my balls off in this place, let's go. We will land in the first village we see to the south and await you, Darkclaw."

"Volkinn are not welcome in Aurulan," Marah answered.

"Look at us." Saudett gestured, stifling a laugh. "I would say none of us would pass for *ordinary* in Aurulan."

"That is the first time I've seen you smile, Saudett." Malix's inverted eyes twinkled with wry amusement. "You look...pleasant when you smile."

Saudett felt her face flush momentarily, and then the image of Hear-fan Skaad flashed before her eyes. That look of disgust for her upon it. Her lips drew to a hard line as she tried to keep them from trembling.

Darkclaw Marah let out a low growl.

Malix's eyes widened in dismay. "Fuck me. I'm sorry, I didn't mean anything by it. You've been through so much."

"It's all right, I'm all right." Saudett lied. The fear was still twisting in her gut. "Let's get out of here before we freeze to death."

"Again, I apologize." Malix clenched all four fists together, an intensity alighting in his eyes. His voice was low and malicious. "I'm sorry my father has made you feel this way."

He means it. He truly hates his father. Saudett let it rest at that. Instead, she flexed her wings and opened them. Then, with a powerful thrust, she leaped into the air. "Head south, Marah!" Saudett called back to the Volkinn as Malix followed her into the gentle snowfall of the grey skies of the North Iron Belt.

Bjarkeld, earthwalker of fire and stone, watched as the three departed. *The Blood of Skaad conspires against Him. He must know of this.* Only Bjarkeld's head had emerged from the ground some twenty paces from where the three had been speaking, hidden to look like the stone itself. They were none the wiser as he had watched and listened. Once the trio was out of sight, Bjarkeld descended into the grey world of the earthwalkers. Back down to the Wayfarers Gate, he emerged into the Skaad Lân.

He did not pause as he entered the Ryk Lân gate. Around him was a swirling mass of dark navy clouds with violet flashes of lightning snaking through it. The spherical cloud was massive, surrounding hundreds of floating islands. It seemed to be slowly expanding.

Bjarkeld moved from island to island. He felt the magical gemstones and crystals of the earth below pulsing with life. *This Lân is powerful. The islands breathe as if alive.* He was tempted to descend and examine one of the pulsing gemstones and take it into himself. *Not yet. I must inform my lord of his son's deception.* The need began to scratch insatiably within. The need to consume what lay beneath. *Is this why our lord does not permit us earthwalkers to come to Ryk?*

A shrill cry echoed in the dim light. A moving stream of flying humanoids, the Nyra, soared overhead, shrieking and clicking as they circled. Each island was swarming with *Children.* Many deformed creatures worked on the bridges between islands, making them wider and permanent crossings. Others pushed massive rune-etched solid black metal cylinders on wheels across the bridges all in one direction, presumably toward the enemy.

Finally, Bjarkeld came to the largest of the floating landmasses; more construction took place here. Immense siege towers jabbed into the skies, and one such tower of twisted metal and wood lumbered across a wide bridge precariously.

As he came to the large tent in the center of the island, the thumping call of the gemstones below him ceased as a new magic overpowered them. *Shadow* emanated from the pavilion's interior.

Bjarkeld moved inside.

The Lord of Shadow sat with all four hands, concentrating on an obsidian gemstone floating between them. Unseen to the naked eye, Bjarkeld was shaken by the shockwaves of energy washing in spherical pulses from the gem's epicenter out through him until it reached the wall of navy smoke thousands of feet away. He nearly fell to the ground under the intense pressure of the magic.

"Earthwalker," The Lord's sultry voice broke through the thundering in Bjarkeld's head. "Your kind are not permitted here in Ryk. You will be consumed by hunger. It's for your own good. This had better be important."

"My Lord—" the words were constrained to come out. "Your true blood son, he conspires with the human woman against you. He has taken her and the hound to the Earste—"

A powerful wave of darkness engulfed Bjarkeld, and he could not withstand it. His conciseness left him.

He did not know how long he had been lost when he finally heard a voice.

"Awaken, earthwalker."

Bjarkeld wavered as he looked about his surroundings. They were on a smaller island within the sphere of dark clouds. No bridges. The Lord of Shadow stood over him along with a half dozen Nyra warriors.

"You should not have let my despicable son take that woman. I'm...*dissatisfied* with your efforts." The Lord still held the obsidian gemstone before him in his lower two hands. His upper two were clenched tightly with inner rage, contrasting with his calm voice. "Is there no one here loyal to me?"

Bjarkeld summoned the will to speak, "I am loyal, my Lord."

"Yet you did not stop him?"

"He would have slain me on the spot, then my lord would still be unknowing of his plot, and it would be far too late by then."

The Lord of Shadow studied him, one hand coming to his chin thoughtfully. After a moment, he nodded. "I suppose you are indeed correct. We can still catch him, thanks to your swift relay."

"I'm unworthy of such praise. I would have dared to stop the traitor if I was stronger. But he is of *your* blood. He is not to be underestimated." The beat-like thumping was again itching at Bjarkeld from below. The overpowering presence of the obsidian gemstone in the Lord's possession had lessened.

"Then you shall be," the Lord said. "Consume this island's power. Then, you will use any means necessary to find my son and kill him. Kill the filthy human woman. Kill the dog. Kill the Wayfarer, Gaelin Yesnala. Kill and destroy all in your path. Send word to those of your Lân, bring them here, and let them feast on the gemstones that keep these islands afloat. Use my *Children* and bring destruction to the Earste Lân. I will soon join you, for I am nearly ready to cleanse this Lân. My armies are ready. We're at total capacity here and will soon engulf that Rykling stronghold in total darkness."

"Your will be done." Bjarkeld sunk into the ground. A light shone at him through the grey—a *rainbow* of light. The gemstone was an opal, its spectral heart dancing with rays of iridescent hues. It seemed to change as he looked at it, from cerulean to jade, crimson to silver, and more. It was no bigger than his hand. He reached out for it.

It resisted.

A pulse thrashed at Bjarkeld as he wrapped his stony fingers around it. It was cold as ice, and he realized his hand had been incrusted with frost. He let go.

It flashed yellow, and a jolt of lightning snapped at him, slashing at his pit-like face.

Bjarkeld's jaws parted wide as he eagerly consumed it.

The island began to tremble, and he felt it crumbling away. It fell away around him. Yet something had changed. Not only did Bjarkeld sense the earth as it dispersed, but he also felt the air and wind around him and took hold of their power, keeping him aloft in mid-air. Even at this distance, he felt the sea splashing thousands of feet below them. He felt the static in the clouds around him.

The Lord of Shadow floated nearby, the Nyra escort flying circles above him. He smiled as Bjarkeld leveled with him. "An opal, a rare gift indeed. You are one with all elements. You will be elevated to the highest level of my *Children*."

Bjarkeld looked down to see that the gemstone had protruded slightly from his chest, shimmering with white light. *I am one with the sky, with the earth. The fire and the waters.* He called flame to one of his hands and ice to another.

"Go now. Find my son. Bring me his corpse."

"Your will be done, my Lord."

CHAPTER SIXTEEN

RESENTMENT

Simon gasped awake as heat blossomed in his chest.

The elderly man, Cygne Caladrius, bent over him, hands on Simon's bare chest.

"Simon!" Kiana's voice came through the confusion.

"Lord First!"

Was that Zahir?

"He's alive!"

Murmurs rippled through a crowd once again gathered around him on the beach.

A burning sensation pulsed through Simon with each pump of his heart; his arms and legs ached, and his head pounded as blood returned to it with each pulse.

"A bit young for your heart to be stopping so suddenly," Cygne said quietly as he helped Simon to a seated position with a firm grip on his hand and back.

Vertigo rocked Simon as he tried to comprehend what happened. "What? My heart stopped?"

"Indeed, it did. I had to assist it to get back into a proper rhythm."

"Skrull's balls, was I dead?"

"As dead as a doornail as they say," Cygne chuckled lightheartedly.

"Very funny," Simon snorted. "That's a new one and not in good taste, considering I *literally* just died!"

"Well, you're back with us now. Skrull hasn't taken you yet." The older man stood and made way for Kiana, who had been waiting impatiently.

Skrull hasn't taken me yet, eh? I didn't even know I was gone. There was utterly nothing on the other side. No Skrull to torment me for eternity. No Hettra embracing me in her bountiful, bodacious breasts. No, there was simply nothing.

"Are you all right, Simon?" Kiana's words broke through his musings.

"Like I said, I just *died*." He rolled his eyes with exaggeration as she helped him to his feet. "I'm Skrull-damned wonderful."

Kiana nudged Simon's arm good-humouredly, though her eyes were full of worry. "You *are* getting old. My dear sister may have to remarry." She paused and then, in a whisper, asked, "But be truthful, are you all right?"

The crowd began to disperse once more as the commotion had passed.

"Skrull's balls, it was your defamatory mother who stressed me out. How can she be appalled at Saudett and I's relationship? We had a wonderful, open, communicative thing going until everything started happening to us. Anora even made you whore yourself out, then gets mad at me for finding a little comfort with someone during this Skrull-damned hell-time we live in."

Kiana nodded knowingly. "My mother is...*irrational* at times. She is so set in her ways that no alternative means can correct her. She also has trouble admitting when she is wrong. It's like it simply does not work within her. She would rather lie to herself and everyone around her than be incorrect."

"But Hasiera is such an open and welcoming community that does not disrespect any walks of life. She helped found Hasiera, did she not?"

"She did. Still, every time I reveled in the long tents, she would scorn me at training the following morning without fail. It seemed that Hasiera's inclusiveness did not apply to her daughter. I was just an irresponsible child to her for as long as I can remember."

"You two are reconciling, at least?" Simon asked, genuinely interested.

"We are. We've had many long talks about the past and the future since leaving on this undertaking to find Hata."

"And what does the future look like for you, Sixteenth Otsoa of Hasiera?"

Kiana smiled, her violet eyes sparkling with excitement. "The Earste Lân...no, *all* the Lân's are so much bigger than Hasiera. I do love my home and my people. Yet, there is much of the world I have yet to experience. Take these beautiful beaches and islands, for example. I would never have seen such a wonder if I had stayed in Hasiera. Not to mention those ships! They're incredible."

Simon nodded in agreement. "The world is vast and wonderful, Kiana. Once this is over, you should explore it without the looming dread of ghastly abominations coming out of otherworldly portals and stalking you through the nights."

"It will not end until Hear-fan Skaad is dead and buried."

"That's the goal, though it seems increasingly unreachable."

"Don't worry, Simon, we're with you. You don't have to do it alone." Kiana seized his arm encouragingly. "I saw you destroy that ship with a single spell. That bastard won't know what hit him once we find him."

Simon laughed uneasily. *I'm nowhere near his match. I could not even contend against his son in the Moreas Lân.*

A horn sounded from the ships in the bay. A black hat was waving from the foredeck of *The Mamba's Mouth.*

Kai must be ready to make way. Simon sighed wearily. His chest still had a faint burning sensation. "Well, dear little sister...are you ready to try your blade at pirating?"

Kiana's violet eyes almost seemed to light up with life, and her grin made the dimples in her bronzed cheeks look ferociously endearing.

She's so much like Saudett.

"I can't wait," Kiana whispered enthusiastically, taking him by the arm and leading him down the beach to the waiting boats.

"I'll leave one of my ships here to patrol and protect this island until we've dealt with Old Keen Eyes." Captain Kai stood on the foredeck of *The Mamba's Mouth* as it departed the island's vicinity.

Simon joined him and looked out on the gently rolling waves.

"It worries me," Kai continued. "If Old Keen Eyes attacked here, he must have raided other seaside towns in my territory. We will sweep nearby populated islands and aim for Keeya's Refuge to gather our forces. This very well could be an all-out war already."

Suddenly, a crow landed on the handrail near where they stood. It cawed, and Simon saw a roll of waxed parchment tied to its leg.

Kai fetched something from a pouch on his hip belt and fed it to the crow as he untied the message. "My thanks to you, friend." He unrolled the small note and immediately cursed as he read it. "Chike's shaft. A fleet has been spotted heading for Keeya's. The bastard's flagship has been spotted. Keen Eyes is coming."

"This is ill tidings," Simon deliberated aloud. "But let's look on the bright side. We won't need to go find him now." He recalled how he had so easily destroyed one of the enemy ships and relished that power. "His vessel will burn like all the others."

"Still," Kai shook his head. "He will be pillaging towns along the way. My people will resent me for not protecting them. I have already failed them."

"That you care so much for them proves your worth," a voice said behind them.

Simon turned to see Kiana, Anora, Brena, and Baal. It had been Kiana's words.

Kai snorted in disagreement, "I should have foreseen this. I should have prepared my towns with more fortifications and stand-by ships. But, Keen Eyes...we *had* an agreement."

"Can you honestly take pirate treaties on faith?" Simon asked sardonically.

Kai spun to Simon and pointed a finger hard into his chest. "You know *nothing* of our people. There's honor among our kind. By Chike's trident, there's a fucking code."

"Honor is the moral compass that guides our actions," Brena Vasara said sternly. "It's the invisible crown we wear, not for show, but as a silent testament to the integrity of our spirit."

Kai stared back at Brena, and a slight grin played on the pirate's lips. "Well said, warrior. Who are you then?" His eyes moved curiously to Baal, who stood beside his partner, though he stared ahead unseeingly, *detached*. "And who is this magnificent orca of a man?"

"I am Brena of House Vasara, Chieftain of the Vouri village of Oitilla. This is my mate, Baal."

"A blessed woman you are," Kai said with a cheeky nod, "and I agree. Sometimes, honor is the only thing that keeps us sane. Well, that and a good fucking romp." Kai's mischievous gaze fell back to Simon.

Anora made a disgusted noise.

"*Mother,*" Kiana scolded in a hissed whisper.

"You have something to say, old woman?" Kai taunted.

"You have no right to seduce my son-in-law," Anora nearly spit the words. "So much for your so-called honor."

"How is that on me? How great is his loyalty to this spouse of his to fail after mere minutes in my company?"

Simon's jaw fell open in astonishment. "Minutes?"

Anora's eyes burned into Simon for a moment before returning to Kai. Her hand went to her deadly tulwar blade, and her words were just as sharp as it. *"Skrull-fucking man-whore."*

Simon watched as Kiana's expression contorted in dismay, and her eyes fell to her feet.

A fury flashed in Kai's eyes in answer, and a cutlass was suddenly in his hand. "Care to test my integrity, ya Xamidian hag."

"With pleasure."

"Please stop this," Simon pleaded.

Both suddenly glared at him, and he rapidly feared for his life.

"You're a hypocrite, Mother; I don't understand you," Kiana said, her voice strained to a whisper. "You cared not when you sold my body to the cause. I thought we were getting over this."

"Stay out of it, child," Anora reprimanded, "this is between me and this pirate *boy*."

Kai sprung forward; blade ready to kill.

Brena and Baal immediately stepped between the two like a towering mountain cliff-side. "Since we do not wish to lose either of you to inner conflict," Brena said with a Baal-like grin, placing a hand on Anora's shoulder.

Simon noted he had not seen Baal himself smile like that for some time.

"I suggest you air your grievances through good old-fashioned fisticuffs," Brena continued.

"She should die for disrespecting me on the deck of *my* ship," Kai growled, hand constricting on his saber.

Anora handed her daughter her sword.

"Please don't do this, Mother," Kiana breathed.

Anora said nothing, returned to Kai, and lifted her hands to the ready.

The captain of *The Mamba's Mouth* sheathed his weapon.

Baal and Brena stepped aside.

Kai sprung forward like the snake of his figurehead.

Anora effortlessly glided into a dance-like evasion, despite being unarmed. With graceful precision, she redirected Kai's wild punch with a swift movement of her body, and then swiftly drove her open palm into Kai's diaphragm, leaving him stunned and breathless. Anora took the opportunity to sweep low and kick Kai's legs from under him.

The pirate fell to the deck with a painful-sounding *thud*.

Then, Anora was atop the captain, the dance gone from her as fury took over her strikes. She screamed as she recklessly bashed Kai's head and face.

Kai took a handful of strikes, but Simon saw him grin a bloody smile. His hands shot out and gripped Anora's greying hair tightly on the sides of her head. Kai pulled Anora's head fiercely, raising his own as he did so, and smashed Anora's face against the hard bone of his forehead.

Anora reeled back, falling off the pirate, as blood gushed from her nose.

Kai scrambled toward Anora on all fours.

"Enough!" Brena bellowed, and Baal grabbed the pirate and hefted him to his feet as if lifting a child.

Kai hissed in frustration, then calmed in the large man's grip and spat blood on the deck. "All right, let go. I'm finished."

Baal looked to Brena, who nodded. He grunted and let Kai drop to his feet.

Suddenly, there was a shout from the crows' nest. "Smoke on the horizon! Smoke on the horizon!"

Kai twisted around and hopped up on the deck rail, one hand on the hood of the cobra figurehead, the other shielding his eyes from the sun. "Fucking hells, they're attacking Keeya's Refuge. Make ready, ya mangy bastards! To arms!"

"To arms!" the crew took up the cry.

Two blue-violet sails came into view, and then a third. The last massive ship flew a colorful flag of an azure-blue field with a golden sunburst at its center bordered by emerald green. Its sails were the same tri-colors.

Xamidian.

CHAPTER SEVENTEEN
OUTCASTS

FROM THAT MOMENT FORWARD, the dragon's essence intertwined with Hata. She found herself attuned to Kulta's emotions and could even discern his thoughts when she concentrated. Following their intense battle, they sought respite together, spending the afternoon in close communion on the island arena, exchanging thoughts and delving deep into each other's psyche.

Taivaseläin had urged Hata to return to *Valon Vuori* before leaving himself.

She declined, her emotions still raw from Raine's deceit, and she had no desire to go back. "Why didn't she just tell me?"

Tell you what, little stone? Kulta's voice inside her head was a deep rumbling of warmth.

"That I'm part Himin-dvergar and Kidekorvat. My people back home are from that bloodline."

The outcasts were banished because they chose to bind themselves together and foster a new race into this Lân. Kulta's great head swung to the side, and his luminous topaz eye observed her as she leaned back on his hide. *I was but a hatchling when those people disappeared.*

"They disappeared?" Hata asked.

Yes, little sister, they had no home among the Himin-dvergar and the Kidekorvat. They were unwelcome to live in their midst. Two of another Lân aided them in leaving Ryk. Many of my kin helped fly them to that gateway, even at the loss of their dragonkin siblings.

"Wayfarers?" Hata stood and began pacing back and forth before Kulta.

The four-armed ones were called that, yes. Those people found a new home in your Lân.

"Hmm," Hata pondered aloud, "I wonder if they came through the gate deep in the mountain of Oitilla. There should have been a record of it. What happened to the original Kidekorvat and Himin-dvergar that came to Oitilla? Their children became the Vouri, but if Taivaseläin and Elder Aerendyl were alive, surely some of them must still live. How long ago was this?"

The Kidekorvat far outlive even the Himin-dvergar, but they are still mortal. I see you seek the truth, little stone, but I know no more than what I have told you.

"Thank you, my brother. My *veli*." Hata came to Kulta's head and scratched under his scaley chin, far softer than the hard stone-like scales of his backside. To her surprise, his tail twitched the more she rubbed, thudding the crystal-cracked ground behind him. Pleasure poured out of the dragon and into Hata.

Oh...yes. More...a little to the side.

Hata added her other hand, trying to reach *all* the spots.

No, the other side! Kulta shook his head and flung it skyward, letting a bellowing cry of frustration loose. After a moment, he returned his gaze to her, and she swore his eyes were laughing. *Jade stones, you missed everything that prickled.*

Hata felt her smile on her cheeks and giggled, "Oh, Kulta, I'll get it next time." Then she sighed resignedly, "I suppose we should return to the mountain, but I just don't know what I will say to Raine."

Raine is your mate? The dragon asked.

Hata paused. *Is she? Is she my lifelong partner? Like Isä and Äiti are to one another.* "I don't know. I thought I loved her, and I know she loves me. Yet I feel betrayed. I think of those who I've loved. Only Silja was wholly true to me." She thought back to her childhood friend. Her brunette locks and hazelnut eyes. That first time, they had kissed in the hayloft behind the longhouse. They had just discovered their attraction to one another when it was all taken away. Silja's husband, Ota Vastaan, had murdered Silja for standing with Hata's family during the honor duel between Ota and Hata's father, Baal. *That vile man has no honor. I hope the Children of Skaad were swift in his demise when they took Oitilla.* She shook her head. *No. That is a terrible thought to have. So many died in my village.*

The thoughts of the *Children of Skaad* brought her back to the desert of The Burning Sea. She first met the vile creatures while traveling with Saudett and their companions. *Saudett. She had treated me like a child, even after we found pleasure together.* Then, she saved Hata from the molten-rock creature who would not stop coming for her during the battle in Hasiera. She apologized and vowed friendship and commitment to her husband, Simon. *I barely met Simon before I was taken to the Alpha...the Proctor, and Joanna.* She pondered regretfully, pensive at the memory of Chanel de Montrichard fighting for her life against the Alpha so Hata could escape from the *Convent Enclosure. I'm so sorry.* Joanna had been left behind in chains. *I left her to die. Did she die? What happened to Joanna? Would the Alpha be hunting me after all this time? It all feels like these things happened to someone else ages ago.*

Then I met Raine.

Kulta's maw yawned expansively, showing off his large, hooked teeth, and he stretched as he opened his wings. He gave a pre-emptive sweep of the powerful means of flight. *Your thoughts are like a river with many outlets, twisting and turning down the mountainside. I require meat. I will join my siblings in the hunt.* He did not relay another word as he took a thundering running start and dove off the island's edge and out of sight.

"Well, now what?" Hata pondered aloud. She stood alone on the damaged arena island, still resolute about not wanting to see Raine yet. But her stomach growled, and dusk had fallen. *Why did you lie to me, Raine?* She stood brooding and lost track of time as the light dimmed when she heard the familiar thumping of a rotor-wing propeller.

The craft circled the island once, then came down and landed a few dozen feet from where Hata stood.

Raine clambered out and hurried toward her.

Hata felt the anger bubbling up, and her brow creased, so she turned her head away. Not wanting to look at Raine's face.

Raine halted a few paces away when she saw Hata's expression.

Hata could still see Raine out of the corner of her eye. Tears immediately sprung to the queen's eyes, and Hata's heart lurched, but she held back the urge to run to Raine and embrace her.

"I'm sorry, Hata! I'm so sorry. I should have told you."

Hata closed her eyes. *Raine knows she was wrong; she has apologized. Yet I'm still so angry...* That anger powered the words that came as she opened her burning eyes. "How could you? How could you keep this secret?"

"Please, Hata, listen to me. I was afraid." Raine took a step closer. "Afraid that you'd look at me differently and leave me."

Hata finally turned, her eyes meeting Raine's. "Raine, I could never leave you. But how can we trust each other if we don't share our truths?"

Raine took a deep breath, seeming to muster her courage. "I want to make things right, Hata. I want to earn your trust again." She took another step forward, the distance between them now just a heartbeat away.

Raine's fragrance enveloped Hata, drawing her closer. "I'm still upset with you," she acknowledged, wrapping her arms around Raine and gently resting Raine's head against her chest. "Rebuilding that trust will take time, Raine. You can start by telling me everything you know about my people."

Raine's tears flowed freely as she nodded into Hata's chest, causing Hata's heart to twist with sorrow at their fight. As Raine looked up into Hata's eyes, she whispered, "I'm so sorry; I'll tell you everything. I love you, Hata."

Hata gazed into Raine's eyes, her voice filled with tenderness as she uttered, "And I love *you*." Gently, she brushed away Raine's tears with her thumbs and placed a soft, lingering kiss on her lips. As their embrace ended, a warm, affectionate smile grew on Raine's lips.

Suddenly, Hata's stomach rumbled audibly once again. She had not had a chance to eat much of anything in the feast hall earlier that day.

"You must be starved to death," Raine said, wrapping her arm around Hata's waist to lead her to the waiting rotor-wing. "Let's get some food in you, and then I'll share everything with you tonight in the privacy of our chambers."

Hata did not resist, and the skirmish against Kulta left her utterly famished. "Let's."

They swiftly found their seats, and after a moment, Raine had them soaring through the air. The night sky slowly filled with glittering stars as the majestic moving mountain of *Valon Vouri* came into sight. Dragons circled the mountain like predatory hawks as Raine steered their craft through a tunnel in the side of it. Shortly after, they emerged into the vast cavern city. As daylight waned, lights twinkled through the ornate windows of the tree-like homes. Raine carefully landed the rotor-wing amidst a fleet of other aircraft in the spacious clearing before the feast hall tree. The Himin-dvergar continued to bustle about, tending to their personal aircraft or socializing as they enjoyed ale together.

"Will they not sleep within the comforts of the Kidekorvat?" Hata asked as they began to walk through the flying machines toward the beautiful crystalline tree. The stark contrast between the two races was evident for all to see.

"They prefer to stay near their rotor-wings. As would I, but as Queen, you and I will partake of the elves' hospitality."

It felt like weeks since Hata had laid on the soft down bedding in their chamber at Keep Crystalia. Raine would be curled up beside her, breathing softly and looking enjoyable. A sudden yearning tickled from below and up Hata's spine to her lips. "The privacy would be welcome." But even as Hata's lustful thoughts grew within, something halted their track. The fact that Raine kept her secrets festered like a wound, and the attraction waned. "Of course, that is after you speak with me of my people."

Raine nodded. "I will tell you everything, and then I will *give* you everything."

Anticipation bubbled within, that desire returning as butterflies fluttered in Hata's belly...and then it grumbled again. "Teras's thunder, before we do anything to one another, let's *eat.*"

Soon, they entered the massive feast hall, the crystalline chandeliers sparkling with magical light. The hall was less crowded than earlier in the day. The elders were nowhere to be seen. But a few of the Kidekorvat and the odd Himin-dvergar were still drinking and eating.

Raine and Hata made their way to a table off to the side. A servant appeared promptly, poured wine, and set out a platter of meats, biscuits, and cheeses. Hata tucked in unceremoniously as Raine picked at her dish distractedly.

Taivaseläin plopped down on the bench across from them, his pointed ears and even-cut cheeks flushed with the red of his wine. His words came out with drunken fortitude, "My good ladies! Dragonkin and Queen! What a formidable pair you are." He pointed accusingly at Hata. "You sure have weaseled yourself into the Ryk Lân. You've seduced *the* queen of all the Himin-dvergar and now formed a dragon bond in a single day. It's absurd! That kinship should have taken years. You disgrace the ways of the *Kidekorvat.*"

Hata and Raine sat staring at him in shock. Hata felt Raine tense, readying a rash rebuke. She entwined her fingers in Raine's and squeezed reassuringly.

Taivaseläin came to his feet and swept away a handful of platters and cups, spilling their contents. Then he clambered onto the table about to scramble toward them.

Instantly, three of the olive-clad servants were upon him. Burlier than the others, one man wrenched him off the table and wrapped an arm around his neck. The others got control of his kicking feet.

"Let me go! It's not fair!" Taivaseläin's desperate pleas echoed through the feast hall as he thrashed and hollered, but his struggles were in vain as he was carried away. His cries gradually subsided into heart-wrenching sobs, filled with disbelief and despair. "I—It's not fair—by Teras, why—" His voice trailed off abruptly as the entrance doors slammed shut behind him, casting him out into the night.

Hata stared incredulously after him. His accusations were not unfounded. *It's true, I am with the queen of the Himin-dvergar and made the dragon bond today.*

As if to echo her thoughts, Raine said, "He does have a point. You are an outsider to our Lân and have found a powerful position at my side along with your new kinship to an Amberheart Drake. What are your goals here, Hata?"

Hata's reaction was immediate and intense. Every muscle in her body tensed as her eyes widened in disbelief. "An outsider?" she blurted out, her voice carrying a mix of shock and indignation. As her emotions swirled, her vision seemed to redden with rage. "I am of both races! I'm far from an outsider." Her tone became increasingly frigid with fury. "My goals? My *only* goal is to protect the people of Ryk from Hear-fan Skaad. And not just the people of Ryk. The people of all the Lân's. How could you even ask me this?"

"Well," Raine hesitated. "I—the elf's words led me to such thoughts. I didn't mean—"

"You think I'm using you to gain power and influence?" Hata stood, releasing her handhold with Raine.

"No, of course not!" Raine stood up, too trying to take Hata's hand again.

Hata pulled it away.

"Why are you being so difficult all of a sudden?" Raine's expression was one of concern but there was a hint of annoyance in her furrowed brows.

"*Difficult?* Me?" Hata's neck began to burn with frustration. "First, you lie to me, and now you accuse me of taking advantage of you! I've had enough of this."

Raine stood staring back at her, her face altered to desperation as her lower lip shivered and the tears glistened in her eyes. "Please Hat—"

"No, don't resort to tears every time you wish to win me back." Hata turned and walked away. Furious. She heard Raine thump back into her seat, and her quiet sobs chased Hata out of the chamber and into the night. Not caring where she went, she walked through the city of tree homes, seeking solitude through what passed for streets between the roots and trunks of massive gem-encrusted trees. The light was dim, and she heard the whooshing of leathery dragon wings and their calls to one another in the darkness above.

The rage came in waves as she thought of Raine. *Never have I felt so betrayed. How could she accuse me of such things? Seeking power? Ridiculous.* As she pondered all this and walked, it took only a short time to reach another clearing. No, not a clearing. It was full of plants and vegetables growing in circular rows. Hata felt an attraction ahead, a warmth, and she found herself weaving through the rows of plant life. Now, there *was* a circular clearing in the center of the field. A dragon of azure blue slept here. *Safiiri.*

A man stumbled about with a skin of wine sloshing in his hand, muttering to himself. "Teras's thunder. She doesn't deserve her dragon."

"Taivaseläin," Hata said brusquely through the darkness.

He whipped around to look at her when another dragon's head suddenly emerged from the earth at Hata's feet.

Kulta slowly pulled himself up and out, rumbling with the effort.

So that was the warmth I felt.

Safiiri's luminous cobalt eyes opened momentarily, shining in the darkness, to take in the newcomers then closed again lazily.

Little stone. I feel your rage like a summer storm. Kulta's voice in Hata's head was curious. *You must ease your rage and learn of Taivaseläin's wounds.*

Hata was about to ask Kulta why when the elven man interrupted their communication.

"Bah! Go back to your queen," Taivaseläin snorted in disgust. He turned to address Kulta. "How could you bond with someone after only a day?"

Kulta's response resonated within Hata's mind. *Let him know, little stone, that your deep connection with your element has strengthened our bond. Through the honor duel, you have shown yourself to be deserving of me.*

Hata took a deep breath and relayed the message.

Taivaseläin snorted again. "We, the Kidekorvat, take years to cultivate our connection with our chosen element." He raised a hand, and a shining sapphire current formed, snapping and crackling through his fingers.

Hata noticed two blue gemstones gleaming slightly in his earrings.

"It took me hundreds of years to build my power. It took hundreds more to become *her* brother." He waved toward the sleeping form of Safiiri.

Hundreds of years? No wonder he is upset that I did it in a day. Hata rested a hand on Kulta's warm side for reassurance. "I'm sorry that my actions, Taiv, seemingly cast aside your lifetime of hard work, but I had no say in the matter. I don't know why my gifts awakened, but I'm still learning to control them and need to deepen my connection with Kulta."

"Kulta, that is his name?"

"Yes."

Taivaseläin sighed, subdued. "If he told you his name, then it is true. Henceforth, you are Hata, Sister of Kulta." He strode back to Safiiri and sat, leaning against the dragon wearily.

"Thank you," Hata said as Kulta settled across from the sapphire dragon. Hata also found a seat against him.

"Wine?" Taivaseläin asked, smiling grimly.

"Please."

He tossed the sloshing skin, and Hata fumbled with the catch before taking a long drag of the spiced wine.

"Don't drink all of it. That's the last of my stores." He held out his hand shakily, asking for its return.

"You've been drinking since we arrived in *Valon Vuori*, so perhaps you should slow down."

"Give it to me!" His face contorted with rage, and a fine blue-white energy sparked around his head.

"Fine. Sorry." Hata tossed it back to his eagerly waiting hands.

Taivaseläin downed the remains of the skin in one go, then sat back, eyes closed, and scowled sickly.

Hata decided to change the subject. "You've mentioned Teras a few times now. He is also the god of my people."

"Of course," Taivaseläin muttered as his eyes squinted open. "He is, just as you are, of Ryk. I am surprised that the bright beard never took hold in your Lân. Perhaps the Kidekorvat who traveled to your world outlived their Himin lovers and enforced the worship of Teras over Luminar. That would be the most logical explanation." He closed his cracked eyelids again.

Teras's stones, he's right. "You were alive back then? When the..." she paused, looking for the proper word, "outcasts left the Ryk Lân? You knew them?"

He remained silent for what felt like an eternity, and Hata feared that he had lost consciousness before he finally spoke. "My only sister fell in love with a Himin man and left us. She left me behind. I was just a young boy at the time, while she was several centuries older than me. Despite the age difference, she loved me as any sister would love her sibling. I don't hold it against her for leaving, as our two peoples did not treat them kindly." Tears welled up in his eyes and slowly trickled down his cheeks. "By the mountain, I miss her terribly. Not a single day passes without me thinking of her."

"Oh, Taiv, I'm so sorry."

"Direct your sorrow to *her*. She was forced to abandon me and her dragonkin—a Malachite Serpent with great healing powers. When my sister, Niemela, broke their bond, her dragon did not take long to die from the loss. We lost too many dragons that way."

"Niemela!" Hata blurted in surprise.

Taivaseläin's eyes shot open, and he leaned forward urgently. "You know her? Does she still live? Where is she?"

"It can't be," Hata contemplated aloud. "She is the old healer woman in my village of Oitilla. I mean, she *was* the old healer woman. The village is gone, and I know not where she went or what happened to her."

"What happened to the village? There is a chance she still lives." Taivaseläin was on his feet now, pacing. Safiiri's glowing sapphire eyes were also open, watching him.

"It may not be her. She was old, wrinkled, and hunched and...*old*. Not like you."

He stopped and looked at her. "Did she have face markings? Hers were of dragon fangs, I think." He tilted his head as if trying to recall her image. "Malachite Serpents are known for their head feathers. Yes, yes, she had feather markings as well."

Hata remembered the old, hunched woman and her faded, cracked tattoos and skin. Fangs and feathers. "But how could it be? You still look as if you are nearly a few decades old. How could she have aged so much."

"I don't know." He answered excitedly and came to Hata, grasping her hands and pulling her to her feet. "And I don't care. My sister is alive! Praise Teras, she lives!" He spun her around in a bit of dance, a broad smile on his lips and tears dripping down his cheeks. "Thank you, Hata."

She may very well be dead. Hata kept that thought to herself.

Taivaseläin let her loose from the spin, and he stumbled drunkenly, falling to the ground face to the earth, ass propped skyward. He mumbled as his eyes closed once more. "No more drink—until I find Nieme..." he trailed into silence, and Hata soon heard his faint snoring.

Hata followed suit, suddenly weighed down by exhaustion from the long, stressful day. She curled up to Kulta's warm side and quickly fell asleep.

CHAPTER EIGHTEEN

STUDIES

THE AIR CHILLED THEIR breath as the three Vouri longships sailed north. As dusk fell, the stars began to sparkle into existence above. Kaplan Mir pulled on his oar, the exertion keeping his body warm. He turned his head to glance back at Jude Nelon's huddled form sitting over Joanna Ohleoc as she lay, still unconscious from the attack of the grey ape-like beast.

Jude grasped her hand and muttered inaudibly, the odd curse reaching Kaplan's ears.

He needs her, Kaplan thought as he returned his mind and body to the oar. She took a brutal blow, but at least she was still breathing.

"She will be fine. My people will take her in and nurse her back to health," Nanuq Tornarsuk announced from the oar across from him. "We have great healing remedies and arts passed down by generations. Seal oil and tusk of the walrus will have her up and fiery once again." He chuckled with his Baal-like grin.

"Fiery indeed," Kaplan couldn't help but smile at the jest at the mage's extent. "Still, I fear for her."

"The journey will take nearly a week to cross the *Hoarfrost Straight* before we reach Nunarat and its ice plains." It was Astrid who spoke. "If we stray too far west from our course, we will be lost in the *North Sea*. The Nunara village of *Qilakvik* is on the southern edge of the ice plains."

"The mage may not make it that long," Kaplan pondered aloud.

"Yes, she fucking will!" Jude's voice was sharp and strained. "Yes, she fucking will..."

"You didn't need to say that aloud, Xamidian," Astrid hushed Kaplan.

"Though we were all thinking it," Nanuq grunted.

"You *bastards,*" Jude hissed. "Joanna saved your fat asses back there in that village, and you will just abandon her to die?"

"We are doing all we can, and all we can do is make haste to *Qilakvik.*" Astrid rebuked. "We row day and night, resting in shifts. It will cut a day or two off our voyage."

"Fucking fucks," Jude cursed in answer. "Gods, I wish I had a teleportation marble. I could take her back to the Aurulan. One of the magi could save her. The Theta, I think."

"Would you be welcomed back with open arms?" Kaplan asked. Through the days and nights traveling with Joanna and Jude, he had heard them speak of how the Alpha would kill them or do much worse for abandoning their quest to find Hata Vasara. They disobeyed him, and he would not take such a slight lightly.

"I would give my life for hers as long as Ebras could save her somehow," Jude muttered, but he sat back broodingly. "No, Ebras Corb would not allow us to die easily. He would have us both, and it would be slow and painful."

"Then you have but one choice," Kaplan reassured. "Get her to the Nunara healers and pray for Qav's luck so that we can make it in time."

Jude grunted in response but did not answer, and there was quiet for some time as they pulled on their oars.

"Teras's thunder, we lost many good people today," Astrid broke the silence sorrowfully. "But thanks to you, we saved many more. Because of the sorceress, even the men working the mine returned in time to escape. I can't imagine the slaughter had those *things* come upon them in the mine tunnels."

"What were those fowl creatures?" Nanuq growled. "Where did they come from?"

"The *Children of Skaad* come from another Lân. They killed many of your kin, the Vouri, causing them to flee from Oitilla and any surrounding villages. Aurulan forces engaged with them, and the enemy scattered. But they're numerous and roam the countryside freely, feeding on any they find in their path."

"Another Lân? What're you on about?" Astrid questioned doubtfully.

"The Earste Lân is not the only world in our vast skies; it would seem. When I was young, I read a tome in the Grand Library of Xamid that studied our skies. It stated that the Earste Lân was a spherical ball spinning through nothingness. The sun is holding us at just the right distance for life to exist here. It speculated other such spheres were spinning through the night." Kaplan lifted his eyes and gestured to the stars. "One of those lights in the skies may very well be where the *Children of Skaad* reside."

There were questioning murmurs from all the rowers.

"Ha!" Astrid let out a hearty laugh. "What nonsense you speak, book man. Spinning spheres. If you were to row to the edge of the Lân, you would fall from it. As you fell, you would see the mighty arms of Teras holding the plate of the world aloft."

"So states *your* religion," Kaplan said. "I tend to heed scientific studies with greater weight."

"Hmm," Nanuq grumbled pensively. "The Nunara believe in nature and nothing more. Perhaps what the book man says is a part of that nature."

"Teras's stones, not you too!" Astrid retorted.

"You studied in the Grand Library?" Jude asked, a hint of suspicion in his tone. "In *the* Sultan's palace?"

"Yes, I did," Kaplan replied frankly.

"Then how did you end up a soldier in Aurulan?"

"Well, that is a long story indeed," Kaplan remarked with a suppressed smile playing on his lips. Inwardly, he mused, *Gods, I have become a teller of tall tales. Perhaps it comes from the reading of fictional tomes. I do enjoy retelling my own travels.* He sighed with acceptance and continued, "But I suppose I have the time to tell it."

The story began with a young boy darting through the bustling market streets of Al'Jalif, his small hands tightly clutching two warm loaves of bread as he navigated the crowded thoroughfare...

Fucking hells. Jude Nelon half-heartedly listened to the ranger's tale as the longboat sailed through the frigid night sea. The biting cold seeped into his bones, and the ache in his leg stump intensified with every passing moment. *And Joanna could die.* He looked down at her pale white face across his thigh. Her faint breath misted pitifully in the brisk air. *Skrull's hell, please don't leave me.*

Suddenly, Joanna cried out as her eyes shot open, and her face twisted in pain.

Jude's voice was barely a whisper as he spoke to Joanna, his heart heavy with the pain he saw on her face. He gently called her name, "Joanna... Jo. I'm right here. It's me, Jude."

She stared ahead, unseeing. Then, she closed her eyes again, and her face went deathly still.

Jude held his breath as fear gripped him.

After far too long, Joanna's small breaths returned, and Jude released the tension coursing through his body. *I can't do anything for her.* Jude sat wallowing, holding back his tears. Then he did the thing he thought he never would. He prayed. *Please, Primus, if you're out there. I will do anything to keep her alive. She didn't deserve this. What can I do to save her?* Anger suddenly broiled within. "Why do you make the innocent suffer so? Are you not all-powerful? Tell your gods to come to her aid! Do fucking something!" The words he cast out aloud into the twilight icy sea air. A desperate plea for someone or something to answer.

Kaplan halted abruptly in his story, and everyone turned to look back at Jude.

It was eerily silent and the gods didn't answer.

"What the fuck are you all looking at?" Jude snarled in frustration.

Kaplan shrugged, ignoring Jude's outburst, and turned back to his oar, returning to his tale as if nothing had just occurred between them.

Son of a—Jude sighed; leaning back, he decided to distract himself from Joanna's pain and his own misery by listening intently to the ranger's words.

"And so, I became scribe's assistant. I studied under the palace scholar Tarvinder Locha, who I later learned was a brother-in-law to the Sultan in the Grand Library of the Dhan Ka Mahal. I grew up as his ward for a half dozen years, learned to read, and learned about science, art, and the wide world. Yet, there were some things I had never learned in that library: Swordplay, combat, and warfare. Tarvinder forbade me to study these things as he deemed it unnecessary for a budding academic to know. Still, I snuck to the royal guard quarter and took up the scimitar. The guard did not turn me away, as I was now a finely dressed young nobleman, and they dared not rebuke me. I was eager to prove myself.

"'I was under strict guidance from my mentor, who closely monitored my access to the library's archives. His prohibition on studying warfare only amplified my curiosity about the subject. Despite his restrictions, I managed to clandestinely acquire scrolls related to warfare-adjacent topics, including martial arts and field medical techniques. If it weren't for his limitations, I might have continued as his apprentice and assumed his position today. Years ago, when I was still an orphan wandering the alleyways, I stumbled upon a thick tome discarded behind an estate garden. Its cover featured a charging horse and rider, but the title and contents remained a mystery to me.

"'As I retraced my steps to Nishulk's warren, the weight of my one wish from the Orphan Queen hung heavy on my mind. It was she who had promised me one wish, and

I had asked for the ability to read. While she may not have directly granted my wish, her guidance led me to the Grand Library, where my newfound ability had been fulfilled. Now, with the tome left behind in Nishulk's den, I had to return to retrieve it.

"'Leaving Tarvinder behind, I navigated the familiar streets and pathways, returning to the door of Nishulk's den. The watchful eyes of orphan children followed my every move as I entered the sleeping quarters designated for the children. The environment was suffocating, the stench more pungent than I recollected, and the number of children seemed to have dwindled since my last visit. Pushing the door to Nishulk's room, I steeled myself for what lay within.

"'To my surprise, Nishulk was nowhere to be found. Instead, a formidable woman sat perched on a cushioned chair. Her face seemed oddly familiar, and I knew exactly who she was when she spoke. 'Kaplan boy, I never thought I'd see you in this place again,' she said. It was Jhuta, the young girl who had discovered me on the streets and brought me into Nishulk's service. 'Jhuta,' I exclaimed. 'Where is the Sultana?' 'I am the Sultana of the Orphans now,' she replied sharply. 'Nishulk is no more.' With a nod, Jhuta directed my attention to one chamber wall. There, the remains of a skeleton were fastened to the wall. Clutched within the long-dead fingers of the skeleton was a book. My book.

"'As I approached the charred remains, I set my sights on my precious book. 'I thought you might return for that,' Jhuta remarked, her tone filled with presumption. 'It was quite clever of Nishulk to confiscate it from your possessions before you departed in pursuit of your wish.' 'I need that back,' I insisted. 'I'm not asking for it.' Jhuta scoffed in my face, just as she had done countless times during our upbringing under Nishulk's reign. 'Kaplan boy, that tome, along with all of Nishulk's domain, now belongs to me.' I gazed at her with a sense of pity. 'Domain of what? A handful of starving children? Things have deteriorated here since Nishulk's tenure. What has become of you, Jhuta? What has transpired here?'

"'The woman died in her bed, too weak to move or even cry out. I held her hand as she passed and finally granted my wish. My wish to take on her mantle.' 'A pitiful wish indeed,' I mused as I retrieved the book from the skeletal remains, causing a few loose fragments to scatter onto the floor. 'Put it back!' Jhuta's furious shriek pierced the air. 'Kala!' A large, unkempt man burst through a door behind the Sultana's throne, his face contorted with a savage hunger as he lunged toward me without hesitation.

"'Now, two very different things are reading a book on martial arts and putting it into practical use. I decided to aim a high kick at the brute's head. He caught the blow with both hands and hurled me against the wall. The very wall that Nishulk hung upon. Her remains shattered and clattered about the chamber. The wind burst from my lungs, and I gasped for air. The book flew from my hands on the impact. The man wrenched me to my feet and wrapped his massive scarred hands around my neck.

"'Who are you?' I heard Jhuta scream. The next thing I knew, the thug's grip on my throat released, and blood suddenly burst from his lips into my face. Slowly, the man's fingers constricted repeatedly on my tunic and trousers as he sank, leaning on me as he died at my feet. I saw Tarvinder Locha, my master, wiping a bloody curved dagger with a linen handkerchief. 'This is why I desired to keep matters of combat and warfare out of your reach, my young apprentice. It is unbefitting of a learned man.' I coughed, rubbing my neck where the man had squeezed it. 'Had I had more training in such things, perhaps he would not have got the best of me, master.'

"'I doubt it. The brute was twice your size and strength. In such callous confrontations, that is all that matters.' There was suddenly a clattering noise, and we both turned to see Jhuta scrambling toward the back door, my book in her hands. 'Jhuta!' I cried out as I gave chase. I heard Tarvinder snort in disgust but looked back to see him following. She vanished into the next room, which I had never been in. It was not a room; it opened into a large courtyard surrounded by square brown sandstone buildings. Cages lined the walls of the yard. People huddled within. *Enslaved people.* It dawned on me that the orphans who grew up in Nishulk's service were eventually sold when she deemed them old enough.

"'Fury boiled within me as Jhuta, far more overweight than she had been as a child, lumbered across the courtyard. I caught up to her with ease and planted my shoulder into her back, sending her tumbling forward into the dirt. The book spun away from her, and I strode over and picked it up. Then I returned to Jhuta and pushed her onto her back with a kick. 'You sell our family into slavery? You're a detestable human being, Jhuta.' I patted her down and soon found a set of keys. I went from cage to cage and unlocked them all. Freeing the young boys and girls held prisoner there. I emptied my purse, providing each with a few silvers to find their way. Then, I returned to the first room in Nishulk's old warren, where the children gathered. I could have given them coins as well, but then what? Send them back out onto the streets? No. 'Tarvinder, we need to help these children.' My mentor watched me earnestly, 'My boy, this was your home? This is where you grew up?' I nodded. 'You should have told me. I would have had the guard gather these children and place them in a proper orphanage and school.'

"'I was shocked and didn't know what to say. 'It never crossed my mind to speak of my past to you. I thought you would cast me out of the palace.' 'Well, I wish to know all, but for now.' Tarvinder dusted his hands off as if to prepare for a day of grueling labor. 'Let me help you find a home for these poor children.' He did just that. All the orphans and many of the older children who had been caged for slavery, Tarvinder found them an orphanage that doubled as a school. However, I did not stay around to see how the children fared. I dusted off the book I had so longed to read. The words on the leather binding finally made sense after all the years— *The Strategist's Code: Artistry in Conflict – Authored by Arjun Varma.*

"'That old text? That is what you wished to read?' Tarvinder asked me. 'I'm sure a dozen of those are kicking about in the Grand Library.' I turned my gaze to him. 'Would you have let me read them?' I'll never forget the moment when my mentor fell silent, gazing at the ground. 'I realize now that perhaps I've been overly rigid in determining what you should and shouldn't be aware of,' he admitted. Feeling a weight in my chest, I responded, 'Master... Tarvinder, I'm grateful for everything you've imparted to me, all the years of guidance and more. However, I believe it's time for me to carve out my own path. I'll delve into this knowledge and much more, I'm certain. Yet, I yearn to embark on a journey of my own. I'm contemplating immersing myself in the military to acquire firsthand experience.

"'As much as I wished I could offer you the gods' blessings, I am not a religious man. But I do have faith in your judgment and the knowledge I've imparted to you. If you're set on gaining military experience, I'd recommend Aurulan over Xamid. Their fervor for warfare surpasses ours by far.' As I nodded in agreement, Tarvinder offered me a warm embrace. Tears welled up as I bid farewell to my mentor of many years. 'Farewell, Kaplan Mir, my son,' he said with a smile.

"'Farewell... father,' I whispered back."

Jude heard sniffles from among the rowers, and then, with mustache draping down his face along with wet tears streaming down, the man of Nunara let out an insufferable sob. "Waah, ha-ha! A heart-wrenching tale to tell. To live a life not knowing one's parents...Oh, my little me-ma. Pa-pa!"

Astrid brushed at her eyes. "There's a bit of dusk in the air."

Jude fumed as the brisk sea breeze chilled his bare head, his frustration palpable. "There's not a fucking speck of dust for Skrull's sake," he muttered, fixing his gaze on

Kaplan. "I distinctly recall you talking about studying medical texts. Can't you use that knowledge to help Joanna?"

"I fear the extent of my ability is to set a bone or stitch a cut, but if it makes you feel any better, I can look at her," Kaplan answered, rising from his seat.

"Please do something, ranger." Jude pleaded. *I can't lose her.* "Anything you can do to help her."

"She took the brunt of that attack on her back," Kaplan deliberated. "Let's loosen her garments, then gently roll her to her stomach to see what we can see. Astrid. Nanuq. Help me."

The burly Vouri woman and mustache man got up from their oars and moved to aid Kaplan. Jude hesitated to let go of Joanna as they cautiously picked her up.

Suddenly, Joanna's eyes shot open, and she screamed in pain.

"Put her down!" Jude cried.

"I need to see her back," Kaplan urged.

The three lay Joanna down, her face spasming in agony. Kaplan took one of Jude's daggers, sliced the fabric down Joanna's back, and pulled it aside. He then traced his fingers along her spine from the neck down. His fingers stopped not halfway down her back, and he sucked in a hissing breath. "It's as I feared. Her back is broken. I think one of the vertebrae has cracked and shifted."

"Skrull, take me," Jude cursed. *Her back is broken? Will never recover from this?*

"We need to straighten her spine and hold it in place," Kaplan continued. "It will take some time, but it should heal if she does not move it. We need something lengthy and solid to fasten to her."

"We can spare a couple of our oars, if need be," Astrid suggested.

Kaplan nodded in agreement. "Yes, two oars wrapped as close as possible to each side of her spine should do. It will not be comfortable to lay upon, but it must be done." Kaplan instructed the group to hold Joanna in a position that was as lengthy as possible. Astrid had her head while Nanuq pulled her legs straight. Kaplan carefully placed two oars along her back and wrapped them tightly around Joanna's body using linen and leather strips. "I would add two more oars a hand length out, near the shoulders, to hoist her effortlessly and not stir the middle brace."

Jude watched as they did so.

"Good, this will have to do for now," Kaplan concurred more to himself than anyone else.

Astrid opened a travel chest, pulled out some heavy fur blankets, and covered Joanna from chin to toe. "Teras grant her fortitude." The well-built woman muttered as she tucked the unconscious Joanna in.

Jude could only stare on, feeling helpless. *I'm a useless lump of flesh. I should've protected her.* He looked from each tired person to the next as they huddled over Joanna with looks of concern and sorrow on their faces. *These are good people.* The words were strained when they left his lips, "Thank you. All of you. For helping her."

Kaplan smiled and gave a slight nod.

Astrid brushed a strand of midnight hair from Joanna's sleeping face.

Nanaq put a fist to his chest and said, "This sorceress saved our lives. Saved our village. It is the least we can do to return the favor."

Jude inched closer to his lover, gazing at her as she slept. Finally, the pained look had faded from her face, and he whispered a silent prayer for better days ahead. Grateful for Kaplan Mir and his teachings, Jude settled down next to his slumbering companion, feeling the weight of exhaustion wash over him.

Chapter Nineteen

TOUCH

Column after column of soldiers snaked through the landscape below. Saudett held her wings aloft and glided slowly downward. The sunlight glinted against shining weapons and armor as she approached. *Aurulan.* The armies of Aurulan were meticulously cleansing the *Children of Skaad* from the Earste Lân. The forces of Aurulan occupied the foothills below the North Iron Belt Mountains. However, the soldiers did not push into the mountains themselves.

Saudett leaned toward Malix, who kept pace with her in the skies. "What should we do?" she called through the chill wind. "Marah will be accosted, perhaps even mistaken to be one of the *Children.*"

"We can't abandon the Volkinn," Malix shouted in return. "See that farmhouse below. It is the first structure I have seen. We will stick to the plan. Even if that plan involves defending ourselves."

Saudett nodded her agreement and closed her wings, pointing herself in a dive toward the homestead.

Malix followed closely in her wake.

Saudett realized that the Aurulan forces had set up a base camp around the farmhouse as the ground approached. Tents lined the fields, and flags of white and yellow waved in the early winter sun. *Hells, Marah will not be able to sneak past the soldiers and meet us. There's no other choice but to inform the Auru and try to negotiate with them for Marah's safe passage.*

Shouts began to meet her ears as she opened her wings and flapped them in a powerful burst to slow her descent. She noticed many archers notching arrows and taking aim toward her and Malix.

"We mean you know harm!" Malix's voice boomed over the course.

Saudett hovered mid-air, readying to flee from a volley of arrows, when a flash of white caught her eye.

A woman emerged from the quaint farmhouse. She was adorned in a breathtaking, ethereal white gown that was tight around her figure and flowed like sheets of snowflakes around her legs, and the garment seemed to shimmer in the fading light. With every step she took, a glistening silver pathway materialized beneath her feet, forming an enchanting icy staircase leading upward to where Saudett and Malix floated in the air. Her cascading white-blonde locks swayed gracefully with each movement, capturing the attention of all who looked at her, including Saudett and the awe-struck soldiers gathered below.

Cautiously, Saudett and Malix glided further down to meet the sorceress.

"Come no further. There flies a friend or foe of our Lân?" the woman demanded as they approached, holding up her hands to halt them.

The air around Saudett and Malix began to shiver, and hundreds of flecks of ice suddenly gleamed and jingled about them.

"Friend!" Saudett blurted, watching the sharp icicles spinning around her guardedly. "I'm Saudett Meridio from the town of Dagad and a Shepherd's Eye Lieutenant."

The woman bent a brow and lowered her hands, and the shimmering ice around them subsided. "Meridio, you say? You're not an Auru like that man who made his plea to the council. How are you related to Simon Meridio?"

"Simon!" Saudett sucked in a breath in surprise. *He lives, and he must be close.* "S—Simon is my...*husband.*" The last word was tense coming to her lips, the deep regret of running from him twisted in her gut.

"Well, well. So, you're Simon's partner?" The woman studied Saudett from head to toe, lingering far too long on certain aspects of her. "Let me tell you, *Saudett.* Simon came to treat with the Council of the Aerie in Nidhaut," the woman said with a casual grace even as her icy blue-white eyes darted over Saudett. "He gave a pretty speech, but I believe his aptitude for magic won the Alpha over to his cause. Though the Alpha Passeriform has now taken command of the situation."

"Why did he need to use magic at the council meeting? Where is he now? Where is my husband?" Saudett rattled question after question, wanting even the slightest news she could get of Simon.

The woman rolled her chilling eyes at Saudett's torrent of words, and those eyes found Malix. She inclined her head questioningly at him. "One of your kind was behind the chaos that commenced during that meeting. Now, another comes before us?"

"One of my kind?" Malix floated forward, closer to the woman, eyes ablaze with violet fervor.

"Stay," she raised her hands again. This time, *thousands* of shards of ice burst into existence around them. "I can freeze the very moisture in the air. Come no closer, Wayfarer. I have no trust for your kind."

Malix halted and even retreated a few paces in the air. "I apologize. I am seeking out one of my kind, a man named Gaelin Yesnala. There is much I need to, uhm, *discuss* with him."

I need to change the subject, Saudett thought. "Please tell me where my husband is."

The elegant woman, clad in brilliant white, studied them silently for a long while. A diamond necklace shaped like a swan decorated the pale skin of her clavicle and sternum. Saudett couldn't take her eyes off it and the particular area around it. Finally, the sorceress spoke, "Well, let us not freeze to death in this chill mountain air. Join me for a warm drink. We have much to discuss." She turned and began to descend her icy staircase, and each step melted away behind her.

Malix looked at Saudett questioningly.

Saudett shrugged and muttered, "What other choice do we have?" Saudett glided down after the woman who was entering the old farmhouse. She folded her wings tightly to her back as she entered the farmhouse; the warm interior was welcoming, and she found the woman seated at the head of a long farmhand table. A clay jug warmed on the hearth, and a serving woman stood waiting nearby.

"Have a seat, Saudett, and..." she nodded to Malix as he entered behind her.

"Malix, the Unsought," he said with a grunt, taking the farthest seat across from the woman.

Saudett took a seat in the middle to be an equal distance from either should any unruly magic start flying from either.

"Malix, the Unsought, and Saudett Meridio. Please let me introduce myself. I'm the Eta of the Council of the Aerie, Nix Swan." She waved to the servant, who then acquired the jug from the hearth using a thick rag against the heat and moved to pour each of them a cup. "Mulled wine helps to ward off the chill of the North Iron winds. It's my very own recipe."

"Lady Swan, please relay a message to your patrolling soldiers," Saudett said, holding her clay mug aloft as the servant poured. "Ask them to be on the lookout for a half-human, half-wolf individual who is supposed to meet us here. If they find someone matching this description, please bring them directly to our location."

"Asking for favors already?" The Eta smiled playfully. "We've only just met, my sweet Saudett."

Saudett startled internally at the woman's words. *Simon calls me that. My mother used to call me that.* "Please, Lady Swan, I will do my best to repay the favor."

Nix Swan arched an eyebrow, exhaled heavily, and turned to the servant with a serious expression. "Please send a messenger to Grand Maréchal Étienne Normand. Instruct him to be vigilant for the presence of this... " Nix paused, casting a cautionary look at Saudett, "being."

The servant bowed and disappeared out the door from which they had entered.

"Thank you, Lady Swan," Saudett said graciously as she sipped the steaming spiced wine. It was delicious. The warmth trickled down within her and emanated outward. She slumped in her chair, exhausted from the cold and the long flight, it threatened to pull her into sleep.

Nix Swan savored her drink and shared, "This delightful beverage is the Warm Wine of Conquerors, known as *Vin Chaud des Conquérants*. It begins with a full-bodied red wine sourced from our expansive vineyards in the southern hills of Aurulan. A harmonious blend of spices, containing cinnamon sticks and star anise for a sweet, woody fragrance, cloves for an enticing kick, and a generous dash of nutmeg for a profound earthy flavor. To enhance its sweetness, honey from the apiaries of Nidhaut is added. The finishing touch is a slice of Xamidian orange adorned with cloves, imparting a refreshing citrusy brightness that perfectly complements the wine's richness. The subtle bitterness from the orange peel adds another layer of complexity to the overall taste. How do you find its flavor?"

Saudett paused after the in-depth description of the wine. *Nix has given this spiel before. Did I taste all those things?* "Uhm, it's pleasant and warming."

"Pleasant and warming..." Nix sighed, a finger rubbing at her temple. "It's that bad? Is it too bitter? Perhaps I should leave out the orange next time? The grapes? Are they too dry? I own the vineyard where they're grown. Skrull's scrotum, I should try a different selection of grapes for next summer's batch."

Saudett was surprised to hear the profanity from the elegant woman and snorted a laugh before covering her mouth.

"What do you find amusing about this, young lady?" Nix tilted her head, taken aback.

"Oh, gods, never mind," Saudett waved the question away and took another swig. "The wine is wonderful." She bent her own brow toward the mage, who looked maybe a few years older than Saudett herself. "Who are you calling young? You look no older than me." She let her eyes trace down the woman's soft neck and cleavage framing that dazzling broach.

The Eta let her mouth drop open in exaggerated shock. "Excuse me, we do not discuss a woman's age in such a social setting."

"Then, should we discuss it in private?" Saudett gave Nix her most seductive smile, the wine warming her playfulness.

Nix blinked, and Saudett saw the woman's snowy white skin flush pink.

"Fuck me," Malix grunted. "We have more pressing matters to discuss than wine. Don't you think so, Saudett?"

Saudett twisted her gaze to find the handsome bearded face of Malix staring back at her with a smoldering ferocity. His *father's* face suddenly flashed across his visage, and she recoiled. She pulled away with a cry and fell from her chair to the ground.

"By the Primus, she is afraid of you," Nix was on her feet, a demanding calm in her voice. "What did you do to this woman?" Shimmers of ice began to form once more in the air.

"No, it's not me, it is my father..." Malix's words trailed off.

Saudett shook herself out of the horror and found her voice. "Nix, please, it's not him. He is my friend, and he is here to help us. Let it be."

Nix slowly lowered her hands and then moved to help Saudett to her feet. Her finger's gentle touch was that of ice, and it sent a shiver across Saudett's rag-clothed body, causing her to gasp. Nix quickly released her grip. "I'm sorry, I always forget that my touch causes such chills." Nix's voice became a whisper in Saudett's ear. "It's been so long since I have sincerely touched someone..."

Saudett's face flushed with desire.

Then, Nix shook her head as if daydreaming. "I'm sorry for my rambling. Let's get you a blanket at least, and then I'll have you all outfitted with warm winter clothing tomorrow." She moved to the back of the chamber and pulled a thick fur blanket from a large bed that did not look like it belonged in a farmhouse. She returned and carefully draped the blanket over Saudett, who had returned to her seat.

"Thank you," Saudett whispered, reaching out and taking Nix's hand for a second. She flinched as the cold shot up her arm, but she smiled thankfully before releasing the hold for fear that her hand would freeze in place.

Nix looked down at her with complete wonder, awe, and a hint of something else. *Yearning?* Then, the sorceress turned abruptly and found her seat. She let her icy glare fall on Malix. "Yes, Malix, the Unsought, we have more important matters to discuss, such as why your father would strike such fear into this poor woman to cause her to recoil from your regard."

"My father is Hear-fan Skaad," Malix said bluntly.

The Eta leaped back to her feet, hands raising. "You've brought an enemy among us!"

"No!" Saudett cried, stumbling to her feet, clutching the blanket around her. "Malix hates his father. He has had a life of mistreatment at the hands of that man, and he will help us in our fight against him."

"Listen to Saudett," Malix urged with a cold ferocity. "I will fight back against him. His unchecked conquest has gone on long enough. He still believes I'm on his side. We can use that to our advantage."

The Eta looked back and forth between Saudett and Malix. "Consequently, you came from his Lân? I was told the gateway had been buried under the rubble of the mountain."

"There's a race of people under his control that are of the earth themselves," Malix said. "We call them earthwalkers. They can move through the ground and grant that ability to others. Lucky for us, he sent me here on a mission. No more of his *Children* should be coming through that gate for now."

"What mission?" the mage asked.

"To find the Wayfarer, Gaelin Yesnala, and bring him back with me." Malix paused, and Saudett could see the conflict in his eyes. "If I did as tasked, my father said he would leave the Earste Lân in peace."

"He's already allowing his abominations to spread unchecked in our countryside, a problem I've been assigned to address," Nix remarked with a touch of disdain. "Could he not have called them back? Many of our people have died or lost their homes. Do you genuinely believe he will leave us be if you bring the Wayfarer, Gaelin, back to him?"

"I don't know," Malix answered. "My father is not a man whose words can be trusted at any time."

"Hear-fan Skaad will bide his time," Saudett said, pushing the wine away from her. *I need to be clear-headed.* "Even if we were to deliver Gaelin to him and he was to leave us alone for the time being, he would eventually return with even more strength behind his conquest. He is currently occupied in another Lân. If we were to strike back at him, now would be the time. It is not only the Earste Lân that is in danger. Many innocent people need our help." She thought back to those short, gruff Ryklings; she had killed a few of them with her own hands, and her orders had killed many more, not to mention the flying beings of the Grot Lân, the Nyra, who are enslaved to Skaad.

"Yet, why should we care what happens in some distant Lân?" the sorceress asked icily.

"If we let him act freely," Saudett pleaded, "this will never end."

"Hmm," Nix suppressed a retort. "The very same argument your husband presented to the council. Indeed, we have already formulated plans to counterattack Hear-fan Skaad. We currently have control of two additional Wayfarers Gates and are mobilizing our forces for a decisive strike. We're only awaiting an alliance with Xamid to augment our strength significantly. However, we have encountered a minor setback in our operation. Gaelin Yesnala is unaware of the location of the Skaad Lân gates and cannot point our gates to his."

"I can help with that," Malix said with a toothy grin of anticipation. He nodded decisively. "These are fair tidings. I'm glad to have come here. It seems my father has underestimated this Lân. Underestimated humanity. He does not guard his gateways. We could take over the Skaad Lân before he even realizes we're there especially if he is preoccupied. First, I must visit your other two portals to learn their paths, then return to the Skaad Lân side to deactivate and aim the gates."

"It's a few days' travel to the Gateway in Aurulan. The Alpha will be intrigued to meet you, Malix, the Unsought." Nix said, picking up her mug of now-cooling wine. "First, you must eat and rest for a day. Recuperate." She took a sip and made an expression of disgust. "It's gone cold."

At that moment, her serving woman returned.

"Ah, good, Marise." Nix waved the servant over. "Please freshen our cups and prepare dinner for myself and our guests."

"Of course, Lady Swan," Marise responded with a slight bow before taking the mulled wine and replenishing Saudett's and Nix's cups. Malix sat with his untouched drink. As the servant woman made her way into another room of the farmhouse, the group could hear the faint sounds of chopping, the clattering of plates and utensils, and muted voices.

"You look half starved to death," Nix said concernedly, eyeing Saudett.

Saudett had become gaunt and wiry from her time in the dungeons of Skaad, eating merely one meal of meat muck a day. Her rags hung loose about her once-toned muscular limbs. "I was being held against my will until Malix came to my rescue."

"And the wings?" Nix asked curiously. "I don't suppose you had those while living in Dagad as a soldier?"

"A token of Hear-fan Skaad's..." Saudett hesitated. "...experiments." *I was the one who asked for these. He tortured and very likely killed one of the Nyra for me to receive these cursed things. I can't let them know I was on his side.*

"Dreadful business, dreadful indeed." Nix swirled her cup as she spoke. "But the wings have given you the power of flight in the least, so there is a blessing to the vile fiend's experimentations. They also give you quite the regal bearing."

"Thank you, Lady Swan," Saudett said, a slight blush rising at the compliment.

"We just need to get some food into—"

A loud knock came to the door, and a gruff voice called, "Eta!"

"Come," Nix answered, standing as she said so.

A moment later, the door swung open, and a handful of soldiers wrestled the hissing, writhing form of Darkclaw Marah into the chamber.

"*Ah oui,* 'tis a contentious one. I have never seen the like of it in all my many years. Though it reminds me of an old tale from my childhood days." A man said with a thick southern Aurulan accent, his grey beard trimmed neatly to his chiseled face. He wore a neatly pressed white, gold, and black uniform, and only a single pauldron of gold decorated his shoulder.

"Marah!" Saudett was on her feet stepping toward the group of soldiers. "Let them go. They're with us."

The man stared at Saudett blankly, and then his bluish eyes went to the Eta.

Nix nodded. "You may do as she says, Maréchal Étienne."

The greying veteran arced a brow suspiciously before he nodded to the soldiers restraining Darkclaw Marah, who promptly released them.

Marah let out a low growl.

Saudett went to Marah as they released them and wrapped her arms around the Volkinn. "It's all right, Marah; we're all allies here."

"Say that to their poles and spears. They hunted us and cornered us like a wild beast before this one stopped them." Darkclaw Marah lifted their canine yellow eyes to the Maréchal. "It brings back a hatred for humans that we thought was long ago buried."

"Ah, *pardon*. Messages take some time to make their way through the ranks and files. I was informed of your approach only half a bell ago. The men were doing their jobs. Which is to hunt any creatures of Skaad that still lurk in the hillsides."

"We're not of Skaad!" Marah spat, their fury palpable. "We were *never* aligned with the likes of him."

The Maréchal lifted his hand's palms outward. "Again, pardon. I apologize. I meant no offense. Skrull's saggy balls, you are a hot-tempered...Ehm...fellow."

"*We* are Darkclaw Marah. *We* are Volkinn."

"Volkinn?" The Maréchal, Étienne, got a distant look on his face, and he took his greying mustache between two fingers and began to twist the hair thoughtfully. "Hmm, that sounds oddly familiar."

"What would you know of us?" Marah asked curiously, sniffing toward the Maréchal.

Étienne shook his head suddenly, then shrugged. "Eh, it seems I lost it in my head somewhere. At any rate, who in the Primus's perfect penis are all you people?"

Saudett snorted a laugh. Never had she heard such a curse in her life.

The Maréchal's amused gaze found her, and the side of his mouth looked like it was trying to hide a smile. "*Qu'est-ce que c'est?* You have never referred to our creator's fantastic phallus in such a manner?"

"No. No, I have not." Saudett answered, quite entertained by the older man. She returned to the mug of wine, hiding her smile as she drank.

"Would you join us for dinner, Étienne?" Nix asked politely. "You don't suppose the Beta would be joining us?"

"Ah no," Étienne answered, finding an empty chair across from Saudett. The large farm table was filling up quickly. "Kuro Raven is taking up the task of clearing up the vermin in Aurulan very personally. He has ranged far ahead of our patrols, leaving nothing but pools of bubbling muck in his wake."

"I see. I suppose I should take such a hands-on approach myself." Nix sat back in her seat wearily.

"Never fear, Lady Swan, had you not been here, such matters as this would not have been dealt with efficiently." Étienne waved to Saudett and company.

"Thank Hettra's bouncing bosoms that the *gorgeous* Lady Swan was here to receive us." Saudett proclaimed, raising her mug.

Étienne gave a wry smile and was the only one to raise his cup alongside her. "Ah yes, she is indeed an elegant woman."

Nix Swan turned scarlet.

At that moment, Marise returned, followed by two more servants carrying platters of finely prepared dishes. They spread the plates on the table and served each person seated, starting with the three famished guests.

Saudett moved to the chair closer to Malix and let Marah have a seat to her left. The Maréchal and Nix Swan chatted idly as they began to eat at their leisure.

Saudett was grateful and *starving*. She could not help but attack the delicious-smelling food. She started with a succulent pork roast with plums, the rich meats combined with the sweet stone fruits, and its juice was splendid. They were accompanied by warm country-style bread to soak up the syrupy gravy. Then she turned her attention to a savory quiche filled with wild mushrooms that made her mouth water with its aroma. When she thought she couldn't eat another bite, the servants brought a platter of upside-down apple tarts. The caramelized apples had a soft texture and melted in her mouth.

Malix poked the foodstuff curiously before tasting a bit of tender beef brisket braised with the famous Vouri dark ale. Saudett watched as his eyes widened in wonder. "Fuck me," he said under his breath.

A sense of bliss overcame Saudett. *When was the last time I felt this pleasant and safe?* She had sometimes felt like that in Hear-fan Skaad's company when she had sympathized with his revenge. He had exotic meals and fine wine in the underground dining room, but nothing seemed to compare. Even their picnics in the Wald Lân had been quite lovely. *No. He is disgusted by humans and was toying with me only to breed more true-blood sons.*

Saudett's mood darkened until Malix took a bite of a crimson cake and made a ridiculous, almost squealing noise of excitement. "Hells, what's this? It's incredible. I've never tasted such a thing in all my life."

Saudett turned to him. "Your father never graced you with the fine dining of his halls?"

"Ha!" Malix snorted disdainfully, then carefully put another piece of cake in his mouth. He mumbled through the mouthful, "Fucks no. I've lived in other Lân's for as long as I can remember. In Fjoer, the earthwalkers sustain themselves by consuming cooling lava rocks. I had to make due by hunting other creatures that lived there. Mostly juvenile insectoids with blue flames sprouting from their backs."

"You ate those things?" Saudett asked in disbelief and began to gag at the thought.

"I did what I must to survive."

"Hettra's mercy, you've missed out on so much."

"Have I?" Malix asked as he leaned back in his chair. He placed his lower two hands over a content stomach. "Perhaps when all this is over, I can take some time to enjoy myself. Does the Earste Lân have many more tasty things for me to eat?"

"I much prefer the spiced foods of my homeland of Xamid. Though Simon cooked more than I did at home, my main dishes were pulao rice and tender lamb kofta with a side of flatbread."

"Pulao? Kofta?"

"Sorry, these are Xamidian words. It's spiced rice and vegetables, and kofta is ground lamb mixed with even more seasoning before being grilled to perfection."

"Hmm, I want to try your *cooking* one day," Malix said with a grin. "What did your husband make in your stead?"

"Ah, well, some of what you see here before you. Simon was well-versed in Xamidian dishes and enjoyed and prepared anything with lentils or chickpeas."

"You speak *of* him as if he were dead and gone. Do you not seek to be reunited with him?"

"I—" Saudett faltered.

Marah made a low noise in their throat on Saudett's other side.

"All finished over there?" Nix Swan interrupted from across the table. "You all must be exhausted after your journey. We have set you up with a single pavilion for your party. A sewist will meet you and take your measurements, and with any luck, fresh clothing will be ready for you by midday tomorrow. As a precaution, we will have guards stationed outside your quarters."

"Ah oui," Étienne added, "and should you require anything else, simply ask one of the guardsmen, and they will see that your need is fulfilled." He stood and gave a sweeping bow to all. "I bid you goodnight." Without another word, he promptly exited the farmhouse.

Saudett and company stood, preparing to follow Marise to their assigned pavilion. Darkclaw Marah and Malix exited after the quiet serving woman.

As Saudett put her hand on the door, Nix suddenly approached her, saying, "Saudett, I would like to speak to you in private." Nix reached out a hand as if to take Saudett's in hers. "I couldn't help but notice your blatant flirtations with me."

Saudett took the proffered hand and enveloped it. The biting chill shot up her arm with the touch. Saudett hid her discomfort and held on with a cheeky smile. "Oh? What did you have in mind?"

Nix's face went flush. "Oh, you know. I want to talk. What's it like to lay with another woman? Or a man, for that matter? I have tried a few times, but after mere seconds of skin-to-skin contact, they are forced to remove themselves from the...*situation*."

"Hettra's mercy, Nix, you must be overflowing with frustrations."

Nix laughed nervously. "Yes, I'm very, uhm, frustrated."

"I'm tired now," Saudett reassured. *I can't get with a babe if I spend my time with women instead.* "But there are things one can do with a partner that requires little physical touch. Besides what's a little cold but to add to the excitement of the act." Saudett winced as her hand was beginning to go numb.

"Oh dear, I'll let you rest." Nix released Saudett's hand and ushered her out. "I'll see you tomorrow night, then?"

Saudett paused. This would be a nice distraction from Simon's looming confrontation. *We don't have to do anything intimate; we can talk as two women do.* She nodded. "Tomorrow night."

A genuine, beautiful smile blossomed on Nix's face, and Saudett was momentarily caught in the pleasure of it before Nix closed the door behind her.

CHAPTER TWENTY

DEATH

THE MASSIVE TRI-COLORED XAMIDIAN ship turned to meet *The Mamba's Mouth* head-on. Above the golden sunburst figurehead, a giant contraption was on the vessel's foredeck. It was similar to a ballista that could swivel and move but more tube-like. Simon stared in awe at the odd thing, wondering at its mechanics. A massive metal cask lay on its side behind the apparatus. Pipes connected to and from the drum. He saw a man hold a torch up to the end of the long swiveling part of the device. Flames burst forth in an arcing geyser of death directly at *The Mamba's Mouth*.

"Hard to port!" Kai bellowed beside him as he called back to the helm.

Silas, the helmsman, was already franticly spinning the wheel. But the turn needed to be faster.

Afléotan. Simon flew into the air to meet the oncoming flames. *Windan!* He fired half a dozen blasts of the cutting air projectiles at the oncoming spew. It slowed the liquid-like flames and even redirected some fire aside, but too much of it kept coming.

Lind.

The fire engulfed him.

Simon disappeared into the flames, which continued through him and crashed into *The Mamba's Mouth's* rear deck. Kiana watched as the fire swallowed the burly helmsman. Then, he was suddenly stumbling, his flesh burning and hissing as he screamed inaudibly. He fell to the deck in a pool of flames that seemed to spread like water, his spasming, kicking, and twrithing going suddenly still.

"Silas!" Captain Kai cried in despair.

"Skrull, take us." Kiana had never seen such a horrible sight.

Suddenly, there were the heavy *twangs* of multiple arbalests firing in unison. The Xamidian ship had come broadside to *The Mamba's Mouth*. Row upon row of ballistae bristled from the side of the enemy vessel. The sharp steel three-pronged bolts drilled into the hull of *The Mamba's Mouth* or burst through the railing with unchecked power behind their shots. Ropes attached pulled taunt, and the two vessels crashed together, sending people tumbling to the floor.

Kiana managed to keep her feet deftly. One massive projectile burst past her by a hair's breadth. She instinctively sheared through the cord line that trailed the bolt in a quick-flowing sidestepping slice of her blade.

Corsairs with bows perched in the rigging returned fire on the Xamidian ship, and Kiana heard the cries as shafts struck true.

The scene was electrifying as soldiers adorned in pointed silver helms and scaled armor fearlessly propelled themselves onto the pirate vessel. Their stunning bright blue, golden-yellow, and jade-green tunics and under-armor attire boldly displayed the distinctive tri-colors of the Xamidian military. With spears, tulwar swords, and crescent moon shields in hand, they let out a thunderous battle cry as they confidently set foot on the deck.

"Stop! We don't want to fight you!" Kiana shouted, but the battle drowned out her cries, overwhelming in the chaos. *We can't die here. We must defend ourselves.* She watched a handful of pirates immediately cut down with the martial precision of soldiers. Kiana breathed and stepped forward into the dance.

The first man lunged; gleaming spear point hungry for her flesh. The piercing point grazed past her side, under her arm, as that very arm drew the razor-sharp blade of her sword across the soldier's face.

He screamed and fell away.

The second and third men advanced towards her simultaneously, holding up their shields defensively and preparing their blades for retaliation.

Kiana stepped in, feinting a strike high.

The man lifted his shield to deflect the blow that never came.

Instead, her blade caught his exposed thigh, blood sprayed out, and he stumbled back, only for two more men to suddenly take his place. Spear tips reaching out.

Kiana gracefully danced backward, facing off against opponents who were clearly skilled and well-prepared. It was clear that getting through them unscathed would be quite a challenge. A *deadly* challenge. Suddenly Kiana thudded into a wall behind her, and she looked up.

Baal looked down at her without expression. He did not smile as he gently moved her aside. He began to chant softly, his words taking on an unfamiliar and chaotic quality. "By Teras's might. By Teras's strength. By Teras's stone." Energy crackled around him, and his eyes blazed with blue fire. "By Teras's honor. By Teras's fortitude. By Teras's courage." The runes on the powerful weapon glowed with blue light, and white lightning struck his war hammer from the sky. "By Teras's stability. By Teras's justice. By Teras's MOUNTAIN!"

Baal Vasara became a massive, unstoppable storm as he charged forward.

The Xamidian soldiers, hesitantly retreating from the imposing figure, tried to mount a defense. However, the thunderous strikes unleashed bolts of lightning that tore through the silver armor of Baal's adversaries, hurtling men through the air, some crashing back onto their own ships or overboard into the sea below.

Then, more Vouri warriors surged up from below deck, where they had been idling as the ship sailed. They joined the fray with a bloodlust. Their mountain-hardened fury overwhelmed even the most trained soldiers.

"The fires! Smother the fires!" Kiana heard Captain Kai's commanding shout. She saw Kai fighting off a half-dozen Xamidian soldiers surrounding him on the foredeck with wild bestiality behind his strikes. Brena and Kiana's mother were fiercely locked in combat with even more of the enemy. Kiana leaped into action, vaulting up the stairs to the higher deck.

One of the men harassing Kai turned to meet Kiana. Another sword and shield user. He did not hesitate and blocked her path as she reached the top stairs. With no room to maneuver on the staircase, the man's shield protected most of his body, and his blade lashed out at precise intervals to keep her at bay.

Skrull's hell. Kiana saw past him as three more soldiers landed on the foredeck, leaping down from the larger vessel. She watched as the Captain of *The Mamba's Mouth*, the Pirate King, vanished under their onslaught.

The heat nearly cooked him alive, even through the barrier of magic. Simon dived. Down and down until he plummeted into the sea waters below; the cool sensation of the waters was an incredible relief. The dark shadow of the massive Xamidian vessel overtook his vision as it sliced through the waves above. It came alongside *The Mamba's Mouth.*

Simon began to swim back to the surface when something grasped his leg.

What? No. He looked down frantically. There was nothing there. He strained to pull himself to the surface.

Another invisible hand grasped him, then another and another.

A voice came to his mind.

It was good of me to keep this failsafe active.

The voice was Gaelin Yesnala's.

Kiana could not get past the soldier blocking the staircase. *My mother and Brena need help!*

Something grey blurred past her, brushing against her. Cygne Caladrius, The Theta, bowled into the man with such force that it sent the soldier flying back with a cry of surprise. Before the man landed on the deck, Cygne crouched over him, an old wrinkled hand touching the soldier's face between his helmet guards. The man began to spasm and scream in pain before going limp on the deck.

The Theta councilman stood, looked back at Kiana, gave her a wink, then blurred in amongst the Xamidian soldiers with superhuman speed. As he contacted them, each went stiff as a board, then suddenly slumped to the ground. He reached the group attacking Captain Kai. He promptly dealt with one last soldier, and Kiana finally caught up.

Kai knelt on the deck, leaning on his dual cutlasses jabbing into the deck, panting with exertion. He was covered head to toe in blood. Countless gashes sliced his face, arms, and chest. Bodies of the slain surrounded him.

Cygne immediately knelt and placed his hands over one of the most significant bleeding gashes. Kiana saw the pirate grind his teeth as the heat must have burned through him to heal the wounds.

"This will take some time, help the others." Cygne urged Kiana as he moved his hands to the next gorge of flesh.

Kiana shook herself from the awe and horror of his healing powers and his ability to *kill* people with a simple touch of a hand. She looked about. Brena and her mother fought back-to-back. They finished off three more soldiers as she watched with the brutal efficiency of a Vouri Chieftain and a Hasieran Otsoa, clearing the foredeck of enemies. Corsairs and Vouri chased and dispatched the last of the enemy from the mid-deck while others tried to deal with the spreading fire. Some tried splashing buckets of water, which, in some spots, did suppress the flames, but in others, it only seemed to spread the fire further.

The enemy was retreating, the lines were being cut, and the massive vessel was drifting away.

"We must take that vessel," Kai hissed painfully. "If they send the fire at us again, we are doomed. Give the order, desert dancer. Grapples and planks. *Board* that vessel."

Kiana turned and took a deep breath, the need for haste and the excitement of command filling her with resolve. "To the planks! To Grapples! Don't let her escape and turn on us! Prepare to board!"

The crew roared in answer, grappling hooks soaring, retaliating against the Xamidian warship, and hooking into the rails of the larger vessel. Pirates in the rigging of *The Mamba's Mouth* began swinging across with savage vengeful cries.

Brena appeared next to Kiana and, with a bellow, flung a heavy grapple up and over the rail of the towering ship's rear deck above them. Brena pulled the line tight and held it. "Go!"

Kiana sheathed her blade and grabbed the line, planting her feet against the hull of the enemy vessel, one foot after the other, she climbed.

Simon could hold his breath no longer. *Gaelin, you bastard! You're still in my head. Undo this spell!*

Indeed? And why would I do that? You're nothing without me. I gave you your powers. No lowly human should be able to wield the vast knowledge of the Iban'mael Wayfarers. Be gone from your mortal coil. Farewell Simon Meridio.

"Gaelin!" Simon screamed the cursed man's name into the salty waters, and bubbles spewed from his mouth. Then...he gasped for breath, and the murky cold filled him...

Kiana crested and bound over the rail.

A half dozen soldiers stood between her and the helmsman who tried vainly to turn the vessel away. A man dressed in a fine long kurta and collared black vest with silver studs stood, hands clasped behind his back as he rocked on his feet, just behind the helmsman. He wore a black turban with silver sunburst adornment in its center. Two majestic, jeweled, curved daggers hung on his belt, along with another longer blade, also finely decorated.

Kiana saw the regally dressed man's lips moving, and the helmsman shouted. "Cut those lines; repel boarders!"

Her mother landed softly next to her. Her face crusted with blood from her fight against Kai. "Shall we dance, my daughter?"

"No. Mother. I feel disgusted by you. I will dance alone." Kiana left her mother standing there.

Anora's look of horror turned to anger as she shouted after her daughter, "Kiana!"

Kiana poured herself into the dance. She twirled and slashed, removing a hand and the sword clutched in it. Kiana twisted and cut; blood gushed from the score across a man's neck. She twisted and kicked, sending another crashing into his comrade. Kiana spun and stabbed, piercing a man through the gut. She whirled and *killed* all before her.

Last was the finely dressed man, who took his ornate daggers in his hands and calmly walked toward her. His longer blade was still on his belt.

Such fine weapons usually mean they don't know how to use them. Kiana breathed and streamed toward him, her sword whispering around her.

His lightning-fast blade cut into her wrist, causing her sword to clatter to the deck. Simultaneously, his other dagger sunk into her side. Then, the other followed, digging deep into her stomach as it twisted.

Kiana heard her mother scream as she fell back on the deck, and a chill began to creep through her as her own blood pooled around her.

Anora rushed to her daughter's side.

The man was fast, *unnaturally* fast. He darted in, his bloody daggers flashing toward Anora.

That's my daughter's blood! Fury overcame her, and she swatted away one blade with her sword. The man's other dagger grazed her arm as she lunged, aiming to plunge the tip of her curved blade through him, but he side-hopped and retaliated. She pirouetted away, and a blade sliced into the linen robes on her back and, again, grazed the flesh.

Try and try, she could not land a blow on the slippery man, and again and again, his blade nicked her. *He is toying with me.* The fury raged as she glanced at her daughter lying in an ever-growing pool of blood.

"Keep your eyes on me, else you lose one," the man said with a mock grin. He leaped at her.

Anora had time to deflect only one of his blades, and the other sliced across her face. Across her eye. Pain burst into existence, and she staggered back, clutching at her eye socket as blood gushed through her hands.

"Bastard!" a voice shouted, and she was vaguely aware of Captain Kai charging toward her, followed by the thumping of many feet on the wooden deck.

"Until next time," the man said as he leaped off the ship's side.

Anora did not hear a splash as she knelt beside her daughter. The pain fled as she dropped her hand from her bleeding face and looked down with only one eye at her daughter. Her dead daughter.

There was a cry from the nearby ship rail, but Anora ignored it all as she stared down at Kiana's pale still face as the muffled words reached her.

"Simon!" Captain Kai's voice was broken. "He's drowned."

CHAPTER TWENTY-ONE

LIES

HATA COULD FEEL THE exhilarating rush of wind against her face as she and her dragon brother, Kulta, glided through the vast skies of the Ryk Lân. His scales held her fast to his back. *Hundreds* of colorful dragons and their riders flew around her, following the small group of rotor-wings and the enormous airship. Hata eyed the lead rotor-wing—*Raine's aircraft.*

Hata had been avoiding the queen as everyone prepared to leave *Valon Vuori*. She stayed with the other dragon riders in the clearing, close to Taivaseläin. Now, he was soaring next to her, his cobalt cloak fluttering behind him as Safiiri's wings battled against the wind. Taiv's vibrant enthusiasm for aiding Hata was palpable in his radiant, cheerful demeanor that morning before they embarked on their journey, despite appearing a bit paler than his usual vibrant self after a long night of drink.

"My sister is alive and well," Taiv had said as he clapped Hata on the shoulder. "We'll cleanse the Ryk Lân of this Hear-fan Skaad and return to your world to find her."

"Pray to Teras we can do just that," Hata answered uncertainly.

Now, they flew to that end. To defeat Hear-fan Skaad and his magical sphere of death along with his hordes of *Children*.

Teras grant us the will and strength to overcome him.

Already, a day had nearly passed as they flew, and Hata feared camping for the night and the inevitable confrontation with Raine. As dusk began to fall, the company of rotor-wings and dragon riders made for a sizeable forested island to set up for the night.

As Kulta *thudded*, non-to-gracefully, to the ground, Hata spied Raine, leading the elders of the Kidekorvat into the immense airship.

Hata desperately wanted to know what they would speak of, yet at the same time, could not bear to be near the Queen of the Himin-dvergar.

Taivaseläin hopped down from Safiiri's back, said a few quiet words, and then patted her.

I will hunt with her. Kulta's voice rumbled in Hata's mind, and the two dragons blasted wind and dust at Hata and Taiv as they covered their eyes from the gale.

"They seem to be getting along," Hata said cheekily, nodding to the fleeing dragons.

"Despite her advanced age compared to his," Taiv replied honestly, "They do have the potential to form a bond and become mates. A young brood of Amberhearts and Stormwings would greatly benefit their community and, in turn, benefit us all. However, it will be years before they even consider it."

"Perhaps we could encourage them?" Hata asked excitedly.

"Dragons are nearly immortal in terms of aging. They do not hasten to do *anything*. Though Kulta seems to have disregarded that hesitance with you."

"What can I say? I'm special."

"Apparently," Taiv said with a smile. "By Teras's thunder, I could really use a goblet of wine after today's long ride."

"Do you remember your last words before you passed out last night?"

He paused, getting a far-off look in his sky-blue eyes. "We spoke of Niemela, my sister. I need to find her."

"Yes, and you gave up the drink in order to focus on that task."

Taiv's brow creased. "No. I never said that. Just a few swigs tonight, then we will be on our way again tomorrow."

"Taiv."

He pointed a finger accusingly nearly into her chest. "*Don't* tell me what to do."

Hata sighed and nodded. "Just try to slow down. It will, in the end, be better for you."

Taivaseläin said nothing as he turned away. Then he looked back with a slight grin. "Shall we see what the elders and your paramour queen are speaking about?"

"I'd rather not. Perhaps you can go and bring me news of what is said?"

"A lover spat?" Taiv smiled knowingly. "Oh, to be young again."

"You look maybe ten years my elder."

"Yet I am hundreds."

"Raine broke my trust," Hata said miserably. "I don't know if I can be with her anymore."

Taiv turned back to her and came and clasped her hands in his. "One thing I know in all my years is that love is trying. It is not a magical meeting of two people. It is not fated. Love is tenacity. It is the resolve to love the other with your whole heart, through thick and thin. Love is a choice we make."

Hata, trying to hold back her tears, asked softly, "Have you ever loved someone, Taiv?"

"I have. I still do. Aerendyl and I have our differences, but we love one another, even if he is too busy to see me when I return to *Valon Vuori* or I'm off on patrol."

"Aerendyl? That pompous—"

"I love him, Hata, even if he can be an ass sometimes."

Hata paused, imagining the regal, self-important elder showing a kind and loving side. "I apologize, Taiv, I was just surprised." She paused again, trying to imagine the two of them, and it couldn't form in her mind. "Aerendyl, though?"

"Yes, Aerendyl," he said, then grinned. "That pompous ass of his is quite fine once it's gripped between one's hands." He motioned as if to hold someone by the waist, and he humped the air before him.

Hata immediately blushed. "Taiv!"

Taivaseläin's laughter echoed through the air, filling the room with warmth and cheer. Hata couldn't help but be swept up in the infectious joy, her own laughter mingling with Taiv's. With a gasp amidst his laughter, Taiv spoke, "I will check on your queen, but it's crucial that you have a heart-to-heart with her. Resentment can fester like a wound. Yet, you must also ponder if she truly complements your spirit." His blue cloak billowed as he turned away, waving gracefully before heading towards the waiting airship.

Hata stood pondering. *Love is tenacity, resolve, and determination. I must choose to love her.* Hata found herself following Taiv up the steel walkway and into the center chamber of the airship.

The elders and Raine gathered around the map table.

"If we take a slight detour," Raine said as she glanced at Hata and continued speaking, "We can be at Zephyrion in a few days and acquire a fleet of rotor-wings to help us against the shadow sphere."

"And what would your machines do against such magic," Aerendyl rebuked. "It's *magic* that will be needed to penetrate the barrier. *Kidekorvat* magic. *Dragon* magic."

"Yes, but we can overwhelm the enemy once we break through," Raine answered with her lips in a hard line. Hata could tell she was holding her true words for the elven elder back.

"We have nearly two hundred dragons here. We don't need any more strength to deal with this threat." Aerendyl looked up and noticed Hata and Taivaseläin standing there. Hata noticed his eyes seemed to soften as they met Taiv's. Then, his gaze returned to Hata. "Ah, kind of you to finally join us, Sunstone, Sister of Kulta."

"I agree with Raine," Hata said bluntly. Their eyes met, and Raine mouthed the words *'thank you.'* Hata tried to return a smile as she continued to speak, "We can't underestimate Hear-fan Skaad and what he may be gathering behind that magic."

"Listen to her, Aerendyl," Taivaseläin reassured.

Aerendyl looked at Taiv for a moment before sighing in resignation. "It seems everyone is against my council. I only fear we will be too late if we delay any longer."

"We did send word to both Zephyrion and Skyforge for aid. We can only pray the rest of my people will come," Raine said hopefully.

"Then shall we or shall we not go to Zephyrion?" Aerendyl said, irritation in his tone.

Raine hesitated.

Hata gently approached Raine and placed a reassuring hand on her shoulder. "My queen, the decision is yours to make. We will support you no matter which path you choose."

Raine stared into Hata's eyes, and Hata felt the despair, longing, sorrow...and *love* within them. Raine turned back to the map. "I will send one rotor-wing to confirm that Zephyrion will come. Can you choose a rider to accompany them to prove our alliance?"

"Taivaseläin." Aerendyl's tone was not a question.

"I would be here for the assault. Safiiri's strength will be needed."

"Precisely why we need her swift wings to take you to Zephyrion with all haste." Aerendyl turned back to Raine. "They may even leave your contraption behind if rapidity is truly needed."

Taivaseläin clenched his fist. "There are a dozen other riders as fast, if not faster, who could go. I'm needed here, Aer."

Aerendyl strode gracefully over and placed his hands on Taiv's arms. He looked at him with such care that Hata knew their connection to be true. "Please, my beloved, do it for me then."

"You would keep me from the danger while you will ride in?" Taivaseläin demanded.

"Of course not, my beloved. You are simply the best choice to go, and should you leave now, perhaps you will still ride into battle with us, along with a fleet of the Himin-dvergar contraptions in your wake."

Taiv kept silent, but he nodded resignedly.

"Only one craft I know of may be able to keep pace with your dragon's wings." Raine broke in. "Rorik Windbeard and Bryn Sparkheart have made some new modifications to their rotor-wing that should very much aid in our need of haste."

Taivaseläin snorted contemptuously, then shrugged. "I will take a few days' provision and set out immediately. I've scouted Zephyrion before. I know the way." He said no more as he turned and left the chamber.

Raine waved another Himin engineer over and whispered something to them that had them scurrying after the elven dragon rider. *Most likely to inform Bryn and Rorik,* Hata decided.

"That seems to have concluded our business. We will rest and resume our flight in the morning," Aerendyl said in an irrefutable tone.

"Aye, Elder Aerendyl," Raine expressed with gratitude. "I'm sincerely thankful for your wise counsel and the alliance we have forged."

The regal elven man nodded slowly and then left, followed by a half dozen others of the Kidekorvat.

Then, only Hata and Raine remained looking at each other in silence.

Raine opened her mouth as if to speak, then held it back. Then again, she started and stopped.

Hata breathed, calming herself. That tinge of resentment was still there. *How could Raine accuse me of coming to Ryk only to gain power for myself?* Finally, as Raine was still trying to find her words, Hata spoke, "You really hurt me, Raine."

Tears burst from Raine's eyes, *as usual,* as did the words from her quivering lips, "I didn't mean to! I shouldn't have taken Taivaseläin's words to heart. You're one of us. Himin-dvergar and Kidekorvat. You came here to help us."

"Yes, I'm one of us, and I came here to help. Initially. Then, I wanted more than anything to be one with *you,* Raine. But first, you lied to me and then accused me of this?"

"I take responsibility for my actions, Hata. We all make mistakes, and I did not mean to cause you harm. Running a kingdom demands my full attention and commitment to the welfare of my people. However, it does not excuse my thoughtless words. Haven't you, too, unintentionally hurt someone you loved? Remember the woman who saved your life and bared her soul to you, only for you to turn away from her."

Hata froze. "What woman?"

"The winged woman, of black armor and brown skin like myself. She was faster than I when the man of violet magic defeated you and stood over you, readying his final blow. She reached him first and took off his head. She said she knew you, that she had pledged to protect you, and she had made a vow to her husband."

"Saudett." Complete shock fastened Hata in place. *How could this be?* "She saved me at the keep? Then why isn't she here with me now?"

"The winged ones took her away," Raine said hesitantly. "She was one of them. She was part of Hear-fan Skaad's armies. I fought for my life against her."

Another secret only now being revealed to me. More lies. Hata's cold rage came with her icy words. "You never told me."

"Who was this woman? She said she loved you, and you cast her aside."

"Lies!" Hata screamed. "All you do is lie to me!"

Raine's usually expressive face turned ice-cold and resentful. The tears that had brimmed in her eyes now disappeared, replaced by a fierce resolve. "I am the Queen!" she declared; her voice sharp with anger. "I will not disclose everything to you. I will act as I see fit. So, Sunstone, answer me this: Did you love her?"

Hata started back from Raine's sudden growth of adversity. "I—I used to love her as lovers do. But in the end, before I was taken, we cared for one another only as companions."

"Do you *still* love her, Hata?" Raine's glare was as cold as her dour face.

Hata hesitated. *I do love Saudett. She was good to me. She saved my life...again. I can't lie to Raine.* Finally, she said, "Yes, as a frie—

Raine's voice echoed through the room, filled with rage. "Get out! I never want to see you again!" With a fierce, determined grip, she ripped the map from the pins holding it to the table, scattering the figure pieces representing cities and armies in all directions. Raine hurled the map toward Hata, who had to scramble to avoid it, before pointing an accusing finger. "Get away from me!"

Hata turned and fled, desperate to escape the seething fury of Raine Stormfall.

Chapter Twenty-Two

TOGETHER

Kaplan Mir's keen eyes discerned wisps of smoke curling into the crisp winter air, signaling the presence of a distant village. As the longship approached further, a breathtaking sight emerged before him - an entire town sculpted from compacted snow and ice. A towering wall of ice lined the edge of the sea, enclosing an inlet wide enough to accommodate a select few vessels at a time. The structures within the town, a mix of square and dome-shaped buildings, rose with an air of practicality, their chimneys releasing tendrils of comforting warmth into the frosty atmosphere. While marveling at the beauty of the scene, Kaplan couldn't help but be reminded of the majestic sandstone edifices of Dagad and Xamid, yet these were crafted from the glistening, crystalline substance of snow.

Fascinating, my dear Kiana would have loved to see this.

A shout greeted them as their longship led into the inlet to find a dockyard cut out of the ice. "Vouri friends, what tidings from the mainland?"

"Grave news," Nunuq called in answer, throwing a rope at the man. "Beasts have overrun the North Iron Belt and forced us to flee."

"Beasts?" The man asked doubtfully as he caught the rope in his leather, fur-lined mittens and tied it to a stake hammered into the ice pier. He wore thick leather and fur hides with beads adorning the hems of his clothing. His long black hair was braided and stuck out behind the thick fur hat that covered his head. Two crescent-shaped blades attached like a 't' to a bone handle gleamed on his belt. He also sported a quiver of jagged-tipped bone javelins on his back. He was broad of shoulder, long of leg, and moved with a lithe step.

Kaplan saw that all the people working the dock were dressed similarly, in leathers, furs, and beadwork. Not long after, a crowd began to trickle down from the icy homesteads to see why three Vouri longships had arrived in *Qilakvik*.

"We need a healer!" Jude Nelon interrupted the greetings, clamoring to the dock. "Her back—it's broken. Can you help us?"

The man tying the rope stood and called out in a different language, and a young boy ran off. He then turned to Jude. "Do not fear. We will care for her, Auru man."

Once the longship was fastened tightly, a group of people came carrying a stretcher of tightly pulled hides fastened to poles of bone and wood. Carefully and at the profane protests of Jude, they maneuvered Joanna onto the stretcher, still attached to her back brace of oars, and carried her out of the ship.

Kaplan aided Jude with a shoulder, hoisting him to his feet, and they followed after the procession.

Jude muttered curses the entire way.

Nanuq and Astrid followed after them.

Kaplan tried to give Jude some reassurance. "She'll be all right, Huntsman—"

"Fucking hells, stop saying that!" Jude cut his condolences off sharply. "You have no idea if she will be *all right*. She may never be able to walk again. She may *die* from this."

"Indeed, she may, but do you not wish to hope for the best?" Kaplan asked, his own skepticism not boding well for the woman. Not to mention her injury, the woman hadn't eaten in the three and a half days it had taken to come to *Qilakvik*.

"I don't rely on hope," Jude grumbled. "I assess the reality of a situation and take action to improve it."

"That's quite rational thinking, Jude Nelon. It keeps us grounded in reality," Kaplan answered. "Still, I cling to hope at times. Like in the stories of heroic adventures and budding love, the fight against a greater evil. There is always an inkling of hope underlying those epics. It is always welcome when the hero overcomes a significant hurdle after struggling against all odds."

"Ah, always lost in your books," Jude sighed, a faint smile playing on his lips. "The heroes triumph over their challenges through sheer perseverance and their own abilities, or with the support of allies. Did you ever read *Tales of the First Land?* The hero always gets the shit end of the stick, but he pushes through with fierce determination and Skrull-damned hard work. Honestly, it's not very realistic."

"*You've* read *Tales of the First Land?*" Kaplan asked in surprise. "That is a sprawling ten-volume classic if I do say so myself. I didn't take you for one to indulge in such fantasies."

"Fucking hells, what can I say? I take great pleasure in finding tranquility in my garden, savoring a steaming cup of tea, and losing myself in the pages of a compelling book or scroll."

Kaplan chuckled as he supported Jude along.

"I'm not some lowly peasant who can do nothing but drink watery beer at the day's end, seeking only solace in his cups after toiling through the shit for pennies."

"No, Jude Nelon. No, you are not." Kaplan answered genuinely. *The man is* definitely...*something*. "Look, we're here."

The group carrying Joanna entered a substantial building. A large door with sizeable bone framing and stretched hides opened into a mud room. Here, the Nunara took turns pulling off their thick fur boots and changing into soft, warm slippers before they entered the next chamber through a leathery curtain.

"Change your footwear," Nanuq said as he did just that, nodding to a pile of beaded moccasins. "We do not track snow and mud into our homes."

Kaplan helped Jude with his single foot before finding a pair for himself. The lining of the slippers was of fluffy fur and incredibly soft. As he stepped, it was cushioned underfoot, like walking on clouds. He had never worn such a comfortable footwear before. Soon, they entered the next chamber. The floor was adorned with opulent fur carpets, each one a rich tapestry of deep colors and textures. Tools crafted from bone, wood, and stone were meticulously arranged, creating an intricate display on the walls. Presiding over the room were the formidable skulls of diverse beasts - a towering bear, the fearsome jaws of a shark, and the grand antlers of a majestic deer - each serving as a testament to the power and diversity of the natural world.

After taking in the decor, Kaplan was horrified by what he saw next. They had placed Joanna on an incline, with the foot of the stretcher secured to the ceiling, her head facing downward, and were securing her ankles and legs together. A rope then was attached to her foot bonds and thrown over a massive bone of some sea beast that acted as a beam support to the ceiling. Two men began pulling down on the rope and extending her legs.

"What are you doing?" Jude cried, stumbling out of Kaplan's grip; he fell to the fur-lined floor.

Kaplan reached for his scimitar. *What are they doing? Torture?*

A hand fell on his shoulder as Nanuq said, "Do not fear. They are righting her backbone."

The man who had met them on the dock turned to them. "We have, unfortunately, dealt with a similar case before when one of our people fell into a chasm in the ice. We will straighten the spine and reapply the brace. You did well with what you had, which will further aid in healing her bone tissue. It will take weeks, even months, perhaps. It will take time to nurse her back to health and teach her to walk again."

"Surely you have some sort of magic that could help us?" Jude pleaded as Nanuq helped him back to his feet.

"Magic?" the man asked curiously. "We have that which the Lân provides. What nature provides. The fish and tusk of the walrus. The ice that carries us across the plains. The fat of the sea and land. We have only nature to aid us."

"Where did you learn this odd technique then?" Kaplan asked curiously. "As it does not seem to be of the natural sort."

"It was...*taught* to us." He turned back, dismissing them.

This man has an air of authority about him. Kaplan wondered if he were more than just a simple dock man.

"Now, you must leave us to our work," the man continued. "We will provide lodgings and vittles for you. Siku, show them."

The boy who had run earlier appeared next to Kaplan. "Come with me," he exclaimed excitedly, a bright smile of wonder on his face. "I've never met a Xamidian or anyone from Auru before. Even though my *ataata* taught me both languages."

"I will stay with her." Jude did not ask permission. "Will she be sleeping here?"

The man turned back. His eyes studied Jude, and then Kaplan saw him glance at Nanuq. Something passed between them, and the man nodded. "The Auru man can stay. The rest of you out." Once again, he turned away.

Kaplan watched as Jude found a seat on a short stool. He sat, hands clasped together, white-knuckled as he stared at Joanna. Kaplan followed the boy, Siku, back into the mud chamber to change their footwear. He couldn't help but ask the boy, "Who is that man? Is he the leader of this village?"

"My *ataata*? Leader?" The boy looked up at Kaplan curiously. "There is no leader of the Nunara. We're a community. A family."

"Interesting..." Kaplan pondered aloud.

"It was virtuous you did not cause conflict with Tuktu," Nanuq said with a grin. "Else, he would gorge you on his antler ulu. He is a mighty warrior of the Nunara."

"By the Primus," Kaplan murmured with a touch of amazement, "the world we live in is so vast. It's amazing how we can continue to broaden our minds, even as we grow older."

"Is why I go to the Vouri," Nanuq nodded. "I love my people but wished to see what else was out there. I departed on the next Vouri trade ship to come to *Qilakvik*. Though I got a little bit caught up in the Vouri way of life to explore further." He slapped Astrid on the back. "I quite enjoy a rigorous walk up the mountain."

"Ha!" Astrid gave him a toothy grin and a more than friendly nudge. "For you are now mountain caste, Nanuq."

"You all coming?" Siku asked impatiently.

"Lead on," Kaplan waved the boy ahead and followed him into the chill air of *Qilakvik*.

Fucking cold, fucking ice, fucking hells. Jude sat uncomfortably on the small stool, his leg stump itching furiously from the chill when one of the Nunara thrust a steaming bowl of what would pass for stew into his hands. Chunks of blubbery pink and white meats and some root vegetables floated in a cloudy broth. He spooned some meat and raised it, dripping, to his lips. It smelled fishy, almost like seawater. His stomach grumbled longingly, and he forced himself to push the morsel into his waiting mouth. It was unlike anything he had tasted before—deep and complex, a taste of the ocean's depths and the tundra's vastness. The fish added a delicate sweetness that balanced the gaminess of the other meat, its flesh flaking apart at the touch of his spoon. What it was seasoned with, he could not tell, even with his hobby of tending herb gardens. The warmth spread through him like wildfire, and he savored it.

By all the fucking hells, I needed that.

After he had filled his gut, his focus returned to Joanna, lying half upside down on the pallet, surrounded by these people muttering in their language. Pity mixed with self-hate battled within him. Pity for Joanna and her injury and the fact that she may never recover. Hate for himself not being able to save her. *I should have stopped her from stepping out that door.*

"It will have to do," the large man who had done all the talking since their arrival said, turning to Jude. "Would you like to help us feed her?"

"I can't even walk," Jude murmured pathetically. "How can I help her?"

"It was I, Tuktu, who broke my back in a fall into the fissure."

"What?" Jude started, looking up at the formidable man before him. "Impossible, how is it you walk about and do what you do?"

"A traveler came with the wind, a blessing of the land. He was here when they brought me in and taught us this technique. He passed on his knowledge even after telling us it was improper for his people to do such a thing. He saved me. Now, his knowledge will save her."

"What does that have to do with me? I lost my lower leg. I can barely crawl toward her, let alone feed her. I don't even know where my fucking crutch got to."

"Have you tried?"

"Tried what?"

"To walk." The man knelt before him, and his crescent blade appeared in his hand.

Jude was startled but could do nothing as the man cut away the tattered fabric around his stump. Tuktu took it in his hands and looked at it long before speaking. "It was a clean cut, and the fire that burned the wound closed was of intense heat. I've never seen such a burn."

"Well, it's still hurts like Skrull-damned hell. Fucking itchy too."

The man said something in his language to one of the others, and a middle-aged woman began working at a table nearby, mixing something. Not long after, she came with a bowl of grey-green muck.

Tuktu scooped it out of the bowl with two hefty fingers and spread it over Jude's stump. The sensation was cold and warming simultaneously, hard to describe. Tuktu then wrapped a clean bandage over it. "Once the swelling and itching have subsided, we will craft you a new leg, one more comfortable to walk on. Now come." He hefted Jude to his feet, and the woman moved Jude's little stool close to Joanna's head. They sat him back down, and another bowl of the steaming stew appeared in his hands.

Jude stared at her face and noticed her eyes blinking open toward him.

"Jude?" It was a strained whisper.

"Joanna," Jude let out a breath he didn't know he was holding, clasping her hand in his.

Then they lowered Joanna's legs and raised her head slightly.

"You must work quickly," Tuktu ordered. "Joanna must stay in the head-down position as much as possible. It would be best if *you* cared for her. Feed her. Clean her waste. Wash her. It will be a long and difficult battle. But you will do it together."

Jude ground his teeth, determination suddenly gripping him. "Joanna, I *will* do this. I promise you I will make you better."

Joanna smiled faintly at him, her blue eyes peeking through heavy lids. "I know."

How can she have such faith in me? Jude lifted the spoon to her lips and let her slowly sip at the broth. To Tuktu, he said, "Get me that new leg as soon as you can. I need to start walking so we can do so together once she is ready."

Tuktu smiled, nodded, turned, and pushed through the entrance's hanging fur skin.

CHAPTER TWENTY-THREE

SHAME

SAUDETT SLEPT THE BEST she had in weeks. The substantial military pavilion had divided sleeping chambers within. Darkclaw Marah had wordlessly come to her in the quiet hours of the night and curled up next to Saudett in the blankets of the cushioned sleeping pad. She had been grateful for the company and warmth her friend provided. Their tufts of fur were soft and tickled Saudett's bare skin, but she slept soundly beside the Volkinn. *Safe.*

Dawn arrived with a military sound off to get the soldiers busy. It had been a long time since Saudett had heard such a call, not since she had quartered in the barracks of the Shepherd's Eye in Dagad before moving in with Simon, and the day always started with combat drills and a quick, hearty breakfast to keep one until the afternoon rotation. Then, she would patrol the dusty streets of Dagad, usually with one or two other soldiers. Life had been simple back then. *Gods, I wish I could go back to that.*

Saudett dressed in the sophisticated, warm, newly sewn garments provided to them. The wings were quite awkward when it came to clothing. The seamstress had fashioned a thick, wool-lined coat that needed to be pulled around her wings and buttoned from the back. She did not fail to notice the rank of lieutenant braided in blue and black on the upper arm of the coat. She tried to rouse Marah, who was still fast asleep, to no avail, so she went to Malix's chamber to find him sitting on the edge of his bedding, shirtless, a new military-cut jacket of crimson and white lay on his bedding beside him, scratching his messy beard and brooding.

"Malix," Saudett said in greeting.

"Saudett," he answered slowly. "What do you think of our situation? It seems this council of magi is formidable and plans to strike back against my father."

"Can you help me with this?" She turned her back to him, awkwardly holding the coat to her chest.

He grunted, and then she felt his fingers on her skin as he pulled the fabric tight and began fastening the buttons one by one. His touch was gentle and warm.

"Why do you philander with the sorceress woman?" Malix asked, his voice gravelly in her ear.

Why do I? Saudett asked herself. "Because I'm afraid, I think. Fearful of being alone. When I see someone attractive, I naturally act on that attraction. It's how I've been for a long time now. It's what my husband and I agreed upon in our marriage." *Even though, after Hata, I vowed to only be with him.*

Malix clasped the last button. "Finished. Perhaps you should put some trousers on."

Saudett turned back to him, feeling her cheeks flush with warmth. His face was only inches away from hers, and she could detect the earthy, masculine scent emanating from his solid, hairy chest. He was one of those attractive people that she would typically act upon.

He tilted his head. "You're not contemplating me now, are you?"

"Uhm," she stammered. "I—you are...pleasant to look upon, but your father's likeness—"

"That is one reason," he cut her off sharply, holding up a finger nearly to her lips, "I could never do such a thing to you or any woman. I cannot follow in my father's footsteps and pass on his blood."

"Not even if you found love?"

He turned away from her. "I would not bane someone with my existence. No one can love me."

"Malix, you're *not* unsought. You saved me. I'll be forever grateful to you. I'm coming to care for you as a companion. Even if it's not love, you can find friendship."

"Friendship?" He bowed his head sorrowfully. "I had a friend once. A brother."

"I know, I felt that bond," she said, touching his shoulder to turn him back to her. His father's visage immediately flashed in her head, but she pushed it aside with a determined ferocity. Then she embraced Malix and she could barely contain her tears as she whispered into his broad chest, "You're not unsought." His skin was unnaturally warm, even hot to the touch.

He stiffened momentarily, and then she felt him relax and his four arms wrapped around her. His chest began to heave slightly, and she realized he was crying, which immediately released her tears. "My mother could not bear me. My father was apathetic to my life. There was only Twade. I've done horrible things for my father." He squeezed her tighter, embracing her as much as he could. His voice lowered in her ear. "Thank you, Saudett. It was *you* who saved me."

She wanted to kiss him. To show him that he could be loved...

"Lady Saudett," Darkclaw Marah's voice came from behind her.

Malix let Saudett go as she turned to see the Volkinn holding the chamber's curtain aside, watching them.

Gods, what is wrong with me? Is my need to be loved so desperate that I can't leave anyone alone?

"We are hungry," Marah grunted, then let the flap of fabric fall in front of them.

"Marah, wait," Saudett called after them but heard no answer.

"I agree with them,' Malix said, his tone suddenly held a hint of excitement. "We should eat more of that intriguing foodstuff and rejoin the sorceress to plan our next actions."

"I don't think camp fare will be what you have come to expect compared to Nix's fine dinner," Saudett said, relaxing at his enjoyment of such a simple thing. *I can love whomever I wish. Nobody else should have a say in it.* The image of Simon laughing as he added some herbs to a pot of bubbling curry returned to her. "One day, I'll have my husband cook for you. You would be a welcome friend in our home."

"Fuck me, I would like that."

Darkclaw Marah awaited them impatiently as they exited the pavilion into a camp bustling with activity as the chill air hit them. The camp was a magnificent display of Aurulan's royal colors, with vibrant yellow and pure white adorning every corner. Silk banners, meticulously embroidered with intricate coats of arms depicting a regal lion and majestic eagle back-to-back in shimmering gold, fluttered in the morning breeze against a backdrop of white and yellow. As the sun rose, its golden rays caught the embroidered threads, causing them to shimmer and glow as if they had captured the very essence of sunlight itself.

The clink of metal against metal echoed through the camp. Armorers and blacksmiths worked diligently, polishing breastplates and sharpening swords. Saudett glimpsed an armored knight adjusting his gilded cuirass, the emblem of a golden eye sunburst silhou-etted by a crescent moon emblazoned on his chest—a *Primus Templar.*

The soldiers honed their skills in a nearby clearing, their swift and precise movements a testament to the disciplined training of Aurulan. The sun's rays reflected off the glistening blades as the soldiers clashed in their swordplay practice. Saudett stretched her arms, sensing the familiar call to immerse herself in the training routine, aiming to restore her body to its peak condition.

Soon, the scent of freshly baked bread and sizzling bacon wafted toward them from a communal cooking area. Malix's step quickened eagerly. Soldiers huddled around open fires; their faces illuminated in the dim morning light by the flickering flames. A gruff, no-nonsense cook, clad in a stained, once-white apron, ladled steaming porridge into wooden bowls.

Saudett's stomach growled with hunger, but she fought the urge to eat. "I'm going to participate in the morning drills," Saudett announced, giving Malix a reassuring pat on the back. "You both go ahead and have your breakfasts."

"Are you certain?" Malix asked, doing a double take from Saudett to the cooking area.

"We will join you," Darkclaw Marah growled.

"No need, I won't be long. I will tire quickly in my current state." Saudett turned and strode away, waving back to them to enjoy themselves.

Malix hurried toward the scent of food, and Marah reluctantly followed him.

Saudett strode into the midst of sparring soldiers. Eyes turned to regard her, some widening in awe at seeing her wings folded pristinely on her back. She went directly to a weapon rack and found a stout pole used to train in the spear. She held it aloft, checking its weight and balancing it on her open palm. Then she spun it about her, the hum a familiar noise to her ears. She caught the spin deftly and brought the pole to rest under her right arm.

Soldiers gapped at her in a semi-circle.

"I need a sparring partner," she announced.

A helmeted man stepped forward, holding a simple training sword casually to his shoulder. He nodded to her and presented his weapon.

Saudett nodded in return and pointed the would-be spear toward him.

He immediately dashed in, trying to get quickly through her guard, and his weapon blurred past her parry.

She sidestepped, and the hardwood grazed her shoulder. She spun away only to find the soldier was relentlessly within her guard once more. She caught his thrust on her shaft and parried it skyward. She danced back again. *Breathe!*

This time, he didn't follow. He circled a moment like a hunting predator, awaiting the perfect moment to strike.

Saudett mirrored his every move. This time, she seized the initiative. With a relentless series of thrusts and swift spinning attacks, she launched her assault. But each thrust was skillfully parried, and every feint was swiftly countered with a precise strike. As the battle intensified, Saudett's breathing quickened, her brow furrowed in fierce concentration, and sweat trickled into her eyes. Undeterred, she launched another furious attack. The clash of their wooden weapons created a thrilling symphony, their fierce battle drowning out the murmurs of the onlookers.

Saudett spun away once more, her senses alert to the advancing figure of the man. His imposing presence seemed to envelop her, and she realized there was no weakness in his stance. As she retreated, the surrounding crowd instinctively made way for her. Despite her weariness, she knew she couldn't give up just yet. The threat of exhaustion loomed, but she refused to succumb. *Not yet,* she thought. *I'm not done yet.* She released her wings and with a powerful thrust, propelled herself forward with a last desperate battle cry, pole aimed at his chest.

At the final moment, he swiftly sidestepped, causing her to hurtle past him. Struggling to regain her balance, she slipped and slid on the slushy ground before turning around to confront him once again.

His wooden blade pressed under her chin. His other hand raised and pulled his helm from his head as he let it fall into the muck. Grand Maréchal Étienne Normand smiled down at her, his breath puffing in the cold morning air. "Tres bien," he said, panting heavily, offering her a hand. "I never miss morning drills."

Saudett flashed a grin at him and reached for his hand. "Grand Maréchal, I never imagined I'd find you here, let alone be so agile for someone of your age."

"Mind your manners, madame, or I'll be forced to spank you again." He pulled her to her feet. "Also, no using wings next time."

"I had no other choice."

"Ah, oui." Étienne began twisting his grey mustache thoughtfully. "I suppose you should use what you have. At any rate, I'm famished. Shall we rustle up some breakfast?"

"Please."

Saudett followed the Grand Maréchal of the Aurulan military back to the communal cooking area. *He does not put himself above the ordinary soldiers. He's a good leader.* Malix and Marah sat on a low bench, devouring bowls of steaming porridge along with a few thick slices of bacon. Malix had licked his bowl clean when Saudett sat down with her bowl, accompanied by Étienne.

"Fuck me, this...*bacon* is delicious," Malix said, licking his lips. "The creamy, grainy mud is different but also quite tasty."

Darkclaw Marah tore a piece of the fatty meat with their sharp canines and rumbled in agreement.

"Ah, oui. We'll soon be out of the bacon if we don't get these creatures of Skaad cleared from our lands. Most of our farmland is in northern Aurulan before the North Iron Belt." Étienne mumbled around a mouthful of porridge. "We've evacuated the fields until we have things under control. Winter is here, and when grain is scarce, they cannot feed their swine; hence, there is no bacon."

"How long have the *Children of Skaad* been here?" Saudett asked.

"It's been nearly a year since the Vouri refugees came from the mountains. We won a decisive battle, and the enemy was scattered. Oh, and the mountain from which the enemy emerged also collapsed."

"Hata did that," Saudett said. "She confronted Hear-fan Skaad and brought the mountain down on the Wayfarers Gate. She was then forced to flee from him into another Lân, where she enlisted the aid of another race of people."

"Hold your words," the Grand Maréchal said, his tone changed to that of a commander. "These are tidings the Eta must hear as well. Come." He stood and did not wait for them to follow.

They hurried after him. Malix looked back longingly at the cook forking a piece of bacon into another soldier's bowl. They soon found themselves back at the farmhouse. Étienne knocked on the door, and the servant, Marise, opened it a crack.

"Give us one moment. The Eta has just awakened." Marise said quietly before closing the door again.

Étienne began to pace restlessly.

"There is no rush," Saudett counseled. "I can make my report at any time."

"No, this information must be relayed to the Alpha swiftly."

The door swung open again, and Marise beckoned them to enter.

Nix Swan was covered in a nearly translucent, silk, white sleeping robe, standing at the head of the table. She left little to Saudett's imagination as Nix's nipples protruded against the delicate fabric. "What's the urgency at such an early hour? Have you already eaten? Or will you join me?" She proceeded to sit and nodded to Marise to bring out her breakfast.

"I could eat," Malix said hastily and found his spot at the opposite end of the table.

"Very well," Nix waved to the rest to sit. "So why have you come?"

"Ah oui," Étienne said, sitting and nodding to Saudett. "This soldier has vital information to report. I wished you present to hear it firsthand rather than have me try to repeat it in my old age."

"Saudett?" Nix's serene gaze found Saudett and a hint of a smile played on the sorceress's lips.

"Well, I was about to tell the Grand Maréchal here about the people of the Ryk Lân, or Ryklings as we called them," Saudett answered, trying to hold Nix's gaze and not let her eyes stray.

"Who are *we*?" Étienne questioned. "You two?" He looked from Saudett to Malix.

"Yes," Malix said. "My father has been at war with the Ryklings for some time now and is struggling to conquer their Lân. I think honesty is key here, Saudett. You were with him far longer than me."

Darkclaw Marah grunted in agreement with Malix's words.

What if they pronounce us traitors? Saudett took a breath and sighed it out. Her eyes found Nix's once again. "I was integrated into Hear-fan Skaad's forces, training troops and commanding the battle for Ryk."

Nix did not so much as flinch away from Saudett's gaze.

Étienne slammed his fist against the table.

Darkclaw Marah sprang to their feet and bared the black claws of their one hand.

"Calm yourselves," the Eta said levelly. "I'm sure our sweet Saudett has a reasonable explanation for this?"

"The nomads of Hasiera, along with my husband, and the Wayfarer, Gaelin Yesnala, fought against the *Children* in the Moreas Lân." Saudett put a hand on Darkclaw Marah's shoulder to calm them. "Marah chased their leader through the Wayfarers Gate, and I followed. We were captured but not ill-treated. I decided it better to play along with Hear-fan Skaad and wait for an opportunity to act against him. I trained the Nyra and was working to turn those people to my side. The Nyra are the winged warriors of the Grot Lân, which Hear-fan Skaad had already subjugated. Where I acquired these." Saudett stood and opened her wings for a moment. "The battle for the Rykling fortress was ferocious. Hata Vasara was there, fighting alongside the Ryklings." Saudett paused. The memory of that battle came back to her. She had been consumed by anger and hatred. She had wanted Hear-fan Skaad to win and destroy all of those people. She had killed Ryklings with her own hands. *I had tried with all my might to kill that woman on the walls of the fortress—that woman whom Hata had claimed to love.* When Hata had fallen, defeated by Trije-fan Skaad, Saudett had acted impulsively to save her. She had killed Trije-fan and been taken back to the war camp. Finally, she spoke, "I killed one of Hear-fan Skaad's true-blooded sons in that battle." Saudett glanced at Malix.

"I had no love for Trije or he for me," Malix reassured coldly.

"The Lord of Shadow took it as it was," Saudett continued, "a betrayal. He had me imprisoned. To await my punishment." She shivered at the thought of Hear-fan Skaad forcing himself upon her.

"Where Malix came to your rescue along with Darkclaw Marah?" Nix asked.

"In short, yes. Now we are here."

"What of the Ryklings? Did they lose the battle?" Étienne leaned forward. "Are they still fighting?"

"The *Children* had retreated when I was taken," Saudett said. "I don't know any more than that."

"I do," Malix said. "He has erected a barrier of shadow magic that will slowly engulf the Rykling fortress. He has amassed his armies behind the barrier should the need arise to utilize them. But with that magic, anything caught in it will not survive."

"As I have said before," Saudett urged. "This is our best chance to strike at him while he is preoccupied."

At that moment, Marise returned with breakfast platters for everyone.

Malix eagerly attacked the food while Étienne pushed his plate away. Saudett took a few bites but felt full from the heavy porridge and bacon. Darkclaw Marah quickly downed the contents of their platter. Nix gracefully took delicate little bites while dabbing at her lips with a fine serviette.

Malix moaned and groaned with pleasure as he ate, dipping a flaky, rolled pastry into his eggs with obnoxiously loud noises and far too much lip-smacking and slurping. Yellow yoke dripped into his beard and clung there.

"Malix, slow down. Your second breakfast is not going anywhere," Saudett suggested gently.

"Did your father not teach you table manners?" Nix Swan asked, a look of mild aversion on her face.

Malix stopped mid-bite. "Uhm, fuck no. I was fed scraps in the kitchens before being sent off to other Lân's. There, I had to make due for myself."

Gods, he is nearly a beast. He was raised by himself in that underground dungeon. Saudett's heart lurched for the cast-aside son of Hear-fan Skaad.

"Lieutenant," the Grand Maréchal's tone was that of his rank. "Is there anything else you should be telling us? Any other information you can provide?"

"I've told you all I know." Saudett hesitated. *Was that true?*

"What does his world look like? Does he have a stronghold? Where do his armies camp?" Étienne rattled off questions.

Malix swallowed loudly and cleared his throat, "The Skaad Lân is a world in eternal twilight. It is covered in water but only up to one's knee. His stronghold is underground, only accessible by a moving platform submerged in those waters. The Wayfarers Gates surround that platform. To attack the underground complex would be suicidal. If you sent a battalion down, they would face floor after floor of *Children* and quickly be overwhelmed. By the time the platform returned to the surface for another group, all previous ones would have been slaughtered."

"Does the stronghold not flood when the platform opens to the surface?" Nix Swan questioned.

"It has never been a problem," Malix said. "I don't know how my father did it, but the shaft that houses the platform runs deeper than all his chambers."

"If we hold the surface," Saudett added, "we can cut off his reinforcements to Ryk. The *Children* ascending from below would have the same problem when they emerged on the surface. They would be outnumbered and quickly cut down."

"Along with an attack on his flank through the Gate." Étienne nodded in agreement. "This is a sound plan."

"Is this not what you talked of last night," Darkclaw Marah huffed impatiently.

"Indeed," Nix said as she stood. "I will take you all to the Aurulan Gate. The Alpha should be at that location, but it is not guaranteed. "Malix, are you confident that you'll be able to handle the Gate and accomplish what you need to?"

"I will," Malix answered assuredly. "Is it a long journey to this Gate?"

"Well, yes, if we were going by foot," Nix said, slightly smiling.

"Flight?"

"You'll see. Now, leave me; I must make ready." Nix's eyes met Saudett's and held them as Marise began to usher the others out of the farmhouse. Marise followed them out, blatantly leaving Saudett behind.

Nix strolled back towards the bed at the rear of the room, then pivoted back to face Saudett. With a graceful gesture, she opened her arms, inviting Saudett to join her.

Saudett hesitated as thoughts of Simon tumbled around her mind. *But it's been so long since I've been comforted, been cared for.* So, she went to Nix; the woman was slightly taller as she embraced Saudett. Saudett's thick new winter clothing limited skin-to-skin contact. She did not feel the chill of Nix's touch, but she felt the shape of her body against her own. She felt a soothing heat blossom within her as they intertwined in a tight embrace, savoring the moment as if it were the first time they had ever held anyone so intimately.

As if to read Saudett's mind, Nix whispered gently, "I've never been with someone like this before." Nix's lips brushed Saudett's ear, sending a cool shiver down her spine.

Saudett blushed as she confessed, "It's been months since I've partaken in such an affection."

"Sit with me." Nix took Saudett's hand, the cold immediately biting prickling Saudett's skin, and led her to sit on the bed. Nix's robe fell from one shoulder, exposing much of her snow-white skin, as she sat and turned to face Saudett.

Saudett winced through the pain that was creeping up her hand and suddenly knew it could not be. She felt terrible for the woman. *There is no way we could be physically intimate if I can hardly hold her hand.* She lowered her gaze, ashamed she could not provide this woman with the affection she needed. "Nix—"

"I know you'll tell me we cannot lay together." Nix released her grasp on Saudett's hand and gently raised Saudett's chin just enough to look into her eyes before letting go. The chill lingered on her chin. "Talk to me. Tell me who you are, Saudett."

"You wish to know me, even if you can't have me?"

"I do."

The words breached like a dam from Saudett. "I'm a terrible person, Nix. I'm selfish and narcissistic and have done too many horrible things. Throughout my life, I have only cared about *my* happiness. First, when my parents abandoned me, I disregarded others around me who loved me. I killed him. A man who loved me like a daughter died to save me. I dissolved my parents' Caravan House and worked for hire on others. I did not wish to continue their legacy after I thought they had left me. Turns out, my father was abusing my mother, and their entire caravan company died in The Burning Sea. My mother survived and lived in the desert for twenty years before I found her again. I still believe she abandoned me, even if she had good reason but I'm working through forgiving her. She was upholding the laws of Hasiera. Hasiera's golden rule, once you join the fold, you can never leave.

"Of course, my husband has since abolished that rule since taking over Hasiera, and the people are free to come and go as they please. He even had plans to integrate the oasis into greater society. He is far more empathetic towards others than I." Saudett paused in her rant, recalling Simon when they had just met. "Gods, Simon, I was happy with our life when we were newly married. Then he had to get bored and curious about himself. After a few years together, he suggested we bed others. I will admit that our intimate time together had begun to feel like a chore. We worked late into the day, him with his architecture and I with the Shepherd's Eye. We would eat a quiet dinner and perhaps have sex lazily if we had much energy left. We both agreed we were not ready for children yet, and he would not release inside me. It became quite tiresome for us, and most days, we would simply go to sleep. Until he had that cursed dream, and we forgot to withhold his seed.

"At any rate, when he suggested we open our bed chambers to others, long before the drowning dream, I leaped at the idea and participated enthusiastically. It was so exciting not being limited to one person. We shared our bed with men and women alike. Sometimes, as Simon did, I would sleep with others outside of our home. It's what we agreed to. Then he was taken by Hasiera, and everything went to hell. I hardly mourned his capture even as I was eager to chase after him, but I was drugged and nearly raped. Then, I met Hata and her family. Hata and I formed a bond, and we found love. But, as we traveled to rescue Simon, it became apparent that Hata was still immature. I poured out my regret to her, and all she did was walk away. It was then that I realized I needed no one else. Simon and I only need each other.

"For a time, things were better. Simon agreed that we could be together. Yet it had become a habit, ingrained in me, to pursue my attractions. I was enticed by Darkclaw Marah just days after making this vow to Simon. Just days together again with my husband, I was already unfaithful. On top of all that, I found I was with babe. I acted foolishly; I joined the battle in the Moreas Lân after cautions from Simon and many others. I took a heavy blow and lost the child. It's all my fault, and I fear Simon will never forgive me." Tears streamed down Saudett's cheeks, and her gut churned with that anxiety of confronting Simon.

"Keep going, Saudett, let it all out," Nix's voice was warm and empathetic.

"In that fear, I ran. I ran from Simon. Afraid to admit what I had done to him. Then I chased Marah through the Gate and found myself in Hear-fan Skaad's control. But it was not a forced control; I volunteered to help him. He lavished me with gifts, fine clothing, and dinners. We spent time together. I rallied to his cause of vengeance. I became one of his. I put on the mantle of Greche-fan Skaad. It was only Hata who broke me free from that control.

"After I betrayed him, I sat in his dungeons for what felt like an eternity, just waiting for him to come into my cage and turn his threat of rape into reality. I sat, flinching at every noise I heard, expecting it to be him." A realization formed within her, both with Simon's horror with her and Hear-fan Skaad's looming threat. She knew it with all her heart. "I don't think I ever want to have a child." Saudett sat in silence for a long time. No more words would come out.

After that silent moment had lingered for some time, Nix spoke softly, "It's *your* body, Saudett; no man has any power over what you do with it. You've been through so much, Saudett; I can see in your soul that you wish to be loved and shown affection. I may not be able to give you physical gratification, but I can listen."

Saudett leaned over and embraced Nix, closing her eyes and ignoring the cold touch as their skin touched in places. She tightened her grasp, never wanting to let go. "Thank you, Nix. Thank you for listening."

"Now I know you, Saudett."

Saudett untangled herself from the woman. She then really looked at Nix. The elegant woman was flushed; there was frost on her lashes and slight icicles frozen to her cheeks. Saudett gasped in awe, "Even your tears have frozen." Saudett's eyes found Nix's lips. She leaned closer and saw her own breath mist before her. *She is so cold.* Without another thought, Saudett kissed those lips, and the chill rocked through her head and body, yet she pushed through for as long as she could bear.

Nix moaned with pleasure, which stirred Saudett to seek more. Tenderly, she let her lips stray down Nix's cheek and neck. There was a hint of warmth growing wherever Saudett's lips touched. Still, it was numbing those lips, and Saudett, as if coming up for air, pulled away.

Nix's let out a contented sigh, "That is further than any have gone before. Thank you."

"Gods, what I wish I could do to you." Saudett paused and backtracked. "I think you were beginning to warm Nix. If I just keep at it, I think we can do this."

Nix's eyes widened in shock. "Are you certain?"

Saudett nodded. "Maybe not this time, but we can keep trying. I mean the warmest part must be here." Saudett let her hand come to rest between Nix's thighs. She began to rub her finger along the silk fabric of Nix's undergarments. Up and down.

Nix gasped at the touch and moaned.

Saudett's brought their lips together again as she continued her up and down motion. Dampness formed beneath her fingers. Warmth blossomed. Saudett couldn't bear it any longer and she pulled Nix's sleeping gown apart, spreading Nix's leg wide and replacing her rubbing finger with her lips and tongue. There was not a hint of chill as she brought Nix to a beautiful, moaning, quivering climax.

Saudett kissed Nix's thigh tenderly as she breathed deeply before unentangling herself from the woman. She sat beside her once again.

Nix's lips quivered as emotion overflowed from her. "I...I never thought I could have that. Thank you, Saudett."

"You deserve it. I would love to please you again sometime. But for now, Nix Swan. Tell me about yourself. I've been selfish. I've gone on and on about me; what about you, Nix? Who are you?"

"Little old me?" Nix asked playfully.

Just then, a horn sounded and broke through the walls of the rickety farmhouse. Shouts began to rise from outside.

They both rushed to the door and clambered out. Saudett stared in shocked horror at the sight she beheld.

Five massive earthwalkers, the size of large hills, tore through the ground toward the camped army of Aurulan. Each seemed to shine with a different color of magical essence—all but one, the largest of the five. The light shining through the cracks of its molten rock skin seemed to ever change in hue.

Saudett fell to her knees in desperation. "Primus, help us."

CHAPTER TWENTY-FOUR
DEPARTED

The little girl's voice was loud in Simon's ear. He groaned and rolled over.

"Mama says if you don't get up, she won't wrestle you tonight."

Simon's eyes shot open, and he sat up straight as a board. "We can't have that my little pumpkin; I must win our match this time."

"Why do you always wrestle after I go to bed in my room?"

"Uhm," Simon hesitated. "We don't want you seeing Mama and Papa fighting, is all. Everyone argues now and then. Isn't that right, Amara?"

"I argued with Cyrah Andiges at the market, and she says her Papa builds homes faster and better than you do."

"Really, and what did you say to that?"

"That she's a liar. She got mad and pulled my hair."

"We all think our Papa's are the best and very special to us. I thought my father was the greatest man alive."

A vision of dust. A man standing tall. Smiling.

"Cyrah loves her father and also believes he is the greatest man alive. We must empathize with the people in our lives and understand by using our lives as examples. I mean, you think I'm the best, right?"

Amara shrugged sheepishly, her black hair bobbing around her small shoulders. "Eh, I guess you're all right. I kind of like Mama better. She says I should have fought Cyrah."

A vision of a woman. She was fighting beasts in a swamp. Spear flashing about her.

"What?!" Simon exclaimed. "What's that Mama putting in your head?"

"Papa, can we play in the River Droe? Mama is on patrol today; we have all day to play!"

"Yes, yes," Simon sighed in resignation. "I'll bring a basket of goodies; we can picnic after we splash about a bit."

"Yay!" Amara grabbed Simon by the hand and pulled him to get out of bed.

"I'm coming, I'm coming." Simon quickly stuffed a few sweet loaves of bread, some cheese, and a few apples on the edge of browning into a woven basket before throwing a thick wool towel over his shoulder. He hurried out the door after his daughter. It was a quick ten-minute walk from their home to the river on the eastern edge of Dagad. He watched Amara immediately dash down and hit the shallow, slow-moving river with a gigantic splash, kicking and squealing delightfully. He slowly bent, placed the basket on the ground, and dragged the towel over it. His back ached as he righted himself. Then he stretched, smiled at his adorable daughter playing in the water, and ran down to join her, spraying her with a wave as he joined her.

They spent the morning playing in the river, uncaring about everything around them. They stopped and ate. Amara eagerly gulped down her food, wanting to return to the water quickly. Simon soon rejoined her. The bread and apples had tasted bland—like nothing. He shrugged to himself and rejoined Anora, taking a face full of river water as he trudged down the muddy bank.

"Well, you aren't having *too* much fun without me now?" a voice called from behind.

"Mama!" Amara shouted and splashed up the bank.

Simon turned to look at his wife.

Captain Kai stared back at him with a look of total dread. His odd hat tipped on his head, and his bones and jewelry rattled as Amara hugged him. "Simon?" Kai's voice was clouded.

Something clasped Simon by the ankle as he stood in the river, staring in horror. "Where is Saudett?"

"Simon?" Kai repeated his name.

Another hand tightened around his other leg.

"Simon." Kai's voice became louder, more urgent.

Simon was dragged below the surface, and sunlight sparkled on the water above him.

"Simon!" Kai's lips were on his, his fists pressed into Simon's chest, again and again.

Simon's lungs expelled a gush of water, splashing onto the ship's deck as a searing pain tore through his chest.

"Oh, thank Chike," Kai gasped as he sat back on his knees, breathing heavily.

Simon gasped for breath, feeling an intense burn in his throat with each inhale. His body felt constricted, immobilized. Muffled sounds surrounded him, and his vision was obscured in darkness.

"She's lost too much blood." A different voice came through the fog. "My powers cannot create blood; I can only use what the body provides."

"Please! You must save her. Save my daughter!" Anora screamed, and the sound came back to life around Simon. He squinted past Kai, who still knelt before him. Kiana lay in the arms of her mother in a pool of blood, looking lifelessly at the sky. Anora's face had a fresh gash over one of her eyes and there were countless other wounds on the woman's body.

There is so much blood. Simon's voice was ragged, "Kiana." He tried to summon the strength to move, to at least *crawl* toward her.

Kai put a hand on his shoulder. "Simon, there is nothing to be done. She's gone."

"No," he rasped. "It can't be."

"There's one thing I can try. It is a great risk to Kiana and the one who would *give* their blood. You are her mother; you have the greatest chance of having compatible blood. If it is not compatible, her body will reject it, and she will die either way. It is worth the risk." It was the Theta, Cygne Caladrius, speaking. Simon saw him kneeling beside Kiana and Anora, his white ropes soaking up the red.

"Please, I'll do anything to bring my daughter back," Anora begged.

"Once your blood is within her and has not been rejected, I can begin the healing of the wound and the revival of her heartbeat as I did with Simon." He paused and looked at Anora steadily. "You've already lost much of your own blood. This process will use too much of your life force, too much of your blood. You *will* die from this."

Anora leaned over, thrust out her hand, and grasped the older man by the collar. Her mutilated eye glared at him. "Then I will die in her place!"

"So be it." Cygne nodded. There was suddenly a tiny scalpel in his hand. "Your wrists."

Anora presented them to the older man.

He proceeded to slice upward along the length of Anora's forearms. Blood welled out, and he pressed her wrists down onto Kiana's stomach wound. Then he put his hands over them, and an amber-red light shone through his fingers.

Simon pushed himself to his knees. "I can—"

Cygne moved one hand to Kiana's bare, bloody chest, pressing one hand to her heart while the other stayed on Anora's wrists, pushing them down. The light was pulsing rapidly, sweat glistened, and veins popped from the older man's forehead. The red-orange light grew nearly blinding.

"I can help!" Simon screamed, but it came out as a harsh whisper. He crawled a foot forward.

Anora's face went deathly pale, and she suddenly slumped.

"No!"

Kiana's eyes shot open, and she gasped, life breathing back into her.

"Hells, it's not enough." Simon heard Cygne curse in frustration. "Her organs have been torn to ribbons." He met Kiana's frantic gaze. "You're awake, but it's not enough."

"Kiana, *my daughter*," Anora whispered, then went limp, falling back and thudding onto the deck of the bloody ship. Her hands lulled by her sides, still gushing blood.

Fury suddenly burned bright within Simon. *Why isn't he saving them? Strangung!* Simon surged to his feet as strength filled him. "What're you doing, you fool?" He batted the older man aside with a backhand and didn't think twice as the man cried out in pain, skidded across the deck boards, and crashed into the railing.

"Simon!" Kai shouted in protest behind him.

Simon knelt before Kiana and pressed his hands to the mostly closed wound on her stomach. *Gehae.* The warm green-yellow light blossomed through his hands and into Kiana. The wound closed beneath his fingers, but he held it there long, letting the healing magic of the Iban'mael work into her internal body. Minutes felt like hours as he held his hands there, staring at Anora lying limp on the other side of Kiana.

"Mother?" Kiana asked hazily, turning her head to look.

"Don't worry, I'll save her too," Simon reassured, still staring at his mother-in-law's limp form.

Anora's lips trembled as she struggled to speak, her voice barely above a whisper. "Kiana... I love you."

"Mother?"

"Tell Saudett... I'm sorry. I love her and miss her dearly. I was an awful mother to you both."

Kiana was suddenly struggling to sit up. "No, Mother, what's happening?"

Simon deemed releasing his spell on Kiana safe and quickly moved to Anora.

"*Simon*," Anora's voice was nearly inaudible as the adrenaline of Simon's pulse pounded in his ears. "Be faithful to her..." the words trailed off into nothing.

Simon tightly grasped both of Anora's wrists. "*Gehae*," he uttered urgently. The light flickered, then abruptly extinguished. "*Gehae*," he repeated, with increasing desperation. His hands briefly filled with a blinding glow before falling dark once more. No healing occurred. Frantically, he shouted the incantation, "*Gehae, Gehae, Gehae!*" Anora lay lifeless, her chest still. She had departed from the Lân. "No!" Simon's anguished cry, a mix of sorrow and rage, pierced the air.

"Anora Ahmadi is gone. She traded her life for her daughter's." Cygne said as he slowly stepped up toward Simon. There was blood dripping down his forehead. "Perhaps I could have saved Anora if you had not cast me aside. We could have worked together."

"They were both going to die because of you!" In a fury, Simon spun on the Theta, and his hands moved independently. He grasped the man by the neck and began to squeeze.

"Simon, stop!" Kai was upon him, trying and failing to pull his magically strengthened arms away from Cygne.

The older man struggled to breathe, his mouth gaping. Then Cygne's hands, which were trying to pry Simon's fingers away from his throat, wrapped around Simon's forearms.

Heat and pain suddenly burned up Simon's arms and shoulders. The pain crawled toward his chest, nearing his heart. Simon immediately released the man and staggered back.

"Rah!" a voice boomed over them. Baal was suddenly towering between them.

Brena joined them, looking about the scene and taking it all in. Her eyes came to rest on Anora's limp form. Kiana was weeping, her face buried in her mother's chest, and Brena's face became grim. "She is gone?"

"Yes," Kai answered sullenly.

Brena's steps led her to Anora's discarded blade amidst the chaos. With care, she lifted the weapon and made her way to where Kiana and her mother were. Taking hold of Kiana's hand, she placed the hilt of the sword in her palm, and then, with a tender touch, Brena guided Kiana's hands to place the sword into Anora's lifeless grip.

Kiana sobbed as the cold fingers of Anora held fast to her cherished weapon on her chest.

"She was a skilled warrior, a dancer of the blade, and she cared for you deeply, Kiana," Brena said gently. "She had difficulty showing that love. We spoke for many long hours while we sought the trader in Nidhaut. She told me of her past and the daughters she had thought she had failed. Did she fail you, Kiana Ahmadi?"

"No," Kiana cried out, her voice trembling with disbelief and sorrow. "No, she didn't. She imparted so much wisdom to me, despite her relentless methods… but I simply can't fathom that she's no longer here."

There was a silence that held. Simon gripped his chest. The pain was lingering there and his arms ached from whatever Cygne had done to him. *Is my heart to stop again? Cygne won't save me this time. Fucking hells. I need to be away from these people. Afléotan.* He ascended skyward.

"Simon, there are still enemy ships!" Kai's voice called after him.

He ignored it. *How am I to tell Saudett that her mother is dead? After two decades lost, they had a mere week together, and now she will never see her mother again. Stupid fool, Simon.* He flew higher and higher. *I got her killed. I should have destroyed that ship when I saw it, but I fell in the water and…Gaelin.* The rage reignited, and Simon turned in the air, pointing toward the island with the Wayfarers Gate. *I'm going to fucking kill you, Gaelin.*

Color flashed in his vision below, and Simon saw two more massive Xamidian ships approaching *The Mamba's Mouth*, which was still entangled with the first Xamidian ship. A handful of Keen Eye's ships were beginning to surround the lone Gilded Crow vessel. *Skrull's hell, Kiana's down there. I can't lose her too.* He moved so he was centered above *The Mamba's Mouth*. Then he began to summon the fire. One flaming sphere for each of the enemy ships. They grew like suns around him. Larger and larger. The heat scorched him. He ignored it as it blistered his skin. *I can heal that later.* "Now…*die.*" Simon released the meteoric flaming spheres all at once.

Kiana instinctively raised her hand to shield her eyes from the blinding light emanating from the eight massive flaming orbs as they hurtled downward. The searing heat seemed to stoke the flames of anger within her, intensifying her emotions. *My mother is dead, and I never got to say goodbye. No, I said she disgusts me…*

The spheres fell, each homing in on one of the many ships that had begun to turn away in frantic desperation from *The Mamba's Mouth* and the Xamidian warship they had confiscated. The magic collided, burning through wood and canvas and flesh. The impact caused the sea to boil and erupt into steam, enveloping the ships in a swirling mist. None of the ships survived the devastating onslaught.

How did this happen? How did she die? The memory of the Xamidian man with the daggers came back to her. *He killed me.* Kiana's hands went to her belly, where the man's wicked curved blade had sunk deep and twisted within her. The next thing she knew, she groggily awakened with Cygne looking down at her. Then, Simon took his place. *It all happened so fast.* Then her mother was whispering nonsensically beside her, and the next moment, she was gone. *Before I could comprehend what was happening, she was gone.*

She looked down on the gashed, stock-still face of her mother, Anora Ahmadi. The woman who had taught her the dance of the blade. The woman who had taught her to care for her people. For Hasiera. The woman who had finally opened up about her past and explained it all to Kiana. From her first husband's abuse and attempt to murder her along with the abandoning of her first daughter, Saudett. To the trials of founding Hasiera with the First Otsoa and Rojas, her father.

"*Father,*" Kiana let his name slip from her lips in dismay, knowing that this would destroy him. The loss of his wife would wreck him beyond grief and sorrow. Yet he needed to know, and she had no idea where her father was.

The chaos of people rushing about the ship's deck was overwhelming as Kiana sat beside her deceased mother, taking in the stillness of her expression. She felt paralyzed, unable to react as muffled voices and gestures from the crowd surrounded her. In the midst of it all, she slowly turned her head to see Simon's return to the ship.

His booted feet touched gently on the stained deck boards. He opened his arms, approached Kiana, and held her tightly. "I'm here for you, Kiana," he whispered. "I'm so sorry."

"Simon." Kiana cried out as the sorrow overtook her and the tears and cries burst from within her, and she gripped his shirt, sobbing into it, trying with all her might to crawl inside his embrace.

Simon held her close, gently rocking her in his arms. "I'm sorry…"

CHAPTER TWENTY-FIVE

DRAGONS

A STORM HAD COME to Ryk. It was the first storm Hata had seen in the land of clear blue skies and crystalline floating islands. Rain cut at her face and soaked through her armor into her underclothes, and the wind would have taken her away without Kulta's scales hardening and keeping her in place upon his back. She could hardly make out the silhouettes of other dragons riding through the storm, visible only when a flash of lightning illuminated behind them.

I am no Sapphire Stormwing. This is not favorable for the dragons of other elements. Kulta grumbled deeply within Hata's mind.

"We can't stop now!" Hata shouted over the howling wind. They had spotted the storm approaching earlier that morning, on the third day of their journey to Keep Crystalia. They were supposed to arrive at their destination today. When she had expressed doubts about flying through the storm despite the Queen and the elders' orders, one of the Himin-dvergar nearby had warned her that storms in Ryk often lasted for days, even weeks, during the peak of storm season. "But there should be an edge to the storm we can breach unless it has engulfed the keep. Try to fly as high as you can, crest the storm."

"This is bad," Hata grumbled as Raine mounted her rotor-wing and began to take off. Hata was just another onlooker now, another follower. She wouldn't dare go near Raine again.

Now, Raine and everyone else were lost in the chaos around her. "Climb!" Hata urged Kulta forward.

I will try, little stone. The winds throw me off course every time I stretch my wings.

"Maybe I can help." Hata focused on the metal of her gem-infused armor. She willed it upward. As she was connected to Kulta via his scales wrapping around her legs, they began to gain elevation.

Yes, this will work, little stone. Kulta let out a roar and vigorously renewed his powerful beating of wings.

Finally, they broke through the darkness of black clouds, and the sun hit them. Hata blinked in shock, her eyes taking time to adjust. Other dragons and riders glided here, and a handful of rotor-wings puttered along almost peacefully. Hata breathed a sigh of relief at seeing Raine's aircraft at the head of the group. But it was not the full force they had entered the storm with. She looked back to see dragons and aircraft appearing out of the storm by the dozens. Then, the giant airship broke through the darkness, mist curling around its eight thudding propellers. There was a smoke trail behind it, and it was lumbering along slowly. There were blackened spots along the ship's hull, and Hata expected lightning had hit it multiple times. She turned back, praying the craft would keep airborne. The next sight Hata saw took her breath away.

The immense magical dome, pulsating with shimmering violet hues and dark navy clouds billowing with swirling smoke, rose above the horizon. The base of the massive sphere was concealed within the dense layers of storm clouds. As they rapidly closed in on it, the magnitude of the thing appeared to expand, looming larger and more imposing than Hata could believe.

We will join the riders. Kulta rumbled and steered them to a gathering group of dragons in a tight formation. Hata saw Aerendyl astride his massive, white, shimmering-scaled dragon. Crystal-clear diamonds grew in rows along the ridges of the dragon's snout, head, and neck. A tremendous white light rose from a translucent gem in the creature's jagged-scaled chest.

Ziraelthir, The White Diamond. Kulta answered her unasked question. *He is one of the eldest among us.*

Aerendyl pointed at the approaching sphere of magic, then raised his hand and closed his fist. Ziraelthir let out an ear-shattering roar and surged forward. The light in his chest beat like a flashing drum.

Kulta winged after him, and dragon after dragon drew closer around them. The gemstones in the mighty creature's chests seemed to beat in rhythm, each a different color than the next. Hata felt the power growing within Kulta, readying to release.

Ziraelthir opened his massive maw, and a beam of white light shot from it, causing a thundering echo. It hit the roiling mist with an explosive detonation of blinding white light, but the beam continued to drive into the magical sphere. Hata watched as violet lightning converged at that point as if trying to hold back the mystical power of *The White Diamond.*

Kulta roared, and molten rock spewed out of his mouth. It struck next to the beam of white light. More violet energy crackled to the focus of his attack. Then, a compressed blast of lightning flashed and burst next to his attack. Followed by a tunnel of fire. Jagged icy shards. A high-pressured continuous burst of water. A focused shockwave of intense soundwaves buffeted the magical barrier—fuming acid breath—black fire.

One after another, each dragon unleashed their power, all converging on that one spot. The violet lightning flashed and sizzled, fighting against the onslaught. There were a dozen blasts of elemental energy, then two dozen. Hata had been learning the types of dragons on the long flight back to Keep Crystalia; Sapphire Stormwings, Amberheart Drakes, Malachite Serpents, Citrine Sunfire Wyverns, Emerald Eyewings, Opaline Frost Drakes, Ruby Flamehearts, Obsidian Nightwings, and many more. She lost count as over thirty dragons beat their mighty wings, hovering in place while bombarding their magic against the shield. Still more moved to join them. Rotor-wings circled overhead.

A smaller dark green dragon spewed a fuming acidic blast as it moved closer to the barrier. It was a Malachite Serpent. Suddenly, what looked like a massive hand made of the smoking navy cloud reached out. The dragon beat its wings, trying to rear away, but was engulfed. Dragon and rider disappeared into the hand's grasp. Violet lightning surged to the hand, crackling, hissing and flashing.

Some dragons around Hata halted their attack and roared in fury, moving toward the hand in a desperate attempt to save their kin.

"No! Don't go near it!" Hata cried as a second hand shot out and gripped a blue-white Opaline Frost Drake that shrieked in pain, its head still visible as the fingers tightened around it.

The first hand pulled the Malachite Serpent into the sphere and was gone.

A handful of dragons turned their breath weapons on the second hand. Dark energy sparked and recoiled. The Frost Drake screamed, and its head lulled on a limp neck. A blast of fire hit the smoking hand, and abruptly, the hand evaporated into nothing. The dragon's once brilliant blue-white hide was blackened and corroded where the hand had grasped it. Scales had melted away. The magic had sunk deep into the dragon's flesh. The rider was nothing more than a charred skeletal form that fell away as both dragon and rider plummeted with a trail of smoke into the storm clouds roiling below.

The dragons released a vengeful cry, but they grew wise of the sphere and kept their distance. Finally, many rallied their attack on the single point that Ziraelthir was still boring away at, a testament to their fallen kin.

A hand stretched out, grasping at the massive white dragon, but it did not reach. Its fingers closed on nothing before it pulled back into the dome.

Hata squinted through the blasts and brilliant lights of the dragon's onslaught that threatened to blind her. Suddenly, a hole tore free in the center of the navy smoke, where Ziraelthir's beam of white light drilled deep.

"It's working!" Hata shouted, but her voice was drowned out by the roaring of dragons and the thundering of their magic. *The barrier is weakening.*

A cacophony of high-pitched shrieks rose from below. Hata looked down over the side of Kulta's rough back to see thousands of winged humanoids bursting from the storm clouds below, streaming like black tendrils.

The whirling rotor-wings swooped down to confront the enemy, their razor-sharp blades cutting through the air with a deafening scream. Some dragons momentarily diverted their attention from the sphere and turned to face the imminent threat. Hata observed as the two opposing forces clashed. Explosions of dragon magic rippled through the ranks of the winged humanoids, but the overwhelming mass of enemies seemed unperturbed as if the magic was a swat of flies against an endless swarm. Amid the chaos, she witnessed a dragon engulfed by the enemy horde, surrounded by a flurry of deadly slashing and thrusting weapons. The dragon eventually emerged from the fray, roaring in agony, while its rider remained motionless, shredded to a pulp by the vicious onslaught.

"We must protect Ziraelthir!" Hata urged Kulta to join the battle.

Kulta ceased his molten breath against the barrier and roared. Then he closed his wings and dove.

Hata became lightheaded as the force of the dive increased. She could do no more than pull herself close to his back as he plummeted.

Kulta opened his maw once again as a river of enemies turned on him. Molten rock melted through armor, flesh, and wings as scores of the flying humanoids died before him. Still, others avoided the burning death and converged on Kulta and Hata.

"Release me!" Hata shouted, and Kulta's scales shrunk back around her. Hata leaped off his back and, taking hold of her armor, came to a hovering stop in the air. Kulta barreled down and arced away with a trail of winged humanoids chasing after him, and he disappeared into the storm below. Far more of the enemy came for Hata.

Hata closed her eyes and pressed her fingertips together before her. The amber gemstone in her breastplate thrummed to life. She felt the metal of the flying creatures' weapons and armor in her mind. As they approached her in a swarm from all directions, Hata breathed and, at the last second, as their blades were mere feet away, Hata threw her hands out and *repulsed* the metal away from her. The spherical shockwave that emanated from her sent weapons and armor soaring, and the bodies within that armor crushed back as if they had flown head-on into a castle wall and crumpled against it. Shrieks of pain filled the air around her as bone snapped and shattered.

Then, a few flying beings slipped through, wearing dark leather instead of their comrades' blackened steel armor. Their weapons had been lost, but their sharp claws, hands, and taloned feet stretched viciously for Hata.

Hata focused on the heavy metal of her vambraces and melded them into long, sharpened blades that extended out over her hands. She then used some extra metal around her gorget and shoulders to grow in curved plates and formed a helm around her head. She met the enemy head-on while maintaining her *push* of other metal away from her. *I only need to deal with the unarmored ones.*

Claws raked along Hata's back, and she spun, bladed hand outstretched and sheared through a wing. The creature screamed, and blood sprayed as it lost control of its flight and fell. Two more blows scratched and squealed along the heavy tungsten of her shoulder and leg. Hata twisted mid-air, swiping and missing as the creature retreated. Three more circled. All around them, the swarm pushed against her magic, and flashes of blue sky peaked through the countless numbers of screaming, jagged-tooth humanoids. She caught sight of the white form of Ziraelthir, surrounded by the enemy.

Teras's thunder, I don't have time for this! Hata propelled herself toward the white dragon. Claws scraped against her, and one flying man didn't move out of her way fast enough. Hata pierced into his gut with both her blades and ripped them apart. She burst through a mist of blood spray and two halves of a body, continuing her surge upward. Ever repelling the other enemies away from her, the flight caused her push to crumple the armor of those who did not move, breaking the creatures like waves on a ship's hull. Weapons were flung from their hands as her magic hit them. Hata gathered those loose weapons in her wake; they trailed after her, cutting, stabbing, and hacking through the vile, monstrous people.

As she came to Ziraelthir's aid, a wall of deadly black iron weapons came with her. She flung them at the enemy, and a torrent of fatal projectiles shot out and killed the winged creatures, harassing the mighty dragon by the dozens.

A beam of white light seared through the air and cut through more like a knife to butter. Hata saw Aerendyl standing on Ziraelthir's back, his hands outstretched, shooting the beams in short bursts from his palms.

A creature dodged and broke through Aerendyl's defense, and Hata watched as the winged woman's spear aimed for Aerendyl's stomach. Hata focused on the spear tip and pushed. It was enough to change the direction, and the weapon glanced off the edge of Aerendyl's silver elven chainmail. He sneered, and his open-palmed hand smashed into the creature's face, then lit with white light. The winged woman's head ruptured into bits and pieces as the beam tore through it.

Hata moved to join Aerendyl's defense of Ziraelthir. The flying humanoids were too numerous, hacking and slashing at the massive dragon's legs and tail. The White Diamond swatted away dozens like flies, never ceasing to release his torrent of power against the barrier. Unfortunately, many other dragons had broken off their attack to defend themselves and their kin. The hole that had opened in the violet-crackling smoke was beginning to close again.

We need more dragons attacking the barrier. The loud thumping of propellers came to Hata as she pondered what to do. She turned to see the giant airship lumbering toward Ziraelthir. The winged people were attacking it as it came, but its thick armor was withholding. A smoke trail followed it, and one of its eight propellers was not spinning. She saw plated latches slide open on the sides of the airship, and heavy crossbows peeked out and fired upon the flying enemies. When a latch opened, the winged ones swarmed toward it, weapons trying to stab into the openings. But the Himin-dvergar staggered their attacks. A latch would open in one place only for the next to open on the opposite end of the airship. The latches opened, fired, and closed so swiftly that Hata expected two of the Himin at each latch, one to open and close the door and the other to aim and fire.

The airship diverted the attention of many of the flying humanoids.

Kulta! Hata sought out her dragon brother as she zipped around Aerendyl and Ziraelthir, slicing through enemies or taking hold of the metals of their armor and crushing them mercilessly. When anyone in leather armor attacked, she quickly disarmed them of their weapon and ignored them afterward. Their claws couldn't penetrate her armor.

They were too quick, dashing, twisting, and spinning about her, many evading her blades easily.

Little stone? Kulta's voice answered within her mind. It was strained, haggard, as if he were struggling to speak.

Are you well? Are you injured? Hata asked worriedly.

I have used much of my magic against the flying insects. They are persistent and unending. The storm has weakened me, and lightning has scored me half a dozen times.

Can you come back to me, to Ziraelthir?

I will try, little stone.

Hata took a lull in the fighting to fly near Aerendyl. "We must regather the dragons and focus the attack on the barrier!"

"We are sitting marks when the dragons are stationary," Aerendyl called back to her, his face strained, and blood dripped down his nose where it looked like a claw had managed to cut him. "The riders will be swarmed and defeated, and their dragons will go into a rage fueled by grief, and we will lose the ability to direct them. We must thin this horde."

Hata nodded in response but faltered. *What can we do? There are too many of them.* Even as she hovered there, she watched as a dragon riding Kidekorvat was cut down from her mount. Her crimson-gold Citrine Sunfire roared and twisted its head around, snapping up two attacking winged ones and sundering their bodies. Then it went berserk and began chasing after the winged ones who retreated...toward the barrier.

The hand seized the Citrine Sunfire, engulfing it and pulling it into the storm. Its cries of rage and heartache were silenced forever as it disappeared into the void.

No more. I need to end this. I need to kill Hear-fan Skaad.

Hata found Kulta leading a tight formation of rotor-wings that soared past them, a streak of flying creatures shrieking in their wake. Hata glimpsed Raine at the head of the V-shaped formation of the Himin-dvergar rotor-wings. The bladed wings of the aircraft were covered in blood and gore. Himin berserkers stood in the back seat of many rotor-wings, dual magically enhanced axes, swords, or hammers crackling with fire, ice, or lightning. If the winged blades of the rotor-wings missed their targets, the berserkers were sure not to miss their strikes as they defended their pilots to the death.

"Kulta!" Hata shouted over the chaos, and it reached his mind. She pointed at the opening that was slowly closing around Ziraelthir's blast. Kulta roared, and the amber gemstone in his chest began to pulse. He veered toward the focal point. Hata shot through the air to join Kulta. The shockwave from her movement sent winged ones tumbling away from her by force. She found her perch on Kulta's back, his scales growing to hold her in place as they aimed themselves.

Kulta let loose his molten breath directly before them.

The air crackled with energy as Hata and Kulta raced toward the barrier. As they approached, the shadowed shield began to give way, just enough for them to pass through. But before they could celebrate, a massive hand of violet lightning and navy smoke reached out to grab them. They narrowly dodged the grip, only to witness an explosion as two rotor-wings collided with the hand. To her surprise, Hata saw the Queen, Raine Stormfall, and her squadron hot on their heels. The Himin-dvergar and a small group of dragons were also making their way through the opening. The battle was far from over. They plummeted into the opening, Kulta releasing his molten breath at the last second.

Then there was darkness.

Chapter Twenty-Six

ELEMENTAL

THE EARTHWALKERS CRUSHED THE armies of Aurulan beneath them. Hundreds died as towering rock-like hands slammed and tore, thundering over the fields and across the scattering soldiers. They could do nothing against the massive mountain-like creatures. One of the earthwalkers spewed fire from its hands across the hills and valleys of northern Aurulan. Another froze people solid with a blast of icy wind, only to shatter them as its bulk moved over them. The earthwalkers were only torsos moving through the ground, their legs not visible in the earth. However, one seemed to hover above the others, a tornado of wind keeping it aloft, shooting blasts of cutting wind down upon the onlookers.

They each control the power of earth, wind, fire, and water. Saudett thought as she stared in horror at the destruction and slaughter before her. She heard the door to the farmhouse slam shut behind her, and to her surprise, Nix was gone from her side. *Where is she going? Is she running away?* Saudett returned to the chaos and noticed one of the earthwalkers lagging behind the others.

The one flying above the rest had inky black tendrils wrapped around its neck. The creature was grasping at the black cords, its glowing white maw open in pain. The tendrils stretched behind the earthwalker, originating somewhere on its backside.

I need to get out there and help. Saudett quickly found a weapons rack and took up a sturdy spear. Then, flexing her wings, she took off. From above, she could see the soldiers closest to the earthwalkers scattering away from them in all directions. A sphere of violet light flashed ahead of her and soared to collide with the most prominent leading earthwalker. *That must be Malix.*

Saudett flew as fast as she could and watched as the massive earthwalker's light changed to crimson, and suddenly, searing flames burst from its mouth and overcame Malix. The sphere of violet-black light around Malix held as he shot out of the fire above the creature. He pointed two of his four hands at it, his dual axes blazed with violet flames in his upper hands. Two strings of violet-black fire snaked through the air and punched into the earthwalker.

The earthwalker roared and swung a massive hand up at Malix.

He casually moved aside, letting the hand pass in front of him by inches. Malix then slammed both axes into the side of the hand, and Saudett saw glowing molten chunks dislodge from the earthwalker.

The earthwalker's glow suddenly changed to a bluish-white, and jagged shards of ice grew from the passing arm of the creature. They converged on Malix and struck him, sending him flipping back through the air. His barrier of light cracked under the force of the blow.

Saudett reached them as Malix righted himself.

"I thought your father would leave us alone?" Saudett called out to Malix.

"It's Bjarkeld," Malix growled ferociously, almost like a wild animal. "He must have spied on us. Fucking hells, I'm a fool. I knew he would not let me go so easily."

Saudett stared down at the massive earthwalker. "This is Bjarkeld? How has he grown so large?"

"Something has changed within him. Look where I struck his hand. The wound heals."

Bjarkeld glowed with a greenish-golden light, and Saudett saw his hand healing along with the holes that the strings of fire had pierced in him. "I didn't know the earthwalkers were so powerful. The one I defeated died like any other being when I stabbed it."

"We don't have time to ponder it. Can you distract him for a minute?"

Saudett leveled her spear. "Gladly." She pumped her wings and dove.

Bjarkeld let loose a rocky groan that reverberated through Saudett's bones, his pit-like eyes alight with azure fire. Charged sparks crackled, and a bolt of energy shot out at Saudett.

She twirled and spun, but the lightning homed in on her spear tip and burst against it. The force of the strike caused her entire arm to tremble with pain but luckily, the lightning did not travel down the sturdy wooden shaft and up her arm. She closed her wings and shot past Bjarkeld's face, her spear cutting and sparking across his eye and face. Molten blood dripped from his rocky skin. *Too shallow.*

Bjarkeld raised both hands as if to splat her between them.

Saudett pounded her wings and flew higher into the sky, narrowly avoiding the thunderous clap at her heels. She looked back to see Malix taking the opportunity to strike at Bjarkeld's neck with his fiery axes.

Malix moved unnaturally fast. Two blades of sharp wind hit Bjarkeld first, and then Malix's axes hacked into the flesh as if it were not made of hardened stone; glowing blood spurted about Malix as he gripped on with his lower hands and chopped savagely with the two deadly axes in his uppers.

Bjarkeld moaned with an eerie agony. "Blood of Skaad. Betrayer." The cracks in Bjarkeld's skin shone with amber light, and suddenly, shards of sharpened stone grew out of Bjarkeld's flesh around Malix and engulfed him.

Saudett dived back down to aid him, but she was struck by a jet stream of water, which sent her careening out of control. The force of the water thrashing her nearly knocked her unconscious, if not for the pain. Her wings stopped responding, and her vision hazed as she crashed through the bows of some black pines, their serrated branches and needles scraping and tearing at her until she finally came to a rest on the forest floor. She lay there, gasping for breath as her entire body ached. *How am I supposed to fight these things? I have no powers like Malix or the magi. Where was Nix? What's she doing right now? We need her.*

The ground began to shake as Saudett slowly found her feet. She held onto a tree as the rumbling continued. She heard the screams of dying soldiers nearby. Finally, the shaking ceased, and Saudett tested her wings. They were wet and throbbing with pain as she flapped them once. Then, she gritted her teeth and took off back into the air.

One of the earthwalkers was pulling its hands from the earth. A massive, jagged gorge had opened before the earthwalker, and soldiers had fallen by the hundreds into the crevice. She could still hear cries for aid, as some had not died from the fall.

Suddenly, from the flank of the earthwalker, a barrage of heavy stones and flaming pitch pots launched and arced through the air toward it. The creature roared as the pot smashed against it, and oil fire spread across its rocky skin. The heavy stones were impacted by powerful *thuds* that caused the earthwalker to recoil, but then Saudett saw that it absorbed the large boulders into its body.

A salvo of heavy ballista bolts rained down on the earthwalker—piercing and driving deep into the being. Its amber-glowing blood oozed from the punched holes in its stony flesh.

Saudett circled above. The catapults and heavy ballista were spread out in a staggered line and were slowly rolling on their sizeable wooden wheels away from the earthwalker who had turned toward them. Even as they retreated, she saw the soldiers reloading their siege equipment. Another volley was loosed from the ballistae, as they were quicker to reload than their catapult counterparts.

The earthwalker roared in fury and sank one hand into the earth; it pulled its hand out with a massive boulder in its grasp. Amber light shone through its cracked skin as the massive being hurled the boulder at the nearest group of siege equipment. The stone crushed man and machine alike as it bounced off the earth, shattering a catapult and skipping over land. Dirt, wood, and flesh were pulverized beneath it. The earthwalker reached for another stone below.

Ice suddenly crawled up the earthwalker's arm, which was elbow-deep in the ground. Sharp shards icicled up its shoulder and engulfed the side of its head. It brought its other hand in a fist down against the shards of ice with ferocity. The frozen arm *shattered* from the impact. Ice and stone flesh alike. The earthwalker released a disturbing wail as its entire arm, from the shoulder down, crumbled into glowing shards of ice.

Still dressed in her nightgown, Nix Swan elevated herself on a pillar of ice before the thrashing being. She raised her arms, and three massive cones of jagged ice formed in the sky above her. Nix slammed her arms down, fingers extended toward the earthwalker. The three stalagmite-like shards of ice impacted at intervals with lethal, grinding noises.

The earthwalker fell back as the first shard sunk deep, the second drove it to the ground, and the third pinned it there. Saudett heard its wheezing wail as it reached out a hand toward Nix as it lay bleeding to death. Barely visible, a small sphere of compacted earth shot out from its palm.

Exactly like Hata used to do.

Saudett descended and could see Nix smile confidently as a wall of ice shot up before her to shield her from the attack.

The earth bullet punched through the ice and straight into Nix's forehead.

"No!" Saudett screamed even as she saw the blood and matter burst from the back of Nix's head.

The woman tottered on her ice pillar and then fell backward, hitting the earth below with a sickening *crunch*.

Saudett stumbled and ran as she landed just after Nix's body hit the ground. She grasped Nix in her arms as Nix stared back at her...with lifeless eyes.

"Dead already?" A voice said behind her. "Such weakness."

Saudett turned to see a man clad in pitch-black robes trimmed with gold. His black hair was slicked back, and he stroked his imperial beard ponderously. He held a leash in one hand, which trailed behind him, attached to a figure wrapped in stained bandages from nearly head to toe. It was a woman—an armless woman. Only her eyes were visible through the wrapped red strips, and those eyes looked *lifeless*.

The man looked at Saudett with a ravenous fascination. "Where did you acquire those mesmerizing wings, woman?"

"Can you help her?" Saudett pleaded, even as a shiver crawled up her spine.

"No," the man said bluntly. "Do you have a magical aptitude to compliment those wings? I would take you into the fold of the Aerie if it were so."

Saudett was dumbstruck, eyeing the woman behind the man. "I think we have more pressing matters at hand." She looked at the form of the earthwalker, like a hill towering over her, its chest struggling to rise and fall with wheezy moans around the massive shards of ice.

"Don't move, woman. I will cleanse the filth that defiles our Lân. Once that is finished, I will return to you, for you...*intrigue* me." He turned to the armless woman, pulled off one glove, and touched her on the head. "Don't let her leave."

Saudett couldn't help but shudder again at the man's impression, but he floated casually into the air, leaving the armless woman with her leash dangling on the ground. Saudett looked away, back down to Nix's still face. Trickles of blood had dripped down her nose and cheeks. Saudett wiped them away with her hands, "You didn't deserve to die. You never knew love. But at least at the end, you felt the touch of it. Hettra's mercy, it's me who deserves to die." For a long time, Saudett sat holding the dead woman. The sounds of intense magical battle grew distant to her senses. She sat there, wishing it were her instead.

Malix flung the flaming sphere of violet fire at Bjarkeld. To his wonder, Bjarkeld batted it aside, sending it to explode into a mass of fleeing soldiers. *Fucking hells, I just killed those men.* The only thing that seemed to work on the massive earthwalker was his axes. *All for the better. I prefer to get up close.*

Malix flinched his head back as a steaming stream of water jetted past his face. He wheeled and turned to see the earthwalker with the blue-white veiny energy shining from its cracks lumbering toward him. *Where is Saudett?* He glanced at a dark mass of tendrils restraining another of the earthwalkers, strangling it into submission. He dodged another blast of water and simultaneously flew higher out of reach. *Two earthwalkers are preoccupied with me.* He surveyed the scene. Another of the massive beings was hurling rocks at a well-planned line of siege weapons. *These humans are adept at war.* He pondered as he found the last earthwalker; the forests, fields, and soldiers around it were nothing but blackened char. Flames licked out in all directions around it. *That one's power is the worst of the four; I will take it down first.* Malix hesitated as the same flames suddenly washed out from Bjarkeld, him as the epicenter. *No, Bjarkeld is different. He uses all the elements.*

Malix dove back down to the battle and he caught in the corner of his eye three massive spikes of ice drilling into the earthwalker that had been throwing boulders a minute ago. *That must be Nix joining the fray. Formidable.* He ignited his axes, and the blood rage filled him.

Bjarkeld roared up at him, and thick, white, hot cords of fire twisted up from Bjarkeld's outstretched hand. From his other hand, a razor-sharp blast of wind fired up simultaneously.

Wincian. Malix blinked in and out of existence as he fell. The deadly fire and cutting wind struck nothing as his body vanished and reappeared again and again. *Maegen.* Malix manipulated the gravitational force of his body, increasing his mass, and he plummeted from the sky with increased force. He roared in fury and struck with both fuming axes down into Bjarkeld's shoulder; the impact and weight caused his blow to sear deep into Bjarkeld's chest. The flesh split like timber and folded outward.

Malix tore himself loose and dislodged himself from the bleeding mess, covered in the glowing ooze that was earthwalker blood. He caught a glimpse of something shining in the chest cavity he had opened up. It shined like a rainbow. *Is it a gemstone?* Then, the glowing blood went greenish-gold almost instantaneously, and the flesh began to stitch back together.

Can't give him time to heal! Malix surged back and landed on Bjarkeld's chest, close to where he had seen the vibrant gem. He began to hack and slash, like digging for gold in the earthwalker's flesh. Malix became covered in green-yellow ooze and he laughed maniacally in his fury of blows.

Bjarkeld gave a dreadful roar, but his healing was too powerful. For every strike of Malix's axe, the stone skin regrew anew.

Malix kicked off and away as a massive hand swatted where he had been a moment before. Out of the corner of his eye, he saw a man clad in black floating toward the earthwalker with the water element. He casually floated up to it...and then *through* it. A massive spherical cavity gaped in the earthwalker's chest where the man had entered. Malix saw him examining a blue-green gemstone in gloved hands, picking it curiously with a finger.

The earthwalker crumbled into rubble behind him.

"NOOOOO!" Bjarkeld's desperate moan echoed over the course. "To me! We become one!"

The flaming one surged over the charred field around it and charged into Bjarkeld's embrace. Bjarkeld absorbed the other earthwalker and seemed to double in size. He was so large that he reached out and touched the earthwalker pinned under the massive shards of ice. He sucked its essence into himself, leaving nothing but three amber-stained cones of ice where it had been.

Impossible. Malix looked in horror as Bjarkeld began to move toward the last earthwalker. He breathed a sigh of relief. The black, inky tendrils shrunk away from the pile of rubble that was once the earthwalker with the power to control the wind. Another man, hooded and black, moved along stilts of shadow to meet Bjarkeld. He raised his hands, and hundreds of pitch-black tendrils shot out of his hands, wrapped around Bjarkeld's wrist, and held it in place.

"Ah yes, Kuro Raven, my first pupil is an acceptable mage," a voice said with a hint of inconsequence, and Malix turned to see the first man in black floating nearby. This time, the man's voice turned to disgust as he spoke, his eyes bright with white light, "Another wretched Wayfarer? You people are beginning to turn up like rats in *my* Lân."

Chapter Twenty-Seven

REVENGE

She's dead. Anora is dead. Simon was still in shock as he tried to comfort Kiana, even though he felt empty inside. Simon slowly guided Kiana back to *The Mamba's Mouth*, followed by Baal with Anora's body in his arms. Brena was close behind.

Kai was shouting orders to scuttle the Xamidian warship as they didn't have enough hands to apprehend it, and he didn't want it returning to the fight. Simon was barely present in his body as the sailors rushed back and forth, frantically disentangling *The Mamba's Mouth* from the Xamidian ship. At the same time, they fought the flames that had earlier splashed on deck. Even the Vouri warriors were hulling on ropes, cutting grapples, and pouring buckets of water on the fire that had somehow been confined to the rear deck.

"Take them to my cabin." Simon heard Kai say mutely even as he stood before him.

He stared at Kai blankly, and Brena nudged Simon forward and through the door to the captain's cabin. They made Simon sit down, his arm still wrapped around Kiana's shoulder, as Kai went to an armoire and produced a large linen sheet. He spread it out on the bed behind them, and Baal laid Anora on the sheet wordlessly. They then wrapped the body multiple times until the sheet was tight around her. Lastly, they placed Anora's blade atop her.

Baal and Brena quietly left the chamber.

Kiana leaned against Simon and wept.

"Simon," Kai said reservedly. "I need you on deck."

Simon did not answer.

"Simon, please don't leave me. You're the only family I have," Kiana whispered with a tremble in her voice.

"If we spot an enemy sail, I will summon you," Kai stated before turning away, leaving them in solemn silence, broken only by Kiana's stifled sobs.

*Be faithful to her…*Anora's last words kept echoing in Simon's head. Saudett was alone in the enemy's clutches, and Simon was conceitedly bedding a pirate king. *I'm a repulsive fucking bastard.*

Kiana's voice trembled as she spoke, "She saved me. I… I wasn't there for her in the end. Moments before she died, I truly hated her. The last thing I said…" her words trailed off, filled with despair.

Simon snapped back to reality, and his hand found hers. Their grip was a lifeline in the vast ocean of grief. "I know that feeling. You remember, minutes before my father was murdered, I told him to fuck off and leave me be. I know that feeling all too well. I, too, never got to say goodbye. But as I watched my father die, I saw him looking at me with unending pride. *You* were her pride, Kiana. Every strike, every parry, she saw herself in you. And in that final moment, she did not hesitate to exchange her life for yours, for she knew the future was safe in your hands."

"How can I go on?" Kiana's voice was hollow, a shell cast upon the shore of despair. "How do I bear this weight?"

"By continuing to *fight*. Anora bestowed great strength upon you, Kiana. The years of training have brought you this far, and they will keep you going. We need to finish this so we can go home and find peace. Go home to live our lives as we wish." Simon's words were just as much for himself as for Kiana. "Her love will never wane. We carry her in our hearts. We will remember her by living."

"I will fight," Kiana nodded against him, and they sat together, bound by blood not of their own.

As will I, little sister…

Simon was startled awake as Kai slammed the door open. *How long was I out?* Kiana leaned against him, also asleep.

"Simon, he's here!" Kai exclaimed. "Keen Eyes is here."

Kiana stirred awake at the commotion, and Simon stood, helping Kiana to do likewise.

"He flies a flag of parley," Kai continued urgently. "We must go speak with him. Should he choose to sully his honor again, I will need you."

Simon's resolve had returned from his time with Kiana. He nodded. "Very well, I shall protect you. I will protect all of you."

"I'm coming too," Kiana said, hand on the hilt of her sword, then she stopped and turned back to the body her mother wrapped in linen. Kiana put her hand on the hilt of her mother's curved blade. "I will fight with you by my side." She took up the sword and gave it a swing before unsheathing her other and holding both at the ready.

They stepped outside, and a warm breeze hit Simon's face. Dark clouds flashed on the horizon behind a fleet of *hundreds* of ships. The largest of the ships was at the center, ahead of the others. Its sails were of black and violet, a deeper violet than the vessels around it. A white flag flew at half mast above it. Over a dozen of the larger, tri-colored Xamidian warships were scattered throughout the ranks of Keen Eyes' blue-violet vessels.

Simon could see the turrets on the forward decks of the Xamidian vessels. *The flame spitters.* "We don't have a chance against them." He breathed aloud in terrible wonder at the sheer size and might of the enemy fleet. *Did I choose the wrong side of this conflict?* To their left, Keeya's Refuge was burning. The coral stone houses were choked out with smoke, and the stone watchtowers burned like candles in the dimming light of the approaching storm. A handful of *Gilded Crow* ships were sunk or burning in the cove, along with a half dozen enemy vessels they had managed to take with them.

Simon turned to see a dozen more allied ships trickling in, joining a tired formation behind *The Mamba's Mouth*.

"This is all we have?" Simon pondered aloud.

Kai grinned wickedly at him. "But we have *you*, Simon."

"I'm pathetic. I couldn't save Anora against one ship, let alone hundreds."

"And your resulting rage destroyed half a dozen because of it. Flame that fury." Kai hopped beside the hooded cobra figurehead on the rail, peering at the lead enemy ship. "We will speak with old Keen Eyes before we kill him. As the code says. He expects us to surrender, but we will meet his dishonor in kind." Kai gave a signal, and *The Mamba's Mouth* pulled ahead while the rest of his formation held back.

The deep violet of Keen Eye's warship, a formidable sight with its towering masts and billowing sails, also began to move forward. One other Xamidian warship, equally imposing, followed the flagship.

Simon wondered what the name of this behemoth ship was called but knew it would only be displayed on the stern of the vessel. Ever so slowly, they approached until Simon could see the sailors of the massive ship gathered in droves along the railing, brutal pirates through and through. They jeered and hollered at the crew of *The Mamba's Mouth* as the vessels came alongside one another. Rope ladders were thrown down to the smaller vessel, and a voice boomed over the raucous, which immediately silenced all.

"Captain Kai of the Gilded Crows! We extend our invitation to you. Let us meet aboard *Rojas's Revenge* to negotiate under a banner of truce. We have much to discuss, you and I, for the tides, are ever-changing, and so should the alliances amongst those who rule the waves. Let us find common ground over a bottle of rum and a horizon view. Make haste; the storm approaches."

Rojas's Revenge? The shock was palpable in Simon's dumbfounded expression.

"Come down and meet us, ya old bastard!" Kai hollered back.

There was a moment of quiet as both crews shifted uneasily, weapons ready. Then the voice boomed out again, "Very well." Then they heard the thudding of booted feet on the deck above, and a dozen pirates leaped out, swinging on rigging, and landed in the center deck of *The Mamba's Mouth*. A massive, broad-shouldered man grinned wickedly as he stood tall, adorned in regal piracy; he wore a long, weathered coat of deep purple, almost black, with intricate gold embroidery that caught the light with every confident step. The coat's tails flutter like the sails of his ship. Beneath the coat, a vest of supple leather fitted snugly over a billowing white shirt, sleeves rolled up to reveal dark forearms marked by the lines of many battles. Around his waist, a sash of black silk held an array of weapons, from lethal-looking daggers to a hand-axe and a sword. But most of all, his eyes were a study in contrast: one, a deep golden brown, reflective and intense, like the turbulent waters of the abyss; the other, a striking violet, captivating...*keen*.

Yet even as Keen Eyes' aura of command reeked over the deck, Simon could not help but stare in horror at the other man with similar eyes as the old pirate. The same eyes as his daughter. The man dressed in the desert garb of Hasiera, his face covered, his two violet eyes peering through the slit of cloth.

"Father!" Kiana shouted and, ignoring all else, ran to Rojas Ahmadi.

Simon heard Rojas gasped in surprise, even as he tore his face covering down, revealing an aged and greying stubbled face. He moved to meet his daughter in an embrace.

"She's gone. Mother is gone," Kiana curled into her father's arms.

"What? What're you saying?" Rojas demanded, his violet eyes darting through the crowd.

Simon called from the back of the crowd, where he observed the happenings discreetly. "Thirteenth Otsoa, your new friends are responsible for your partner's death. Why do we find you siding with our enemy?"

Rojas's mouth hung open, moving, but only found one word, *"Anora?"*

"Brother?" Old Keen Eyes' throaty cadence rumbled as he tilted his head curiously. "You never told me you had a wife and child. After all these years apart, you would hold secrets from me. Even after I agreed to aid you in your plight against this threat of Skaad? To join an alliance with Xamid on the condition of ridding Tal'tulu of these blood-hungry Gilded Crows. I took you in as my long-lost brother who vanished all those years ago. I returned home with our father to find my poor mother dead there, along with a young woman whom this town is named after. A young woman who was taken from her homeland, from Tal'tulu, to die on Xamidian soil." Old Keen Eyes waved a hand toward Keeya's Refuge in the distance. "You came to me as an emissary of Xamid and your so-called desert country of Hasiera. Yet you have not been wholly honest with me, brother."

"Ravi Ahmadi...my brother," Rojas's voice was near a whisper. "My wife, Anora...who could have done this?"

"The fucks should I know? Any number of my captains would be a fatal adversary to some measly, weak woman. Ha har!" Keen Eye's crew echoed his laughter and hollered insults from the above deck. Ravi motioned for calm, and everything went quiet once again. "The last ship they engaged with was a Xamidian warship; don't blame me. These things happen in war. And for that matter, why was your woman even here?"

"She was *not* a weak woman." Rojas's voice was devoid of warmth, sending a shiver down Simon's spine as its icy tone cut through the air.

"I meant no offense, dear brother," Ravi said with a grin. He then turned to Kai, who stood with teeth grinding, looking ready to spring upon Keen Eyes at any second. "Do you still have the body of my dear brother's spouse?"

Captain Kai nodded, scowling.

"Go, Rojas, see your lover," Ravi ordered. "I will speak with this young upstart."

Rojas did not even glance at Simon as he hurried past, Kiana still clutching her father as they went toward the captain's quarters.

Skrull's balls, he has some explaining to do, though I imagine this elder brother is about to do so in his stead. Simon stayed back among the other sailors and Vouri warriors, trying to look inconspicuous.

With his striking violet eye, Ravi slowly swept his gaze across the deck, taking in the eclectic assortment of individuals gathered on the creaking vessel. "Quite an interesting mix of characters you've assembled on your little ship, Kai Bahari."

"That's *Captain* Kai Bahari," Kai retorted. "Surrender and submit to execution for the betrayal of our pirate alliance; it will be the Gilded Crows who will aid the world in their plight against Hear-fan Skaad."

"Ha har!" Ravi hooted obnoxiously, and his crew followed suit. "You and a handful of ships? We've scuttled nearly two dozen of your squawking crow wrecks on the voyage over. It's time you learned your place, young charlatan. Xamid came to me; The Sultan sent my brother and members of his court to treaty with *me*. I'm sure you remember that my father was Xamidian, and he used to own these seas. Captain Arnav Ahmadi. They called him the Terror of Tal'tulu. He negotiated with Xamid after they murdered my mother and, as I used to think, my little brother." He shrugged as if it mattered little to him. "Lo and behold, he lives."

"Xamid is taking too much from Tal'tulu; they would leave us with nothing," Kai asserted angrily. "They are extinguishing the very life of the sea."

"The fuckin' fish be boundless," Ravi rebuked. "What you say is impossible. The death of a few *sea elephants* matters little when the world is apparently in danger of invasion."

"There are fewer and fewer sightings of the *Erin Okun*. They take years to breed, and there will soon be none left. And it's all for a few barrels of oil?"

"Oil is wealth, little *Captain* Kai. Unimpeded trade with Xamid will be a great boon for Tal'tulu. You only need to stop taking their ships. Turncoat to my colors and serve under me; we need not shed more blood in these seas."

"I will never serve under a half-breed who cares more for Xamid than Tal'tulu."

We find ourselves vastly outnumbered in this place. Simon deliberated. *It is clear that Keen Eyes would be the superior option when facing the impending danger posed by Skaad. It's evident that Kai harbors a deep-seated animosity towards the Xamidians. Is that why he fought with Anora? I'm beginning to question whether I made the right decision in picking his side.*

"My brother, Rojas, treated with the Sultan of Xamid, and he brokered a deal. He is to rid the Isles of Tal'tulu of the pirates who attack Xamidian vessels on sight. Then Xamid will join the battle against the outside threat to our Lân. That, and the generous Sultan will pardon Rojas for his murder of a couple of Xamidian royal guardsmen some two decades ago. The merciful Sultan left it in my brother's hands to determine how to proceed with that daunting task."

There was a shout, and the Xamidian warship that had followed *Rojas's Revenge* was sending a boat with a delegation of Xamidians aboard.

"Chike shaft, we don't be needing more of them on board to discuss this," Kai growled. "We can finish this blade to blade and be done with the parley."

"Of course, we *need* them, Captain Kai. They're the key to this alliance," Ravi said with a friendly gesture to the gathering. "All are welcome to add their voices to the parley of pirates. I see Aurulan and even Vouri heritage here. Speak up, you all."

"Your people attacked us without warning, without even trying to see who we were. You broke your alliance with Captain Kai and the Gilded Crows." Brena stepped forward, Baal shadowing her. "I do not wish to join with someone who would dishonor their agreements and fight only for the reward of pillaging."

"Ah ha, I've heard tell the Vouri people are slightly fanatical with their honor." Ravi chuckled heartily, and then he shrugged. "What can I say to that, warrior? We're bastard buccaneers. We take *what* we want... *when* we want it."

There was a clamor, and a half dozen Xamidians were helped over the side of the ship where their boat had landed. All were exquisitely outfitted in fine jewels and brilliantly colorful turbans to contrast their equally rich saris or knee-length jackets with intricate designs stitched into them. However, there was only one woman among the newcomers.

One of the men stepped forward, his turban black as night with a silver sunburst pinned to it. His clothing was also made of black fabrics and silver embroidery. Clean-shaven, the man's smooth features gave him an air of playful arrogance. Simon couldn't help but find his eyes wandering to the jeweled hilts of two curved daggers at the man's waist.

The man bowed deeply. "My uncle, the compassionate and charitable Sultan of all of Xamid, Jhanda Muzumdar, sends his warmest regards and wishes us to resolve the matters of Tal'tulu wholly and swiftly. I am Prince Arjun Singh Rathore, and I speak on my uncle's behalf regarding said matters."

"You were on that warship we fought. Are you not the one who nearly killed Kiana?" Kai whispered, his hands tightly gripping the hilts of his cutlasses, his rage barely contained. "You leaped over the side like a coward."

"Kiana? Warship? Whatever do you mean?" Prince Arjun's brow creased as he looked about the gatherers with a ponderous gaze.

"The gracious princeling would never leave the safety net of my fleet to engage in battle on his own," Keen Eyes reproached. "Could you imagine if a prince of Xamid were to die in my care? This fickle alliance would be shattered."

"He killed your brother's wife," Kai snapped. "I know it was him. He turned tail and ran when we arrived on the scene."

"Brothers wife?" Arjun scoffed. "Your brother is quite on in years, correct, Ravi Ahmadi? Did he take a much younger wife?"

"Only my blood brother may speak my true name," Ravi snarled, "for you, I am Keen Eyes."

"Of course, Great Captain Keen Eyes," Arjun made another extravagant bow, his hand brushing the deck as he bent. "I admit, I was on that ship, but the poor young lass I gutted was only in her early third decade if I were to judge."

Bastard. He's the one. Simon was readying to lose a *Bael Cnytells* through the prince's forehead.

"Brother!" Ravi's voice boomed over the course. The winds had begun to pick up, and the darkness of the storm was closing in. "We have found your wife's killer!"

The door to the captain's quarters kicked open with a slam, and Rojas and Kiana rushed out with weapons at the ready.

"You!" Kiana shouted; her sword and late mother's both wielded in expectation.

Arjun blinked and tilted his head. "I'm quite sure I did kill you. How is this possible?"

"You murdered my spouse; you must now face the consequences." Rojas's violet eyes seemed to flare to life as he pointed a spiked morning star in one hand at the prince.

"Now, don't be hasty, dear brother," Ravi interrupted. "Should Arjun die, the alliance will be torn asunder, don't ya know. All that hard work will be gone like a school of mackerel startled by a pod of jumpers."

Rojas did not hesitate. "I care not. My love—my poor Anora is dead..." Rojas suddenly leaped forward to bring his mace down on Anjun's head.

Daggers appeared in the prince's hands, and he crouched low, poised to strike.

Kiana began to move forward.

Suddenly, everything became sluggish, like time had slowed to a crawl, and Simon knew all hell was about to break loose. *It will be a bloodbath for both sides, and nothing will be accomplished.* Even as this thought came to him and he watched as Rojas slowed down mid-air, he saw Captain Keen Eyes moving unimpaired, even as everyone else looked to move through thick molasses. Then time sped up, and Ravi caught the shaft of Rojas's mace in one hand, wrenched it from his brother's grasp, and flung it away; rattling across the deck.

"My Brother, please." Rojas grasped Ravi by the coat. "He *must* die for what he has done!"

"No,' Ravi said, his voice elevating as he repeated the word. "No, no, no! Enough of this fuckin' bickering. I grow tired of it, and there is only one way to resolve our matters most swiftly. The *pirate* way." He turned to Kai, who had unsheathed both cutlasses when Rojas had leaped to action. "Ah, I see. You bore arms against me foremost; therefore, our discussion is forfeit. *Time to die.*"

Everything slowed around Simon again, and he watched in horror as Ravi Ahmadi strode up and behind Kai.

The Captain of the Gilded Crows had his mouth wide with a battle cry and his curved cutlasses brandished to rush to the spot where Keen Eyes had been standing.

Simon, frozen in place, could do nothing but watch as Old Keen Eyes stabbed Kai in the back.

Chapter Twenty-Eight

SHADOWSTONE

Hata, sister of Kulta, broke through the barrier into a thickly shadowed dome. Azure blue fires burned below, giving off an eerie musk. To her horror, Keep Crystalia was partially engulfed in the navy clouds of the magic dome. The dark movement of the *Children of Skaad* roiled in the city streets of Aerion below the fortress, which floated higher above. Odd cylindrical black iron tubes shot arcing blue-flamed projectiles up at the keep's walls. Massive siege towers had been pushed up to the lip of the upper island, tall enough to reach the platform that led to the main gates of the fortress. *Children* flung themselves by the hundreds against the massive barred metal of the gates. All the floating islands around the city were crawling with the enemy horde—like masses of black ants.

I pray the city's people evacuated before the barrier swallowed them. Hata thought as she heard the screaming wings of the Himin-dvergar aircraft breech through the hole in the barrier behind her. She looked back to see the sizeable hole beginning to shrink. The light from Ziraelthir's beam dimmed on the other side. As the last rotor-wing broke through, a half dozen dragon riders trickled after them.

A Ruby Flameheart made it through.

The inky smoke narrowed.

Then, a second dragon, an Obsidian Nightwing.

The light through the hole was barely a pinprick to Hata's distant vision.

A third and fourth made it in time.

Then, the way was shut. The last of the six dragons disappeared and did not emerge. Second to last was an Emerald Eyewing. It was caught by the tail just as it cleared the shadowy smoke. It halted abruptly, shrieked in pain, and flailed wildly. It slowly sank back into the shadows of the barrier as violet lightning crawled across the mist to converge on the trapped dragon.

The Flameheart immediately circled about and roared its sweltering breath weapon directly at the blue-black darkness where it held the Emerald Eyewing. Crimson-yellow flames penetrated the shadows, and the smoke retreated.

The Emerald screamed a cry of thanks to its kin, and, almost as if limping in the air, it lumbered up to join the formation of dragons and rotor-wings circling the vast armies of Skaad below.

"What do we do now?" Hata wondered aloud.

Look there, little stone. Kulta reared his head in the direction opposite Keep Crystalia. A violet light emanated eerily from one of the islands in the distance. Waves of power pulsated out from the light, each pulsation strengthening and stretching the reach of the navy-black cloud of magic.

"It's him, Hear-fan Skaad," Hata breathed aloud, and fear twisted in her guts.

Then Raine's rotor-wing flew close beside Hata and Kulta, and the Queen pointed at the violet glow.

Hata nodded, the fear lessening at Raine's nearby presence. "Kulta. Tell the other dragons to thin the horde. You and I will fight him together, my brother."

Kulta released a mighty roar, and Hata listened as the five other dragons echoed their battle cry. As one, they descended, each dragon taking their place over the *Children of Skaad,* unleashing their fierce power.

The fire of the Ruby Flameheart burned a line of blackened flesh and charred earth as it spewed death through the screaming horde below. It focused on the enemies at the gates of Keep Crystalia, and Hata hoped it would be enough to save those still within. An Opaline Frost Drake breathed a hoarfrost mist that froze the abominations of Skaad into statues of ice. The black fire of the Obsidian Nightwing corroded flesh with an unquenchable desire. The Emerald Eyewing swooped over an island churning with *Children,* and emerald dust drifted down upon them. As the dust touched the earth at their feet, barbed plants and roots sprung up and entangled the creatures, sawing into flesh until their bones snapped under the force of the constricted holds.

Lastly, a second Amberheart drake, like Kulta, plummeted into another island, teaming with the enemy. It was the large one that Hata had first met when she had come to *Valon Vuori*. The Amberheart vanished into the earth as if diving into a lake of water, its jaws and claws biting, locking, and pulling one of the enormous insectoid creatures with blue flames into the ground. The Amberheart was triple the size of the burning beast. Hata saw the entire island begin to shake and then it shattered into a million pieces. The torn corpse of the blue-burning insectoid was broken as if it were a part of the earth when it shattered. Stone-like chunks of bleeding flesh rained down. The horde atop the island itself shrieked and wailed as they plummeted out of sight into the navy smoke of Hear-fan Skaad's spherical barrier.

Hata focused on the violet light ahead. "By Teras's Mountain! We'll take him together, my brother! It's time to end this!" They approached swiftly, aiming directly for the light, but Hata saw *him* sitting cross-legged as they closed the distance, floating a few feet off the ground. His snow-white robes hung about him, and his blue-grey skin glistened with sweat. His white hair flowed back over his head and was tied into a tail. In Hear-fan Skaad's grasped before him was the obsidian amulet hovering between his lower hands. The magic pulsed in waves from the dark stone. His eyes were closed, and his upper two hands were held with his fingers in an odd pattern.

None of his *Children* were around him. There was only *him* and the remains of a military camp, with scattered canvas and poles strewn about.

"Somethings not right," Hata hesitated. "He's goading us."

Then he's a fool to underestimate dragons and their kin! Kulta roared in her head even as he roared a bestial cry aloud. Molten rock disgorged from Kulta's gullet and melted through the ground in a track before it engulfed Hear-fan Skaad. Kulta swooped low overhead of the spot where the man had been.

Hata had to crane her neck to look back.

The lava hissed and popped around Hear-fan Skaad, but it did not *reach* him. His violet barrier shimmered around him, and his black inverted eyes were now open, reflecting the chaos around him. He smiled wickedly as he casually pointed a finger of one upper hand at them, his long, lean, pale finger contrasting with the dark energy of his barrier.

"Watch out! Kult—"

The violet string of fire tore through Kulta's wing. He bellowed in pain, and his flight began to career downward in an uncontrolled spin as fuming smoke billowed from the burning wound.

Hata willed Kulta to release her from her bind to his back, fearing he would crush her in the fall. He did so, and Hata leaped from his back just as the dragon's bulk collided with the earth. But instead of crashing against it, it was more like a splash as Kulta vanished underground.

"So, there *are* dragons in this Lân, and they have the same ability as the earthwalkers of Fjoer. I'm surprised that the Iban'mael surveillance was accurate. I should have subjugated this world centuries ago. They would have been my most potent *Children*. Don't you think so, Hata Vasara? Or should I call you...The Sunstone?"

Hata wheeled about to face Hear-fan Skaad, who floated slowly toward her, his legs still crossed as if easing into a warm meal. "We will never surrender the Ryk Lân or the Earste Lân! We will triumph over you!" Hata slowly descended to the ground, the *earth* reassuring under her feet.

"Ha! The Earste Lân burns as we speak. That's the problem with you horrifically hasty humans: even if by some miracle you manage to cause my retreat, it will only take a few years for me to regather my forces and reinforce them with new magics and technology that I have attained from the egotistical Iban'mael. I will do this *incessantly*. Forever. Time and time again, I will return; long after you have died of old age, I will return."

"I won't let you run. This ends now, Hear-fan Skaad." Hata slammed her hands to the ground, and a massive wave of jagged, sharp stones rumbled into existence before her, rolling toward the Lord of Shadow.

Hear-fan Skaad clapped his upper two hands together in front of him, sending a shockwave of sound slicing through Hata's rockslide as if it were made of water. The powerful spell surged directly at her.

She stomped her foot, and a pillar of earth launched her diagonally into the air.

Two strings of violet fire scorched through the air after her.

Hata took hold of the metals in her armor and painfully jerked herself in the opposite direction, narrowly avoiding the flames that could penetrate any material. Then she pushed herself down, back to the earth. *I need to stay in touch with the ground. I have nothing to fight him with when I'm in the air.* As soon as she landed, two violet-tinged blades of wind converged on her in a crossing pattern. *I can't evade this!* Just then, something yanked her below the earth, and Hata was taken aback to see the shadowy figure of Kulta maneuvering through the gray underworld.

Together, little stone. Kulta swam away like a great sea serpent and out of Hata's vision.

Hata looked up to see if she could figure out where Hear-fan Skaad was. It wasn't him she could see; instead, it was the obsidian gemstone in his hands; his form flashed white every time the magic pulsed from the gemstone. *There you are.* Hata used the same tactic she had used against Kulta; she circled, quickly picking up speed while gathering hardened gemstones and minerals around her fist. Her vambraces were still shaped into long blades extending out over her hands. She edged the blade in gemstone dust and encrusted her fist in a concoction of minerals. Then she released that pent-up power and burst out of the earth directly below Hear-fan Skaad. As she surged upward, it felt as if time slowed. She caught his eye as he slid sideways, her gem-coated blade grazing his cheek, a thin line of dark blood oozing out.

He smirked cruelly at her, then blinked out of existence. He appeared ten feet away and laughed contemptuously. "Fool! Where else would an earthwalker strike from but below—"

Kulta's jaws snapped closed on him from behind. *Entirely.*

"You got him!" Hata cried in surprise.

No, little stone. Kulta's voice was strained within her head.

Hata saw Kulta's maw slowly open, inch by inch, as Hear-fan Skaad pushed with his upper hands and feet.

This is your chance, little stone; strike him down while I have him!

But I'll hurt you. Hata answered with concern.

Quickly, little—

Violet fumes suddenly gushed from Hear-fan Skaad's hands into Kulta's mouth. They corroded away teeth, tongue, and flesh as Kulta convulsed, releasing his hold and slamming his head down on the earth.

Kulta rolled away, spasming and shrieking in deformed draconic cries of agony.

"KULTA!" Hata shouted in despair and flew toward him.

Hear-fan Skaad blinked into existence before her, and one of his fists *slammed* into her. She just managed to catch the blow with the flat of one bladed hand.

The blade snapped.

Hata swung with her other hand, aiming to take his head.

Hear-fan Skaad casually batted the attack aside, which caused Hata's arm to slap painfully behind her. He struck again with blinding speed directly into her breastplate, where the amber gemstone sat. There was a resounding *crack* and lines splintered through the gemstone even as Hata shot through the air away from Hear-fan Skaad. She bounced not once, not twice, but three times before coming to a skidding stop, her entire body reverberating with pain. Her vision blurred. The blood tasted of copper in her mouth. Her connection to the earth felt...*weakened*. She turned her head to vaguely make out the form of Kulta in a frenzy as he rolled over the island's edge and vanished.

Hear-fan Skaad's ornate, white-shoed feet came into view; no longer floating along cross-legged, he walked like any other man.

That's right. He's just a man.

"Is that it?" His melodious voice was disappointed. "Is this all the mighty Sunstone has to offer?"

With a surge of energy, Hata gathered all her strength and pushed herself to stand. Focusing her mind, she commanded the earth to rise and ensnare Hear-fan Skaad's legs, but his violet personal barrier glimmered and held firm against the advancing soil and rocks.

Hear-fan Skaad continued to walk casually toward her, uninterested in her attempts to halt him as he sneered disgustedly. Occasionally, his eyes darted down to the dark gemstone in his lower two hands, and his jaw would set. Then, a pulse of magic would wave out of it through Hata and toward the dark navy smoke of the enormous barrier.

He is preoccupied with maintaining the sphere. Hata thought as she launched away from him with a column of earth below her feet. She slowed her fall as she touched the ground a few dozen paces away. Then, she called upon an old method, manipulating tiny spinning spheres of the earth. She carefully selected the hardest materials available - specks of iron, copper, hematite, peridot, jade, and emerald. Skillfully crushing the minerals together, she watched as the tiniest marbles took shape. With a flick of her wrist, she set them into a rapid rotation, swiftly superheating and melting them into scorching projectiles. In a swift motion, she unleashed them in his direction.

The Lord of Shadow scoffed in contempt as he continued strolling forward. The projectiles began to pelt against his magical barrier—one after another.

Hata moved about as she continued to create the hardened marbles and attack the shield.

His steps slowed.

The barrier hissed and crackled as the first jagged fissure of bright white light crawled across his defenses. *Snap. Hisst.* A second line snaked out from an impact. Then, a third.

"Enough!" he bellowed, saliva dripping from his lips as the rage overtook him. He shot into the air as a hundred more hardened marbles zipped past below.

Hata continued firing even as Hear-fan Skaad soared skyward; she skated about using the earth to drive her feet as she slipped and slid across the ravaged island. She would not give in, but it was becoming difficult to keep up her barrage. She glanced down to see her amber gemstone dimming as magical energy seemed to seep through its cracked surface and dissipate.

Suddenly, a violet-burning meteor brightened the sky where Hear-fan had stopped mid-air; it was nearly as large as the island they fought upon. It fell toward her unhurriedly, but it was so massive that it would swallow her and most of the island with it.

She touched the gemstone with one hand and launched herself diagonally away, using a thick column of earth to propel her. Then she pushed herself as fast as possible, gripping her armor with her mind. The heat washed over her as the meteor approached. The armor on her back began to heat, and she screamed in pain as it touched her skin.

The searing fireball tore through the earth and ravaged the floating island, devouring everything in its path before plunging into the abyss below. Miraculously, a third of the island remained, now bearing a precarious semi-circular shape that seemed on the verge of collapse.

Hata collided with the ground and slid, her face taking the brunt of the impact as she skidded to a rest. She screamed and squirmed as her metal armor still burned to the touch. She scrambled to her feet and forced the metal away from her body, leaving only the cracked and faint amber gemstone in her hand. Her under-armor garments had charred marks, sizzling holes burned through them, and painful red-white blisters pocked the skin beneath.

Hata fell to her knees with exhaustion, her magic nearly spent.

Hear-fan Skaad touched down gently before her, smiling with a triumphant impression added to his stride.

He's too strong. The *sunstone* in her hand pulsed feebly. Hata tried to reach out and feel for any other magical gemstones she might use around her. Malachite perhaps to heal her? Diamond to strengthen her? She felt only one other gemstone nearby. *Obsidian.* It was still clutched between Hear-fan Skaad's lower two hands. The silver metalwork of the amulet that housed it contrasted brightly with the deep blackness of the stone. It truthfully was a *shadowstone.*

"I expected more, to be honest. You're nothing more than an irritating insect, just as all you humans are. It's a wonder your species is the most similar to the Iban'mael, as you are practically primates. Even the apes of the Wald Lân are more formidable foes after I have enhanced their bone structures. You humans are at least a step above these Rykling dwarves. Inferior little things. What do they call themselves?"

"The Himin-dvergar...and we will *never* be enslaved." Raine's flaming sword hacked into Hear-fan Skaad's side, lopping off one of his lower arms.

The Lord of Shadow shrieked, and black blood squirted from his stump.

Hata immediately reached for the *shadowstone* with her mind, taking hold of it and the metalwork around it, and yanked it from his grasp.

"NO!" Hear-fan screamed furiously as it slipped from his fingers.

Hata caught it in her free hand, *sunstone* in one, shadow in the other. She willed the *shadowstone* to connect with her. At first, it resisted as if it had a mind of its own, but then the connection *seeped* into her like creeping darkness. It was sickening and, at the same time...*remarkable*. Hata's gaze dropped to witness the creeping darkness snaking through the veins of her hands, slithering up her arms and encroaching upon her neck. She could feel the blackness seeping into her eyes, consuming them entirely. Hata knew then that she now controlled the massive sphere that Hear-fan Skaad had conjured around them. Hata dispelled the darkness with a wave of her hand, and the swirling smoke and crackling violet lightning vanished into thin air, revealing a stunning sunset. In the backdrop, a thousand rotor-wings and hundreds of massive airships stood silhouetted, led by a single majestic sapphire dragon.

Hata heard the outcry from the *Children of Skaad* on the surrounding islands as the amber sunlight began to burn their flesh.

"Give it to me!" Hear-fan spun, and his backhand swing collided with the flat of Raine's sword as she tried to stop the blow. The strike powered through and crushed her guard, sending her flying, tumbling through the air to land with a stomach-turning *thud* two dozen feet away.

"Don't touch her, you bastard!" Hata tried to step toward Hear-fan Skaad, but the darkness thickened her vision. She couldn't control her arms or legs.

Hear-fan Skaad wheeled on her, and his three hands found the obsidian gemstone in her two. As his fingers touched it, some of the darkness abated. His face grimaced with malicious hatred as he stared hungrily into the darkness of the stone.

He could've just killed me instead of trying to take the stone. Hata mused as she felt her sense of self returning to her.

A different voice drifted through her mind—a warm voice.

Destroy it. It is not of me.

Hata Vasara did not think twice as she poured the last of her power from the sunstone into the shadowstone. As the energy surged through the obsidian, fissures of vibrant amber light rippled across its surface, starting as tiny fractures and then expanding into larger, more drastic crevices.

Hear-fan Skaad's eyes widened in astonished realization. "No... What are you doing!?" He painstakingly pulled a hand away from the gemstone as waves of violet and amber magic pulsed from it outward. Inch by inch, he pointed two fingers directly at Hata's forehead.

Hata emptied *all* of herself into the stone.

Hear-fan Skaad let loose the violet string of fire...just as Raine's hands wrapped around his outstretched arm and pulled it down away from Hata and into her own chest.

The *shadowstone* collapsed. Then, both *shadowstone* and *sunstone*...detonated.

Chapter Twenty-Nine

Heart

Malix had lived for a century among the earthwalkers in the Fjoer Lân and had never seen any display such power as Bjarkeld did now. *It's that stone in his chest. Where did he get it?* Even as he thought this, he dodged away from a broad torrent of pressured water emitting from Bjarkeld's massive open maw.

Bjarkeld's rocky, cracked skin glowed blueish-green as the geyser gushed past Malix.

Malix narrowly avoided it and stretched out his hand. *Scua Liegetu.* Violet lightning arced from his fingertips into the water flow and surged up it to detonate into Bjarkeld's open orifice. It hissed and smoked as chunks of the earthwalkers stone flesh erupted from his face. Bjarkeld wailed unnervingly in pain, and his glow changed to green-yellow, and the flesh instantly began to heal.

"Fuck me," Malix breathed, soaring higher away from the battle. "I can't get through his healing."

"Perhaps you should let those of this Lân be the ones to defend it." Malix turned to see the robed man in black. He held out a hand, and the other man, hooded and cowled in black leather, his facial features hidden, stood in the air on an invisible platform.

"Hells," Malix grunted with a shrug as he scratched at his beard. "Be my guest."

"I am Ebras Corb, the Alpha Passeriform of the Council of the Aerie. As is The Beta, Kuro Raven. You Wayfarers, you, *Iban'mael.* You will come to respect and dread the power of humanity." The Alpha raised his hand, which had been held out to Kuro Raven, and pushed it toward Bjarkeld, who had just finished healing his facial wounds. The Alpha flung Kuro Raven directly at the earthwalker.

Kuro dove toward Bjarkeld as a dozen tendrils of darkness shot out of his hands before him; like honed spears, they pierced into Bjarkeld.

The earthwalker screamed.

Poor thing.

Kuro used the hardened shadows to move himself, shooting one after another of the spears, pin cushioning Bjarkeld from all sides. Kuro Raven seemed unable to fly, but he used his power to push himself off the ground or wrap the inky ropes around tree branches or the bulk and limbs of his enemy to pull himself and swing through the air.

Malix watched as the Alpha joined the Beta. Kuro's shadow tendrils fastened Bjarkeld in place, and the earthwalker roared as Ebras Corb approached his massive head. Ebras raised one hand, and suddenly, a *chunk* of Bjarkeld's head was gone. Something had punched through the earthwalkers face in a circular shape.

Again, Bjarkeld wailed in pain but then began to glow with crimson fury. Abruptly, like the volcanoes of the Fjoer Lân from which he came, Bjarkeld erupted. Molten earth burst from the cracks in his stone skin, melting away the tendrils of shadow and overflowing in a wave up toward the two human magi.

Kuro flung his hands back, and shadows reached for some trees not far away. He pulled himself through the air as the lava splashed and singed around him.

Ebras Corb did not move as the wave of melted rock swallowed him, but a few seconds later, he stood in the air, unphased. He raised his hand again in retaliation, and another spherical mass punctured into Bjarkeld's shoulder and out the other side.

Bjarkeld groaned eerily and glowed green-yellow, beginning to heal once more.

The Alpha hovered close, unleashing strike after strike of invisible energy into the earthwalker, shredding him.

Malix couldn't help but feel sorry for Bjarkeld as he watched the earthwalker bleed and wail in pain. *He's just another pawn of my father who had the misfortune of meeting these Earste Lân magi.*

Yet still, Bjarkeld's healing kept him standing; this time, he maintained that healing glow as a different color came to his massive hands raised over his head. It was green-blue. Dark clouds thundered into existence above them, spinning rapidly. The wind picked up and buffeted Malix, where he stood mid-air. Those enormous black whirling clouds began to twist toward the ground where the Alpha hovered.

Malix retreated, the wind threatening to pull him in. He glimpsed Ebras Corb as the man also tried to flee but was sucked into the cyclone. The storm raged as lightning flashed through the gale, and Malix could do *nothing*.

Saudett stared down at the motionless face of Nix Swan in her arms. *She's dead. It's my fault; I brought these things here chasing after me.* The sounds of battle raged about her and she felt the vibrations of the fight through the ground beneath her. She heard a faint babbling mutter and looked up to see the armless woman staring with her bandaged-wrapped.

"Leave me be!" Saudett shouted. "Go away."

"Ha..." the woman's words were slurred as if she struggled to say anything.

"You laugh at this woman's death? At me? Of course you do. I'm pathetic. All I do is hurt those around me...Simon, Marah, Nyxal, and now Nix. And Hata, poor Hat—

"Hata..." the armless woman moaned, and she twitched toward Saudett.

Saudett stood abruptly, Nix's body still in her arms. "Do you know Hata?"

At that moment, a wall of lava poured through the trees around them, burning and consuming the trunks, stones, and growth—everything in its path.

Saudett pumped her wings and struggled with the added weight of Nix. She looked back to see a spinning gust of wind at the armless woman's feet, thrusting her into the air. The woman soon overtook Saudett as they ascended.

A ghastly roar echoed through the air, and Saudett turned to see the massive earth-walker raising its hands aloft. Storm clouds twisted and thundered, lightning flashing in their midst. The wind took hold of Saudett and began pulling, pushing, and tossing her about. She strained to keep her hold on Nix as they tumbled through the darkened skies.

Suddenly, the wind stilled around her, and the armless woman was beside her. A sphere of green-tinged wind repelled the storm around all three women.

"Thank you!' Saudett called as the weight of Nix burned in her arms and the muscles of her wings. "I need to take her away from here!"

The armless woman cricked her head and moaned, "Ha-ta...she lives?"

Saudett nodded. "Yes."

The woman's voice was hoarse, nearly a whisper, but she seemed to find more words as she spoke, "My—my mind is gone. But *her* name pierced through like a light. I can't remember anything else."

"Please help me," Saudett pleaded. Nix began slipping from her hands. "I can't hold her."

"You should leave her and flee." The woman's voice strengthened as her words became almost regal. "The Alpha is a vile man and has taken an interest in you. Get as far from here as possible."

"I can't leave my companions." *Malix and Marah are here somewhere. I need to find Simon and my mother. Simon is working with these council members, and I should, too.* "I must fight. I must save Hata."

"So be it. But I warned you." The armless woman let out a horrifying scream and flew through the air directly at the revolving black clouds.

The wind immediately picked up as the woman left the vicinity of Saudett, and she was forced to descend. In the high winds, she found an old oak clinging to the earth. She knelt at its trunk and held on to the sturdy tree with one arm while, with the other, she held Nix's lulling corpse to her chest.

Malix watched in awe as a bandage-wrapped, armless woman appeared from nowhere, unphased by the wind as she streaked through the air and plummeted into the roiling tempest. He caught flashes of greenish light through the spinning clouds, and suddenly, the tail of the tornado was moving, twisting up like a snake rearing its head. It surged forward and *drilled* into Bjarkeld's chest.

The earthwalker wailed as the cutting wind continued to burrow deeper into him. His glowing returned to healing colors but struggled to keep up with the massive slicing and tunneling wind storm.

This is my chance! Malix dived, axes blazing with violet fire.

The Alpha appeared, his slicked-back hair disheveled and his black robes stained with wet soil. The white light in his eyes burned furiously as he reached out his hands, grasped the air before him, and *yanked*.

One of Bjarkeld's arms tore from its socket, glowing green-yellow blood spraying from his gaping shoulder.

The Beta, Kuro Raven, was suddenly above the earthwalker, and inky tendrils wrapped around Bjarkeld's neck, who shrieked and tried to claw at the black restraints with his other hand as they tightened around him.

Malix collided with Bjarkeld's chest, axes first, where he had seen the rainbow gemstone, just feet away from where the tunnel of wind spewed glowing blood in all directions. It splattered across Malix's face as he used one axe to hook into Bjarkeld's rocky flesh to steady himself. He hacked, chopped, and tore into the earthwalker with the other. The fuming *Scua byrnsweord*, the violet fire of his axe melted away stone and flesh alike. Then he saw the opaline gemstone thrumming with dancing colors of light.

"Blood of Skaad! You are no *guardian!* You betray all of Fjoer." Bjarkeld roared, and the gemstone flashed; a bolt of lightning spat out and struck Malix, stunning and biting into his shoulder.

Malix shook off the stun and ignored the pain as he stretched his fingers toward the gemstone with one of his free hands. It changed to ruby red, and fire spewed out into Malix's open palm and around his arm, charring his flesh. The agony ripped through him, but he ground his teeth and *reached* through it.

A shield of ice formed over the gemstone, halting Malix's efforts.

"*Strangung!*" Malix bellowed as he pulled back his fist and struck the ice, shattering through it. His fingers found the opal. He wrenched it free, the stone pulsing like a heart in his hand.

"Betrayer!" Bjarkeld let out one last desperate wail as his power of healing left him, and his wounds overcame him before he unceremoniously crumbled into rubble and dust.

Malix floated away, ashamed at the death of such a mighty patron of the Fjoer Lân. A place Malix had called home. A place where the same earthwalkers had named him Guardian. "I'm sorry, Bjarkeld, walker of the earth. You didn't deserve to die in the service of my father. I swear, one day, I will free your Lân from his hold."

The wind subsided, and the sound of battle quieted. Saudett sat, her wings wrapped around her and Nix Swan protectively.

"You survived, and you didn't flee; I'm surprised. Indeed, this is excellent." The man in soiled black robes strode over, pulled a glove from his hand, and touched Saudett on the temple of her head. "I have plans for you."

White light bloomed and engulfed her vision as her memories rushed from her head and into *his*.

CHAPTER THIRTY

UNCLE

SKRULL'S HELL BROKE LOOSE on the deck of *The Mamba's Mouth*. Time returned to normal, and Captain Kai fell to the floor as Keen Eyes pulled the bloody dagger from his back.

"No!" Simon cried out as a battle cry drowned out his voice, as hundreds of Keen Eyes pirates poured from the massive *Rojas's Revenge* onto the deck of *The Mamba's Mouth*. The battle erupted simultaneously with the coming of the storm. Rain and wind rocked the ships and their crews even as men and women killed one another.

The Gilded Crow Corsairs converged to their captain's aid, fighting tooth and nail to reach Kai, who lay, bleeding on the deck.

Kiana flung herself at Prince Arjun, dual curved blades humming about her.

Baal and Brena faced off with the formidable men and women who had first come on board with Keen Eyes—presumably his officers.

Rojas vanished from Simon's sight as he looked for his discarded morning star.

"This is a lost cause," a voice said next to Simon as a hand fell on his shoulder.

Simon turned to see Cygne Caladrius.

"Should we not aid the Keen Eyes pirates? They have the backing of Xamid. Perhaps you chose the wrong side of this conflict. The Gilded Crows are broken."

"I know! Fucking hells, I know!" Simon cried. "But I can't simply leave them to die. I can't leave Kai. Can you save him?"

"Possibly, but you must deal with Old Keen Eyes. His magic is powerful. Did you see him move with such blinding speed? He is dangerous."

"Leave him to me. Get to Kai. Don't let him die this time." *Lind. Afléotan. Strangung.* Simon incanted the spells within and leaped from the deck, over the heads of the fighting, toward Captain Keen Eyes. Toward Ravi Ahmadi. The wind from the storm immediately blew him off course. He crashed into the center mast of the ship, and his *Lind* barrier reverberated with the shock. *I can't fly in this wind.* Simon released *Afléotan* and internally incanted a different spell. *Maegen.* He increased his weight to give him a sure footing as he hurried to find Ravi. He ignored all else, the rage building and burning in his neck. *Kai is a good man. I chose the right side.* Weapons dashed against his barrier as he hurried through the turmoil, and he ignored them. The fighting raged about him, but he could only see Keen Eyes standing tall and proudly grinning over Kai's body.

Simon began to run. He pushed through a group of pirates murdering one another, and they bounced off his *Lind* shield. He shouted incoherently as he broke through and had a clear shot at Keen Eyes. He raised his hand, pointing two fingers. *Bael cnytells.*

Ravi Ahmadi turned toward Simon as the strings of white flame shot out at him. He cocked his head, and at the last second, right before the fire struck, time slowed.

Simon followed Ravi with his eyes as he sidestepped, then walked casually up to Simon, the rain floating in bubbles around him or soaking into his deep violet coat as he walked through them. Ravi tested his dagger on the *Lind.* It sparked a golden light, and he quickly pulled the blade away. Time returned to normal, and the rain gushed like a wave. It had built up in a torrent around them for that split second. "Who are you? Ravi asked inquisitively. "My brother told me that the leader of his desert tribe was a powerful mage. Be you he?"

"It doesn't matter. You will die, and Kai will unite the Isles."

Ravi shrugged and waved his dagger at Kai's body. "My knife says otherwise."

"Fucking bastard!" Simon shouted and flung his hands at Ravi. *Windan.* Two blades of razor-sharp air hissed out...and then *slowed.*

Again, Ravi stepped aside. He sheathed his dagger this time and took a brutal-looking hand axe from his belt. He proceeded to slam it into Simon's barrier.

The *Lind* shield flickered and crackled around him.

Ravi attacked repeatedly as Simon looked on, his mind following what was happening, but his body was frozen in slumber. Those around them, along with the rain, were also slowed to a crawl, and then Simon glimpsed Kiana a few dozen feet away, whirling and dancing, locked in heart-pounding combat with the man Arjun. Simon craned his eyes upward. A dome was formed where the rain slowed above them.

His power is limited. I need to get outside his range.

A crack snaked through Simon's barrier as time resumed with a downpour of water splashing across the deck.

"How bothersome," Ravi pondered, absently picking at a nick in the blade of his axe. "If this threat to our Lân is so significant, losing one with your powers in the coming battle against it would be a shame. I have thousands of men to throw at the enemies of our Lân. Xamid has offered me a significant sum of coin, along with our trade agreements, in exchange for joining the fight and disposing of the Gilded Crows. What does young Kai bring to the table? A few damaged vessels and their remaining crews? Has he omitted the fact that most of his ships and their crews have already chosen to align with my cause?"

Simon didn't want to believe a word out of Ravi's mouth, even if those words made sense. *If I keep him talking, perhaps I can distract him.* "I can't believe I'm saying this, but you make a good point. Still, from what I have seen, Kai is a good man, and his people love him. I don't think you are being truthful about his crew deserting. He wants what's best for Tal'tulu, and Xamid has abused their power."

"He's a reckless *boy*. His plundering of Xamid ships harms Tal'tulu more than it helps. He's an ardent supporter of Chike, a fanatic, and is enamored with the sea creatures. Saving sea elephants from hunters means a loss of wealth for the people of Tal'tulu."

"He respects the traditions of his people, unlike you." Simon circled the pirate cautiously. *I can't make distance by flying away in this wind.*

"Ha ha!" Keen Eyes hooted. "My father was Xamidian, and he believed in amassing as much gold as possible. I'm carrying on his legacy."

"Your gold means nothing if the world is lost to shadow." Simon found his back to the ship rail.

"More superstitions," Ravi snorted. "I only agreed to the alliance to rid Tal'tulu of Kai and his crows. Then I will be the sole king of the Isles."

"We do not lie," Simon answered gravely. "The next time Hear-fan Skaad comes to our Lân, it will be to destroy it."

Ravi shrugged indifferently. "I don't give a damn about Hear-fan whoever the fuck."

Suddenly, a massive wave crashed into the ship, threatening to capsize it. The crews were caught off guard and slid to one side, some losing their grip and disappearing into the dark, churning sea. The two ships, once bound together, now bobbed in the ocean like two apples in a bucket, desperately clinging to each other. The true storm had arrived, and they were no longer on its edge.

Simon's *Strangung* and *Maegen* spells kept him on his feet as he grasped the railing, and water washed over him. His *Lind* barrier deflected most of it, but water still rushed through the cracks that had formed. It splashed in his face and eyes, causing him to cough and splutter. Finally, he got his bearings and looked to Keen Eyes just as time slowed…again. Simon's mind took it all in; the bubble of time that had before been a few dozen feet in circumference now engulfed the entirety of both ships. *Gods, he was holding back before.* The sea splashed up against the barrier of time, and waves of roiling water froze in place. Lightning cracked toward the mast of the ships and slowed to a crawl as they penetrated the sphere.

Simon saw Cygne crouched beside Kai, holding him as the older man clung to some rigging after the ship had rocked perilously. A dim red light was glowing on Kai's back.

Keen Eyes approached Simon but seemed almost to follow Simon's train of thought. He tilted his head and then turned to look at Cygne and Kai. He rolled his shoulders, axe in one hand; he unsheathed a jewel-hilted sword in his other and strode toward the two men.

Simon could do nothing but watch in horror.

Her movements were fluid and precise; Kiana danced with her twin blades, always mindful not to give the man who had killed her an opening. He was swift, but she was swifter. With her mother's blade and her own, she weaved a deadly dance. The rain, a mere backdrop to her grace, splattered in lines along her blades as they sliced through the air. Kiana became the storm, a whirlwind of cutting edges.

The man, Arjun, darted in with his double-daggers, but her longer weapons reached out, threatening to remove his hands if he came in too close. He leaped back as one of her blades grazed his arm.

This time, I won't let him get close.

But as Arjun hopped away gracefully, he sheathed one dagger. "I don't usually have to use this. But since I already killed you once, I'll do you the honor of not holding back." With a flourish, he pulled his longer sword from a wide scabbard. It was wide because the razor-sharp blade tip was hooked forward, like a small sickle. He grinned presumptuously, flipping his dagger in his off-hand to a backhanded grip as he prepared to attack.

At that moment, Kiana felt a vibration to her side. The rain slowed in a sheet around a dome of invisible magic. Inside was her uncle, walking forward to Simon, who stood in place, though Simon's barrier of golden light shielded him from her uncle's dagger strike. As she gazed into the magic, something stirred in her vision, and her eyes burned with intensity. Kiana's attention snapped back to Arjun, and she saw the billhook blade, ghost-like transparent, as it sliced through the air toward her and through her parry. Then she saw it repeat itself exactly, and the blade was definite this time. Kiana caught it and retaliated with a diagonal upward strike at Arjun's other side.

She saw his dagger catch her attack with a counterstrike of his offhand.

But it was a ghost.

She twitched her blade back in a feint.

The dagger swept through nothing where she would have struck.

Kiana's bare foot planted in his gut, sending Arjun stumbling back.

"Fucking bitch woman," Arjun grunted in pain and frustration as he began circling.

There was another reverberating *pulse*, and Kiana peered over Arjun's shoulder to see Ravi Ahmadi slamming an axe against Simon's shield while everything else was frozen around them. Kiana's eyes throbbed at the sight of it. *He can slow time. How?*

There was no time to ponder it as Arjun dashed in.

Again, she saw his movement before it happened. Kiana ducked below the deadly hook on the end of his sword, and she stepped through his guard, only to see a blurred dagger aiming for her abdomen once again. The shadow vanished into her. *It's going to hit. I need to be faster. I need time!*

Arjun's blade slowed to an imperceptible crawl.

Or have I sped up? Kiana thought as she danced away, and her violet eyes burned into her skull. A pounding headache began to *thump* behind them.

His dagger swiped through nothing as it returned to normal speed. "What in Skrull's hell?" he gasped. "How did you—"

Suddenly, the ghost of a massive ocean wave struck the hull, and Kiana saw the ship begin to keel over, phasing through her.

She dove and wrapped her hands in a line of thick rigging.

The actual wave struck, and water washed over everyone on board. Arjun screamed and vanished as the torrent crashed over him. People were swept past her and over the side.

Baal was holding a man aloft with one hand when the massive force knocked him off his feet and sent him plunging into the surging water. As the chaos subsided and the ship stabilized, Kiana saw Baal dangling over the rail, saved only by the miraculous presence of his mate, Brena. With a mighty roar, Brena pulled him back onto the deck, and they both collapsed, panting for breath.

The pulse reverberated through Kiana once again, and time slowed around *everything*. Engulfing both ships. She saw her uncle turn away from Simon and walk toward Kai and Cygne, who were frozen in place. Kiana pushed herself to her feet and stepped toward her uncle as even the rain hung in suspended teardrops about her. Her violet eyes ached with power as she shouted, "Uncle!"

Ravi Ahmadi flinched and turned to her, and a look of wonder spread across his dark, scarred face. Then, as he found her eyes, he understood. "You're my niece? You, too, have the power of the Tal'tulu oracles. You, too, can see into the future."

Kiana's gaze found her father, who was near the captain's quarters, stuck in the pose of running toward his brother. She couldn't help but ask, "Why doesn't my father have this ability?"

"Ha! How the fucks should I know? I've spent years with…" he paused for a moment, tilting his head in thought. "I suppose she would be your great-grandmother. Anyways, she taught me the ways of an oracle. Rojas has not cultivated this power, or perhaps he does not carry it. Though it is doubtful with those vibrant eyes of his. I know not how you awakened yours."

"Please stop this uncle. My *only* uncle. We can all work together."

To Kiana's surprise, Ravi's face softened. "No matter how many women I've bedded in all these years, none bore me a child. *Uncle* Ravi. Hmm, it does be rolling off the tongue nicely."

"Will you finally put an end to this? I'm begging you, please spare any more lives."

"Alas, my dear niece, Kai cannot live. I will rule the Isles and unite them. They will prosper under an alliance with Xamid. Join me. Convince your father. Sway this mage." Ravi waved his axe at Simon.

Kiana hesitated, looking at Kai and then at Simon. Simon's face was struck with fear, and his eyes were on Kai.

Then…his eyes *flicked* to Kiana.

She nearly gasped in shock, but instead, she circled so Ravi's back was to Simon, and she was between Kai and her uncle. "I'm sorry, uncle, I can't let you kill him."

"Well then, that's a shame. 'Tis a shame, indeed. After just meeting my delightful little niece. What was your name? I don't think I heard it."

"Kiana. Kiana Ahmadi. Daughter of Rojas and Anora Ahmadi. Sixteenth Otsoa of Hasiera. I'm sorry, uncle. You'll not get through me."

"I beg to differ." Her uncle's scarred face contorted in rage as he charged her.

Kiana breathed and leveled her swords. *I need to keep his attention.* She rushed to meet him and slid on one knee through the wet, parrying the downward strike of his saber and stabbing out with her other blade. Kiana's arms vibrated painfully as their weapons scraped against each other, and the sparks flashed and slowed around them.

His axe caught her jab, and their weapons entangled together.

She surged up and cracked her forehead into his jaw.

He took a step back, grimacing in pain, then struck with both axe and sword.

Kiana leaned back, his blades cutting through the slowed raindrops, narrowly slashing her face. She turned her lean into a twisting slice of both blades, sending her feet over her head as she flipped back.

His velvet-black tricorne hat tumbled off as he stumbled away. Time flicked into existence, and the entire ship shook with the build-up waves that suddenly slammed into the vessel. Only for a second, then the bubble expanded once more from Ravi.

"Fucking hells, I'm losing my touch. I haven't had to fight anyone for decades because of this," Ravi Ahmadi grumbled with heavy breath as he waved at the dome of the slowed storm and sea about them. He bent, took up his hat, and propped it back on his grey and balding head, nearly turning toward Simon. "Someone taught you well, my eager little niece."

"It was my mother!" Kiana roared and leaped toward him. *I won't let him lose focus on me.* She glimpsed a dim light behind her uncle as they clashed once more. "She's dead because of you and your Xamidian ally." The anger overtook her, and her dance became a brutal symphony of unchecked bloodlust. She struck again and again. He could only defend himself as she released a flurry of never-ending strikes upon him.

He was tiring, his blocks lowering each time she struck.

Again. Her mother's words in training echoed in her head.

"Fucking bastard!"

The white light was growing brighter behind him.

Again!

"Please, my niece, let me live," Ravi pleaded under her onslaught.

Again! Get up and do it again! Anora's voice drowned out all else.

"I don't need an uncle. I don't *want* an uncle."

His axe clattered to the deck, and Ravi Ahmadi bent over and leaned on the point of his saber in defeat. "I surrender."

Kiana lifted his chin with the tip of her mother's blade.

"Make it quick," Ravi breathed. "I'm sorry, Rojas, after all these years, I thought you lost, and now I am to die at the hands of your very own daughter."

Kiana hesitated.

Her uncle's thick, scarred hand flashed out and gripped her blade, and blood gushed through his fingers. He wrenched her toward him, his sword coming up awkwardly to strike, but they were too close. Instead, he dropped the weapon and slammed his fist into the side of her head.

White light bloomed in her vision, and she dropped both swords as pain stunned her. She blinked blearily as two solid and slick hands wrapped around her throat. *Are they wet from the rain, or was that blood?* She thought absently as she struggled to breathe.

The grip loosened ever so slightly, and a rotten breath drifted over her as her uncle spoke into her face. "Maybe I won't kill you. Maybe I'll chain you to my bed and have my way with you until you die of it. My brother did brood quite the pretty little whore."

Kiana's sight cleared slightly. Yet there was still a white light silhouetting her uncle. He had lifted her off her feet with both hands, and she saw the string of white fire crawling through the slowed time, and it was just feet away from drilling into her uncle's back. "P—Please, uncle," Kiana rasped. "I will serve you willingly—*all* of your needs. I now see you are the strongest of Tal'tulu. I would fight for you. You can use me. Use my body. My mother drove me to more than just the sword. You're right. She said so herself. I'm nothing but a whore."

His clasp on her neck loosened further, his head tilted back, and he roared a victorious laugh. "HA HA HA!"

"Let me prove it, uncle," Kiana whispered submissively. "Kiss me, my pirate king." Kiana Ahmadi removed herself from her body as his greasy lips suckled hers. She often did this in *La Maison du Paon* with undesirable patrons.

Her uncle began ripping her clothing away with a savage hunger as they stood there. In his bubble of time, he would have her. Her breasts tore free from their linen wraps from his thick, clawing fingers. Her sick, repulsive, degenerate uncle did not even notice the bright white light as it cast his bulky shadow onto Kiana.

The white fire drove high into his back. Ravi jerked, and time crashed into reality. The snaking fire burst from his chest and straight into hers.

Neice and uncle fell, holding one another on the deck of *The Mamba's Mouth* as a tidal wave of build-up ocean surged with nature's fury and crashed into the two pirate vessels. *The Mamba's Mouth* and *Rojas's Revenge* were tossed and overturned by the storm's relentless power of sea and sky.

Chapter Thirty-One

UNITE

THE TREMENDOUS FORCE OF the detonation threw Hata off the crescent-shaped chunk of the island, sending her hurtling through the air. As she tumbled, her mind reeled from the shock, and her body seared with pain. She knew she had exhausted all her physical strength and magic abilities at that moment. She had no armor to take hold of, allowing her to soar to safety. The *sunstone* was gone, destroyed in the blast along with the *shadowstone*. Hata fell toward the roiling storm clouds below. She nearly closed her eyes and accepted her fate until she saw another person free-falling. Their body limp.

"Raine!"

Hata twisted mid-air and tried to angle her fall toward Raine, but she was hundreds of feet away. She tried to reach out with her earth sense to feel anything that might help her. A faint hint of Raine's armor came to her, and Hata tried to pull on it. It was a feeble attempt as the magic fizzled out. Then, a different sensation itched within her mind.

Little stone?

"Kulta!" Hata cried out in surprise. "I need you!"

I cannot fly, little stone. I float like a log in the seas below.

"I'm about to join you, along with the queen!"

I can't save you... Kulta paused, and an affectionate draconic growl echoed through Hata's mind. *My mate is close, little stone.*

There was a piercing cry and the rumble of something else at that moment. Hata's eyes widened as a rotor-wing sliced through the air, leaving a fire trail in its wake. It surged towards the queen, and Hata spotted Rorik Windbeard and Bryn Sparkheart at the helm. Hidden behind dark goggles, colorful bandanas, and round spiked helms, they hurtled through the air, Bryn standing in the seat behind Rorik, directly pointed at Raine.

A majestic dragon trailed after the aircraft—a brilliant blue creature with a rider adorned in a cobalt cloak. Safiiri and Taivaseläin had returned, and the mighty blue dragon descended towards Hata.

When Raine collided with Bryn, he was jolted and flung back into his seat from the force of the impact.

Taivaseläin reached up one arm as he and his dragon leveled with Hata's fall.

She reached out and grasped it.

Taiv pulled her in and shouted, "Hang on to me!"

Hata maneuvered to find herself clinging to him from behind, arms wrapped around his waist. She pressed her face to his sturdy back as exhaustion suddenly overwhelmed her. *We're safe. Raine is safe.*

"It's not over yet!" Taivaseläin shouted and pointed to the sea of enemies on the island that housed the city of Aerion. The *Children of Skaad* still assaulted Keep Crystalia in force even after the bombardment of dragon fire. Dusk had fallen, and the *Children* were not succumbing to the light. *The Children of... Skaad?*

"Where is he?" Hata cried with realization. "Where is Hear-fan Skaad?"

"I never sighted him," Taivaseläin answered over his shoulder. "I saw the blast on that island, and we made haste to come. We found only you and the queen."

"Where did he go? He can't be dead."

"No time to ponder it. We rejoin the battle."

Safiiri roared, and the wind beat around them. Hata felt her hair stand on end as the imposing Sapphire Stormwing lifted her head and sparking compressed energy charged in her maw. Then it released with a high-pitched shriek, and a beam of lightning shot through the air and tore into one of the massive siege towers that connected the city island to the keep above. The beam thinned to a line, and then the head of the black siege tower exploded. Chunks of metal, corpses, and gore hurled through the air.

Rotor-wings shrieked overhead. Most engaged with the flying humanoids of Skaad. The massive airships formed a line, thumping along with their numerous propellers. They all landed simultaneously on the edge of the island city in a row. The large side doors of the aircraft slammed into the earth to form ramps. Himin-dvergar charged down the ramps and into battle. The magic weapons of savage berserkers tore a clearing in the enemy as a wall of shielded pikes formed behind them. Just as the berserkers looked to be overwhelmed by the *Children,* they fell back to the safety of the pikes as they parted to let the tired men and woman regroup and rest behind them. The prickling line of pikes marched forward, skewering all in their path. Airships lifted off, and others replaced them, reinforcements pouring out to join their kin in battle.

Dragons released their elemental weapons, killing *Children* by the hundreds. Compressed lightning. Molten rock. Acidic fumes. Black fire. A few dragons landed on the edges of the pike line to join the battle with tooth and claw, ripping into the murky flesh of the *Children of Skaad* with eager relish.

The massive gates of Keep Crystalia swung open, and more Himin-dvergar rushed out to meet the enemy. Upon the walls, crystal-powered ballistae swiveled and fired up at the winged humanoids or turned their aim down on the *Children* below with extreme force.

Hata was too tired to do anything other than hang on for dear life, but she observed the slow and tedious battle as Safiiri periodically breathed lightning into the midst of the enemy. A horn sounded above, and the winged humanoid suddenly disengaged and fled in clouds of shrieks and pounding wings. They fled toward the Wayfarers Gate.

"We can't let them escape!" Taivaseläin called back to her and reigned Safiiri after the fleeing creatures.

Other dragons joined the pursuit, unleashing blasts of dragon magic that dropped hundreds of the abominations from the sky.

Rotor-wings soared and sliced through flesh.

Suddenly, the enemy came to an abrupt halt. The Wayfarers Gate stood inert and empty. One could see right through it. The way was shut.

"How?" Hata asked in astonishment. "Did someone close it from the other side? Or from this side?"

"We may not understand how these portals function," Taiv responded with a frown. "But one thing is certain – our enemy is completely trapped. We can wipe them out."

As the words left his mouth, the flying creatures landed on the island with the gateway and a few surrounding ones. They fell to their knees and dropped their weapons. They sang a wailing song of despair as every single one of them surrendered.

Hata couldn't believe her eyes.

Dragons and rotor-wings circled the submitted creatures, seeming unsure as to what to do.

"We should end them," Taivaseläin said through clenched teeth. "They killed many of our people, Himin and Kidekorvat alike. Many of our dragon siblings lost their lives today."

"They have submitted, but at what cost? How did Hear-fan Skaad secure their allegiance?" Hata consoled. "We can't stoop to his level and execute those who have surrendered. It's time to return to the keep."

Taivaseläin grunted then leaned toward Safiiri's neck and patted her gently. The dragon wheeled about, and they soon returned to the battle.

The city of Aerion was in ruins. Smoke billowed skyward all across the island, and many buildings had collapsed. A clearing had formed before the airships as the Himin-dvergar pushed inland.

Taivaseläin guided Safiiri to land gracefully, and Taiv helped Hata down from the perch behind him. Once she was safely on the ground, Safiiri and her elven dragon rider took to the air again and began sweeping over the enemy with destructive discharges of her lightning breath.

Hata sank to the ground, gazed up at the darkening sky, and watched as stars slowly began to appear, twinkling into existence. Exhaustion overcame her. "Just for a minute," she thought as she lay on her back, her hands touching the earth. Despite feeling distant, the connection was still there. With that comforting thought, she surrendered to sleep.

Sometime later, Hata awoke to the sounds of revelry. She sat up dreamily to see that numerous massive bonfires had been lit to brighten the night. Himin-dvergar and the taller silhouettes of the Kidekorvat danced together around the flames. The city of Aerion lay in ruins, its once grand structures now reduced to rubble. Yet, amidst the devastation, bonfires blazed, casting a warm glow over the city's remnants. Hata smiled in wonder at the Himin-dvergar and Kidekorvat, united by their triumph, gathered around the fires, their spirits high.

The Himin-dvergar, with their soot-streaked faces, clinked their mugs of ale, their hearty laughter echoing through the night. The Kidekorvat, elegant and ethereal, joined in the revelry, their dragons resting nearby, their scales shimmering in the firelight.

Taivaseläin was suddenly helping Hata to her feet, a tankard of wine in his hand. "Hata, sister of Kulta!"

Hata's eyes widened in horror. "Oh, gods! Kulta!"

A groggy voice answered her within. *Little stone, I am here. I am safe. I am resting.*

"We fetched him soon after we dropped you off," Taiv answered enthusiastically. "It was quite the feat; we needed ropes and chains, and I felt that if not for the Himin machinations of the pullies and whatnots connected to their perplexing airships, it would have taken much more effort to fish him out."

"Thank Teras," Hata breathed in relief.

Taivaseläin led her to some makeshift seating near one of the bonfires, where people danced and cheered. He fetched her a drink. Hata noted the ale and smiled fondly that her long-lost comment on preferring ale had not been forgotten. Taiv sat beside her, drinking and chatting.

Soon, another Kidekorvat joined them. The regal elven elder had blood-stained bandages around his head and arms, and his robes were in tatters. Aerendyl stood a few steps away, cleared his throat, and held his arms out.

Taivaseläin leaped to his feet and embraced his lover. "I nearly didn't make it in time," Taiv whispered into Aerendyl's disheveled blonde-white locks. "All would have been lost had I been delayed but a minute."

Aerendyl took Taiv by the shoulders and looked into his eyes. "You came. I put my trust in you. I knew you would succeed."

"I thought I would lose you."

"Not yet, my beloved. Not yet." Aerendyl pulled Taiv in and kissed him.

They lingered there in caress as Hata's cheeks ached from smiling. Then, she noticed someone on the edge of her vision.

Raine stood staring affectionately at Hata.

Hata felt a strange sensation nagging at her subconscious. Just as she was about to confront Raine and sort out their lingering issues, Bryn Sparkheart and Rorik Windbeard crashed into her, sending her tumbling from her seat and landing unceremoniously on the ground.

"Sky-lass!" Rorik bellowed. "By the bright beard, you're alive!"

Bryn pulled Hata to her feet. "Luminar's light, I can't feckin' believe we got here in time. Snatch the queen right out of the sky, we did." He tossed his dark, curly head around. "We dropped her with the healers and got right back into the thick of it. They said they'd fix her up right away."

Hata looked to where Raine had been standing. She was gone.

Suddenly, a hush fell over the crowd. A Himin-dvergar bard stepped forward, his handcrafted lute in hand, and began to play a melody. An elven minstrel joined him, her voice clear and haunting. Together, they sang a song about unity and hope that would forever bind the two races.

From the depths of the sky, where the islands float high,
The Himin-dvergar toil, with machines they rely.
In the shadows they fought, with courage and might,
Till the Kidekorvat came, on dragons of light.

Together we stand, as one we unite,
Himin and Kidekorvat, in the firelight.
With hearts intertwined, our spirits soar free,
In the ruins of Aerion, our bond is the key.

The crystals we mine, the dragons they ride,
In the face of the dark, we stand side by side.
Through the battles we've won, and the losses we've mourned,
A new dawn is rising, a future reborn.

Together we stand, as one we unite,
Himin and Kidekorvat, in the firelight.
With hearts intertwined, our spirits soar free,
In the ruins of Aerion, our bond is the key.

Let the fires burn bright, let our voices ring clear,
For the shadows have fled, and the dawn is near.
With the strength of our kin, and the courage we've shown,
In the heart of the ruins, a new world is grown.

Together we stand, as one we unite,
Himin and Kidekorvat, in the firelight.
With hearts intertwined, our spirits soar free,
In the ruins of Aerion, our bond is the key.

The song ended, and for a moment, there was silence. Then, a cheer erupted from the crowd, and the celebration resumed with even greater zeal. The Himin-dvergar and Kidekorvat danced and sang long into the night, their newfound unity a beacon of hope for the future of the Ryk Lân.

Hata reveled in her friendships and their hard-earned victory, leaving all negative thoughts for later. She wished Raine were here. *Is she all right?* The memory came back to her. Raine's hands gripping Hear-fan Skaad's arm. Violet fire. Hata stood abruptly. *I need to go and find Raine, apologize for everything, and make sure she's all right.*

A mellow horn blew at that moment, and silence suddenly washed over the festivities.

"What is it?" Hata asked her companions. "What's wrong?"

Bryn's lips quivered, and his mouth opened and closed repeatedly. No words left his lips.

"The Queen is dead!" Rorik wailed as he clutched his head and fell to his knees.

Hata looked ahead in utter shock. "No, it can't be. I just saw her in the crowd," she whispered. She started running and called out, "Raine! Where are you?" She ran and ran, screaming and crying, "Raine!" The silent crowd parted around her, guiding her to a stone slab elevated above the onlookers where Raine's body lay.

Still, cold and lifeless…

Chapter Thirty-Two

SOUGHT

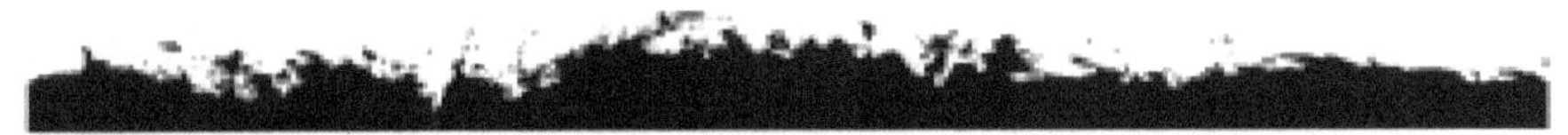

"Saudett?" a voice asked through the haze.

She blinked, and a bearded face of rough pale grey with strange inverted eyes looked at her. He had four arms. *Is that right? Is that natural?* She lifted her two hands to look down at their warm brown skin. *Are these mine?* She flipped them over to look at her palms. They were calloused and rough from years of use with something. Her back was oddly heavy.

A voice came from behind the strange-looking man. "She seems to have taken a blow to the head and lost her memory. Allow me to take her into my care, Wayfarer. We will have her back to fighting shape in no time."

"What?" she asked aloud. "Who're you people? Who am I?"

The four-armed man straightened from where he had been bending to look at her. He turned to the man behind him, clad in black robes trimmed in gold. "Can you help her?"

"Of course,' the man said, a gloved hand stroking the pitch-black hair of his chin.

An odd moan came from another direction, and she looked to see an *armless* woman clad in bandages.

"What is going on? Where am I?"

Everyone ignored her.

"Please help her," the four-armed man said.

"I will do all I can." The man in black nodded and moved toward her. "Report to the Grand Maréchal; I will fetch you momentarily, Wayfarer. First, I will bring the woman to the safety of my facilities."

A crack of light suddenly tore into existence in the space before her. The black-clad man raised a hand, and the bandaged woman approached him and stepped through the light. He then placed his other hand on...*what was it he called me? Saudett?*

"Come now, my dear, let's get you fixed up."

He pushed Saudett through the light, and she found herself on a flagstone garden path that led toward a domed structure. The bandaged woman led the way as she followed, the man close behind, his hand never leaving her shoulder.

Massive oaken doors groaned open, and they stepped inside. Another dome, draped in burgundy silk sheets, took up the center of the room, and she followed the bandaged woman inside to find silk bedding and pillows.

A metallic *clang* rang out behind her, and she turned to see the man in black closing a black iron cage and locking it with a key.

"What are you doing?" she asked. "What's going on?"

"It's for your health, my dear," the man said, grinning. "Be patient; I *will* return."

The bandaged woman groaned and huddled in the corner of the cage.

The man turned, and the curtains fell, shrouding them in maroon-colored light.

Malix found the Grand Maréchal in a command tent not far from where their battle had taken place against the earthwalkers. *I hope Saudett's memory returns. I will have to trust in these human magi and, I admit, their notable skills.* He pondered this as he strode into the tent.

"Ah, oui, Malix, was it?" Grand Maréchal Étienne said upon his entry. "You put on quite the show out there with those terrible monstrosities. We lost many good soldiers, but thanks to you and the council members, the Earste Lân is again safe. You have our eternal gratitude." The aging officer gave a curt bow with a hand on his chest. Standing again, he asked, "And where is your lady friend?"

"Yes, where is Lady Saudett?" Darkclaw Marah growled from the corner, which startled Malix. He hadn't been aware of their presence.

"She took a hit to the head and has lost a bit of memory. The Alpha councilman has taken her to be healed."

"We should be with her. You should not have let her go alone," Marah rebuked gruffly.

"Fear not, my friend," Étienne reassured. "She is in the most capable hands in all of Aurulan. What of the other council members, where have they strayed off to?"

At that moment, the cloaked figure of Kuro Raven entered the tent with Nix Swan's body in his arms.

Étienne's mouth fell open in disbelief. "No, it's impossible..." his words trailed off as Kuro gently laid Nix on the map table.

The Beta then pulled back his hood to reveal short dark hair with three white scar lines across the left side of his face, an eye with blindness, and an ear cleaved and missing a chunk. His single tawny, ovate eye glistened in the dim light of the tent. He was of a pale golden complexion. "Those damned demons got her." His voice strained with frustration.

"Hettra's mercy to us," Étienne exhaled regretfully. "I never thought one such as her could be defeated. She was good to the soldiers. We will give her a proper burial."

"I'm sorry for your loss," Malix mumbled, unsure what to say.

Kuro Raven turned to him. "Why can't your kind stop meddling in our affairs? First Gaelin and now you. We had it under control. We didn't need your help out there."

"Fuck me," Malix snorted irritably. "It seems Nix would say otherwise."

The Beta's face contorted in rage, and he sprang at Malix. Inky tendrils snaked out from his hand.

Wincian. Malix blinked out of existence and reappeared behind his attacker. He grasped him with three of his arms and pressed the blade of one axe up into Kuro's throat; a thin line of blood began to trickle there. "Far more would be dead had *I* not resolved the situation. As I explained to the late Eta, I've come to put a stop to the conquest of Hear-fan Skaad. I've come to *help* humanity. Even if my aid is unsought." Malix recoiled within from his own words. *Not even these humans want my help; I'm such a wretched fool.* He unconsciously tightened his grip on the man.

"Pardon, my friends, do not fight amongst ourselves—" Étienne started.

"The Grand Maréchal is correct." The tent flap swung open, and the Alpha strode in. His previously soiled clothing from the battle had been changed to clean, luxurious garments, and his once disheveled hair had been combed and slicked back against his head. Another man followed behind him.

A man with four arms.

Malix released Kuro and let him stumble forward.

The man stopped at the sight of Malix, his grey robes rustling about him. "Threnn? No...too young. Who're you?"

Malix felt his entire body tense with anticipation. *Gaelin Yesnala. This is my chance. I could disable him and return to my father. Prove my worth.* He glanced at the Alpha and Beta. *They are powerful. I don't think I could take all three at once.* He shook his head. *No. I'm no longer my father's pawn.* "Malix is my name. Malix, the Unsought."

"Nymira's little bastard? It can't be...." Gaelin's face twisted in a mask of rage. "You are responsible for all of this! You caused my home to be destroyed. You led to Threnn's banishment. You are the reason for his revenge. How many people were killed in the Hiel Lân? How much knowledge was lost?"

"I—"

"You don't deserve to live. We should have executed you the moment that whore woman birthed you, but Nymira pleaded for your life. Instead of that, we decided to send you to him. It's just as much your mother's fault as yours – if she hadn't seduced my friend and provoked him to act on those impulses."

Malix was stunned into silence. *I'm the reason for all of this. I've brought so much death to countless worlds.*

"Alpha, this man is a blooded son of our enemy," Gaelin urged, turning to the man Ebras Corb. "He will not be of aid to us. He must die."

Perhaps it is for the best. Malix thought as he closed his eyes. *No one needs me. No one loves me. I'm worthless and only cause hurt and suffering. I truly am unsought.*

"No, Gaelin, you sniveling coward," the Alpha rebuked. "You never fight your own battles. I should let the two of you settle this in conflict, but knowing you, Gaelin, you'll simply pout about it and do everything you can to avoid it. This man, *Malix,* has already displayed more aptitude than you have yet to show me, Gaelin. All you've done is shot down a defenseless old priestess."

"Ridiculous!" Gaelin squealed. "I single-handedly cleansed the Moreas Lân of Skaad's abominations."

"You had Simon for that, another man who has shown me his value. You're increasingly wearing on my patience, Wayfarer."

"I—I built the Gates all over this Lân." Gaelin stammered. "That was no simple feat. It required a mass of resources to build them."

"You built those gates, and hence let the enemy in. And how exactly are these portals created? What resources are used in their construction?" Ebras's face was sullen, his lips in a cold line.

"Indeed? Oh, never mind the method, Alpha; it's just a bit of bone of a sentient being and some complex incantations. Fresh bone works best."

"Where did you get this... *fresh bone*?" The Alpha's voice held an eerie, emotionless tone.

Gaelin laughed nervously. "Oh, here and there. No need to concern yourself with the details."

Kuro's eyes widened in shock as he exclaimed, "You've been harvesting humans?"

"Absolutely not!" Gaelin reassured, his four hands moving in a calming gesture. "I did a bit of grave digging and rescued the occasional beggar at death's door or some criminal from a prison cell. But never did I take live, healthy specimens."

"Enough of this. You will tell us how to destroy these gates. We will do so, and upon the last one, we will send you and all your kind," Ebras looked at Malix as he said this, "away from our Lân."

"As is your right." Malix nodded in agreement.

"There's no way to destroy the Wayfarers Gates. They're indestructible." Gaelin urged. "We must deal with the threat of Skaad and make your Lân and all Lân's safe because of it. We must eradicate him and all his *Children*." This time, it was Gaelin who looked to Malix.

Ebras Corb put two gloved hands to his temples and rubbed circles. After a long moment, he snapped, "Fine! We will continue with the plan. Kuro."

Kuro's back straightened as his name was uttered. "Yes, Alpha."

"You will not leave this man's side." Ebras gestured at Malix. "Both of you will finish aiding the Grand Maréchal in cleaning up the North Iron Belt of the *Children*. I do not want a single one of those abominations still running rampant in our lands. Once this task is complete, return to me."

"Yes, Alpha." Kuro bowed with arms tight to his sides.

With that, the Alpha waved a hand, and a crack of light opened before them. Ebras looked at Gaelin. "Wayfarer."

Sheepishly, Gaelin Yesnala entered the portal, but not before glaring hatefully at Malix.

Ebras Corb followed the Iban'mael in, and the crack of light vanished.

"Well," Étienne cleared his throat awkwardly. "I don't enjoy a minute in the Alpha's company, but King Guignol Gaucher commands us to obey him. Long live the king, as they say."

"We should not delay; the longer we take to eradicate this pest, the more innocent people die." Kuro Raven muttered, pulling his hood up. He then turned to Malix. "Malix. We will acquire packs and supplies and set out immediately into the mountains. Send your troops after us, Grand Maréchal."

"But of course, Beta," Étienne quickly saluted, and then he turned to Darkclaw Marah who had been hiding in the shadows. "Would you care to join me, Volkinn?"

Marah growled but nodded and followed the old veteran out of the command tent. They heard his shouts as he began directing troops and runners.

Anxiety churned in Malix's gut. *These people don't see the man, Ebras Corb, in a good light. Was it right of me to send Saudett with him?*

"Let's go, Malix. It's a daunting task that awaits us. I don't care what your motives are or who your father is. Thank you for helping us destroy those colossal creatures. We have our work cut out for us and must save as many lives as possible. You aided in that goal today, and we continue to need you now."

"I would do anything to right my father's wrongs," Malix said, scratching at his beard. "If hunting and killing his *Children* is a part of that, let us make haste."

Kuro nodded and pushed the tent flap aside.

I'm needed here. Malix thought as he followed the mysterious cloaked man into the dusky light of an amber sunset. *I am sought.*

Chapter Thirty-Three

LOST

Simon gasped to wakefulness, coughed hoarsely as he rolled onto his side, and splashed his hand into the sea. He realized he was on a handful of planks nailed together precariously as it drifted through the waves. The memory came back. The ships had been destroyed as the built-up tension of crashing waves had all been unleashed at once. His spell had caught Ravi Ahmadi in the back, and then cold and darkness had engulfed everything. Kiana had done well to keep him distracted as the *Bael Cnytells* had inched through the air. *Kiana.* She had been able to move freely in Ravi's bubble of time. *It must be her eyes. But Rojas couldn't do it?*

He floated for a long time, pondering the brutal battle. How many had been swallowed by the ocean? *Where are my friends?* Simon vaguely recalled surfacing after the ship had tumbled. He had used *Strangung* to pull himself onto a piece of board as the storm flung him about for hours as he clung to it. Exhaustion finally took him as the sea settled and the storm rolled on.

"Is anyone still alive?" he croaked aloud. He sat up and nearly capsized his makeshift raft as it tipped under the shift of his weight. He scanned the horizon and saw no sign of others floating on the seas. He vaguely made out a dark swell in the distance. *An island, perhaps?*

"Kai!" Simon hollered into the vast, endless sea. "Baal! Brena! Anybody!"

A large dark fin surfaced nearby and began circling his raft. He winced and pulled his feet out of the water. Again, the debris nearly flung him off at the weight shift. The fin vanished at his movement. "Well, I don't want to find out how many teeth that thing has. I guess I can't stay here. *Afléotan.*"

His toes lifted off just as the massive shark burst from below him. Rows upon rows of teeth sheared through the board and chomped down where Simon had been sitting a moment ago.

"Skrull's scrotum!" Simon yelped as he flew higher into the sky, leaving the beast to choke on the driftwood. He aimed for the island in the distance. The sun was setting to his right. That means this island is northward. "Qav, grant me luck; I have no idea where I am." He mumbled in prayer. It grew dark quickly, and he nearly missed the island as night fell around him. Finally, Simon found himself on a soft, white sand beach. *Leoma.* An orb of light floated about him as he gathered some dry driftwood around. He lit the pile with *Byrnsweord,* a short burst of flame in the shape of a knife that he plunged into the firewood, which caught quickly under the magical flames.

"Hells, I wish there was an incantation for food." He sighed as his tired body urged him to lie beside the warming flames. Simon soon closed his eyes as his mind cleared of all that had transpired or was still to come.

Skrull's hairy balls, will this ever end...

Kiana opened her eyes to the rattling of chains and the sight of bodies in tattered, waterlogged clothing lying about her. Some of them moved and groaned, while others were as still as stone. Groggily, she sat up and observed the bars of her cage.

"Remarkable. You yet live. How many times would you have died on this little expedition by now? Though your hearty constitution may have fortified my efforts. It was almost as if the bleeding had slowed to an unnatural speed this time."

Kiana turned to see Cygne Caladrius huddled in a corner. Captain Kai lay unconscious before him. "Where are we?"

"Picked up by one of Old Keen Eyes ships. None of our leaders, Simon or otherwise, have yet to be found. At least by this ship. They could be imprisoned by another. Or perhaps they made it to safety. Or perhaps..." Cygne trailed off.

"They drown?"

"Well, you need not be so morbidly blunt about it. I do detest death and violence."

"Is Kai all right?"

"Oh yes, he'll pull through. He is resting now. You should do the same."

Kiana couldn't argue with the old man. Her eyes and head were pounding with each beat of her heart. She closed them and tried to block out the moans of pain and the rattling of chains, instead focusing on the sound of footfalls on the decks above and the distant shouts of sailors. She drifted in and out of sleep, wondering where this ship's journey would end.

Jude Nelon spooned the fishy stew into Joanna's mouth. She slurped at it, and he dabbed at a drip of broth on her chin. "You're doing excellent, my flame," he reassured, "just a few more bites."

Joanna Ohleoc smiled weakly back at him.

It had been weeks, maybe months, since coming to the icy town of the Nunara people known as *Qilakvik*. Jude hadn't left Joanna's side during that time. The Nunara provided food, clean leathers, and furs, but Jude was responsible for feeding and cleaning Joanna. She could not walk, stand, or even roll onto her side for long. He tried to hold in his poor gag reflex as he cleaned her piss and shit away and then wrapped her in a clean fur blanket. There was no sense in dressing her in clothing as it would simply get soiled once again.

Every time he hobbled around her, wiping her down, Joanna began to sob, tears streaming down her face. "I can't believe you would care for me so." She stammered through her drawing breaths.

Fucking hells, I can't believe it myself, he thought. *But it's true.* "I would do anything for you, my flame. You will recover, and we will be together. Two disabled wretches till the end of our days." He took her hand and kissed it gently.

And so, the days went by. Tuktu had fashioned Jude a comfortable new leg for his stump, made of bones, gut netting, and skins. Thick fur cushioned his leg attached to the prosthetic. It had a broad, webbed base where his foot would've been, making balancing on the snow-packed ground more manageable than a peg leg, which would punch through it. *At least I'm able to walk now.*

Kaplan Mir came to visit every few days or so. He would chatter about going on sea hunts with the Nunara, trekking across the tundra to stalk a white snow bear, or helping cut ice blocks to build new homesteads. The man was far too enthusiastic for Jude's liking, but he didn't mind the company. Joanna had very few words to say in her state and slept most of the time. Kaplan enjoyed telling stories; he even recounted the events of the desert and Hasiera and how they had journeyed to Nidhaut seeking Hata Vasara. He talked in great detail about his past as an orphan in Al'Jalif and working in the Sultan's palace. Jude almost had a mind to put ink to paper and write Kaplan's stories if not for the lack of parchment and pen in *Qilakvik*. Kaplan was Jude's elder by a decade or so and had done much with his life.

And what have I done with mine? Made money by capturing young people and forcing them into servitude to Corb. *No longer. When Joanna's in good health, we will find somewhere warm to settle down and be together.*

As he sat there dreaming of a life with her, he heard the gentle swish of the leather curtain leading into the chamber.

Jude groaned as he stood to greet the visitor. *Kaplan, come to tell me another story?*

The knife sunk into Jude's gut. The figure was clad in black studded leather; she grinned wickedly as she pulled the knife free of his flesh and whispered into his ear, "Huntsman to Huntsman, the Alpha does not abide traitors."

EPILOGUE

Hear-fan Skaad crept through the Wayfarers Gate of the Ryk Lân, invisibility cloaking his departure as the battle raged in his wake. His arm dripped blood where the Rykling woman had sheared it from his body, and he had no time to heal it. When the *shadowstone* exploded, he was blasted away through the air. In a daze, he had incanted flight and invisibility. Without the *shadowstone*, his magic was drained to near nothing; he could not close the wound while maintaining the other two spells. *I must close the portal. I must regroup and rebuild.*

Luck was with him as he entered the Skaad Lân without confrontation. He then turned and placed his hands upon the Wayfarer's Gate. He closed the portal, and the rolling grey mist dissipated as he stared through the archway at the endless wading waters of the world he had been banished to. The world of endless starry skies. The world of *nothing*.

"They cannot follow. They do not have the powers of the Iban'mael to control the Gates. They are stranded in their Lân. I'm safe for now. But that woman, Hata Vasara. Such a revolting, meddling human," Hear-fan vexed aloud as he began healing the bleeding stump of his arm. "I will need a new one fashioned. I must plan my retribution." He went to the platform that descended into his underground labyrinth but paused as his eyes fell on one other of the Wayfarer's Gates. It was pointed at his home world of the Heil Lân. *Perhaps there is something yet to be used of the Iban'mael technologies. An influence to annihilate armies. A force to level cities. A power to destroy worlds.*

Hear-fan Skaad stepped back into the world where he had been born and began picking his way through the ruins as deafening silence enclosed him. He walked the streets where his once great people had laughed in their arrogance—the people he had meticulously eradicated. *I will do so again, beginning with every human being. The Earste Lân will be nothing more than a burned-out husk.* He smiled with certainty; his resolve renewed as he continued toward the central citadel of the Iban'mael Wayfarers.

FREE NOVELLA

Greetings,

Thank you for reading. I hope you enjoyed this story and wish to continue following the Sunstone Saga of Hata, Saudett, Simon, and their companions on their journey into new Lân's. If so, please sign up for my reader group newsletter. I send out a monthly update on my progress on upcoming books in the series and any special offers or events I may be attending.

If you sign up for my newsletter, you will receive a **digital** copy of my novella *Caste of the Mountain*. A prequel story following Baal, Brena, and Hata before the events of *The Shepherds of the Sunstone*.

THE SUNSTONE SAGA NOVELS

Book One - The Shepherds of the Sunstone
Book Two – The Children of Skaad
Book Three - The Wayfarers War
Book Four – The Storm of Sea and Sky

PREQUELS

Prequel One – Caste of the Mountain

9 781738 282807